MASQUE OF THE

RISING MOON

A TWIST OF POE MYSTERY

Also By

VELDA
BROTHERTON

TWIST OF POE MYSTERIES
The Purloined Skull
The Tell-Tale Stone
The Pit and the Penance
Masque of the Rising Moon

THE VICTORIANS
Wilda's Outlaw
Rowena's Hellion
Tyra's Gambler

THE MONTANA SERIES
Montana Promises
Montana Treasures
Montana Dreams
Montana Fire
Montana Destiny
Montana Legacy

OTHER TITLES
Beyond The Moon
A Savage Grace
Once There Were Sad Songs
Stoneheart's Woman
Wolf Song
Remembrance

MASQUE OF THE RISING MOON

A TWIST OF POE MYSTERY

VELDA
BROTHERTON

LAGAN

OGHMA CREATIVE MEDIA

www.oghmacreative.com

Library of Congress Control Number: 2018944179

ISBN: 978-1-63373-289-6

Interior Design by Casey W. Cowan
Editing by Gil Miller

Lagan Press
Oghma Creative Media
Bentonville, Arkansas
www.oghmacreative.com

This book is dedicated to my daughter,
with all my love and thanks for being who you are.

Love you, Jeri.

ACKNOWLEDGEMENTS

There are consistently many people to thank for each of the books in the *Twist of Poe* Series, mostly those I worked with, interviewed and wrote about in my long years with newspapers. So if you see yourself in the pages of this book, then know I utilized you with the greatest of respect and thanks for being my friend and sharing your stories. Even if you become the villain, it is with that same respect that I recreate your personality, even if I had to twist it a bit.

Thanks also go out to the best publisher in the world, Casey Cowan and Gil Miller, a super editor who keeps me on the straight and narrow.

1
CHAPTER

A tow-headed kid burst out the exit door from Walmart and ran full tilt into Jessie. Knocked her up against a display of potted plants that went tumbling, dumping soil and flowers everywhere. He stopped, eyes wide, stared at her as if his world had ended. For a moment their gazes locked. An understanding there that surpassed her surprise and his fear, a connection formed before he grabbed what he'd dropped, stuffed it inside his jacket, and took off. Something pink and frilly. A girl's garment of some sort. A crowd gathered around her. A man bent to help her up from the mess, and a tubby fellow in a blue Walmart vest ran out to join them. For a second he paused, eyes pointed toward the fleeing kid, then swiveling toward her. Perhaps gauging whether he should see to her or chase the boy.

"Someone catch that little bugger." He made up his mind and took off, leaving her to paw her way out of the soil and scattered plants.

The "little bugger," maybe pre-teen, all gangly legs and arms, leaped into a van on the access road. Tires squealing, the blue vehicle sped onto the street and away. The kid needed help. It was in his eyes, his body language. The terror of the pursued, the lost. She squinted to make out the tag on the muddy van, but only got a letter and two numbers.

73G.

Fat raindrops splatted dots of mud in the spilled soil on the parking lot. The small crowd scattered as if they'd melt. She brushed off her jeans and t-shirt and allowed a helpful guy to lead her out of the pile of broken pots and dumped flowers. Now she'd have to go home and change.

Blue jacket reappeared. "What a fucking mess." He glanced at her. "You see that getaway? Oh, I'm so sorry. Are you sure you're okay? Do you need me to call someone?" The fellow was definitely more disturbed about the destroyed exhibit than he was her or catching the kid.

Why would a boy steal something like a pink dress? Oh, sure, he could swing that way, but even if he did, the dress was small and he was almost as tall as her. Oh, well, just another exciting day with *The Observer*. Her first story of the week and she hadn't even arrived at work yet. The past two weeks had seen several shoplifting events pulled off by kids, so there might be a growing story there. She thanked the man and left without going inside to buy drinks for the fridge at work. Home first, then on to work.

The story would beat her to the Red Bird. Nothing could happen at Walmart but what everyone in Cedarton knew about it. So why bother writing it when it would be all over town before the paper came out Wednesday? Cause everyone would expect it, that's why.

The rain continued as if unconcerned. She pulled keys from her jeans pocket and headed for the Jeep, thankful she'd left her backpack containing her new Panasonic locked inside the vehicle. If she'd been carrying it, no telling what might have happened to it. She'd lived on beans and potatoes to buy that camera. A trickle of customers trotted toward their cars to get out of the rain. Her phone jangled like wind chimes. She unlocked the Jeep and crawled inside before answering.

"Where you at, girl?" Mac sounded frazzled.

Poking her key in the ignition, she told him. "Why?"

"Could you come by for a few minutes? Got something to talk to you about."

"Sure. Do you need anything from the store while I'm here? It's Walmart, they've got everything."

"Nope, I'm good."

"Okay. Well, I have to run home so it'll be a few minutes, but I'll be there soon."

Overhead a wall of black clouds swallowed half the sky, leaving the rest shimmering with sunlight. To the east a double rainbow appeared, sprouting from the Ozarks like a blooming arch. It took thirty minutes or so for her to get home, change clothes, and convince Brad he didn't want to go outside in the storm. The cute little pit bull was convinced he should accompany her everywhere, especially when it involved a ride in the Jeep. He always called shotgun.

"Gotta go, Brad. Stay home and guard the place." She closed the door and hurried through the steady downpour. Better get over to Mac's and see what was up. He sounded troubled. She was more than happy to keep him company. Sitting around home watching the grass grow had to bore a man accustomed to action. A shame he'd been temporarily sidelined as sheriff. There was something screwy about that.

His tidy house sat on a sloping plot a few blocks south of the courthouse, and he waited on the front porch. The rain passed, the rainbow smeared across the blue sky. A light breeze greeted her when she parked and got out. He met her halfway across the yard and wrapped her in a hug. After her grandfather's death, his best friend Mac had informally adopted her and she had happily agreed to the arrangement.

"Glad you could come. Sorry to bother you. 'Spect there's lots of things you'd rather do than cater to an old man."

She walked beside him through the wet grass, soaking her moccasins. "Don't be silly. Want to sit out here?" On the front porch, she paused where there was a swing and a rocking chair. The cooler air smelled fresh and sweet and she drew in a breath.

"Nice, ain't it? But let's go inside. I have some things I want to show you."

His tone was way too serious and she studied him closer. The crease between his pale eyes deepened, wrinkles ran downward from the corners of his mouth. This business with his job was really getting to him.

Under his hands the screen door creaked open. "Don't suppose you've heard from that contrary Dallas? He hadn't ought to have left us like that. And especially not you, seeing as how you were courting."

Mac's old-fashioned way of putting it wasn't quite accurate, but close enough. Her involvement with the Cherokee lawman had never been conventional, but there *had* been plenty of hot sex wherever and whenever they could have it. She wanted to kick his ass for leaving her so abruptly. Eight months and counting since he'd disappeared. And no, she hadn't heard from him, but if she opened her mouth to discuss him, she'd either cry or have a tantrum. Dumb to feel that way over a man, but there it was.

"Boy ought to know better than to leave all his friends without a cotton picking word. Sure do hope he's okay."

Me too. Me too. Unable to speak past the lump in her throat, she stepped into the living room crowded with mementos of Mac's long life in law enforcement.

He beckoned her to sit next to him at his desk and pulled out a sheaf of newspaper clippings from the weekly newspaper up in Nolton County. Stories of a rash of home robberies around Bee Rock and Cave Springs. Small towns with little law protection save a thinly spread county sheriff's department. Much like Cedarton and Grace County, break-ins up there were normally rare. The really odd thing was food was taken. Reports of snack items that could be carried, and once in a while food straight from the fridge.

"What do you think, Mac? Sounds like something going on that needs fixing." She lay down the last short clipping and faced him.

"I'm worried, girl. It's not so much these piddly little things. I think we got us a big problem and the two probably related. That boy picked up the other day had a tattoo on his arm, which of itself isn't much nowadays. But I been checking and Sheriff Kimble said several of those over in Nolton County carried the same mark. A straight line with a half circle at the top."

Maybe she wouldn't mention the earlier incident at Walmart. If it hadn't been on the scanner he wouldn't find out about it and he was upset enough as it was.

He barely took a breath, then went on. "Kids. Dammit, kids ought to be in school or playing basketball down at the park, not shoplifting or stealing from neighbors. I don't like it."

"Been listening to the scanner today?"

"It's my job. Course I been listening. Just cause they've laid me up and put that idjit Arthur Couch in my place don't mean I'm letting my county and my men down. I'm on the job, whether they like it or not."

"And you're afraid there might be someone behind this? Like that cult up in Nolton County?"

"Exactly. You don't think those fellas left the country, do you? They just settle in somewheres else and start over. We got the perfect setup for them, right here in Grace County. Lots of wilderness, back roads where no one lives anymore, not enough deputies to patrol, deep hollers where they can grow their weed. We don't even have a decent DHS program. Kids get overlooked when they run away and it wouldn't be hard for these yahoos to grab em up and promise em all sorts of things. They ain't got folks, or if they do they're worthless."

Petty thefts didn't exactly point to cult activity, but the same tattoo on a few kids caught stealing could mean a gang organization of some kind. The stuff they were stealing, it didn't make sense to link it to a cult or a gang. A real puzzle. She stared out the window that framed the neat neighborhood. Cedarton was a good place to live. The junior college brought enough money into the area to keep businesses running, entertainment was plentiful. Bowling alley, miniature golf, an arts center where the kids could put on plays and art exhibits. A Walmart where everyone could hang out, and the Malco theatre that showed 3D and first run movies, for goodness' sake. There were even Little League baseball teams. It would be dreadful if what Mac feared was actually happening in this peaceful wilderness county with what went on in all the larger surrounding communities. Casinos to the west and south. To the north bars lined the streets of larger towns where once no liquor was sold. He constantly fussed about how much longer Cedarton could remain peaceful, what with the new highway from Tulsa to Branson bringing in outsiders.

"So what are you thinking of doing?"

"I don't know. Thought you might have some ideas. Maybe write some stories in the paper for people to be more vigilant, demand more care for kids so they don't get in trouble. Tell these people in this cult or whatever it is, that we won't tolerate their sort of tomfoolery. Stuff like that."

"Well, Mac, it's not that easy. I can't just create that sort of story out of—well, *nothing*."

"Nothing? Kids committing crimes in broad daylight. That ain't nothin. Not how I see it. We stop these people now, run em out of our county, hell, out of the state. Once and for all. It wasn't too many years ago members of that cult up north ended up murdering a highway patrolman. And who can ever forget the Alamo bunch down south?"

"Of course we'll write a story, but we can't write about cults we know nothing about. I can't add my opinion to a news story or make wild accusations with no sources of proof. You know that. I can quote what you said about people being more vigilant, taking care of their kids. Your opinion carries a lot of weight. But I can't go lecturing on my own. Parker would have a fit. He writes the op-eds, not me. He might come up with something. Maybe I could get some more good quotes from our temporary sheriff."

"Fat lot of good that'll do. That prick can't get off his butt long enough to follow up on anything. Might be I'd say more than most would want to hear. But you put something together and I ain't afraid to comment." He ran gnarly fingers through a thatch of white hair, paced around the cluttered room muttering under his breath. Stopped and stared at her. "I gotta get back on the job, try to put a stop to this nonsense, that's all there is to it."

His breath came faster, and he clutched his chest.

She leaped up, the clippings fanning out on the floor. Mac sank to his knees, grabbed the arm of the sofa. She ran to his side, eased him up onto the cushions.

"I'm calling 911. You just sit there."

"Ain't nothing." He gasped a couple times. "I'm okay, no need in that."

Ignoring him, she spoke to the dispatcher who answered. It was one of the young deputies recently hired. Much to Mac's dismay her friend Tink, who usually manned the phones, was working in the field since Arthur Couch came on as sheriff.

Mac had thrown a cussing fit when he'd found out a female deputy was in a patrol unit.

The dispatcher promised first responders on the scene immediately. The small volunteer fire department was proud to have cut down their response time to under five minutes within a five-mile radius of town. It would take a bit longer for an ambulance from Harrison. A siren sounded within a couple minutes of the call.

Meanwhile, she got Mac to settle down his breathing and gave him an aspirin to chew. By the time the responders arrived, he was feeling better, but they checked him out on the machine they carried.

"Well Mac, you aren't having a heart attack, but I think you ought to let us call an ambulance. Take you to the hospital." Michael Henley was the EMT who had helped Dal after his accident last year.

"No, blast it. I ain't never had a heart attack. I'm just agitated, that's all. Plumb agitated. And I ain't going off down there to the hospital."

Henley grinned at Jessie and she took Mac's hand. "Then let's see if we can't get you un-agitated, or they'll haul you in."

"Not without my say so, they cain't."

He was right there, but she figured if he didn't feel better soon, she would persuade him to go in to see Doc at the clinic.

After several checks of his blood pressure, oxygen, and pulse, he was pronounced okay.

"But you ought to go in and get looked over, just to be safe." Henley repeated his earlier request, but Mac glowered.

"I'll go. Soon. Anything to get rid of you. I'm fine. You done a good job getting here and all, but I'm fine." He made a sweeping gesture with one hand. "Next time, maybe my babysitter won't be here to bother you."

Henley got on the radio and stopped the ambulance from making the trip from Harrison.

After the last of the responders tromped out, she fixed Mac a bowl of soup and left him grumbling but spooning up the hot chicken noodles.

After a stop at the sheriff's office to get information on a pot bust, she headed for work. Plopping her bag on the cluttered desk in the office, she slumped into the chair.

"Just saw Mac and he's, as he puts it, plumb agitated. Can't say as I blame him. I don't like Arthur Couch one bit. Further, I don't trust him."

Wendy leaned out around the corner from where she was opening mail. "Well, he is a man."

"Much worse than that. Besides, his name doesn't even sound like a sheriff. Sounds more like something you lollygag on. And there are dozens of other reasons why I dislike him. The biggest one is I just found out he's a liar and a drunk."

Wendy stepped out in the open, one hand filled with manila envelopes. "Are you sure of that? The drunk part, I mean. Liar's a given. Never met a man who wouldn't lie even if the truth would suit."

"Here now," Parker muttered from his office.

"With one exception." She grinned at Jessie. "What'd Couch do this time?"

"I caught him drinking and lying both. This morning when I went in no one was at the front desk over at the jail and I was supposed to interview him about the marijuana plants they destroyed last night, so I tapped on the door and went on in. He had a whiskey bottle in his hand, trying to hide it in the drawer before I saw it. Then he spins this big story about taking it off a guy he caught sleeping in the lobby when he came in to the office earlier."

"What did you say?"

"What could I say? Just pretended I believed him. Why didn't they let Les or Burt take over for Mac? We don't need some guy who doesn't even know the county that well, even if he's sober as a judge. He hadn't ever served as a deputy anywhere. His last job before he retired was patrolling a stretch of highway up north in Benton County. A totally different place, almost all town. Sure nothing like our tiny place. If I'd a told Mac what I saw he'd have been more than plumb agitated."

Wendy laughed. "That's the truth. Did you get your story anyway?"

"Oh, sure. He answered all my questions about the drug bust, posing like some big city boss, throwing out sound bites like he was doing a television interview. I think I'll fix his wagon and not quote directly anything he said."

"Not a good idea, Jess." Parker stood in the door to his office, a twinkle in his dark eyes. "You sure Mac is okay?"

"Just fuming. Mike said he ought to check with Doc, though. I'll see he does. Tell you what, I'll give you my notes on the marijuana bust and you can see how pretentious that Couch is. Bet you won't use anything he said either."

"Just the opposite. Fools spin their own traps. He'll look more a fool if you quote every word."

"As long as I have your permission, I'll be glad to do just that. He'll be the laughingstock of the entire town."

"So be it." Parker headed for the tiny kitchen in the back. "Smells like the coffee is ready."

She joined him and Wendy appeared in the doorway too.

"Hank dropped some cinnamon rolls by earlier when he delivered this week's ads."

Jess dug them from a brown sack. Parker wrapped one up in a paper towel. Jess let Wendy go next, then took one, leaving several for stragglers.

The paper had grown over the past year or so, and now it wasn't laid out and taken to Harrison for printing until Tuesday night. So the next two days would be long and harried. But that's the way she liked it.

She trailed Parker and Wendy back into the main office, each carrying a steaming mug and a napkin-wrapped fragrant roll from LaNita's on the other side of the square. They were baked fresh every morning.

"Mac say anything about when they might let him go back to work?"

"No, but he's liable to just come back and kick that old fart out, he's so vexed. He thinks by the time he's allowed on the job Cedarton will be in the midst of the worst crime wave in its history."

Parker chuckled. "I believe that was last year, wasn't it? Speaking of, though, you want me to call Couch and get something on the kids and their shoplifting sprees?"

"I wish you would. I was up at Walmart and literally got run down by one of those little felons. Funny thing though." She paused and took a bite of roll. "This kid, he looked right at me like he was about to bust out crying. So sad." She went on to relate the event in its entirety.

"You sure you're not just empathizing with the little brat?" Parker had no patience with anyone who broke the law for whatever reason.

"Maybe, but why would a pre-teen boy steal a girl's dress? It doesn't make sense."

"Where was your camera when all this was going on?" Parker took a last bite of the roll and wiped his lips and fingertips.

"Out in the car. Who expects to run into a story at Walmart?"

"Well, you bought yourself that expensive doodad. I was hoping you'd use it to get us some extraordinary photos." His words were half teasing and she shot him a frown.

"I will, don't worry about that. Still, I'm curious."

"You're a reporter. You're supposed to be curious. So follow the story and quit mooning over Dallas. He'll be back, crazy as he is about you."

She sat down at the empty desk and took a big bite from her roll.

Maybe Dallas would be back and maybe she ought to quit thinking about him. But he probably wasn't near as crazy over her as Parker thought. And last year was the worst she'd spent here since returning home from California, what with Dallas getting pushed off the mountain and nearly killed, and then his leaving town. Not to mention her shooting her ex-boyfriend Steve. Thank goodness neither of them died, but both men lit out. Maybe she ought to consider that she might have been responsible for both of them leaving. Could be she was too much for any man to handle. No one had heard one word from the Cherokee lawman since then, either. When he came back, she was gonna kick his gorgeous butt right up between his shoulders then haul him off to the nearest private place and jump his bones. As for Steve, good riddance.

Part of the enjoyment of working for a weekly newspaper was the variation of duties. Wendy took care of phone calls most of the time. Jessie handled overflow. Wendy typed submitted columns into the Quark layout on the computer. Jessie helped with editing. Hand-delivered last minute items went to whoever looked up from their computer more than three minutes at a time. That was a joke Parker often made, and it was almost true. If the fire truck across the street took off Jessie did too. Same if the scanner emitted a police call for anything from a minor dispute between neighbors to a traffic accident or TA. There was no police department in Cedarton, nor in the county for that matter. Only the sheriff's department. Deputies took care of everything except speeders on the state highways.

By the end of Monday the office looked like a tornado had hit. Finding room for everything was a hassle. Forty percent of each page was devoted to ads to support the paper, which then dictated how many pages there would be overall. Sometimes some stories had to be picked up off the AP wire to fill the gaps or a few had to be left out. Parker was pretty good at estimating the final count as the day wore on, though.

Jessie loved every minute of it. Even her so called days off when she could be called in at any time if something came up that had to be covered. Her life was never boring.

Late Monday afternoon Parker brought in a fax and tossed it down on her desk. "This came in off the wire, might be worth looking into for next week. Just run the release as is. We'll make room, then you can do a story next week if it turns out to affect us."

Rolling her eyes, she picked up the fax and read the first line.

In the wake of recent Nolton County arrests the DEA has announced investigation of several county sheriff's departments in north Arkansas and southern Missouri.

The phone rang and she dropped the fax into her box. Nolton County was against the Missouri state line to the northeast. Probably nothing there for *The Observer.* Yet it was possible Mac's suspension could be related. Sometimes the DEA liked to make a sweep of two or three small counties with only deputies to cover them all. It could turn into a big story. After lunch she'd cut it down to fit.

Around six, Parker went to the Red Bird Café and brought back burgers, fries, and Cokes for everyone. As always, he insisted they take a break while they ate at the empty desk.

"End up with mustard and ketchup all over our keyboards if we try to work and eat." A mantra he used more than once.

Monday and Tuesday were a blur of writing, editing, phone calls, and drop-ins. It was 11:30 when Jessie dragged herself home, arriving at the small cabin a few miles outside of town close to midnight. Brad waited for her on the front porch, wiggling his hind end all the way inside. Hadn't she left him in the house that morning? The little imp had found a way to squirm his way out, no doubt.

She scratched his ears. "Guess you know what I've got, don't you?" She unwrapped the burger Norma, the waitress at the Red Bird, always sent him. He gulped down the patty in four huge bites while Jessie locked up and trailed through the house shedding her jeans and t-shirt inside the bathroom door and stepping into the shower. Her shoulders ached from sitting hunched over a desk most of the late evening and she let the hot water pound the muscles until it cooled down.

Settled in bed, she propped her head on three pillows and dragged out her Kindle to read a while. Brad's nails clicked across the living room floor. Taking up guard duty near the door. Warm summer air drifted through the open window, caressing her naked body. In the midst of reading a hot sex scene, her fingers drifted across her stomach and between her legs, sending a pleasant sensation through her weary muscles.

Times like this when she craved some loving was when she missed

Dal the most. Before he took off they'd been going at it pretty hot and heavy. If they weren't fighting over whether she belonged at his crime scene, they were wrapped in each other's arms in heated passion. Then he was gone and she was beginning to think he wasn't coming back. Three years ago he fled the violence in Dallas and landed in Cedarton, hoping to find peace. Somehow, what he sought eluded him. No doubt because he carried his guilt with him, whether in Dallas or Cedarton. So he took off late last fall, and there'd been nothing from him at all since.

The Kindle plopped down onto her belly. She startled awake, shut it off, and turned over to imagine being in his arms.

Next thing she knew, bars of sunlight warmed her legs. This morning she had an appointment to interview Alicia Woodson, an attorney who had recently opened a practice in town. Should make quite a story. Woodson had left a large legal corporation in New York City. Talk was she wanted her husband to have a quiet place to live. He had been wounded in Afghanistan. Theron at the Red Bird said the poor fella was blind, his face all scarred up. He said the lawyer had bought the old Hermitage place, a plantation-style house on the side of the mountain looking down on the town. It would be plenty peaceful up there, being about three miles from the main road and no other houses out that way.

Jessie chuckled. Living in a small town meant information flowed all the time. Still, it had to be checked out. She didn't know any of that for sure, and she'd verify it with the interview. Hopefully, things would be quieter this year than last. Compared to New York City, Cedarton probably appeared real laid back to the Woodsons. An attorney would be welcome in town, seeing as how there wasn't one. Unless you went to Fayetteville or Harrison. And everyone said half of them were crooks.

After a morning spent sprucing up the house, changing the bed linens, and doing some laundry, she hopped in the shower.

She resisted the urge to dress up and show this New York City woman she knew good fashion. Instead she wore a denim skirt, an embroidered peasant blouse, and moccasins. She tied her long, sun-streaked hair back with a bright blue scarf. At LaNita's, she ordered a pitcher of lemonade and one of tea, told Amy Lou she was expecting Alicia Woodson and they would eat out back to take in the view of the mountains.

"Oh, that's the new lawyer lady, idn't it? She's real nice. Has took to eating here some days when she's in town. Spends most of her time up at that new place they bought. Has an office up there too, but I don't think clients are welcome there. Her poor husband, you know. I'll bring your drinks and menus back in a sec." The tiny, dark haired girl flitted away, ponytail swaying with each step.

So much for introducing the town to Alicia Woodson. Jessie had to smile at the way word got around.

"You must be Jessie West." A low-pitched voice with a slight back-east accent interrupted her woolgathering.

She turned to greet a tall, thin, striking woman with chocolate eyes and shiny brown hair cut in a bob that touched her jawline. She wore a navy blue pants suit and loafers.

"That's me." Jessie stood and shook her hand. "I've ordered us something to drink. Oh, here it comes now."

Alicia eyed the two pitchers and laughed pleasantly. "No martinis?"

"No, I'm afraid not here in Cedarton." Jessie studied her to see if she was mocking their way of life. Sure didn't look like it. Just something to say. She ate here, she knew no alcoholic drinks were served. Though you might score some weed out back.

Amy Lou poured Alicia lemonade and raised her eyebrows to Jessie, who nodded. She left the menus and took the pitcher of tea with her.

Alicia leaned back in her chair and studied Jessie over her glass. "This town is precisely what I wanted for Jeff. Have you been here long?"

"Well, not this time. I'm from here originally, but my folks moved to California when I was in my early teens. I only came back about three years ago. Seems I'm related to half the county. In a lot of ways it's a good feeling." She laughed and the attorney joined her. "How did you know I hadn't grown up here?"

"You have a bit of a West Coast twang to your Arkansas drawl."

"I do? That's funny, I didn't realize that."

"I see you're not married."

Jessie busied herself unrolling her silverware from its paper napkin. The statement didn't need an answer and she didn't want to explain that whole mess anyway. "Somehow I feel as if I'm the one being interviewed."

"Oh, I'm sorry. I didn't intend to—"

"No, no. I didn't mean it that way. Usually people just sit and look at me waiting for me to ask questions."

"It's the lawyer in me. We start off by asking questions of our clients, and so it's a habit. Please ask and I'll answer and I won't pry anymore, I promise." The dark eyes gleamed with mischief to show she was teasing.

Jessie liked her, especially the friendly way she presented herself. Before she could ask her first question, though, Amy Lou came back to take their order. They all chuckled because neither of them had opened their menu.

"Maybe I'll just have the usual," Alicia said playfully.

Jessie broke up. That's what everyone at the Red Bird said when they wanted burger and fries. Dal had thought it so much fun when he first went in there to just order the usual.

Never do that in Dallas, he'd teased. *No telling what you'd get.*

God she missed him. The way his cheeks dimpled when he joked around with her. The green eyes that went so dark with passion when the two of them made love. She blinked to stop the tears.

"I'm sorry. I asked what you wanted." Amy Lou looked at Jessie.

"Oh, bring me a chicken salad with ranch dressing."

"So, that'll be two usuals." She hurried off, laughing.

"Now, who do you love?" Alicia had waited till the waitress left to ask that one.

Jessie glanced up quickly and took another sip of lemonade.

"There I go getting nosy again and I promised I'd let you do the interview. It's just that you looked so sad there for a minute. I couldn't help but wonder what some man had done to you."

"It's nothing, really." She fussed around in her bag, brought out a pad and pen, and started the interview.

It was true, what Theron had said. Alicia's husband was blinded when an IED blew up in his face. Though he'd learned to deal with being blind—at least to the point where he could get around pretty well—he suffered from bad dreams and flashbacks so that he needed to live away from people.

"Sometimes his shouting disturbed our neighbors who lived on the other side of the walls. All the other sides. It's just better for him here. He spends a lot of time out in the barn. And frankly, I didn't mind one bit leaving the city. If I had to listen to one more claim of innocence from some pierced, tattooed hood, no matter what, I think I might've shot someone and pleaded innocent myself. I want to practice family law here. Take care of folks with financial problems, elderly care, defend people against stupid lawsuits, less violent things. You know, 'your tree limb fell in my yard and smashed my petunias' sort of thing."

"You may have come to the right place. We tend to shoot our violent lawbreakers. Saves lots of money and time."

Alicia's eyes widened and she stared at Jessie for a long moment before Jessie laughed. "Teasing. More or less. Why don't you give me some background like where you were born, where you went to school, what you think of our small town and its residents, and tell me how much of what you just told me you don't want in the paper? In that order. And maybe a bit more about your husband, if you don't mind. We're a patriotic bunch around here. And we honor our veterans, especially when they've given as much as he has. One of our newest deputies, Colby, is a veteran. He served three tours in Afghanistan. Been here about eight months. He seems to really like living here, but then he's an Arkie anyway."

Alicia filled her in on where Jeff went to school, that he was an architect prior to being injured. "He wants to be an artist. Likes to sketch in charcoal. Claims he can feel it on the paper, see it in his mind's eye. He's amazing in ways you wouldn't believe." Love shone in the woman's brown eyes.

How fortunate they both were, even considering his injuries. She fought a touch of envy, wondered how he could possibly tell when he had a drawing the way he wanted it. Now that would make a terrific interview. Their meals arrived and they continued to get acquainted while they ate.

They both ordered pie, but Alicia only ate a couple of bites, asked for the rest to be boxed to take home to her husband. "I like to taste sweets, but I've never quite recovered from a bout with anorexia when I was young. Still can't convince myself I'm not fat. That, by the way, is off the record."

Jessie laughed. "Everything you say to me is off the record unless I tell you it's for the story. Big difference from city newspaper reporters. Dal always has such a hard time with that. Getting people to reveal secrets then publishing them for everyone to see is a no-no around here."

"Maybe that's because people already know them." She laughed, then sobered. "Dal? Is that who made you almost cry a while ago?"

"You're too sharp. You ought to be the reporter."

"Not me. I could never do that. Guess it's cause I have to keep everything a secret. And you might like to know, off the record, that I've already been made privy to a few really interesting secrets that will kick off my law practice quite well. So far, I'm happy."

"Well, you wouldn't believe the stories I have hidden inside me. Believe me, I can keep secrets with the best of them. And I do. Could I get a picture of you to run with the story?"

"Sure. Right here be okay?"

Jessie took out her camera and snapped a dozen or so shots. "It's been great meeting you. Hope I never need a lawyer, but if I do I have a feeling it would be you. I hope we can have lunch together again sometime soon."

"I'd like that." Alicia rose, wished her a good day, and threaded her way between the tables.

Nice to meet someone who might make a good friend. Tink would like her. Since Tink and Burt married, Jessie didn't see as much of her, but they did get together when he pulled an evening shift or was called out late. Sheriff Mac tried to only use the single guys for night calls, but it wasn't always possible. Couch wasn't that considerate.

Since Sheriff Mac had been sidelined and Arthur Couch brought in to take his place, things had remained pretty quiet, but all hell could break loose at any time.

Alone in the office, she was typing away on her article about the new attorney in town when the scanner went off. Three kids had charged out the door at Brown's on the square after being spotted on a store camera stuffing video games inside their baggy clothing. A blue van was described as having scooped them up. Colby answered the call.

Jessie paused in her typing to see if he was in pursuit, but he soon broadcast a BOLO for a faded blue Ford van with a mud-coated license tag that couldn't be read. Sure sounded like the van from this morning at Walmart except for the mud on the plates. What was going on in their quiet town?

Earlier this spring the cult that had been raided by the DEA and Marshal services over in Nolton County was found to be using kids to pull robberies in the posh side of New Castle, a retirement village. Sheriff Robert Kimble was under investigation.

Ah well, nothing there for now. Time to get home to her empty house and feed Brad. She missed Dal the most on days like this. Sometimes they'd spend the entire night making love and talking.

God, she wished he'd come home where he belonged. More than that, she wished he'd at least get in touch so she'd know he was okay. He'd been in a dark, dark place when he left town last fall and she was worried sick about him.

2
CHAPTER

On the way home Dal stopped at the small grocery, picked up some perishables, and bought a copy of the *Arkansas Times/Gazette* from the rack outside the door. At the gas pumps Aileen gassed an old pickup. She grinned and waved. Kind of cute, in a grubby way. Always had oil smeared on her face and hands, and her figure hidden inside a pair of oversized coveralls. Still, he got a bit of a buzz on when she grinned at him like that. Probably cause he'd been without a woman for eight months, two weeks, and three days. But hell, as they said, *WTF?* After all, he didn't know how many hours it'd been.

"You doin okay there, handsome?" She shook the nozzle free of a few drops and eased it back in the pump, threw him a look that tightened his groin. Sticking that nozzle in there like that. She knew precisely what he was thinking. Little minx. He couldn't help but laugh. Here he was covered in sweat and sawdust, shirt and pants clinging to his soaked body. Had to stink and she's flirting with him. Must be desperate. Too young and too innocent for his taste. He gave her a nod, climbed on his four-wheeler, and ripped out of town before he could change his mind about her.

When he fled Cedarton he'd rented a tiny cabin in Frog Pond—well maybe not literally in the pond but close by. It was only a wide place in the road in the center of nowhere. He chuckled. He once considered Cedarton the center of nowhere. It was all in his perspective. Thrusting hard on the hand pump in the yard, he dunked his head under the icy water's flow and washed away the sweat and sawdust, then stripped out of his shirt, kicked off his boots, and peeled out of his britches. A bar of soap waited on a three-legged stand. He palmed it and scrubbed from head to toes, filled the aluminum bucket, held it high, and poured it over himself. Gasping from the shock, he dug a comb from his discarded shirt and ran it through his long hair before tying it back with a strip of leather thong. An okay shower for summertime. Better than the washtub sitting in front of the potbellied stove during this past winter.

So far, this life suited him, if only he could stop feeling so damned lonely and black out the nightmares that had followed like an *anasgi`na*, the dark spirit trailing along in his wake. He missed Cedarton and his friends, but he refused to think about who he missed most. She didn't figure into the place he was in, nor would he ask her to. Besides, he couldn't handle all the problems that went with her life. Chasing after every damned killing or disturbance. Plunging into danger. All for a story, and him afraid she'd revert to her own dark past.

Granted, one or two murders a year beat the hell out of three or four hundred, like Dallas. Still, when he was shoved off that mountain by the man she'd betrayed, something inside went all black. It liked to killed him, fired his buried guilts to life, and on top of that uncovered just how vulnerable he was. He hated that worse than anything.

Damn, he carried as much, if not more, baggage than Jess did and that was the real trouble. Not just her. Shit no, they fit together like two jagged edges. Slashing away at each other while sparks flew enough to set the world on fire. Enough to leave permanent damage.

Okay, end this trip down memory lane right now. It gave him a damned hard-on just thinking of her. Images of her fine features, the dusting of freckles and sun-streaked hair that tickled his skin like strands of silk. Slipping inside her hot, wet, sweet... oh, shit. Stop. Oops. Too late.

He came with a flash of incredible dismay that drained him so that he leaned on the pump for a moment. Dammit, he had to quit this. Falling back to earth, he grabbed the towel hanging on a nearby bush and rubbed down real good. He wadded the dirty linen with his discarded clothes and darted into the house where he stepped into a clean pair of jeans. The climax left him feeling empty, dissatisfied, yearning for her touch. Goddammit, would he ever get over her? Just like him to hang on to the most damaging of memories.

Shirtless and barefoot, he started a fire in the stove to cook some supper. A steak he'd bought at the grocery soon sizzled in a cast iron skillet, a can of corn and another of green peas steamed in two small enameled pans he'd picked up at a flea market. Butter waited on a bag of ice inside the plastic chest. He unwrapped a round of homemade bread Rema gave him before he left working on her house, set the table, and flipped the steak over to sear the other side. It had to run red when cut, and he waited two minutes before sliding the chunk of thick meat onto his plate. He set the pans of vegetables on pads as red as splashes of blood on the white painted table. Weary, he lowered himself into the single wooden chair.

The steak bled with the cutting, butter melted in the veggies and on the bread he'd warmed in the oven. Toting two-by-fours and four by eight sheets of plywood and wielding a hammer all day left him hungry as a wolf. Eased his desire to pound someone over the head. He took his time savoring the food. When he finished it was going on toward dusk and he placed a pan of water on the stove. While it heated to wash up his scant eating utensils, he picked up the paper and relaxed near the window where light from the dying sun lit the pages.

The article was buried in the out-of-county news. Way out-of-county for the *Gazette*, though a Fayetteville issue was printed as well as the one distributed in Little Rock. Why did he always search for these small news items? As if he would never be quite done with Grace County and Cedarton. Deep down, the idea that might be true ate at him.

Why is Grace County Sheriff on Leave?

The official version is that Mac Richards, Grace County's sheriff for the past decade, has been put on medical leave. But this reporter has uncovered another possible reason. Nolton County Sheriff Robert Kimble was recently suspended when he was accused of taking bribes from a reputed Islamic Cult. A hearing has not yet been scheduled. It has been surmised that perhaps the same thing is going on in Grace County, thus throwing suspicion on Sheriff Mac Richards.

With the smallest population in Arkansas, Grace County has in the past had its problems. Mainly countless arrests of marijuana growers who are then released after being fined. Could it follow that the cult, recently run out of Nolton County, did not go far? Perhaps there are more secrets hidden in the wilderness of Grace County than we know about. This reporter could not learn if there is an ongoing investigation of Richards at this time, but it is a distinct possibility considering his discharge from the Grace County Sheriff's Department.

"Goddammit." Dal slammed a hand down on the spreadsheets of the newspaper. "Son of a bitch." Grandfather would frown at his use of white man's curses, but his undercover occupation had educated him quickly in the nuances of such language. The Cherokee limited their swearing to turds, farts, and comparisons to animals.

Sheriff Mac would never take bribes. Worst he did was let a lot of growers go free after imposing a fine cause he knew growing marijuana was the only way some folks could make a living. It had replaced the stills of another era. Putting growers in jail just created another family without a breadwinner plus extra mouths to feed in the jail. Far as Mac was concerned, he'd done his duty when he caught them and the court fined them. That kept the county coffers filled. Besides, he didn't have enough deputies to police everyone twenty-four/seven. Just a fact of law enforcement in the sprawling wilderness of the Ozarks. Anyway the feds and their helicopters kept watch during growing season, and they hauled in a goodly amount of the wicked weed. There were better ways to utilize his deputies' time.

So what in the world was going on with this deal? Had the reporter reached too far in his suppositions? Or had Mac fallen off the wagon? Maybe the old man decided he was fighting a losing battle. Dal would bet on the reporter making up the story before he'd believe Mac had done anything like was being hinted at.

He read the short news clip again, then sat until dark staring out the window. This reporter cited no sources. A good reason to figure he was blowing smoke. Mac was a good friend, as were some of the other guys in the department. Then there was Jess. Dal didn't make friends easily, and yet he'd got to know and like several of the men, including Sam Watson, the retired deputy, as well as Les, Burt, Colby, and the EMT Mike Henley. They could all get dragged into this mess. What Mac needed was an experienced investigator outside his deputies to root out the truth. That could be him. But what about Jessie? How could he avoid her? Answer was, if he went home to Cedarton, he couldn't.

He fetched a clean shirt, slipped his bare feet into moccasins, and went out to fire up the four-wheeler. In town he stopped at the café, the only place in town with a public telephone. To his amazement cell phones had invaded even the wilds around Frog Pond, killing the need for public ones. He dropped in a quarter, punched in a number he knew by heart, and it rang several times before it was picked up.

Jessie lay stretched out on the couch eating an apple and reading a James Lee Burke novel when the phone rang. The incoming number was foreign to her. It was in the area code, but she almost didn't answer, then thought what the hey and picked up. Might be good for some entertainment on this lonely night.

"Jess?"

Her heart skipped around in her chest and she saw black. Must be asleep and dreaming.

"Dal?" She could scarcely get the word out, but the next ones poured forth. "Are you okay? Where are you? My God, it's good to hear from you."

"You too. You doing okay?"

The knot in her throat swelled and for a minute she couldn't reply. Just like that, he calls. After leaving her nearly nine months ago. She cleared her throat, still couldn't speak. Hell no, she wasn't doing okay. Not where he was concerned. But she didn't say so.

"I'm calling about Mac. How's he doing?"

Heated anger flushed her face like a fever. "Why do you care? You just up and walked out on all of us. Now you call out of the blue about Mac?"

"Jess, I—"

"What?" Dammit. Tears wet her cheeks and dripped onto the pages of the novel.

"I didn't know who else to call to find out anything. I'm worried about Mac. There's an article in the *Gazette* that practically accuses him of taking bribes from some weird cult. How is he? What's going on? Who's checking this out? And who is running the department?"

Shoulders raised, she did her best to sound distant. "He's fine, very angry. He had an anxiety attack earlier today. Mike said it wasn't a heart attack. So far he's just on medical leave. I don't know what's going on except we got kids stealing stuff all over the place. I imagine the deputies are checking it out, but it's not a good sign. Arthur Couch, a retired statie, has been put on the job as sheriff. Is there anything else you wish to know?" She covered her mouth so he couldn't hear her sob. All she could think was, damn you, Dallas Starr, come home so I can kick your butt.

"What do you mean, kids stealing stuff?"

"Why do you care? I guess we can handle it without your help." Her crying definitely muffled those words. What a wuss she was.

"Jess, I'm sorry." So soft she hardly heard him, then an almost silent click and he was gone.

She sat straight up, rechecked the area code of the number he'd called from. Eight seventy. Same as Grace County, but how many counties did it include? Grabbing the thin telephone directory, she opened it to the front page with area code information. The map in the phone book showed the area code covered all the eastern plus a portion of the southern and northern parts of the state. Not much help in locating him. The least populated per square mile section of the state but huge in size. It included Harrison and Cedarton, but he wouldn't be that close. Too many people knew him, especially in the sheriff's department. If he wanted to stay hidden, he'd be holed up in some holler deep in the wilderness. In a place where only beasts and few men tread. Closer to what they referred to as the Grand Canyon of the Ozarks. In these mountains there were hundreds of scattered settlements where people lived who were set on leaving no footprints and they didn't nose into anyone else's business for fear of causing attention. Most had no electrical power and remained off the grid.

Grace County was still that way in many respects, but with the new highway from Tulsa to Branson cutting through its corner, a few more people were taking up residence around the county seat.

Okay, Jessie, you're an investigative reporter. Investigate. Working for *The Observer* had dulled those skills. Not difficult to learn anything in a town where everyone knew everyone's business. Still, she'd heard no gossip about where these kids, like that boy at Walmart today, came from and why they picked Cedarton. Only wild suppositions. But back to Dal. Call the number, see who answers. If it's him, hang up. But maybe he's using someone else's phone. It wasn't his cell number.

Her fingers shook so badly she could barely punch in the number. Got it wrong the first time and had to start over. There, now it was ringing. She held her breath. It must've rang eight or nine times. Might as well hang up.

"Yeah?" The voice came through short tempered, not Dallas.

"Could I speak to, uh, to Dallas Starr please?"

"Nope. Don't know the guy." Click. And just like that the connection was gone. What had she heard in the background? A bell or buzzer. A voice whooped, another said king me. That was all. Sure not much to go on. King me? What in the world? Someone playing checkers?

Dallas.

Why did you call if you're not coming home? Or even if you are. Dammit. Now she was upset all over again. She picked up the book, tried to get interested in Dave Robicheaux, but it didn't work and she finally put it down and crept out onto the deck, plopped into one of the lawn chairs, and stared up at the star-splattered sky. They'd spent more than one night out here together. Her and that stoic Cherokee. His viridian eyes black in the night while he kissed her, eased into her, gentled her tight against his muscled thighs and held her there ever so long, stirring inside her, hot and hard while sucking on her earlobe and neck, his moist breath raising goose bumps.

"Oh, God." The tortured moan accompanied an orgasm that bowed her body. But how did one enjoy something that should feel good when it was birthed by a bitter emptiness? That night she dreamed of children wandering the woods, crying, fighting with each other.

The sun shining through the eastern window woke her. A wooded peak blocked the rays till after nine o'clock. She stretched and sat, pulled her knees up to prop both elbows on them. Angry that she missed him so much, angrier that he had called and brought those feelings back to the surface when she'd about had them tamped down so they only came out occasionally. Just plain pissed off.

Even though no one would be in the office, she'd go in. Maybe she could come up with another story for the coming week's issue. Try to find out more about this cult in Nolton County. Probably a story about it in the *Gazette*. She'd stop and pick one up when she got a cinnamon roll from LaNita's. Would Colby know something? He patrolled a lot of the county. Liked to be out and away from everyone. Odd, but men who came back from war were often that way. Be damned if she'd ask that Arthur Couch anything.

Brad gave his two-bark request when she left the house, twisting all over to convince her he could ride shotgun. She opened the door of the Jeep, looked back at him and patted her thigh.

"Well, come on, then. But you have to be good while I work."

No one would be in the office, so it wouldn't matter. What harm could one pit bull do?

Especially one as sweet as Brad.

The top was down on the Jeep and he sat in the passenger seat, head high, tongue lolled out, tasting the wind and taking in the sights all the way to town. Occasionally she silently thanked whoever discarded Brad near the college last fall. He'd taken up with her and followed her back to the newspaper. They'd been together ever since. No one ever claimed him, even though she ran a notice in the paper for three weeks. By that time, she was in love with the funny looking dog with a curl to his lip.

Parked at the office, she gathered her copy of the *Gazette*, her backpack, and the sack containing a lone cinnamon roll and headed inside where she gave Brad a bite of roll, started a pot of coffee, and went to her desk to read the paper while it made.

It was nice and quiet in there. Folks rarely called on Thursday and if they did she could let it go to the answering machine. The police scanner was silent, like the universe maybe wanted her to have some peace and quiet. Even so, she couldn't help wishing the phone would ring and it would be Dal and all would be forgiven.

Stop this nonsense, woman. You aren't defined by that man. You can live without him. Or at least she wanted to think she could, just in case. That didn't mean her current life was enjoyable. This yearning for his companionship just wouldn't stop.

The article about Mac was buried in the back section of the paper and after she finished reading it she muttered a few curses. At one time she might have written just such a piece. Today she knew better. To make unfounded guesses like that was one thing in private, quite another when published in a newspaper. People tended to believe what they read, and the way this was worded people could easily believe Mac had already been convicted of taking bribes while steering the law away from an illegal organization that stole not only possessions but children. As far as she knew nothing of the sort had even been suggested. He certainly hadn't been accused. But no one would ever forget they read it in the paper.

The brief article went a long way toward explaining Dal's call of the previous night. Whether it would be enough to bring him home or not was another question. And whether she could handle him coming home was definitely questionable. She was mad enough at him to box his ears and that wouldn't set too well with him.

The morning after reading the piece about Mac in the paper, Dal stuffed some jockeys, a pair of jeans, a t-shirt, boots, and a few essentials in a duffel, rode the four-wheeler to town and pulled under the sloping tin roof alongside the gas station. Aileen wandered out carrying a cup of coffee.

"Mornin. Something wrong with it? Want me to take a look?"

"Nah, thanks. I have to go on a short trip and it's not licensed for the highways, so I wondered if it'd be okay to leave it here till I get back. Hate to have to walk back home. You can use it while I'm gone if you want."

She gazed up at him, a smear of grease on her chin. "Sure. Could charge you rent I guess, but it don't take up much room. Going home for a visit?"

"What?" He wasn't really listening, already wondered if he was doing the right thing, going back to Cedarton, even for a little while. "Oh, no. Got some business."

She snickered, looked him up and down. "Business? You're kidding. Well, if it's none of mine I reckon you can tell me whatever you want."

"No, I'm really a rich guy hiding from my family, see, but once in a while I have to show up or lose my fortune."

She laughed. Her throat was long and graceful when she tilted her head back. Interesting that he'd notice. Maybe he ought to—nah, that would be foolish. She had too many questions and doubts for his taste. Besides she couldn't be over twenty. He didn't like anyone knowing too much about him and wasn't real crazy about silly young women. True, Jess had poked her nose in where it didn't belong just like a damned reporter. They were always hunting for secrets that were none of their business, always writing lies when they were too lazy to dig out the truth. But then he had to go all nuts about her.

"How you gonna get there?" Aileen's question brought him back with a jerk.

"Thought I'd hitch."

"Tell you what. I've got to run out to Harrison for some parts today. I could take you wherever you're wanting to go if it's in that direction."

He studied her, the eager expression on her face. "Thanks, but I'm going the other way. Appreciate the storage. I'll be glad to pay you. See you when I get back. I don't know how long I'll be gone, but I wrote down the café's phone number in case I need to get in touch."

She pulled a cell out of her pocket. "I've got this, too... if you want the number."

He took a couple of backward steps. "No, that's okay. See you later."

Her smiling expression sobered. At the curve in the road, he turned to look. She stood near the road staring after him.

Three miles later at the highway, a box truck stopped and picked him up after about ten minutes. The driver immediately explained that he never picked up hitchhikers but he was lonely and it was a long drive to Fayetteville, and where was he headed? Everything spoken in one long drawn-out sentence.

"As luck would have it, you're going my way. Where Highway Twenty-two heads south, that's where I'm going."

"Got folks living there?" The guy shifted gears before Dal pulled the door shut. Everyone wasn't nosy, it was just considered friendly to ask personal questions.

"Yeah, they own a hog farm down the road a ways from there."

"Oh, well? Guess they's good money in that nowadays."

"Yep, they're just rolling in it."

The guy shut up and glanced at him. Then he busted out laughing. "Oh, the old joke. Rolling in pig shit. Damn, you're a funny guy."

"So I'm told. I do appreciate the ride, though."

"Oh, that's okay. Like I said."

"Yeah, it's lonely out here. You drive this way often?"

"Once a week. I haul all kinds of stuff back and forth. Loads of furniture, pecans, flooring, whatever I can pick up. They's plenty of smaller businesses don't like to wait on a semi to fill up before they send stuff to their other stores, or customers. So they call me and I can make a run with smaller loads at a decent price whenever they want."

"Interesting. Never thought of that as being a good business."

"Oh, sure, I do all right and I can always say no if I don't want to make a run, though I'm usually accommodating."

"Tell me, you ever haul any, uh, illegal stuff? I mean, hell, there must be a lot of money in that."

"Hey, you mean drugs. Hell no, wouldn't catch me doing that if I was starving. Besides, those folks are plumb scary to deal with. They'd shoot you soon as look at you. I've been approached a couple of times, but I steer real clear. I didn't fall off no damned turnip truck."

"Yeah, I get that. I used to live in Dallas and it was real bad there. Drugs everywhere."

"Yeah, well the real drug route through this country is down on I-Forty. Shit, betcha every third or fourth vehicle is carrying drugs of some kind."

"That right? Man, I wouldn't have thought that."

"Oh, yeah. This country is going plumb to the dogs where drugs is concerned. And they's way too much money in it for the government to get serious trying to stop it either. But you won't catch me going nowhere near that stuff, no siree. I'd rather haul wetbacks as drugs." The guy gave him a quick glance. "Sorry, you ain't Meskin, are you? Your dark skin and all. I didn't mean nothing by wetbacks."

"No, I'm Cherokee. Better be careful, we sometimes take scalps." He gave the guy a minute to absorb that, then went on as if he hadn't mentioned scalping. "Wetbacks, huh? Way up here? You'd think we'd be too far north for that."

"Sheeit, no. But I ain't never done it, you know. They's enough ways to get in trouble without breaking the law, you know." He tilted his head toward Dal. "Cherokee, huh? Taking scalps. Now that there's funny. Say you're kinda far off the reservation, ain't you?"

Dal laughed and so did his host driver. The guy had the kind of warped sense of humor he dug.

The conversation wandered all over the place during the three-and-a-half hour drive to where he got off. Stomach rumbling from hunger, he crawled out, waved at the disappearing truck, trotted across the highway, and headed south on 22. Once in Grace County, he'd probably be spotted by someone who knew him, so he cut off through the woods on an old logging road that would take him close to town the back way. Maybe he could make it to Mac's house without anyone recognizing him. Once there if lucky he could learn there was nothing to the story and be on his way back to Frog Pond without having to see anyone else. Couldn't be helped Mac would blab to everyone he knew. By then, though, he'd be long gone on his way out of town.

No such luck. He came out of the woods only half-a-block from Mac's. By then the sun was bearing down, soaking his shirt with sweat. He stopped to wipe his face with a red bandana, and who comes driving down the street but Seth Parker, esteemed editor and publisher of *The Observer*. In his nosiness, of course, he spotted Dal right away.

He honked and slowed to match Dal's walking speed. Put his elbow over the window frame and hollered. "When did you get back in town?"

Caught, Dal stopped. "Just now."

"Does Jessie know you're here?"

"I don't reckon. Won't be here long. Just come to see Mac, make sure everthing's okay."

"Oh, well, it isn't. Looks kind of bad, though a lot is conjecture. Mac could sure use a hand getting this straightened out. One reason I'm out here today is to go see him, see where we can get a photograph. I've got an idea for an article to help put an end to this nonsense."

"Thought the paper went out already this week."

Parker grinned. "Oh, it did, but in the newspaper business there's always the next issue. Maybe you could come up with something to put the hiatus on this stupid deducing. I've tried to run down this reporter's sources, but they're just not there. Still, the bell's been rung and even if we can prove otherwise, it can't be un-rung. Everyone's talking and taking sides. Couple of fist fights over it already."

"I know Mac, he had nothing to do with anything like that."

"Well, then, maybe you can step back in your deputy shoes and help out in that regard. He don't need folks running away."

Though he hadn't run away from that particular thing, Dal swelled with anger. One thing no man wanted was to be thought a coward. He'd drop in on Mac and figure out what he might be able to do to help the old man. Now he'd been spotted by nosey Parker, there was no way to keep his appearance from Jess and the whole damned town.

Shoving Dal's call to the back of her mind, Jessie called the sheriff's office to find out about the kids who'd been picked up in several different incidents. Got the new young deputy. She'd forgotten his name and asked.

"Howie Duggan, ma'am."

"Well, I'm Jessie West, reporter for *The Observer*. I was wondering if Colby is available."

"Let me see where he is. Hold on please."

Silence while she was put on hold.

She tapped the desk top with her pen till he came back on.

"Sorry, ma'am. I have a notification here that reporters calling have to go through Sheriff Couch to get any statements."

"How do you know I want a statement?" She was not too happy with the assumption, though it was true. "Never mind, put me through to the, uh, Couch then." Be damned if she'd refer to that asshole as sheriff. She hated referring to him at all, and dealing with him was even worse. After a long minute he came on.

"Couch." When he spoke he sounded like a dog growling. Seeing as how he was built like a fireplug, she could visualize all sorts of things.

"This is Jessie West. From *The Observer*? Are you preparing a press release on the recent shopliftings?"

"Nothing to release. A few of em got away, we caught the last little bugger. We'll get the others too, in time. All juveniles. No names to release."

"Is it true the others were picked up by a van?"

"That information isn't available at this time."

"May I quote you on that, Sheriff?" She drawled out the title, planned on quoting him nevertheless. Like Parker said, the man managed to make a fool of himself whenever he opened his mouth.

"Certainly, if you must."

"Thank you." She hung up before she could snort in the man's ear.

What a fool. She had enough for a story after stopping by Brown's and Walmart and talking to a few clerks and some customers in the store yesterday. But she'd quote the ignorant fool cause he sounded so dumb. Probably been hitting that bottle in his desk. He needed some schooling in running a sheriff's department.

She tapped out the story on her computer, saved it, and closed up. The more she thought about Dal's call the more upset she became. The phone rang before she could do anything about it. It was Parker.

"Has Dallas been in touch with you?" When he called he always just started talking without a greeting. Usually caught people unaware.

"Well, yes. He called me yesterday, but I don't know where from. It was an eight seventy area code, so at least he's still in Arkansas. He'd seen the article in the *Gazette* about Mac. Why? Did he call you?"

Short pause. Yeah, for sure, he knew something else and couldn't decide whether he should tell her or not.

"Parker, what did he say to you?"

"He's in town. I was driving down the street on my way to the Red Bird and he was walking along the sidewalk, big as you please. Said he was headed for Mac's."

She gritted her teeth. Damn him. Why had he cut her so completely out of his life? If he was coming to town, why didn't he just say so? She'd really like to see him. After all, they'd been a bit more than just friends. Obviously he didn't feel the same though.

"You there, Jessie?"

"Yes, I am. Did he say how long he'd be in town?"

"Nope, and I didn't ask. Might be best to leave that boy alone. He's obviously got some deep set problems to deal with."

"Oh, I'm going to leave him alone. Don't you worry about that. He shows up at my place, I'll throw water on him unless of course he's on fire. Then he gets nothing."

"Why don't I come out to your place tonight? We can play cards or watch a movie or something."

She took a deep breath. Not really in the mood for company, yet she didn't want to turn him down. "Okay. I'm so pissed I won't be good company, but it'll make me stop thinking of what's pissing me off, anyway."

Parker chuckled. "Well, I guess that's as close to an invite as I'm going to get. Want me to pick up something? Food, a movie, a hair shirt?"

"Ha ha. Bring us a pizza, but I'd just as soon chat as try to concentrate on a movie. I'd like to talk about this latest development with investigating county sheriffs, especially Mac."

"Want me to make notes or record our session?"

"Smart ass."

"See you later, then. I'll try to come up with something to put out the fire. We can discuss that."

Since Dal had gone Parker had taken to dropping by occasionally, but never without asking first. It wasn't like they were dating, it was just that they had so much in common to talk about. One Sunday he invited her to go horseback riding with him, and that had become an almost weekly event. She enjoyed it a lot, and he never pressured her to repeat the events of the night they'd spent together during that Steve business. She made it clear that she didn't want a sexual relationship after Dallas left, and so far he'd honored her wishes. Occasionally, when she had the urge, she almost wished she hadn't asked for his promise on that, but wasn't sure how to broach the subject with him again.

Now that Dallas might be back, she was relieved she hadn't done so. If they could ever renew their relationship she didn't want to have to explain it to Dal or Parker. What a muddled mess that would be.

3
CHAPTER

The front door rattled, not quite a knock. Mac put down the Smithsonian Magazine and peered through the curtained window. Hard to make out who it was, across the room like that. Tall feller with long hair tied back. Who did he know like that? This time a knock and a voice saying his name.

With a sigh he rose and shuffled across the room. From there he could see his caller but didn't quite believe his eyes. Maybe he'd fallen asleep reading and was having a wishful dream. Just looked like Dallas cause he wanted him here so bad. Couldn't be him, though. The hair wasn't right.

Under his hand the knob twisted and the door swung open. Sure enough, there stood Dallas Starr, minus his snakeskin cowboy boots, wearing moccasins, jeans, and a white t-shirt. Long hair tied back with a leather thong, he carried a duffel slung over one shoulder and had a smile on his face.

"Well, gawdamn me, git yourself on in here, boy."

The tall Indian stepped through the door and embraced him, flung his arms plumb around him till his feet left the floor for a minute. "Hey Mac, how you doing anyway?"

"A whole lot better now. Put that bag down and come set. Get you some coffee or something stronger? A beer, maybe? It's sure hot out there." The big fan going in the corner kept the shade-covered house cool though.

"I'd take a beer, been a hot, dry day. Looks as if tales of your demise have been exaggerated."

Mac chuckled on his way to the refrigerator. "Yep, they have. Sure enough have. Yours too, it would appear. After all this time we had our doubts of ever laying eyes on you again." He grabbed two bottles by the necks and carried them into the living room, made his way through the clutter of chairs, a well-worn couch, several tables, and a doily-covered bookcase filled with western paperbacks and Zane Grey books.

Dal sat on the couch and took the beer eagerly, sucked half of it down before speaking. "Damn, that's good. Next time I take a trip I'm going to carry a canteen of these around my neck." He held up the bottle, took another sip, and lowered it.

"Don't believe beer does well in a canteen. Imagine it'd half squirt out first time you opened it. They's other stronger drinks carry well, though." After a sip or two from his own beer, Mac could wait no longer. "So, I suppose you heard the latest news is why you're here after almost a year of total silence. We was worried about you boy, you shouldn't do such. You got friends around here care for you." He drank again, pinned a gaze on Dal's somber face.

"Maybe not so many anymore, but I'm sorry. It was only a while over eight months. I had some things to work out. Didn't see any use in making everyone else miserable cause I was. I did hear the news. Well, at least what was printed in the paper yesterday. That's all a crock of bull. I know that, and that's one reason I came on over to see what I could do to help."

"Well, I thank you. So you're back home to stay, I reckon. If Ina Mae can't find a empty spot over to her park, you can stay here. Place ain't very big but there is a second bedroom right yonder." He pointed toward the front corner opposite the small kitchen. "Course, I'd understand if you had another place in mind for staying while you're here." He glanced through lowered brows at Dal, who didn't meet his gaze. "I spect she's going to be mighty pleased to see you."

"I wouldn't be too sure of that. But I appreciate your offer, Mac. I noticed a new motel out on the highway. Figured I could stay there if I needed to be here more than a day."

"Well course you can. Come all this way only to leave the same day? That don't make any sense. Neither does staying in a motel when you got so many good friends here who'd love to have you."

Dal put down his empty bottle, careful to set it on a coaster he pulled from under a stack of magazines. "I want to hear about this cult business. What do you know so far?

"Not a whole lot. I think Couch's got Colby and Tink on the job right now. Would you believe, the first time my back is turned, that new sheriff sends that little gal out in the field where she could easy get shot or socked or hit over the head? Or worse. Bad things happen to women who work amid the criminal element."

"Now Mac, that's just the way things are now. Are they keeping you in the loop?"

"Not so far they ain't. That Couch fella keeps a pretty tight rein on who they share with."

"The hell he does. Where's your phone?"

Mac gestured toward a small corner table. "Keep thinking I'll get me one of those cordless outfits, but never get around to it."

"Thought you had a cell phone."

"Did, but it's run down and now I'm not an active sheriff anymore don't see the need for one. Use that one. Who you calling?"

"To start with? I'm calling the sheriff's office to try to get ahold of Colby and Tinkerbelle. Then I'm going to call Parker, and against my better judgment, Jessie. I think we all need to get together and arrange a come to Jesus meeting with the new sheriff, the fire chief, and the mayor about this situation and get it ironed out. I'll bet I can think of a few more before we're done. Tell me, are you acquainted with any folks involved with this so-called cult? Or does it even exist?" He snapped his fingers. "Oh, and do you happen to know the disgraced sheriff of Nolton County? Couldn't hurt to find out just what he does and doesn't know about this situation. And there's Sam Watson. He retired from the department some years back, but he's always got his nose in all the goings-on in town."

"Well, hell boy, why don't we just open up city hall and have a town meeting stead of messing about with those few? And before I forget, since I'm getting old, what's with the hair?"

"Didn't want to listen to a damn barber, that's all. That city hall idea, sometimes that only ends in a big fight that splits the town. Before this is over we're gonna know all there is to know about this so-called cult in Grace County, I can guarantee you that."

By the time he made that declaration, Dal had the phone in his hand and was punching numbers.

"Hey, it's me again." At that point he shut up and listened for a while. "You done yet?" He sounded vexed. "Look, Jessie, I'm here to help Mac and we're gonna need you and Parker, so if you want to help, could you come on over to Mac's tonight? And why don't you get a hold of Tinkerbelle and ask her and Colby to join us? This new sheriff isn't real friendly, and especially not with strangers." He listened again, interspersed uh-huh a few times, then, "Okay, see you at seven then."

Mac stared at him. "You're working fast. What'd she have to say?"

"Not real happy with me, but she'll be on your side, that's for sure. I decided maybe it'd be a good idea to leave Couch out of this till we get our strategy figured out, but I asked the rest of em here, hope that's okay."

"A little late to be asking, but hell, why not?"

"I'll run to the store and get some more beer, some pop, and what else do we want? Pizza, a bucket of chicken or burgers?"

After Dallas left to make a food run, Mac straightened up the living room, swiped through the bathroom and kitchen, and dug out some paper plates and napkins. By the time Dal returned, the place was presentable. Mac'd let the place go a lot since Marsha died, and that he couldn't do much about, but he did clear out the middle. Time he hired someone with a shovel to come in and clean up. Maybe he'd do that next week.

Dallas stood at the kitchen table and unloaded his loot. Pizzas went in the oven to keep warm, the beer and pop in the fridge, a stack of Honey Buns near the microwave. He glanced up at Mac and grinned.

"For breakfast."

It was so blamed good to see that boy's face and with a grin on it to boot, that Mac whooped. "Well, I reckon we must be in for an all-nighter."

Off in the distance, the sound of a siren. Mac went to the corner of the room and turned up the police scanner.

Dispatcher. *"10-14 at 1416 S. Cedar Lane"*

Deputy. *"Car 4 responding"*

Mac stared toward the front windows. "Hell, that's just up the road, top of the hill. That's Colby and Tink responding. Sally Carthage lives there. What in hell is she doing taking someone in custody?"

"Shall we check it out?" Dal followed Mac into the living room.

Together they went outside. Neighbors stood in their front yards, all staring up the road to where the blue lights lit up the night sky.

Mac tapped Dal on the arm. "Let's hike on up there and see what's going on."

Dal followed Mac, and when they arrived Sally Carthage was on the porch talking to Tinkerbelle, who had a small, skinny kid in custody. Couldn't've been over ten or eleven.

"I'm saying I don't want to press charges," Sally said. "He's just a kid."

"He broke into your house, was fixing to carry off your computer, your Kindle, a stack of DVDs, and no-telling what all else if you hadn't caught him."

"But officer, he's a child. He's probably hungry. Do you have a place to sleep, honey?" She turned to the boy, who stared at the ground and said nothing.

"You don't have to press charges, ma'am. We'll take him to child services for the night and let the judge talk to him in the morning."

Tinkerbelle took the kid to the patrol unit, put him in the backseat, and shut the door. When she turned back she waved at Dal and Mac. Even in the darkness, she looked more happy than Dal had ever seen her. Marriage suited her, and perhaps part of it was getting to do the job she'd always wanted.

Dal met her halfway and swung her off her feet.

She squealed. "You big hunk of gorgeous, when did you get back? You staying? Have you seen Jessie yet? She must be ecstatic. God, we've missed you."

He didn't try to reply to her questions. It usually wasn't necessary where she was concerned. Just ask one and shut up. "Do you know the kid? Has he said anything?"

"Never saw him before. He hasn't said a word to us. Maybe to Miss Sally. She heard a noise, saw the flashlight downstairs and called us, then, bless her heart, goes down to talk him out of stealing. Time we got here, she was giving him cookies and milk and explaining to him why he should live the good life."

Dal cocked his head. "Do you think he's part of this ring of kids put out to steal, supposedly for a cult?"

"Don't know anything yet, Dal. Not really. Miss Sally tried to get us to let him go. Course we can't do that. This is the fifth burglary in the last two days pulled off by kids. It's looking bad."

The impromptu meeting was delayed a while because everyone Dal had asked to attend the meeting at Mac's ended up at the latest burglary. It took a while to sort them all out, let them do whatever job they had to do, then filter on down to Mac's place. But at last he had everyone in the same house, at least. Les, Tinkerbelle, Colby, Jessie, Parker, and of course Mac and himself. The fire chief and mayor couldn't be reached and Sam didn't answer his phone. He might be down in Florida visiting his kids.

"Pizzas are in the oven, probably a bit dried out around the edges, there's pop and beer in the fridge. Help yourselves."

He'd just got them all settled and quieted down from questioning him about where he'd been and what he'd been doing, when there was a rap on the door. Colby was closest, having squatted on his heels beside the end of the couch where the women sat with Mac. He rose and opened it to let in Tink's husband Burt Sample and Mike Henley, who'd been delayed with the kid they'd picked up.

Dal grabbed their hands and shook them, got out some more beers, and showed them to the table and what was left of the pizzas. "Mac, why don't you tell everyone what's going on so we can get some notion what we can all do?"

"Who here hasn't read the article in the *Gazette* about Nolton County and our part in this mess?"

There was a general discussion for a minute or two that determined they'd all read it.

Parker added his two cents right then. "Y'all must've noticed that there were no sources quoted in that article, so it's not worth the weight of farts in a wind. However, people reading it are liable to take it for the gospel since most folks tend to believe everything they read in the newspaper." He grinned. "Sometimes that's good for me. Anyway, there are a bunch, though, who prefer not to believe anything they read, which leaves them hard to convince of anything. However, we'll prepare an article with sources for all the information and have it out next week. But we need to do some damage control before then if we can. And that means everyone here should get to checking every source they might have to get some good information on this cult thing, especially as it affects Grace County." He peered around the crowded room. "And spread it to the gossip tree."

General agreement came from the group in nods and yeses.

Dal nodded. "Thanks, Parker. Does anyone here already know anything for a fact? And let's not hold anything back cause it might offend a friend or family member."

Mike raised his hand and everyone laughed including Dal. "Yes, Mike. You may speak." This brought a second laugh.

"Couple weeks ago we had a nine-one-one call to a place buried deep in Riley Holler just a few miles out of Hooper Valley. We liked to never found it. There was a girl there, about nine or so. They claimed she had fallen on a knife. She was bleeding bad. We tried to bring her in to the hospital, but they wouldn't allow it. Just wanted her fixed up. So we did, but I've seen lots of stab wounds and accidental ones when someone does trip and fall, and it looked the world to me like she'd been stabbed by someone. There's quite a few trailers in the place, some of em in such bad shape they might be empty. The only folks present when we arrived were a man and woman and the bleeding girl. With all the trailers, it surprised us and made us suspicious when we saw not one head pop out of any of them.

"The man kept saying they were the only ones living there, that they had moved in recently and no one else had ever come around. Well, we took it at face value then, but hearing what's been going on, maybe it'd be a place to check out. Reckon we ought to have reported it, but you know how things go in those instances."

"What I want to know," Burt interjected without raising his hand, "is how we gonna prove Mac ain't taking bribes from anyone? That's what's worrying me the most."

Everyone joined in with agreement.

Parker spoke up. "Actually, they have to prove he is. And in that vein we need to find out what evidence they've got and who is doing the investigating. I'd guess it's ATF, DEA, ICE, and DHS. Maybe even the FBI and US Marshals. One or all of them."

"Sounds like goddamned alphabet soup. Why them?" Tink asked.

Dal raised an eyebrow, glanced around the room. "I'd guess they're looking for firearms, drugs, aliens, and lost kids since we've had meth, marijuana, and children mentioned. And guns are always involved, it seems. I'm afraid we could be dealing with human traffickers taking kids down to Mexico. I'd hate to think it, though. There are various reasons to traffic kids, the most profitable to put them up for sale. There's even sites on the Internet where they can be bid on."

"But that sounds more like a big city deal. Doing something like that here in Grace County wouldn't be too profitable, I wouldn't think." Mac took another pull on his beer.

Everyone looked to Dal. "Kids are used for a lot of things because when they get caught they don't go to jail, and they're usually way too scared to rat on the people they work for. They've been told their families will be killed if they do. But there's worse things going on with these kids I'd hate to think of.

"The word here is that the sheriff and his deputies are taking bribes to turn a blind eye to the stealing, and to other stuff like transport of drugs out of the county, illegals doing the work, and so on. Add the possession of illegal guns, and we've got one holy mess. And since Mac and Grace County have been dragged into it, we need to put a stop to it before it gets that bad, and quick."

Mac had sat pretty still up to this point, but his temper got the best of him. "It's a big fat crock of shit, and anyone who knows me and my deputies knows it cain't be true. But I don't have enough men to sweep this county the way it'll have to be swept to make sure we catch these people, if they're here. And from what Mike says, there may be some here already. We got lots of hidden hollers where folks could stay out of sight a long time. There must be a way to find em and get rid of em."

Dal looked around the room at the worried faces. "I have a few ideas, but we'll need the help of more people than we have in this room. We do have to be careful, cause these ole boys are smart enough to infiltrate any public meetings we might have."

"Excuse me, Dal, but does this mean you're going back to work for Grace County sheriff's department?" Tinkerbelle's pretty eyes turned on him with pure innocence.

She always had been that way. Put you on a spot and not turn loose, but look so sweet it didn't even make you mad. Dal stared at her for a minute, trying to come up with a smart ass remark. But glancing around the room, he saw every eye turned in his direction, including the one he wished would stop staring at him in that way she had. All waiting.

"Well, I guess I can stay for a while, at least till this gets worked out. Then I've got a job to get back to." He turned his gaze directly on Jessie who had not said one word during the entire discussion. She glowered at him, picked up her familiar backpack, and shoved her way across the room to stand toe to toe with him.

"Well, don't let us keep you if you've got better things to do." She whirled and was gone before he could come up with a comment, smart ass or not.

The first thing that came to his mind was an urge to go after her, sweep her into his arms, and carry her off, find some dark, quiet place, and fuck her good and proper. Damn. Every time she made him mad, that was the first thing he wanted to do. What did that say about their relationship? Not much that was healthy, that was for sure.

Trouble was, she was more than half right to be pissed off. He'd gotten up and walked out on her without an explanation. Had she done that to him, no telling what he might have had to say.

Okay, enough of that. He wasn't here to make up with her, he was here for Mac and the other deputies who would get muddied by what he saw coming. If they weren't very careful all hell was going to break loose in this little nowhere county. And it wouldn't be caused by something as insignificant as a cult. This had the scent of something a lot worse and he didn't want to see that happen.

He turned to find everyone in the room staring at him. He looked the other way.

"Mac, have there been any charges made against you?" This from Colby, who hadn't spoken till then.

"Nope. Not officially."

"Well, then, I suggest we all work at putting out any fires this article may start and doing as Parker suggested. Once his story comes out next week, we can get a feel about how folks are taking this. Everyone should keep in mind anyone who can maybe help us locate any cults or the like that might be settling in."

The meeting broke up on that note and Mac retired for the night. Dal straightened up, trashed empty bottles and the like, then sat out on the front porch for a while, staring into the night. It was good to be back. Perhaps he had made a mistake leaving these people in the first place. They were the nearest thing to family he had. And they were about to be in a shitload of trouble.

All the way home Jessie nursed thoughts as dark as the surrounding night. The Jeep's headlights cut a bright tunnel along the road. Eyes flashed and she slowed. Deer often spent the night wandering the roadsides and she didn't want to hit one. Sure enough, it was a sleek doe meandering along the shoulder. She crept past. Might be a fawn nearby, but she didn't see one. The deer lifted her head, studied Jess as if she were an interloper, then leaped gracefully over the ditch and into the brush. Sometimes they ran into cars instead of away from them. Not unlike some humans, who spent their time daring bad stuff to happen to them.

Sounded real familiar. She had to stay away from Dal at all costs, for she was like one of those foolhardy deer that runs into traffic. But she so missed his arms around her. Stop, Jessie, think about what's going on and what she might do to help. Offhand, there were two people she knew who could be able to contribute to their efforts to find and get rid of any threats to Mac and his county.

One, strangely enough, was a fellow she had only met last fall, but he had saved her life and Dal's as well. The memory of Dal lying helpless on a mountain and her at his side, holding him close to keep him warm and safe, only sent pain through her.

Dammit, didn't she have any sense at all?

Nick Snow, a reclusive mountain climber, had rescued them, and she had a real good feeling about him before that terrible night was over. He could and did go places in the wilderness where others didn't. Maybe tomorrow she'd pay him a visit. Probably ought to talk to someone else about him first, make sure her impression of him was shared. Parker might know him, or Mac. And there was someone else too. Someone who would be privy to what was going down. But could she trust him? US Marshal Trey Ledger had been involved in last fall's investigation of the murders connected to the WITSEC case and she had formed sort of a bond with him. But he did represent the law and might not be able to help.

The next morning she had breakfast on the deck. Summer was her favorite time of the year and despite being a natural blonde, she loved the sun. Took it in safe doses and wore a golden glow because of it. Her cell rang while she finished off a huge mug of coffee. It was Tinker.

"Got your scanner on?"

"Nope, I'm at home. Don't have one here."

"I thought you'd be jacked after last night's meeting and at the newspaper office with Parker."

"It's the weekend, and I just got up. What's going on?"

"Oops, sorry. The kid they picked up at Miss Sally's last night? Looked and dressed like a boy. Well, guess what? It was a girl and she's gone. Little squirt managed to break out of juvie and just flat disappeared. No one can remember seeing her anywhere."

"Crap. I was hoping they could get something out of hi—er, her. So what's Parker doing at the office?"

"He's working on that story to contradict the one in the *Gazette*. Has been online since dawn trying to track down people who might have some knowledge of anyone involved in that cult in Nolton County who might have left it. You know there's always some that grow discontented and are willing to talk. That's a good idea, if you ask me. A great place to start."

"It sure is. Parker's a pretty bright guy." She scanned the woods, hoping to see a deer.

"He is that indeed."

Movement in the woods caught her attention and she didn't reply.

"Well, you coming in, or you gonna lay around on your lazy butt all day?" Tinker chuckled.

"Okay. Maybe I can shorten Parker's search somewhat. Both of us looking is a good idea." She sighed and let go her planned lazy day. Getting busy would do her good. Take her mind off Dal's presence.

"Great. Let's have lunch together at the Red Bird. Ought to pick up a lot of good gossip there today."

"Yeah, might not even be able to get a seat."

"Meet you there at one, maybe the worst of the lunch crowd will be gone by then."

She agreed and hung up. Maybe she could stay home and search online, but might be a lot of wasted effort without knowing Parker's results.

When she arrived at *The Observer*, she leaned into Parker's office. He was so entranced by what he was doing he startled, then grinned.

"Good thing you had no intentions of shooting me, I'd be dead."

"Heard about the kid taking off and how you came in at dawn to start researching online. Thought I could give you a hand. How's it going?"

"Hell, this town doesn't need a newspaper. It's got its own spy system."

"Well, let's hope that comes in handy."

"There's some downright scary stuff out there. A few years back some cult members shot and killed a Missouri State Trooper and they were found hunkered down here in Arkansas. Not Grace County, but close. Cops had to take a SWAT team in to get em out. Good thing it didn't turn into another Waco. Those that didn't flee were arrested and many are now serving time for a variety of charges from drug dealing to sexual abuse to kidnapping. But some scattered. I'm trying to find a couple of families that came forward back then. Appeared on a bunch of late-night TV shows to tell their stories. We could probably use quotes from some of their remarks in those interviews, but damn, I'd like to talk to at least one of them myself. I won't use someone else's interview results."

"What about the Nolton County cult? Any chance we could get in touch with some of them?"

"I'm not sure I want to. They sound way too dangerous."

"What if we could actually infiltrate one of these so-called cults locally? I mean, if not Grace County, why not one nearby?"

"Talk about dangerous."

"Not if we could get someone who's been undercover, who knows how."

He glanced up, dark eyes sharp. "You're surely not thinking of Dallas Starr?"

"No, as a matter of fact, I wouldn't ask him to pour water on me if I was on fire." Why had she said that? It was like a betrayal. He was burnt out and had no business doing anything like undercover work. She cleared her throat, went on. "No, I meant Trey Ledger. He's a US Marshal and that's what he does. Looks like they'd be interested in the possibility of cleaning out a nest of those crazies. Do marshals get involved in stuff like that?"

"They mainly search for fugitives, which technically might apply. Reckon we could find out. You really looking to ramp this up, aren't you?" He glanced away from the screen.

"If we can, we need to. Mac could be next on the list. I found a form online where people who feel they may be in a cult situation or are in danger in one can report it. There's several people have reported leaving local cults and telling what all they were doing. But most of these are religious. Do you suppose all cults claim religion to get more people involved?"

"Well, it does keep the law at bay."

The office phone rang. He gave a what-now look, and answered. Kept his eyes aimed at her while he talked.

"Good morning, Mac. You sound frazzled. Did we keep you up too late last night?" He listened a moment. "You what? This morning? On a Saturday? When do you have to appear? Well, they didn't waste much time, did they? Yes, she's here."

He held out the phone. "He wants to talk to you."

She took the phone. "What's up?"

"I have to appear at a preliminary hearing next week as a witness up in Nolton County against Sheriff Kimble. Witness to what? Is this a joke? Did you leave me a card from that lawyer woman you told me about earlier?"

"Alicia? Yes, I did. I'm not sure you need a lawyer, but it's best to find out from her what she thinks."

"I've never given two hoots and a holler for lawyers, but I'm afraid of what they're going for. Best to protect myself and Kimble, I reckon. I can't find the blamed thing. Dal is about to blow out a window or something. That boy hadn't ought to be armed jest now, but I'm not the one to disarm him."

Her stomach flopped over and she took a deep breath. "He'll be okay. You can trust Dal. Hold on, I've got her name and a phone number." With trembling fingers she rummaged in her backpack, in the special pocket where she kept stuff like that, and came up with Alicia's card. Gave the number to Mac. "You ask Dal to take you to see her. You don't need to be driving and it'll give him something to do. He's just upset something bad will happen to you. She's in the bank building on the square, has an office upstairs there. Call her first and make an appointment."

She slammed the phone down. "If I knew some fitting words, I'd say them now, but nothing I know is good enough. They're getting around to charging Mac, I just know it. Want him at a hearing over in Nolton

County against Kimble. What's next? Can he be forced to testify against himself? Where they getting their information, anyway? What sort of proof does it take to hold a preliminary hearing?"

Parker tapped his blue pencil on the desk. "A lot less than you'd think. I agree, I don't think at this point he needs a lawyer. I think they're coming in the back door, trying to see just what he might know about this Nolton County deal and somehow connect it to something here in Grace County. You like this Alicia gal? Think she's honest."

"That was my take. Course I've been fooled before. Maybe you ought to meet her as well."

"For what reason? You've already interviewed her for the newspaper."

"You could tell her the picture I took wasn't any good and so you'd like to drop by and get another. That would do it, wouldn't it?"

"You really think that's necessary?"

"It doesn't hurt to cover our butts, now does it?" She studied him for a minute. "I'd feel better to get your take on her."

"Give me the card and I'll give her a call. You want to get ahold of Trey Ledger? See if he's heard anything about investigating cult illegal activity in Grace County?"

"Okay, that's a good idea. Tink and I are meeting for lunch at the Red Bird, we'll keep our ears open to gossip, see how things are going."

"And Jessie? Why don't you give Dal a break?"

"You too? Everyone seems to think what happened was my fault. It wasn't. He picked up and left and I never understood why. I was always there for him, no matter what happened. I stayed with him on the side of a mountain in the cold dark. Dammit, Parker, he broke my heart. What kind of break should he get for that?"

"One that understands that bad things happen sometimes and we can't always control how we react to them. You both went through hell, what with Steve coming after you and the shooting, his killing my horse and pushing Dal off a mountain. Not everyone deals with things like that the same way."

Tears ran down her cheeks. She wiped them with her fingertips.

He came out of the office and leaned over her, holding out a handful of tissues. "I'm trying to be a friend here. You've been miserable ever since he left. I think all it would take is a sit down between the two of you to talk it out. Find out what went on, what's going on now."

"I don't know if I can do that."

"Sure you can. I've watched you do things that took a lot more strength. What could it hurt?"

"It could break my heart all over again, that's what it could hurt."

If only things were as simple as Parker made them. He reasoned things out in a way she couldn't fathom. Dal crawled out of their mutual bed, walked out, and didn't come back. No goodbye, no note, only silence for almost nine months. Just told her he was going, then left, but what good was that? Best thing was for her to stay as far away from him as she could till this thing with Mac was settled and he went back wherever it was he had run to like a coward.

4
CHAPTER

Dal slid into the driver's side of Mac's unit, moved the seat back as far as it would go, and glanced at the old man beside him. How feeble his friend had grown since he left last fall. He'd missed the old fart much more than he'd thought he would, and being with him now, staying in his house, helping out with chores, made him homesick. Shit. He should never have come back. Cedarton and the people who lived here had grown on him more than he'd intended. It felt way too good, like he was home.

So why was he fighting it so?

It was tough seeing Jessie last night. Too many memories slamming around in his head. She was so strong, self-assured, pretty in a way that surpassed mere beauty. When she'd turned loose on him he'd almost grabbed her up right there. He'd missed being around a woman possessed with courage who wasn't afraid to show it.

"This lawyer, she's in the bank building on the square?" He backed Mac's car out and headed up the hill.

"What Jessie said. Brave of a woman to open a law office in a town like Cedarton, ain't it?"

"I suppose. But if she's any good it'll save folks a lot of trouble getting legal stuff done without having to drive down to Harrison or clear over to Fayetteville."

"Well, I trust Jessie, but I'm gonna give this shemale a good going over before I sign anything or pay her."

Dal chuckled. Even though he did look older, Mac hadn't changed and he never would.

"You be in there with me?"

"Sure, if that's what you want."

Right off the bat Alicia Woodson assured Mac that at this stage all he needed to do was answer questions as truthfully as he could and not offer any more than a brief reply. "I'd be glad to sit in on the prelim. They are open to the public. But it'd just be to get a feel for why they've called you as a witness for this other sheriff's department. What's his name, by the way?"

"Kimble. Robert Kimble. They call him Rob most of the time. I've known him for years, but just in passing. I wouldn't say we're friends."

"That's good, though, that you're not friends. Can you think of anything that's gone on between the two counties where you might have seen or heard something, been involved in an arrest or known anyone who was arrested by one of their deputies? Let anything suspicious get past you?"

"I've wracked my brain. Once in a while a speeder or someone wanted for other crimes has crossed from ours to theirs, or vice versa but there's never been any problems settling. And frankly, it's been pretty quiet between us till this whole thing blew up about him and some of his deputies taking bribes. Truthfully, I never would've thought him the type. But then I ain't exactly the type neither."

She nodded, made notes on a pad. "They've not accused you, either. Remember that and don't get shook. Do not presume they're trying to blame you. Don't offer excuses."

After Mac decided he liked her and wanted her to be his lawyer if and when he needed one, she opened a file.

"Well, I think the best thing to do is appear at the prelim, like I said tell the truth, and we'll see what comes of it. I'll make sure to be there. Meanwhile, go on with whatever you're doing."

Mac snorted. "Not doing much of anything. I'm on so-called medical leave right now, and that reminds me, I was so upset over this other thing I forgot. Can I sue that blamed paper for writing that I was going to be arrested for taking bribes? Ain't that libel or something?"

She smiled. "Suing a newspaper successfully is pretty tough. I'd advise you not to bother at this stage. It wouldn't hurt to call the editor and ask that he retract the statement. Nicely tell him you think the reporter was mistaken and had no basis for what he wrote. Request they publish sources."

"I can do that?"

"Of course, or write a letter to the editor, stating your side of the case. He may not retract, but he'll probably print your letter if for no other reason than to start people taking sides and buying more papers. And it won't hurt you any as long as you don't call names or accuse them of lying deliberately. If you'd like, I'd be glad to read your letter before you mail it."

"What would you charge me for that?" Mac raised his hip and reached for his wallet.

"Put your money away, Mister Richards. What we're doing now is a free consult. Reading your letter will be part of it. Then if you have to hire me for real, we can talk about my fee. My flat rates for services are quite a bit lower than your big city attorneys' hourly billing, believe me."

Mac stood and stuck out his hand. "Well, I thank you for your free time, Miss Alicia."

She stood, shook hands with him, then glanced at Dal. "It was good to meet you too, Mister Starr. Thank you for bringing Mister Richards by. Starr? Any kin to Belle and her Sam? I'm partial to western history, sort of a hobby of mine. Some outlaws in your family tree, I'd bet. Cherokee, aren't you?"

Dal smiled. "Yes ma'am, I am. And I've no doubt my tree hangs heavy with outlaws."

She laughed. "Well, if you ever need an attorney, I'm available."

"Thanks, ma'am. I appreciate the offer. I'm going to try to behave myself, though. Old Mac here might run me out of town on a rail."

"I'll bet Mister Richards could do that very thing."

"Reckon you could call me Mac or Sheriff Mac? It's plumb stiff your calling me mister."

"I'll do that, and if you decide to write that letter, give me a call to make sure I'm in before bringing it by. I don't have an office staff as yet. And I'll see you at the preliminary hearing."

Out on the sidewalk, Mac headed toward his car, nosed up to the curb nearby. "Right nice lady, don't you think?"

"Seems so."

"You hungry?" Mac dropped into the passenger seat and buckled up. "We ought to go up to the Red Bird, visit with everyone. We can learn a lot there."

"I could eat. I've missed my usual. Figure Norma remembers what it is after all this time?"

Mac guffawed. "That woman ain't forgot an order in twenty years, I don't reckon."

"Well, let's go on over there then. I'd sort of like to see Theron and Fudge and them."

It was past the noon rush when Dal parked outside the Red Bird, but there were plenty of cars still there. All gathered to jaw about the latest breaking news, no doubt. Inside, he followed Mac and returned greetings and waves the length of the café to the very back table where Mac took a chair scooted up into the corner. A habit that always tickled Dal. Mac told him once that if a lawman like Wild Bill Hickok could get hisself shot cause he was foolish enough to put his back to the door, then it could happened to him as well. So he'd be careful. Dal learned early on not to argue with Mac's odd leanings. Besides, he kind of enjoyed them.

So that put Dal's back to the door at the table for two. Sure hoped he didn't get shot just so fate could prove Mac right.

Fudge, Banjo, and Theron were at the booth next to them, and right away started up a conversation asking Dal where he'd been, was he back for good, would he still be a sheriff, and on and on. He'd long ago stopped correcting them about his title. Mac never had. Once those answers were out of the way, talk centered around the crime spree and the kids responsible.

Fudge remarked that they were likely homeless kids from some big town figured they'd do better here.

Banjo snorted. "If I ever had kids I'd dang sure run em off by the time they reached the age of back-talking."

Theron added his opinion while digging in his overalls for money to pay for his dinner. "I figger it's a spillover from Nolton County.

You know, when you dig up a ant hill, them little critters just run ever which way fast as they can."

Fudge nodded. "Yep, it's for certain we can expect even more trouble down here."

Banjo, who seldom had too much to say, squinted his eyes. "Made a clean sweep up yonder."

"Ain't no telling what'll go on now. I hear the FBI and them US Marshals is gettin thicker'n ticks." Theron tossed a few bills down on the table. "Got to get back to work or my mater plants'll be run over with weeds. Gonna be a good crop this year, looks like, less it quits raining."

Fudge and Banjo followed Theron out. Both of them usually worked for the older farmer during growing season, and laid out the winter. If Dal had to pick tomatoes all summer he'd lay out the winter too. It was a back-breaking, dirty job that turned your hands a blackish green by the end of the day.

Norma brought water and silverware. "Well, howdy Dal, good to see you back. Reckon you want your usual? How about you Mac?"

"Me too." The old man gave Dal a wide told-you-so grin.

Colby and Tink wandered in, saw Mac and Dal, and settled in at the table across from them.

Colby immediately turned toward Mac. "Hey, Sheriff. We picked up that little girl that run off from Miss Sally's last night."

Before Dal or Mac, or anyone else for that matter, could respond the door swung open and in came Jessie and Parker. It was clear she didn't spot Mac and Dal in back until she had reached Tink and Colby's table, then it was too late.

Jessie's gaze shifted from Dal to Tink, then held it there for a long moment. She ought to just turn around and walk out.

Mac made it impossible. "Well, lookee who's here. We need to shove our tables together, that way we can all visit without anyone craning."

Parker pulled back a chair and helped Mac and Colby rearrange the tables, deliberately fixing the seating so that Jessie ended up cornerwise from Dal. Her knee touched his and it was like someone hit her with a cattle prod. She jerked away. He cast her a puzzled glance, then gazed down at his plate. After every one was seated, Dal fiddled with his silverware and avoided looking at her. Too bad she couldn't do the same. All she could do was watch him.

Norma came back to the table with more water and took the remainder of the orders, giving Jessie time to calm down a bit. She really wanted to hear about them picking up the runaway. Besides, it was childish to act so, uh, well, childish.

"So, what's that about them picking up the girl? Have they learned anything from her yet?" Parker aimed the questions at Colby, who had evidently been there when it happened.

"They're waiting for someone to come on over from DHS in Harrison. Seems she's ten years old and tough as a knot. Ain't saying nothing." Colby laughed. "I heard she stomped on one of the deputy's toes when he offered to get her a pop. So far she won't tell her name. The only way they found out her age was one of the guys said she looked to be about eight and she heard him. Shouted out that she was not eight, she was ten. She is little though. Too skinny like she's maybe not well fed. They've got Doc looking at her right now, but she ain't a bit happy about it. I took it Doc wasn't real happy either."

Jessie sucked in a deep breath. "Poor little thing. She must be terrified."

"Mad as a wet cat is more like it. Didn't see no fear. I sure hope we can find out something from her before they haul her off down to Harrison." Colby took a long drink of water. "They've got an advocate for her. She'll eventually talk to a shrink. But that may be too late."

"Can't they go ahead and question her, maybe find out where she came from or something?"

Everyone stared at Tink, who sounded none too sympathetic.

She shrugged. "Sorry. Misbehaving kids tick me off."

"I'll bet you were a little hellcat." Colby gave her a grin.

She elbowed him. Everyone laughed. The two had been partners since Couch took over the sheriff's position, and they were getting to act like brother and sister, always fussing with each other. None of the other deputies had partners, and Tink wouldn't for long if Couch had his way. He expected her to pull her weight just like the men once her six weeks of field training was over. More than once she'd told Jessie she respected that about Couch.

Her and Mac had never gotten along real well because of his penchant to make her man dispatch or watch the jail. She once called him a misogynist in his hearing and he reamed her out for cussing him, saying as long as he was sheriff no woman would be put in danger on the job even if she did cuss him out on a regular basis. After quitting three times, she gave that up, because she loved the idea of the job so much.

Jessie looked for her to get pregnant and quit, now that she and Burt were married, but so far that hadn't happened. The couple got married right after Dal left Cedarton. And there she went again. Couldn't seem to keep from placing everything that happened to before or after Dal left. She ought to reach right over there and smack him upside the head. Knock some sense in him. This was where he belonged. Couldn't he see

71

that, sitting at the table with everyone laughing and talking, teasing and having a good time? Took that crease out from between his eyes.

"Hey, Dal. I like your hair. Always did like a man with long hair. Isn't it pretty, Jessie?" Tink batted those big eyes and it was her Jessie was ready to smack.

"Men don't have pretty hair," Mac grumbled. "Looks like it'd get in the way of things."

"Yeah? Things like what?" Colby chuckled. "I don't believe Dal's been real busy lately."

Jessie expected Dal to speak up. Say what he'd been doing in defense, but he remained silent.

Norma approached with their orders lined up both arms. How she did that, Jessie would never figure out. She couldn't even carry a cup of coffee in one hand and a plate of food in another without spilling one. Everything got distributed, ketchup went around for the fries, silverware rattled, and the conversation quieted a bit so they could eat without talking with their mouths full.

When they were finished, Dal ordered a piece of apple pie with ice cream, Colby did too. Jessie caught herself watching Dal's eager expression when he cut into the pie and took his first bite. He closed his eyes with pleasure. Probably the first decent meal he'd had since he ran away. Served him right. She couldn't take it any longer, watching those dimples when he chewed, the sparkle in his jade green eyes as he did away with the dessert. Eyes that refused to light on her and just swept right past. Anger grew inside till she could take it no longer.

She scooted her chair back. "I think I'd better go. Gotta get to work."

That was a lie. It was really her day off. In anger she rose and got the hell out of there before the tears flowed. Like a fool, she searched for her

Jeep, then cursed. She'd ridden over with Parker, and was left to sit in his new black Rover and wait till he came out. Which the ornery devil didn't do till they were all through. He did that on purpose, making her sit out there like a naughty child.

"You owe me eight-fifty," he said when he climbed behind the wheel. "I left a dollar tip."

"Thank you." It was all she could manage before sobbing uncontrollably. He patted her on the shoulder, then peeled out of the parking lot before Dal exited. She was grateful for at least that one thing.

How in the world was she going to continue to work and visit and live here with Dal coming and going? Damn him, anyway. He'd gone and ruined her happy home.

Back at the newspaper office, she fiddled around putting a story together about the little girl, but there was so much missing she gave up.

"Do you think Couch can figure a way to get that child to tell him something about the cult that young'un runs with?"

Parker grinned. "Well, Mac would be able to cajole something out of her real quick, but I don't know about this Couch."

"I'm going over there, poke around, see what I can find out."

"Um, yeah, okay. Just don't get put in jail."

"Why? Cause you'd just leave me there?" *The Get Out of Jail Free* card she held against Couch was valuable and she had to be sure and use it when she needed it the most. This could be that time.

Parker snorted and gestured for her to get on out so he could work. She left. He hollered before she shut the door. "Want candy or gum when I come to visit?"

Rather than move the car two blocks onto the square she stalked off down the street. It was a beautiful day, and she couldn't stay mad.

Flowers of all colors bloomed in yards butting up to the business district and all around the square in well-tended beds, their fragrance thick in the warm air. Dogwood trees offered creamy blossoms hanging heavy over the sidewalks.

At the jail, she skirted the front door and headed out back for the exit that was kept locked to the outside. Sooner or later someone would come out and she could sneak in before the door closed. That would put her just down the hall from the cells. They'd have to keep the child in one of them till someone from DHS came over and that could be late this evening.

She wasn't much for making plans. Every time she did something came along to mess them up.

It wasn't long before one of the cleaning women sashayed out. Jessie kept her eye on the woman till she rounded the corner, then she dashed over just in time to slip inside before the door clicked shut. Down at the end of the hall, the new deputy stood with his back to her, talking on a cell phone. She crept forward and eased through the opening that put her in an empty hallway.

This wasn't her first secret foray through these halls, and she soon found her way to the entrance of the jail proper. On tiptoes, she peered through a window with bars.

Quiet and empty.

She slipped through and walked along the cells past a couple of drunks sleeping it off and a fellow sitting in the corner, holding his head in his hands and muttering. Then some empty cells, and finally, the child sitting on the floor hunched into the corner of the one closest to Couch's office. Thankfully there was a solid wall between so the man could work without listening to any caterwauling from prisoners.

The door was closed, probably locked since the kid was so much trouble. Jessie crept along the concrete floor and seated herself on the floor with only the bars between the two of them.

"Hi, how you doing?"

The kid turned, glowered at her. "I'm in jail."

"Yeah. Sucks, doesn't it?"

"Who are you?"

"I'm a reporter and I'd like to write your story. What do you think of that?"

"Where's your badge?"

"Reporters don't have badges."

"I don't believe you." The girl crossed thin arms over her chest and stared in the other direction.

"Don't you want your story told? Like how these big bullies ganged up on you and threw you in jail when you didn't even do anything bad?"

"Well, I didn't."

"I believe you. Why don't you tell me what really happened?"

She cocked her head, dirty hair hanging in strands. "What's your name?"

"Tell you mine if you tell me yours."

She nodded briskly.

"You first."

"Okay. My name is Jessie."

"Mine is Lily."

"Jessie West."

"Lily is all I'm saying."

"Why is that?"

"Cause, that's all. Cause. I was only looking at that stuff when they said I was stealing it. Not supposed to get caught, so I run hard but I got caught anyways, then I kicked that one in the legs and got away. Supposed not to go home case someone is following."

"Sounds like a good plan. So where you supposed to go?"

She shrugged.

"Is it far from here?"

Again a shrug.

"Oh, come on. How can I tell your story if you won't tell it to me?"

"New Daddy tells me what to take and what to do with it. Promises I won't go to jail if I do get caught. Says if I'm good and proper the angels will look after me. Looks like he lied to me, don't it? You think maybe me stomping the cop's toes is why I'm here? I did something wrong and the demons will have me now." Tears streaked down her face that someone had washed so the skin was cleaner than any of the rest of her. "Can you get me out?"

"Maybe, if you tell me the truth." Angels and demons? A cross between religion and supernatural? She regretted having to lie to the child, but it was more important than telling the truth at the moment.

"There's this big bunch of caves and they keep us there sometimes when they go off." Lily zipped her mouth with her fingers. "We can't tell about the caves. It's a secret."

No doubt with the angels and demons. Her heart thumped hard. Us and secret jumped out at her. "Us? Who is us?"

Her little head shook and she glanced around with wide eyes, like someone might be listening.

"Who is us?"

"Les see. There's Mary, and Annie and Janie, a new girl they just brought in, and some boys too mean to tell their names. This pretty lady—I don't know her name, New Daddy calls her honey—she brings us food and water and stuff, and watches us when New Daddy takes us to town to snatch."

"Snatch?"

"Yeah, don't you know nothing? Snatch. We snatch the stuff, take it to this old house that sets back off the road on the way out to the caves, and wait there till they pick us up."

"Why do you go back? Why don't you run away from New Daddy?"

"Cause he says if we do demons will kill everyone we know. Mommy, Daddy, brothers, and sisters, and even us."

She stared at the frightened little girl for a long while. "Where does your family live?"

Lily grabbed her hand. "Please help us. We can't get away and we're scared of what they're going to do to us. To our moms and dads."

The little girl turned wide brown eyes up at her.

"What the *hell* you doing?" A heavy masculine voice stiffened her back.

That damned Couch had caught her. Lily screamed and hunkered into the corner, little fists covering her eyes.

Jessie scrambled to her feet, glanced back at the door. She'd run, but he knew who she was so that wouldn't do much good. He'd just come get her, so she stood her ground.

He loomed over the two of them. "Shut up that caterwauling fore I give you something to holler about. And you." He pointed at Jess with a sausage-sized finger that shook with anger.

She glared at him. "No need for you to be so mean. Me and Lily were just talking. It'd do you to stop hollering at her and maybe you'd learn something. Kind of like the other day when I learned about something secret in your desk drawer." She slanted her eyes in his direction.

Couch glared at her then down at the girl. "Shut up, Lily."

The child stopped screaming, but continued to sob quietly.

He turned on Jessie. "You're that gal works for the newspaper, ain't you?"

"That's me."

"Don't you know I can throw you in jail for this?"

"Really? Looks like I'm already there. We were just talking. I didn't break in or anything. What would you arrest me for? Besides right now I'm keeping your secret, but I won't for long."

"Interfering with an ongoing investigation." He gritted his teeth but appeared to cool off. "Don't you go threatening me."

"There are kids being held captive and all you want to do is arrest me? I want my lawyer. I want to tell her about our so-called sheriff, nothing but a drunken—"

He spluttered and took her by the shoulder. "I'll make you think you want your lawyer. Don't you know you can't believe anything these kids tell you? A bunch of little liars."

"Alicia Woodson is my attorney. I want to call her right this minute. That is, if you're arresting me."

"You git on outta here, and don't let me catch you here again. Or you'll need that lawyer."

The little girl's pleas for her to come back in her ears, she ran ahead of the angry sheriff, shoved her way out the door at full tilt, and ran smack into Dal, who grunted and caught her in time to keep her from bouncing back and going down.

Without turning loose, he gazed down at her. Still held on. Her stomach turned over and she couldn't speak or pry herself from his grip. Like they were frozen in time, both remained in place. His gaze swept her from head to toe, then back up to her face.

Her insides went all jittery.

Well, say something. Do something. One or the other of us.

Best be her, and so she tried, but her voice caught somewhere down in her throat. All she could do was stare into those jade green eyes and wish like hell he'd just pull her up close and never turn her loose again.

He finally spoke, leaning down near her ear so his minty breath ruffled her hair. "Up to your old tricks, huh? Did you get anything out of her?"

Still mute, she nodded.

Dear God, *move*. Say something. *Do* something.

"Well, anything useful?" His lips touched the flesh behind her ear and she closed her eyes tight.

Place lips together, form words, one after another. "P— p— probably. I'm not sure."

He turned her around, kept hold of her arm, and guided her to a bench under an umbrella of pink and cream dogwood blossoms near the sidewalk. "Well, sit. Tell me."

Before answering she glanced around. The sheriff had disappeared inside. Dal continued to watch her, his eyes all soft and warm.

"I, uh, she told me they keep some kids in caves, talked about an old house along the road on the way where they wait to be picked up after they run away from town. She's afraid for her family. Called the man who has them New Daddy and said he tells them about angels and demons who will kill her family if she doesn't do what he says, or if she runs away." Well, she got all that out. Good girl.

"Angels and demons? Not good. Sounds like what we thought. Some kind of cult. Well, it's a start. Tells us they're being held against their will, so we can go in legally with a warrant."

With enormous effort she scooted away from him, met his gaze. "But DHS will take her away before we can find out anything more.

Unless one of the deputies does something about it. Or maybe we could kidnap her."

He studied her for a while, a grin threatening to send those dimples popping. "Kidnap her? You would think of something like that. Threatening kids with angels and demons. Goddammit, how can people be so cruel?"

"Dal?"

"I don't know if it's enough to find these people, though. Do you have any idea where these caves could be? I would think—"

"Dal, I need you to tell me why you left like you did." She trembled all over, sitting there, thigh touching thigh and him babbling on like he was talking to Mac or Parker, but certainly not her.

He stared at her. "Jessie, I'm sorry. Truly sorry about that. I never looked at it the way you did."

"Well, you should've. I know I shouldn't presume you have feelings for me, but we did have some good times and I thought we were friends. For you to go off like that without a word of explanation. You hurt me."

"I didn't mean to do that. I just needed gone from what was haunting me, and I never thought once about how it might hurt you."

"Well, did you leave it behind here in Cedarton, or did it follow you? I always thought our troubles went with us everywhere we went. Look at me. Read my mind. Please don't shut me out. We're one."

"One? No, we can't be one. It's too dark where I live."

"Are you happy there? Where you live?"

He brushed her cheek with his fingertips. "I have to admit I've missed you, Jess."

She closed her eyes, forgave him in her heart, but would not do so aloud. Not yet. Even though all she wanted at this moment was to be in a quiet room in his arms, his mouth devouring hers. Gathering her backpack, she rose shakily to her feet.

"I have to go. It was good to see you again. I wish you well."

Dal watched Jessie walk away, the wind blowing her long hair. Inside, that part of him he could never control yearned to follow her. Go somewhere away from everyone and lay down with her close. Never let her go again.

That desire frightened him. He had to get out of here, leave as soon as this business with Mac could be settled. Being with old friends today had left him yearning to return to this life, to see Dave and Kathy and Burt and Les. Maybe sit down and visit with Sam Watson, who always had good stories to share.

Violence brought the restless spirits back into his life. He wanted them gone forever, yet when they were he missed his grandfather, who must be somehow attached to the asgi`na and anasgi`na. Probably perched out there in the woods just waiting to jump into his life again if he stayed. Fill him with the fear that things would spiral out of control. That he couldn't stop bad things from happening to people he loved.

Sighing, he rose and went inside the jail where he'd been going when he collided with Jessie. The swelling in his groin warned him of one thing. He'd better beware or he'd jump in bed with her first chance he had, or drag her to one of those crazy places where she enjoyed making love. And now that he'd sat down and talked to her, one thing was for sure. Whatever it was between the two of them, it hadn't lessened one bit while he'd been away.

With a great deal of effort he turned his thoughts to what she had learned from the little girl. It sounded bad unless the child had made up the story. Could be a vivid imagination at work. Surely this new sheriff, Couch? Surely he'd investigate such a story.

Could it be that this secret bunch of loonies were the ones Mac would be accused of taking bribes from? Money meant to keep him quiet and allow them to carry on their dirty deeds. The least of which were the thefts, the worst of which was what he could only guess at. Had to be a lot more to it than the few piddly things they'd stolen.

He made his way to the sheriff's office and rapped on the closed door.

"Hang on. Who is it?"

"Dallas Starr. Wonder if I could talk to you a minute."

"Starr? Don't know you. Check with the deputy at the desk. I'm busy."

Dal leaned his forehead against the wood for a minute. A Number One asshole. "I just want to speak to you a minute. I used to be a deputy here."

"Oh, yeah, I remember who you are. See my deputy. I don't have time for that sort of nonsense. Never understood why Richards hired someone like you in the first place. Go talk to one of your spirits."

Well, shit-fire. Dal turned the knob and shoved the door open so hard it hit the wall behind it.

The man sitting at the desk leaped from his chair, palm over the butt of his weapon. "What in hell you doing, boy? Looking to get shot?"

"You shoot unarmed men?"

"When they kick my door in, I might."

"Try again. I merely shoved the door open. No kicking done."

"I suggest you get your Injun ass out of here fore I call for assistance in throwing you out."

He couldn't help himself, he laughed. "Did you call me an Injun? My

God, what century do you live in? I'm sorry I bothered you. I'll be taking this up with the US Marshals who I believe are currently scouring 'your' county for illegal activity."

Without allowing the sheriff to say a word, he turned and stomped on down the hall to where a deputy he hadn't seen before sat behind a desk, staring at him as if he had two heads.

By the time he reached the astonished guy, the sheriff barreled down the hallway toward him. Dal's hands balled into fists and he turned to meet what he expected to be a physical attack. He towered over the man by five or six inches and outweighed him with muscles versus fat. He could whip him in a fight. Not something he wanted to do, cause he would end up in a cell, no matter how it went down from this point. And no way could he help Mac then.

"Why don't you come back to my office, Starr? You caught me at a bad time. I'd be glad to talk to you about this mess we all find ourselves in. We can probably come to some sort of agreement on how to proceed. I'm the last person to want to see a lawman with Mac Richards's record in trouble. Would you want a cup of coffee before we sit down?"

Speechless, Dal stared at the idiot. Seeing silence as the better part of valor, he went with the ass into the break room where the two of them filled mugs with some black, oily stuff that vaguely resembled coffee. He then followed him back to his office where he was invited politely to sit.

This was someone he would watch very closely. Hated like hell to invoke any powers that might help him, but given half a chance he'd dig around in that ignorant brain and see just what he was up to. He might be a bit out of practice, but if he had to be cursed with strange powers, he might as well use them. He was still the grandson of Lone Bear Stands and he hadn't forgotten what the shaman had taught him. For Mac he would reach into that dark place.

He just hoped he didn't come out in worse shape than the last time.

5
CHAPTER

Before leaving the newspaper for home, Jessie called the sheriff's office and asked the new deputy Howie Duggan if anyone had come for the little girl to take her to Harrison.

"No'm, she's still here. Just sitting in there staring a great hole through the wall. I feel kind of sorry for her. She shouldn't be in a cell."

"Wonder if maybe someone could take her home with them, just till DHS can pick her up."

"Wouldn't know about that."

"Is Sheriff Couch there?" Damn hard to call the man by his title. It wasn't right he was even in Cedarton. That ought to be Les or Burt, or better yet, Dal, sitting in that office taking care of town business. Couch didn't know his ass from a teakettle about Grace County.

Her thoughts were interrupted by a grumbly voice. "Couch here. What can I do for you?"

"This is Jessie West from *The Observer*. I'm inquiring about the little girl you have in that jail cell. Don't you think someone could keep her overnight at their home till DHS can get up here from Harrison? It's cruel to make her stay behind bars."

"I wouldn't have that authority."

"Well, couldn't you call someone who does down there and get permission?" Stubborn asshole. "I know we could find a good place for her to spend the night if you would kindly do that."

His grumbling resonated in her ear, but she hung on. "You people are certainly a strange lot. I've worked in law enforcement for a lot of years and never run into the like. First I get an Injun with no authority kicking in my door wanting to drag people out scouring the woods for a danged cult, now you want to tote home an ornery little thief. A gal who talks of demons and such, and actually keep her in a Christian home? Gotta be something in the water."

"At least it's water affecting our actions." She cleared her throat and let that sink in, then went on before he finally regained his thoughts. "Actually, it's called giving a damn about other people. I think that's known as the Christian thing to do, but I could be wrong. If kindness is in the water, then we need to be exporting it all over the place, don't you think? Now, would you do me a favor and make that call? You know, it might do for a nice article in the paper, the sheriff caring enough about a child's welfare to go the extra mile to get her taken care of. On the other hand…." She deliberately left that hanging.

Silence for so long she almost clicked off, then this huge sigh like he was being asked to hang the moon or something. "I'll make the danged call, but don't get your hopes up. Those folks are pretty strict."

"Well I'll bet if you explain to them that a ten-year-old child is waiting in a jail cell, they'll give us permission to take care of her."

"Fore you hang up, young lady, I want to know just one thing. You gonna take her, or you got the name of someone who will? I believe I'll just need that fore I go asking these folks for favors."

She swallowed hard. How did you go about taking care of a kid? The only one she'd ever been around was herself when she was that age. She could probably find some kind mother or older lady with experience, but since he was wanting a name now, she just gave him hers and crossed her fingers.

She went ahead and loaded up in the Jeep, but sat in the parking lot waiting for him to call back, in case she had to be the one to go over and pick up the girl. Oh, Lord, what would she do if no one wanted to help out? She didn't know the first thing about child care. She called Norma but she was going out of town to visit her sick sister. Working her way through several others, she gave up. Everyone was ultra busy. Even Dave and Kathy had some sort of thing to attend in Kansas City over the weekend.

Parker had gone on home after the get together with Mac and the crew, so she had no one to discuss this with. Maybe Tink was still in town, she'd grown up with little brothers. No one answered her cell, just voice mail, so she left a message for her to call back. Then she tried texting her, but still no reply. Her and Colby must be out following up on something.

Then her cell toned. It was the sheriff's office. Asshole himself.

"Well, young lady, a feller down there told me if we could verify someone was qualified to have overnight custody of the girl, it would be okay. You need to call this number and give them your information. Then you can come on over here and pick her up. Glad to be shut of her, if you want the truth. She's a handful."

She took the number, made the call, and gave them the information they wanted about her. No way did she want her overnight but it looked like it was that or go on a guilt trip about leaving her in that cell. They gave her a case number, told her to leave that number with the sheriff as well, and she could pick up the girl. Before heading on over to the jail, she called a couple more people she thought might take the girl for one night. Everyone was otherwise tied up, so she gave up and drove the few blocks to get her.

Lily was her name. She remembered that when the sheriff accompanied her back to the cell where she sat in a corner, overall-covered knees pulled up to her chin, dirty blonde hair sticking out in tangles. Doing her very best not to cry. Relief was evident in her expression when she looked up and saw Jessie. A familiar face in this most scary of surroundings.

"Come on, Sweetie. You're breaking out of this joint." Jessie held out her arms, not knowing anything else to do.

Lily jumped up and ran to her. Motioned for her to lean down and whispered in her ear. "I needed to pee and he wouldn't take me, so I wet in the floor, back in that corner over there. Don't tell him, he might make me stay here."

"You're coming with me." Served him right. Without saying a word to the sheriff, she led Lily through the halls and out the exit to the back parking area. The sun had set, flaring the blue sky with a rainbow of colors that shifted and flashed, reflecting in the long narrow windows of the bank along the east side of the square.

Lily climbed into the Jeep and leaned back in silence.

"Fasten your seat belt, honey." Jessie followed her own advice and glanced around to see Lily trying to get hers to lock.

The odor of urine in her nose, she leaned over and fixed it for her. "Did they feed you anything?"

"Nope."

"You like hamburgers, fries, pop?"

"Everyone likes them, but New Daddy says we shouldn't eat meat, or white bread, or French fries, or pop."

"Gracious, doesn't leave much, does it?"

Lily giggled, surprising Jessie.

"Well, I won't tell if you won't. I don't keep much food at home, so let's go to the Red Bird and get us a couple of burgers, some fries and what do you like to drink? Coke? Pepsi? Sprite? We'll take it home with us."

She nodded with vigor. "Am I going home with you to live?"

"First we'll stop by Walmart to pick you up some clean clothes." The little girl's question sent her heart right to the bottom of her stomach with a painful thud. "It's just for the night, honey. And I want you to know I've never had kids around me and you make me very nervous, so unless you want to witness a complete meltdown you'll be a good girl. It would be an ugly sight."

Again Lily giggled. Did ten-year-old girls giggle all the time or just most of it? Even with the dreadful fix she was in, this little girl found things to laugh about. How scary it must be to be taken from your parents, told if you didn't do terrible things they would be killed. Maybe she could find out more about the situation, stuff that would help locate this bunch of perverts, once she got Lily home, bathed, fed, and in a comfortable bed. What else could she possibly need?

Later that evening she found out there were things she didn't know about a child's needs. First off, she hadn't anticipated Brad's reaction to a pint-sized human invading his space. He took one look at her, did his up and down foot stomp, then ran about three circles around her, barking with delight.

Lily clapped her hands and started hollering at him, so he added more barks to the frenzy. Enough was enough and Jessie stepped into the fray.

"Okay, stop, both of you."

Her plea did little good so she shuffled Brad outside where he stood at the door and barked.

"Let him in. I want to play with him." Lily's voice turned screechy when she wanted something.

In an effort to put a stop to that, Jessie opened the bag from the Red Bird and put out the hamburgers and fries. Norma had added a patty for Brad without being asked and she tossed it out on the porch to him.

Lily wolfed down the food, so that was a success, despite Brad's swallowing his whole then demanding to be let back in again. Ignoring the dog, Jessie cleaned up after their supper and told Lily to undress to take a bath. While the tub filled Jessie tried to unfasten the filthy overalls that had made her appear like a boy early on.

"Don't touch me." Thin arms flailed, she scratched and bit, hunched out of Jessie's grip and glared at her.

"Okay, I won't. You do it then." The Walmart bag was on the floor and she opened it, held up a pair of blue shorts and top. "Look here. This is yours. Take off those britches. The tub is steamy hot and smells good. You're not sleeping on my clean sheets dirty and stinky as you are now. If you won't take a bath and put on clean clothes, well then you can just sleep on the floor."

"That's not very nice." Lily stomped her foot. "I hate you, and I don't want a bath."

She eyed the brat, reminded herself what she'd been through. Besides she wasn't taking her to raise. "Okay, do what you want, then. You're going to sleep on the couch. I'll get a big towel to put under you so you don't get it dirty."

Lily balled her fists, held them to either side of her body, and proceeded to scream till the sound reverberated painfully in Jessie's ears. Brad didn't care much for it either and he replied with high-pitched howls. It was enough to send Jessie running from the house, leaving them to it. On second thought she might just grab Lily up and paddle her little behind. Not a good idea. At one time, that would've been okay. These days she could end up in jail. Instead, she took her firmly by the shoulders and marched her into the living room.

"You wait here. Don't you dare move."

Lily glared at her, but appeared to have settled down some. Probably had screamed her throat raw. Jessie ran to the linen closet at the end of the hall, grabbed one of the oversized towels and hurried back to spread it on the couch. The room was empty.

Where had the brat gone? She appeared to be nowhere in the house, neither in closets or under beds, nowhere. Jessie called her several times, threatened her with dire circumstances if she didn't come out. Then she stopped, listened. Too quiet. Brad was no longer barking.

Oh, dear God. She ran out onto the porch. No Brad and no sign of Lily either, and it was getting dark. This was a fine mess. Though she called and called the pit bull, he didn't come.

Now what should she do? Ought to've known better than to take the kid on in the first place. Should've left her in jail where she was at least safe.

For a while she sat on the porch steps, hoping against hope that the two would appear out of the growing shadows. When they didn't, she went inside, grabbed her phone, and tried Tink.

Still no reply.

She tried Mac and his went to voicemail. Since he rarely checked that until someone reminded him, she tried Colby. He replied but he and Tink were fifty miles to the southwest answering a disturbance call. He suggested she call Dal since he would be available. All the other on-duty deputies were out on calls except Howie, who was still stuck with dispatch duty.

"Does he have his old cell phone?"

"I reckon. He had one on him last time I saw him. Try his old number. Let me know if you don't get him. That little girl could get way lost overnight in these woods."

She punched in Dal's old number. It rang three times and he answered. "Thought you were too pissed at me to be calling. What's up? Must be really important."

"It is, or I wouldn't bother you." She told him what had happened in short spurts and ended bursting into tears.

"I'm coming. You home?"

"Yes."

"Settle down, I'm in town, won't take me but a few minutes. You got some good flashlights?"

" Uh huh."

"Okay. Stop crying Jess, that's not like you. I'm on my way. Already gone five miles just since I picked up."

She chuckled through her sobs. "Be careful, please. I don't... I can't... Dammit, Dal."

"I know, darlin, I know. Keep talking if you want, just get those flashlights ready and toss in some spare batteries so we don't get caught out. You should see my headlights in just a few. If you want to stay on the phone, do. It's okay. This isn't your fault. Things aren't always someone's fault. Things just happen."

"But I don't know the first thing about taking care of a kid. I should never have brought her home with me. I just didn't know what else to do."

"You did right. Not your fault she bolted. She's survived out there before and it's not cold. Not like there's grizzlies or the like in those woods. We'll find her, or better we'll trail her right to those bastards."

She rummaged through her junk drawer, found a handful of batteries, and stuffed them in the pockets of her jeans, all the while talking to Dal. Having him on the other end of the conversation kept her from going nuts. He kept talking her down. He was good at that.

"You think that little dog went with her?" Headlights were on their way up the lane from the main road.

"Yes. He wouldn't just go off and he was ecstatic when I showed up here with her."

"Okay, I'm here. I'm getting off the phone now so I can gather up some stuff. I'm driving Mac's unit, he's got flashlights and batteries and, oh, good, under the seat, a forty-five. He always kept one tucked away."

Why would he need a gun?

The random thought went right on through her head, chased by worry about Lily plus the trouble she herself would be in if they didn't find her.

Superhero to the rescue. Dal almost climbed back in the car and drove off when he caught sight of her silhouette against the lights of her cabin. Stay away from her. Let her handle this any way she could. How she would if he were still living over at Frog Pond, blissfully ignorant of her troubles.

But he wasn't, was he? All it took to stop him was her running his way, and him standing there like a fool waiting to take her in his arms. Which of course he did, having no other choice when she threw herself there.

Good God, it felt great to hold her. Her body pressed tight against his, arms curled around his neck, her face hot and wet with tears rubbing on his shirt. And him, getting a hard-on just holding her, his mind conjuring up all sorts of visions of the two of them.

Did he not have a brain in his head? Well, not in the one giving him trouble anyway. It was like he'd never left. Him wanting to holler at her or kiss her every moment that passed.

"Okay, while there's still a little light on the ground, let's circle the place, see if we can find where she left the yard and headed into the woods. Walk next to me about three feet away and swing the light back and forth slowly on the ground. I can look for a telltale track of some sort. Can you do that?"

"Yes." She snuffled a few times, then did as he asked. Together they made a slow circle, beginning straight out from the front porch, each moving the powerful beams slowly back and forth in a good-sized swath.

"It's getting dark."

"I know, keep going, let's at least find which way she went into the woods. She'll tend to follow animal trails rather than stomping through briars and wild roses. Once we pick up that trail, it'll be easier."

"Brad, here Brad!"

"Good idea. Keep calling him. He just might come back or bark."

About three-quarters of the way around the perimeter of the yard Dal stopped and bent down. "Come here. Shine your light here next to mine."

Dried leaves from the winter lay thick on the ground, except for a spot where they had been disturbed like someone had run through them. The light beams showed that same disturbance toward the undergrowth where large oaks and saplings thickened into woods. A path through dry leaves led to a gap in the undergrowth. He moved slowly, trusting her to follow.

"Watch the edges of this little trail, probably left here by deer, then followed by coon and possum and no telling what else. If she leaves the trail we might see her tracks, or we could lose her. If we do lose her, we'll mark the spot and come back in the daylight to see if we can track her down."

"Leave her out here all night?"

"Nothing out here to hurt her, and if she's as tough as you made out, she'll do just fine. I'll bet she's spent nights in worse places, and it's better than spending the night in jail."

Dal soon gave up seeing any more sign of the child and dog. It was too blasted dark, even with the flashlights. No moon made it even worse, so he stopped. Jessie stumbled into him.

"Oh, sorry, I was looking down." She didn't move away, just stood there, so quiet he could hear her breathing.

From a stream somewhere frogs filled the night with their songs. Overhead, leaves whispered in a soft breeze. Her breath touched the back of his neck, sending goose bumps across his shoulders and down his spine. Still, she didn't move away or say a word.

He shut off his flashlight and turned toward her. Her firm breasts trailed across his shirt front. A shudder ran through him, making the contact even more sensual. In the glow from her flashlight, he traced fingertips down her jawline and over her lips. More than eight long months without a woman, any woman, but most especially without this woman, and he was a prime target for whatever she wanted.

Who was he kidding? It wasn't only what she wanted. Every inch of his body yearned for her till he hurt all over. No common sense in the world would stop him. The flashlight fell to the ground, joined hers with a thud. Reflective light cast eerie shadows that enveloped them. His hands crept under the hem of her shirt and up to cover her bare breasts. One filled each hand. He groaned, shoved his hips tight against her. She had not uttered a sound until that very moment when she unfastened his shirt, one slow button at a time.

This was what he liked. The way she used foreplay to make each sexual encounter so much hotter, sweeter, exquisite. Then prolonged it with afterplay. She'd taught him that word, those special acts she always used to extend their lovemaking.

His shirt open, him still holding her breasts, she nibbled across his chest and caught a nipple between her teeth. Almost but not quite hard enough to hurt. After a while, she moved to the other one. He leaned his head back, his body trading tension for passion. Being with her was like throwing away something bad and replacing it with something delicious.

Tongue following a trail down the center of his chest and belly she fumbled the belt buckle loose and traced the zipper opening with a hungry mouth. The sound he let go with was at the same time guttural and musical.

Inside his gut clenched. Stop this now, before it's too late. Before it all starts over again. You don't need this. She doesn't need this.

He grabbed her hands, resting on the waist of his jeans. Held on tight. "Stop, Jess. Now. We have to stop. I'm a mess, a frigging mess." His voice broke on the words, but he didn't loosen his grip. "No good for you."

Her fingers crawled up his chest. She tilted her head to gaze up at him. "Look at me. I'm pretty much a mess too. I betrayed Steve then shot him when he tried to get even. Thank God I didn't kill him." Her head dropped to rest against his bare belly.

For a moment he hesitated. Ought to take her in his arms. He sure as hell knew how she felt.

"Somehow when you and I are mixing it up it's like I'm living a good life. Is that so bad?" She kept touching him. Ought to push her away. "Don't tell me you don't feel the same when we're together?"

Damn her to hell. She wasn't going to let this go. Didn't know how dangerous it was to love him. If it came down to it he couldn't protect her, couldn't save her. He didn't save Leanne, so how in hell could she expect any more from him? He pushed her off, hands gripping her shoulders. Remained so for a long moment unable to speak for the knot in his throat.

"Damn you, Dal Starr." She went limp against him. "Damn you to hell. What's wrong with you, anyway?"

"Way too damned much to get into tonight. Let's just stop it. Now."

She shoved him back so hard against a huge maple that his head thudded against the bark and he saw stars. For a moment he took deep breaths and leaned on the tree, till some sensibility returned.

By then she had snatched up the burning flashlight, whirled, and ran back the way they had come. The leaping beam went out of sight around a bend in the path. He waited till he could no longer hear the rattle of leaves under her fleeing feet.

Sorry, Jess. Dammit, sorry I ever came back, ever put my hands on you. Ever involved you in my crazy life.

Still a bit dizzy he bent down, picked up the other flashlight, and moved along the trail, searching for where the girl might have walked. He came around another loopy curve, and there where it turned back almost the way it had come, the leaves were churned as if kicked underfoot. The girl had gone straight off the path and down the steep incline. The undersides of the disturbed leaves were still damp. He tried calling Brad, but nothing. A branch hung head high and he broke it so it would hang down and mark this spot.

In the morning he would get a couple of people to help and they'd try to track the child in the daylight.

The lights in Jessie's cabin were out when he emerged from the woods. Too bad he couldn't tell her how sorry he was, but he didn't dare go to that door. Imagining her lying awake in her room sent him hurrying all the faster to the car, where he drove off before he could change his mind.

Back at Mac's, he snuck inside, hoping the old man was in bed asleep. He was in no mood to explain what had happened. As it was the people at DHS were going to have a conniption fit over them losing Lily. Jessie would be in a heap of trouble over this, and he hated that.

"That you, boy?" A querulous question from the back bedroom.

"Yes. You feeling okay?"

"I'm fine. Just tired, so I came on to bed. Help yourself if you're hungry, or get a beer or whatever."

"Thanks, will do. See you in the morning."

He hooked a beer from the fridge and went out on the porch. Settled in the swing to stare into the night.

"You all right, grandson?"

The question floating out of the lightning bug-speckled dark startled him. He should've known, though, that coming back here would awaken the ghost of his grandfather. It was guilt that stirred them up once more. They didn't exist in the real world. He must be crazy in the head to believe this shit was really happening. Still, his subconscious replied to Lone Bear Stands. One was not rude to his elders.

"I am not all right. How are you, grandfather?"

"Pleased to see you."

"Let me ask you one question before you leave. Why is it you are only here?"

"I am everywhere. I choose not to appear at times."

"I don't understand."

"You will. You must remain here. The children will need you. The woman will need you even more. Do not leave."

"Aw, shit." This he said aloud in reply to the conversation in his head.

Why did the old man have to be so vague? Why did he have to be here, period? He should be resting in the spirit world instead of pestering him. Why did he speak in riddles no one could solve? Children? What children? This was why he wouldn't stay any longer than it took to lead the trackers to the place where he'd broken the limb. Then he would go back to Frog Pond where he could at least find some peace.

"The peace you find will be here, my grandson. You have to look in the right place for it."

Furious and puzzled by Grandfather's words, he refused to converse any longer, but finished his beer in silence, like a pouting child. After a while he rose and went inside, careful not to awaken Mac.

The *asgi`na* and *anasgi`na* followed him into his dreams, pulling him in many directions while he searched for the lost children. An ugly darkness drove him to hide from happiness and seek reasons for existing. Or perhaps for not existing.

Confusion and fury drove Jessie from Dal's arms and back to the cabin. Understanding men proved to be nearly impossible, even with the best of them. They were wired differently from women, no doubt about that. One could almost say men and women were from different species.

And that child. Talk about impossible. That's what she was really concerned with right now. What in the world sent her running off in the dark like that? She had turned to Jessie for help, only to go off into the unknown the first chance she got. Perhaps that had been her plan all along. She was on the verge of the age known for being manipulative to say the least.

Jessie snatched up her phone and called Tink again. This time she answered, and she poured out her story in fits and starts.

"Wait a minute. She ran off into the woods… in the dark?"

"Almost like she knew where she was going. Tink, you don't think…?"

"That girl knows exactly where she's going. I'd bet my bottom dollar on it. She would never have just run off in the night. She's going home to that New Daddy she told you about. He's probably got those kids so hypnotized to his will they'll never be the same again."

"She sure fooled me, then. Do you suppose this is a religious cult or one of those communes where they raise marijuana, or worse, cook meth?"

"How far did Dal track her?"

"I don't know. Maybe a quarter of a mile or so. Then I… he, uh, we had a fight and I ran off. Earlier he told me he'd be ready to start searching again in the morning."

"Give him a call and see when he needs searchers and we'll get some rounded up to meet him there."

Before she could suggest Tink call him something scratched at the front door. "Hold on a second." She crossed the room, peered out the window. A dog barked, a bark she recognized, and she flung the door open. Brad bounced in, ran around her feet two or three times, then stood on his hind legs to paw at her britches.

"Where have you been, you naughty dog? Running off like that." She held the phone to her ear. "Brad just came back."

"That's interesting. Now we have a dog who knows where she went, or at least knows where she's headed. Is he smart enough to lead us there in the morning?"

"I don't know. I didn't even expect her to run off, sure didn't expect him to go with her. We'll just have to wait and see."

"Well, it's a possibility anyway. Honey, you sound sort of upset. I thought you'd be happy Dal is back."

"He's not. Not really. In fact he can't wait to return to wherever he was. Soon as we clear up this mess with Mac."

"I don't believe that. You two were, well, tighter than new jeans before he left."

"Well, that's old news. He wants nothing more to do with me, and I'm not sure I know why. I knew he had some things to sort out when he left here, but he's so mixed up he doesn't know whether to laugh or cry. I wish I could help him."

"Aw, honey. Don't worry. He'll come around after he's here a while. The way you used to go at each other, I can't believe he doesn't care for you at all."

"Well, sorry to say, it appears he doesn't."

"Burt just came home. I have to get supper on the table. You find out from Dal when and where for in the morning, then let us know. We can round up someone to help out. Colby and I are off tomorrow unless something turns up. We can be there."

"That would be great. Why don't you call Dal and tell him. I don't feel like talking to him anymore tonight. Please?"

A long pause. "Sure, honey, I can do that or maybe I'll have Burt do it. I might give that Dal a piece of my mind for making you cry if I have to talk to him."

"Don't do that. I'm just being a baby. There are more important things to think about right now. I'll put on my big girl panties by morning. Thanks, Tink. Love you."

Tink said goodbye and hung up.

It was still dark when the phone rang. Jessie pawed around on the bedside table, found the cell and mumbled something indistinguishable.

"Jess, that you?"

"Mac?"

"Hell, yes, it's Mac. Who'd you think?"

The old grouch. They needed to change his meds. "What's wrong? What time is it?"

"I need you to come over first chance you get."

"Well, okay. Do you know what time it is?"

"I didn't call you to tell you what time it was."

"Then why did you call me in the middle of the night?"

"To ask for your help. I think I finally figured out why they think I been taking bribes."

She sat up, switched on the lamp, blinking against the light. Had the old man been dreaming or what?

"Well, won't it wait till morning? There's nothing we can do about it tonight, is there?"

"You remember a few months ago when I arrested that old boy for dealing drugs and he threatened to get back at me?"

Obviously it wouldn't wait. Who in the world was he talking about?

"Not sure." Let him talk some more.

"Well, I just recalled that he's a cousin to Sheriff Kimble up in Nolton County."

"The one they're fixing to charge?"

"The very one. What if he's figgered out a way to prove I'm taking money and letting this cult or whatever it is get by with whatever it is they're doing?"

It sounded pretty far-fetched to her. "What does Dal think?"

"Hell, I don't know. He's asleep."

"Mac, hang up and go back to sleep. We'll talk about this in the morning. You need to get some rest. Okay?"

"Well, if you think that's best. I'll talk to you in the morning."

She put down the phone and turned off the light. It was a long time before she went back to sleep, what with worrying about Mac's mental health, Dal's insistence he didn't deserve love, and that little lost girl wandering around in the woods. That was entirely her fault. She would show up tomorrow to help search, even if it meant she'd be around Dal. If anything happened to Lily it would be on her. All on her. Not something she wanted to face.

6
CHAPTER

Thunder woke Dal from a hellish nightmare and he sat straight up, fists hammering the air. Sounded like gunfire in the distance. In the gloom of early morning the clock on the bedside table glowed five-thirty. Sheets of rain washed the window panes. Lightning cracked open the ashen sky, thunder rattled the glass and shook the bed. He rubbed a hand over his sweaty face. What was that dream-scare all about? As usual, meaning had fled into the dark recesses of his brain. Poised there to appear again in the middle of some future night. Not remembering was a good thing. He was in Mac's house, that much he knew.

Jeans lay in a pile on the floor and he slipped them on, then pulled the crumpled t-shirt over his head. Barefoot, he crept to the bathroom, tried to avoid the mirror. Tangled hair and puffy eyes.

Looking real good there, buddy.

On to the kitchen. No sense in waking Mac. He'd rather be in a motel where he could scratch where he itched, but the old man needed him around. Pawing through cabinets, he came up with coffee and started a pot. The rich aroma filled the room. He opened the back door, breathed in the refreshing rain-scented air. A bad day for a search, but a worse day for a kid to hunker down in the woods. They had no choice but to get out there and try to find her.

Colby and Tink would meet him out at Jessie's. Not a place he wanted to be, but there wasn't much choice. They had to gather as near to where Lily'd disappeared as possible. Tink had offered to call a few more people, but he told her that too many could only muck up the tracking. He'd rather just a few go. He could only hope Jessie had other plans for this dreary Sunday and would remain absent, but somehow he doubted that. She'd feel like losing the girl was her fault and insist on helping out. If he knew anyone, he knew Jess. Damned if he wished he didn't. Being around her strained his control to the breaking point. Hard to forget the time they'd spent in each other's arms.

Mac stomped into the kitchen and caught Dal pouring himself a cup of coffee. "Smells good. Give me some of that, son."

He slumped into a chair at the table. The old man had aged ten years since Dal'd been gone. That was a worry. He was pale with dark circles under his eyes and his clothes hung loose, like he'd lost some weight. Be damned if he'd let these sons of bitches ruin Mac's reputation and cause him pain. Whoever had started this had better watch their asses, cause he intended to put a stop to it. And they hadn't seen this Indian on the warpath.

"Want something to eat?" Mac glanced around as if there might be something hiding in the room they could eat.

"I'll pick up something at LaNita's. She'll be open and her cinnamon rolls are good. Listen, Mac, I'm going to be working today, or at least this morning. I could make you some eggs or something before I leave."

A frown wrinkled Mac's face and he waved away the suggestion.

"Okay, but you eat something. I'll be back later in the day to make sure you're okay."

"Well, sure I'll be okay. No need in anyone babysitting me. There is something I want to talk to you about, but I spect it'll wait. I've lived a long time without anyone to mollycoddle me. So you're taking a shift today?"

Dal peered closely at him. Decided not to try to remind Mac that he hadn't been a deputy for a good long while. "Okay if I take the unit?"

Mac nodded toward the front door. "Sure, I'll just stay home. That's a nasty storm out there. You sure you have to go out in it?"

"Yep, I better. You eat something. Okay?"

Mac nodded and Dal finished dressing, hooked a mackintosh off the coat rack, grabbed Mac's walkie, and stuck it in his pocket. Funny, even after eight months without it, all of a sudden he felt naked not carrying his .45. Dangerous to go on the job unarmed. Though the thunder and lightning had abated some, the rain hadn't let up one bit when he ducked off the front porch and ran to the patrol car. Inside, he punched Tinker's number in his phone. Hadn't wanted to talk to her about the search in Mac's hearing.

She answered on the first ring. "I'm on my way. Colby's with me. Where you at?"

"Going to town to get coffee and rolls for everyone. Why don't I meet you out at Jessie's?"

"Okay, but you sure you want to go out there? She's mad enough to take a shot at you."

"Yeah, well, she can get glad the same way, or stay home, and I don't think she wants to do that."

He hung up to the sound of Tink's laughter. By the time he arrived at

Jessie's cabin, they were all gathered in her kitchen waiting. At least she wouldn't take a shot at him with witnesses. Brad barked an announcement of his arrival. Dal went in without knocking, distributed cups of coffee and the giant cinnamon rolls, leaving puddles on the floor.

"Figured you wouldn't have enough Honey Buns to go around. When did he come back?" He threw the question toward the dog without meeting her glare.

Tink cleared her throat and lit into a roll and coffee. Colby looked like he wasn't sure what was going on and Jessie acted as if she hadn't heard him. Didn't thank him for the breakfast or explain Brad's presence.

Well, he really didn't care. Just wanted to get this done and over with. Find that little lost girl, clear Mac's name, and go back to Frog Pond where he could hunker down all alone. Hide like the coward he was. Didn't look like that would happen very soon.

They gathered on the porch, snapping raincoats closed and pulling the hoods over their heads.

"Reckon he'd be able to track her?" He pointed at Brad, who watched the action with some tail-wagging anticipation.

Colby scratched Brad's ear and made doggy sounds. The pit bull went ecstatic. "Looks like if he could, he'd already have took off like in one of them Lassie movies, barking and coming back to urge us to follow. He don't look like a tracker to me, and sure doesn't have a hound's nose."

Jessie picked him up without adding to the opinions, set him inside, and shut the door. That settled that.

Within twenty minutes or less they trudged in a line behind him toward the animal trail where they'd last seen Lily. A line of figures encased in yellow plastic like some weird gathering of aliens, hoods pulled over their heads to ward off the steady downpour. Dal led them to the broken limb that marked where the girl left the animal trail the day before. The canopy overhead spat heavy drops that popped onto the raincoats. Underfoot, rivulets ran down the incline, slopping over their boots.

"Watch your footing." The sound of the storm muffled his warning. "These leaves are slick. I'm afraid we're not going to find any tracks in this mess. Best we can do is follow the path of least resistance and hope she did the same. Jessie, she knows you, why don't you holler for her ever once in a while."

Still not talking to him, she followed his instructions while he scanned the area, searching for any sign Lily'd been through there. He led them around a mass of thorny blackberry bushes. What looked like a torn rag hung from one of the long brambles. He pulled it off and they gathered around.

"This look like what she was wearing?"

Jessie fingered it. "A piece of that ragged shirt under her overalls. I tried to get her out of them to take a bath. Yes, at least we know she got this far."

"Holler for her again. She could be holed up anywhere."

They all waited while Jessie cupped her hands around her mouth and shouted for Lily. The rain fell steadily, but the thunder and lightning had drifted to a distant rumble. Looked like the downpour was set for an all-day affair. Thick timber kept them from being drowned.

"Tell you what, let's go on down to the next logging road. I might pick up her trail there if it's not already standing in water. Then we can decide if we want to give up and hike out to the road, or keep looking."

Emerging into the open, he needed wipers to clear his eyes. Swiped a hand down over his face, scanned the area for some sight of a small human. She could be huddled under the shrubs thick along the slopes, or hunched behind a tree. Hiding.

Colby stared into the shadows. "Looking pretty iffy. Hate to go off and leave her, but there's only so much we can do. She could be plumb off the other side of the valley by now. How about tracking dogs? Maybe after it quits raining."

Dal had his doubts they'd find her, rain or shine. "I guess we could try, but by the time this gully washer gets done, all signs of her passing will be gone. I have a feeling that little gal knew exactly where she was going when she lit out from Jessie's. She's hightailed it straight home, and she's probably back warm and dry with that bunch of yahoos that sent her out to steal in the first place."

Tinker wiped rain from her face. "I'm with Dal. I say follow the logging road out to the main road and hike back to Jessie's. It's not like this child is four or five years old. We do track her to those folks, we probably can't bring her in. We ought to do it right. Take what we know to Judge Smith, get a warrant, then track them down legally."

No one disagreed, and Dal led them on down the side of the hill, hanging on to saplings to keep from losing his footing. Memories of nearly getting killed tumbling head over heels down the mountain last fall kept him extra careful. By the time they reached the flat area where loggers drove in to cut and haul out downed timber, about halfway above the bottom of the gorge, he was more than ready to call off the search for the day. There had been no further signs of the girl, and though they all spent a good long while searching the logging road, none of them found any trace.

He glanced at his watch. They'd been out a bit more than four hours. He had Jessie call for Lily while they trudged along the weed-covered lane, but there was never an answer.

"It quits raining, we'll see if we can get some dogs out here and check it out, but I got my doubts we'll find her."

109

"You don't think she's dead, do you?" Jessie ran up from behind to slog along beside him, her expression one of misery.

"No, I don't think so. I think she's back with her people. The little imp used you to get out of jail and she knew exactly where she was going from the minute she left your place. It isn't your fault. None of it."

He felt bad for Jessie, who would blame herself no matter the outcome. And the DHS people weren't going to be too happy with her, either.

Jessie stood on the front porch waving goodbye to Colby and Tink. Dal sat inside finishing up a mug of coffee. He didn't seem anxious to go. It better not be cause he had something he wanted to chew on her about. Bad enough she blamed herself for Lily getting away from her like that, without him adding to it by laying the problems between the two of them at her feet. At least he didn't fault her for the escaped child.

Hugging herself, she moved inside and shut the door against the chilly wind following the storm. Dal sat in one of the kitchen chairs, Brad at his feet sharing a bit of stale Honey Bun.

They both glanced up as one, the male human grinning to show those blasted gorgeous dimples. "Sorry, he's so ugly he's cute. I can't resist his begging. And I'm starving. Knew you'd have some of these somewhere."

The male dog did his best to look innocent, a scrap of sweet roll protruding from his mouth.

She ought to smack the male human right square over the head. That was their shared joke, those stale sweet concoctions. From a happy time for both of them. Right this minute, she'd bet a hundred dollars he had some in his cabinet. That was a long time ago, when he lived down at Ina Mae's trailer park. Not now. Now he was gone from here. From her. Only back to help Mac, which she was more than glad about. Still, his presence kept giving her goose bumps just thinking about their history together.

"Jessie, I'm sorry. I truly am. I didn't mean to make you unhappy. You can talk to me. Hell, you can scream at me if you want, but please stop going all silent on me and glaring like I shot your pet dog."

Saying something like that to her took some nerve and she let go on him. "I don't know what you expected when you came trailing back in here like you'd never been gone. Hope you'll excuse me if we can't just be best friends and to hell with what's happened between us."

He turned his mug round and round on the table, then took a big gulp and rose to his feet. "Okay, it's however you want it. I'll be on my way. Sorry I bothered you."

In that brief moment before she regained her senses, she almost ran to him and threw her arms around his neck. He looked so miserable.

The raincoat over one arm, he went to the door in sock feet, picked up his boots, and stepped out on the porch where he sat in a chair to put them on. The sound of him stomping down the steps, squishing through the soaked grass, the car engine moving away, leaving behind silence, brought tears chased away by anger. At herself, at him, at this whole fucking mess.

Why couldn't he just go back wherever it was he came from? How would she ever be able to stand him being here for weeks, or even longer? All the while knowing he couldn't wait to leave again? Seeing him all the time. Covering stories and him hovering about like some ghost out of the past.

Stay and love me, you bastard, or get the hell out of here.

Damn him. He wouldn't do this to her. She had a job, stories to write as this latest occurrence played out, friends to be with. This was her home and be damned if he'd make her feel so bad. What she wished for more than anything else was that she was madly in love with someone else and she could show up with him everywhere Dal went so he could see what, by God, he was missing.

How petty. Fury curled a knot in her belly and she reached for something, anything, to throw. It turned out to be a plastic salt shaker. When it hit the cabinet door, then went skittering across the room, Brad barked and ran round and round in circles snapping at the silly thing.

"Oh, shut up." She sank to the floor and cried while the crazy pit did his best to lick the tears from her cheeks.

The next morning, on her way to work, eyes swollen and heart aching, who did she see but a familiar face she'd never expected to see again. A man she could love, if her heart was so inclined. But it wasn't, no matter how hard she tried. He was driving an unmarked pickup and he couldn't be undercover since everyone in Cedarton now knew Trey Ledger was a US Marshal. No, correct that. A US *Deputy* Marshal. These lawmen and their titles. She drove past the jail, sunlight reflecting off rain-washed tree leaves, the air sweet.

Trey slid from a sleek black club cab with tinted windows. Looking sharp as could be dressed in blue jeans with a badge on the waist band, a western shirt tucked in, a silver Stetson, and shiny black boots. The last time she'd seen him he'd had shaggy hair, needed a shave, and could've used clean clothes. Pretending to be a druggie down on his luck living in a shack on the edge of town. This morning he had a shave and a haircut, the thick brown hair curled over the collar of his shirt.

Scolding herself for acting like a woman on the prowl, she beeped her horn and waved when he looked up.

He waved back and shouted, "Howdy, Jessie."

Seemed more than one man was back in town for this latest crime wave. Pumped and not sure why, she hurried inside *The Observer*, put her things on her desk and leaned into Parker's office.

"Words out we might have a big story brewing. I just saw—"

She stopped when she spied the glowering woman sitting across from his desk.

"Come on in, Jessie. This here is Missus Drummond. She—"

The angry Missus Drummond rose from the chair, the action cutting Parker off midsentence. Jessie didn't blame him. Her eyes followed the unfolding frame. The woman must be six feet tall and wore a dark suit that accented her height. Jessie considered herself tall at five foot eight, but this one towered over her and she was fit to be tied.

"So you're the one who talked Sheriff Couch into giving Lily over to your incompetent hands?"

Jessie darted a quick glance Parker's way. Palms up, he shrugged. Dang his hide, he didn't bother to make any excuses for her. She was obviously on her own.

"I'm afraid that is me. I might remind you that we called your office for permission. I didn't steal her. She is a tricky little thing. Led me to believe she trusted me, sure had me fooled, cause soon as I turned my back she was off and running. We hunted for her several hours during the rainstorm yesterday."

"As well you should. Who's out looking for the child? The sun's shining."

"I'm not sure. I understood some of the deputies were going to—"

"I've been there already. They seem of the opinion that she went back to her family."

"Oh, well, then your job must be done."

Drummond glared at Parker like he might be able, at the very least, to shoot Jessie, then shifted a hard gaze to her.

"Anything happens to that child, it's your fault. Entirely."

With that dire promise, the woman stomped on skinny legs from the office, through the newsroom, and out the door.

"And that to you too, lady." Jessie glared at the empty entryway.

Wendy stood. "Well, my goodness gracious, that was interesting."

Jessie cleared her throat and Parker smiled. "Never a dull moment. What was it you said about a big story brewing?"

"Uh, oh, yeah. US Deputy Marshal Trey Ledger just arrived in town. He's over at the jailhouse right now. Wish I was a fly on the wall."

"Get on over there and play like you are. Find out what's going on. That's what you do, isn't it?"

"Uh, oh, yeah." She was repeating herself, but could think of nothing else at the moment.

"Go, woman." He waved a hand.

She scurried from the room, grabbed up her pack, and hit the door running. Should've thought of that herself when she spotted Trey. Then she would've been over there at the jail instead of in the office getting her butt chewed off by Wonder Woman.

Inside she came up against a brutal truth. Couch didn't think as much of her as Mac did. When she tried to get in his office to find out what he and Ledger were discussing, he told her to wait outside till they finished, then if she had some questions he would talk to her.

Howie Duggan manned the booking desk. Might as well find out what he might know, so she moseyed that way. He turned out to be another newbie who thought he was supposed to keep his mouth shut around the press. This town was getting too damned big for its britches.

How was she supposed to write news stories if no one would talk to her? Maybe she should just go over to the Red Bird, listen to the latest gossip, then go back to the paper and write it up so everyone could argue with her over what she got right and what she got wrong.

To add insult to injury, she was still hanging around in the waiting room like some rookie reporter when Dal came busting in. He didn't see her till after he asked to see the sheriff and was told the man was busy.

Then he turned and hauled up short. "Won't let you in either, huh? Place may never be the same again."

"Yeah, well. It doesn't do to try to enforce the First Amendment. Best to keep everything secret. Wouldn't want the public to be well informed."

"Ho, boy, does that sound like a seventies protester."

"Ah, well, of course we now have the National Securities Act so everyone can choose to keep their mouths shut, no matter what."

He hooked his thumbs in the waistband of his jeans, not quite so new as Trey's, but sexy anyway, those eyes sparking like fireworks. "Bet if we wanted we could keep this up all day."

Instead of taking the bait, she filled him in on what he might've missed. "US Marshal Ledger is in there with him, even as we speak." She nodded toward Couch's closed door. "Reckon what they're up to?"

He took her elbow, guided her toward the row of benches against the wall. "I need to talk to you about something."

Not sure she wanted to listen, she hung back.

"Come on, it's important. Mac said something to me this morning. I need your take on it."

"Turn loose of me and I'll go with you."

He glanced down as if surprised that he gripped her arm. "Sorry, I guess I'm a bit upset."

"I think we all are." She managed a smile and followed, sitting next to him, thighs touching so she felt all shivery. She didn't bother to move away.

The touch must've affected him too, cause it took a minute for him to clear his throat and begin.

"Mac said he arrested a fellow last fall for growing and selling weed, and he turned out to be a cousin of Sheriff Kimble. He thinks maybe Kimble is the one who cooked up this attempt to frame him for taking bribes. If he did then it backfired on him. Sounds pretty thin to me. Do you know the man?"

"Did he tell you his name?"

"No, just said Kimble's cousin. I thought maybe you might've written a story on the arrest and would remember."

She thought a minute but couldn't come up with it. "I could call Parker, he might remember."

"Would you do that, please?"

"Sure." She pulled her phone from an outside pocket in her backpack and punched a button.

After a while, Parker answered. She asked him about the story.

He was silent a moment or two, then came back. "Yeah, I do remember that. Reason you don't is, you were working on a series and so I covered it. Let me think now. The guy's name was Lannigan... no, Lundigan, Royce Lundigan. His mama was a sister to Sheriff Kimble. Don't recall her name."

She nodded at Dal. Handed him her phone. "Talk to him. He remembers and you can ask whatever you want."

"Hey, Parker, did you talk to the man?"

She watched Dal nod his head. Then he went on. "Did he seem to be the kind that might be vengeful, do something to get back at Mac?"

He listened a minute. "Okay, thanks. We'll do that. Yeah, thanks." He handed back her phone. "He said he'd find the issue if we wanted to come by and pick up a copy."

"He wanted me to stay and find out what's going on between Ledger and Couch, so guess I'd better. There was a woman from DHS there when I went in this morning. Tore me a new one about letting Lily get away."

"Oh? I hope you didn't let her get to you."

"Not really. It's not like she can put me in jail or anything." She glanced up at him. "She can't, can she?"

"Hell, no. Well, I don't think so."

"You don't think so? That's encouraging."

He pulled his leg over just a bit so their thighs were no longer touching. She acted like she didn't notice. Be damned if she'd let him get to her. "Thought you were going to talk to Parker about that man."

"He's gonna find the article. Said I could pick it up anytime. I'm curious too." He tilted his head toward Couch's office.

A sadness lingered in his eyes, so even when they sparkled she saw it. That entire episode out on the mountain last fall had been hard on him. Not to mention herself, skinning down that rope till her hands were bloody. Their time spent together till help came didn't count anymore for some reason.

Without speaking to her again he took off down the hall in the direction of the break room and the jail cells. Where was he going? With a sigh she slumped back onto the bench. If Couch ever came out she had a bunch of questions to ask him about rumors there was a hoard of people running around in the county using kids to commit crimes for them. It sounded about as ridiculous as the idea that last night's storm could've soured all the cows' milk.

The door to the sheriff's office opened and she rose, anticipating a face-down. Trey scooted out, hat in hand followed closely by a frowning sheriff. Both swept past her like she wasn't even there and took long strides to the sheriff's vehicle, where they climbed in, turned on the siren and lights, and lit out of there.

Dal came trotting back, glanced at her, then followed them. She hurried out on his heels and was right at his back when he opened the door of Mac's car.

She scooted around its rear end and took hold of the passenger door handle. "Am I going with you or are we wasting gas?"

"I expect you'll get in anyway, so get on in and fasten your seat belt."

It didn't surprise her one bit when he turned on the siren and skidded sideways onto Mountain Street and around the square in hot pursuit. "Funny they both went in one car without fighting over it first."

"Same goes for us, I reckon." He hauled ass out onto the highway in the same direction as the patrol car.

She didn't answer. Honestly couldn't' think of anything much to say. It was best just to get a good grip on something with fingers and toes and hang on for the ride.

About a mile out of town, Couch side-slipped onto Dog Town Road and cut the siren to drive alongside a pasture filled with grazing cattle. Clods of mud kicked up from the flying black and white. Dal followed suit like it was some sort of contest to see who could throw the most mud clods.

"Dang, wish I knew where they're going in such a hurry."

He didn't look at her, for which she was glad, fast as he was going. "Wonder what happened?"

"Nothing on the radio. Did the phone ring while they were in there?"

"If it did I didn't hear it."

Brake lights flashed and Couch skidded through an opening in a white wooden fence, in and out of a puddle sending up rooster tails, and down a white graveled road toward a big fancy house that looked like a southern mansion from *Gone With the Wind*. The mailbox read Bainbridge. A man stood in the yard.

Dal stopped at the entrance gate and left the engine running.

"Well, go on up there. We can't hear what's going on from out here." She leaned forward as if that would make the car move.

"No, and they can't run us off either. In case you forgot, I'm not a deputy anymore and this sheriff doesn't have much use for you or your newspaper. We go up there, he's liable to shoot at us."

"Well, how we gonna know what's going on?"

About that time the radio came to life. Sheriff calling dispatch.

Dal grinned at her and she grinned back, then both sobered. He didn't want to be there with her and she was supposed to be mad at him. In silence they listened to the call.

"Ten nintety-seven, we have a ten fifty-seven."

"A missing person?" They both said the words, then waited.

No call for assistance.

The two lawmen bailed out, talked to the man in the yard for a moment. A woman came out on the porch screaming so loud Jessie could hear her from where they sat at the gate. She had a strange, vibrating voice.

"We need you, Number Four. Get on in here."

Breaking protocol on the radio was fairly common in backwoods counties, but Dal showed surprise at being summoned. "That's us."

Jessie did too. "What do you suppose—?"

"You tell me." Dal shifted out of park and barreled down the long driveway, scooting to a stop in the wet gravel.

She bailed out dragging the backpack, but he beat her to the porch. Someone opened the door. She couldn't make out who till she slipped in behind Dal, expecting someone in there to toss her out on her duff. They didn't. Trey shut the door and stood with his back to it.

Couch stared out the big double windows into the sunny day and the man and woman sat side by side on the couch, holding hands. Both had been crying.

"This here's Taylor and Susan Bainbridge. The girl you let get away yesterday. That her?" He glared at Jessie and pointed to an eight-by-ten photo sitting on a bookcase against one wall. A pretty blonde with short curls and blue eyes. She looked so perfect she could've been a model.

Jessie moved closer and Dal followed. He let her reply. "Nope, that's not her. Lily had a butchered haircut and dark eyes. She was skinnier too, almost emaciated."

The woman burst out crying.

"Ma'am, your daughter's been missing for what, three days? Why did you just now call us?"

"She's done this before. Gone off to see her sister in Bee Rock. We just thought she was there but she's not. We figured she'd be back like she was the last time, so we didn't report it. But all this uproar over these kids scared us. Have you found out what's happening with these kids? Where they're coming from? Will you try to find her before she gets caught up in whatever that mess is? Please?"

Couch looked down for a minute before facing the woman. "No ma'am, nothing has come up as of yet, but we'll keep you posted. We'll do our best to find her. I'll take the picture. What's her name?"

"Rebecca."

"What's her sister's name?"

"Jennifer Mason. You got any ideas about these kids? Someone kidnapping them or they runaways?"

"We're still trying to sort things out, but we'll keep you apprised of our progress."

The asshole preened around and asked her a few more questions, took some notes, and ran his thumbs around the belt of his pants. "I assure you, we'll do everything we can to find her. Now, don't you worry."

He scurried to Dal and Jessie, herded them from the room. Trey brought up the rear, bidding the couple goodbye.

"How come someone's not staying here in case she gets in touch?" Jessie whispered to Dal.

"I don't think this idjit has ever handled a missing child case." Dal headed for Mac's vehicle. "You coming with me?"

Out in the yard, Trey was holding a conversation with the sheriff and Taylor Bainbridge, who had followed them. Jessie wanted to hear what was being said, but she didn't want to be left behind so she joined Dal and climbed in his car.

"Where we going?"

"Before that incompetent asshole gets started, we're going back where we found a piece of this girl's shirt and starting over. I should be able to connect to her if she was frightened." He gestured toward the house. "They're lying about something. I'd like to talk to them without so many people around muddying up the works. We need to concentrate on finding Lily, cause I have a feeling she's gone home and home is that blamed cult."

Jessie refrained from asking him why he hadn't connected with the child when they found the tattered cloth. He probably had a good reason.

"But this little girl isn't her. What do you suppose is going on?"

He shook his head. "I think we're close to learning what's going on with these kids running around stealing things all over town. But I'm not sure yet. I need to get back where we lost track of the other child. There's something strange going on here."

She didn't like the expression on his face at this very moment. He looked like he dreaded what he would have to do.

CHAPTER 7

Backing around so he could get out ahead of Couch, Dal slammed the shift into drive and tore ruts in the grass. Looked like in order to learn what was going on with these kids he'd have to connect with the *asgi`na* and *anasgi`na* once again. Goddammit, he didn't want to put himself in that dark place. After succeeding in shutting them down while at Frog Pond, going about his life without any of that mindfucking business, would he be able to handle the upheaval caused by such dark linking? Could he handle it without going over the edge?

Almost dying on that mountain last year had affected him more than he could believe. After being involved in those deadly shootings in Dallas he thought he was up for just about anything. Till he and death met up out there a second time. Twice now he'd escaped it.

Why?

What was he supposed to do that could be so damned important?

Then he came face to face with a woman who cared so much for him she put herself in danger to find him. He didn't need any of that shit.

But if it meant he could save some kids, he'd have to go there again. Grandfather had told him as much, so he had to follow the signs.

Even as he sped down the road, he released the blocks he'd erected against those ghosts and spirits. And here came Jessie's thoughts, sneaking in to hit him with a vengeance. Her fear for the child, guilt at being responsible, and helpless despair that she could do nothing about the situation, poured through his mind. He massaged his temple with the heel of one hand. The car swerved. Not a good idea to drive at the moment. Foot jammed on the brake, he slid to a stop. The car slanted to block the road, rear wheels in the muddy ditch.

Great performance. Just when he might have convinced everyone he wasn't really crazy.

Jessie yelped in surprise, her mounting grief at losing Dal fading from his thoughts. She reached over to touch his thigh. "What happened? What's wrong? Did we hit something? Dal?"

Flesh torn by barbed wire, bloody palms, him cursing and leaving her stranded. Him lying on the side of the mountain, bloody and broken. The images shot from her mind to his.

He slapped a hand over hers. "It's okay, Jessie. Sorry. I didn't mean to frighten you. And no, I'm not going to leap out and get torn up battling a fence or fall off some damned mountain."

She cast him a wide-eyed gaze.

Shit. He'd read her mind and she'd caught him at it.

Someone banged on the window and he twisted. A wide open mouth shouted at him outside the glass.

"What the hell's going on?" Sheriff Couch, furious, impatient, filled with murderous intent. The man was plain dangerous. A vicious mass of threats swirled through his brain.

Dal hit the button to roll down the window. The guy might just belt him one across the mouth, the anger he was dealing with. Something pent up in that twisted mind that he had plans to deal with, and soon. This was what Dal hated about his so-called gift. It was as confusing as hell, being dropped in the middle of someone's anger issues.

While the idiot shouted obscenities at him, he gripped the steering wheel so tight his fingers turned white. Emotions poured through him at a pace he had trouble sorting. All the peace he'd carried for so long exploded from his brain, leaving behind a blackish mist. He muffled the flood of emotions spewing from Couch. It was that or bust him one in the mouth. Thank God Couch couldn't tell what he was thinking at the moment.

Deputy US Marshal Ledger appeared, touched the sheriff's arm, and he calmed down. Glanced around as if embarrassed by his actions. That didn't last long. He was like a volcano shooting lava, then cooling, only to erupt again.

"You're driving a sheriff's vehicle, mister. Who the hell are you?" Couch leaned forward, breath stinking of liquor. "And what are you doing following me around?"

The marshal spoke in his soft voice. "Sheriff, I know this man. Let's dial it down a notch or two, if you don't mind. He's Deputy Sheriff Dal Starr with Grace County. He's been on leave. He came back to lend Mac a hand straightening out this mess that's growing around him." Ledger peered in the window at Dal, mind transmitting thoughts that said he'd better be right about this.

Dal nodded in thanks. Smart of Ledger to put that slant on his introduction. Might cool this pea brain off some.

"Doesn't give him the right to take over. Since I'm acting sheriff, the thing for this man to do was introduce himself to me before he started poking around in an active case." He swung his attention back to Dal. "For your information, and I'm making this clear to all my deputies, you are to stay out of this investigation and they aren't to assist you in any way. You got that?"

So much for his hopes of a cool-down. He stared beyond the man's shoulder and nodded without meeting his eye. Couch had no right to tell him what to do, but he wanted this nonsense to stop.

Couch wasn't ready to let it go yet. "And why in hell did you drive into the ditch?"

"Well, I haven't been drinking. And if you recall, I attempted to introduce myself back at your office. You were too busy at the time."

The man glowered, and for a minute it looked like he might go for his gun. He sure didn't like being put on the spot, especially in front of a US Marshal. "Just keep in mind what I said. It goes for you and all your friends."

How this fool was appointed to carry out Mac's duties was more than he could understand. But then he wasn't in much shape to prejudge anyone till he got himself under control.

Jessie leaned across his lap. He had to grin. Just like her to take over to settle things down. "Sheriff, you remember me? Jessie West. It sounds like we have at least two more children caught up in this. Have there been any others reported missing recently?"

"You're that newspaper lady. Even if there had been, I wouldn't release that information to you." He switched his indignation her way. "Now, if you'd kindly get your friend here to move the car out of the road, I've got work to do."

Dal keyed the car to life. "I'm not deaf or crazy. You could ask me yourself. But to save you the trouble of being polite...." He spun the rear tires so they flung a sheet of muddy water, pulled onto the shoulder, and parked. He'd leave, but his hands continued to shake so badly driving wasn't an option.

Reflected in the rearview mirror, Ledger managed to skedaddle out of the way of the spray, but Couch took it full in the face. He stood there shaking a fist in the air and shouting.

"Looks like you made yourself an enemy." In spite of her tone, she chuckled. "But he sure does look good covered in mud." The chuckle grew to a full blown laugh, then she gazed at him in that familiar way she had of making him feel good all over. "You okay, Dal?"

Without answering, he climbed out, crossed in front of the car, and jerked open the passenger side.

"Please drive."

Mouth open to speak, she took one look at his expression, got out, and ran around to get in behind the wheel. Good thing too, for it appeared Couch was actually considering going from yelling at them to shooting.

It was debatable just how much Dal wanted her to know about what was going on in his head. Best he kept quiet. She took the car out of park, pulled sedately onto the road and he kept his mouth shut.

There were things other than their personal life that they needed to consider at the moment. How much of his last nine months would he ever reveal? She already knew more about him than he wanted by being with him on the side of the mountain while they waited for Nick Snow to rescue them.

Aw, hell, he had to face it. She had done some digging around in his psyche while he was, in effect, out of his head. Her knowing so much about this dark side wasn't good. Considering she had not only found him on the side of that mountain when no one else could, she had remained with him, holding him close till the rescue team arrived. In spite of everything, he owed her big time. A debt he probably could not repay. What a disturbing emotion love was. Admitting to that four-letter word left him even more powerless.

The sheriff blew by them like they were standing still, leaving them in a thick curtain of dobs of mud.

Jessie didn't say anything for a minute or two, then, "That man is crazy as a shit house rat."

Ah, hell. He burst into full blown laughter and felt way better than he ought to. She was just too much and tough to stay mad at. "Glad to know you haven't mellowed much in my absence."

Eyes sparkling, she tried to remain stern but couldn't. "I have a feeling it's a good thing I can't read minds."

"I'd rather not myself. I hear the weirdest things. If you had any idea what it's like to wander through the perverted thoughts of people who do the awful things some do, you wouldn't even consider wanting to."

"Sorry, Dal. No, I can't even imagine what it's like. You helped people, you know. Lots of them, in fact, and put away some bad guys as well. And it often occurred to me how bad it might be. You just never said and I—" She glanced at him. "You okay?"

"Yeah. *Hell* yeah. That couple back there? Could you tell what they were thinking?"

"No, of course not. What?"

"You sure you want to hear this?"

"Yes."

"It has nothing to do with the missing child, which is way weird. Hubby, he's thinking how, if his wife wasn't such a narcissistic bitch, she wouldn't have spent all their money on such a godawful house. The chatter inside the place, coming from that asshat Couch and that woman, who was so furious with hubby over something I couldn't get a handle on her thoughts. They were a complete mess that made no sense at all. I think she wants to kill him or someone, but I could be wrong. I'm concerned that neither one of them had one thought about the missing girl that I could sift out. Violent ideas and thoughts always overpower all else when I open up, and I had to shut down in there before I went crazy. You got any aspirin? My head is about to split."

"In my backpack. I carry everything in there."

He dragged it from the backseat. "My God, is it full of bricks?" He pawed around and came up with a bottle of Tylenol. "This'll do just fine. We need to get this settled and fast and get Mac back on the job. I wouldn't be surprised if Couch started the rumors about him taking kickbacks from folks breaking the law in Grace County. And the sooner rid of him, the better. He's dangerous. And there's something going on between him and Bainbridge." He palmed three pills and dry swallowed them.

"You don't know it for sure about him starting the rumors?"

"My brain's not like a vacuum cleaner, sucking everything in that's there. But he's sure as hell guilty of something, and I intend to find out just what he had to do with all this."

"Please don't shut me out, Dal. I want to help find these kids and uncover whatever dirty is going on before it ruins our town."

"First thing I'm going to find out is where that little girl went. And you're going back to *The Observer*." He held up a hand. "I'm not shutting you out. You need to do your job. Put us ahead of the curve. I'm tired of chasing my tail and learning nothing. We need to put a handle on this."

"Okay. I'll go back and see what I can find out. Just be careful and let someone know where you're going. Would you please?"

He did not make that promise, but went on. "I have some ideas about running Lily down. I'm not sure about Rebecca. From what I learned there, she may well have run away to escape those nut jobs."

"If you won't take me with you at least let me know what's going on. Even if you won't admit it, you know the media can help uncover dirt."

"Dammit, Jessie. Pay attention. That's what I'm trying to have you do."

"Okay. It'll be fun working together again."

"We never worked together. We fought every inch of the way. You for your story and me to catch the bad guys. That's what we're still doing."

"Well, okay. But still, Dal, we shared what we learned, more or less. And you have to admit it was fun. I've missed you like crazy. You can't tell me you haven't missed me."

He didn't say anything, but it was good she couldn't read minds, cause he was remembering one dark night when they'd run across each other at a crime scene and ended up fucking in the woods till the world tilted on its axis. Strange they'd both avoided mentioning anything like that.

One thing was for sure, they always got along in that respect, even if they fought like badgers the rest of the time.

And that was what he liked about her the best.

She stood toe to toe with him and never backed down. He didn't have to read her mind to find out what she really thought. Okay, so he did like her. A lot. So what? He could be a real bastard sometimes and it took a woman like her to handle that. Not that he was sure that he wanted handled. They both carried too much baggage and it sure mucked up getting along.

"Doesn't matter. I'm dropping you off before I go looking for Lily. Do what you like about that."

"Don't do this all alone. What about Colby and the others?"

"I'm not getting them involved. Couch would fire every one of them, but he can't hold that over me cause I don't work for him."

She gave him a long, burning look, but didn't say anything.

Hard to do, but he shut out what she was thinking. No way was she going with him on this adventure, no matter what she thought.

Jessie drove back to town without another word passing between her and Dal. Mostly because she didn't know what to say. She had no clue about him and what he thought. Sitting straight in the seat, he gazed out the window. How badly she wanted to touch him. Just reach over and spread her hand over his hard, flat belly, see what he did. But she resisted because she didn't want to use sex to get her way with him. It didn't appeal to her for some strange reason.

At the sheriff's office she parked next to the Jeep, grabbed her pack from the backseat, and bailed out. Let him go do his thing. She had to go to work anyway in spite of her earlier words. He crawled out of the car, went around to the other side, climbed in, started it, and drove off. Without one frigging word. Damn him, anyway.

Back at the newspaper office, she went to work. Normally, she would've called Mac for a release on the little runaway, but Couch would stall till the paper was off to be printed. He'd done it before. Instead she hammered so hard on the keyboard Parker stuck his head around his open door.

"Take it things didn't go so well."

"How'd you guess? That so and so bastard Couch. I'd like to tear him a new one. Okay if I write the story from my viewpoint since I was present when all this happened?"

He grinned. "I sense a battle between the Fourth Estate and our sheriff's department. Write it, I'll go over it. We'll see."

"It's half done." She barked the statement at the computer screen and frowned. Deleted half a line and rewrote it. Without looking up, she sensed Parker had gone back to work. Maybe she was learning to read minds too.

She read what she had written so far.

Who is stealing our children... and why?

Saturday night this reporter accompanied deputies Dallas Starr, along with Tinker and Burt Sample in a search for a ten-year-old girl. She escaped while being held for the Department of Human Services after being picked up for shoplifting. Though we tracked her part way down the mountain, darkness kept us from continuing the search. Sunday morning we began looking again despite the storm, but no sign of the child could be found. Her name is Lily, she has brown hair and brown eyes. She was wearing overalls and a ragged shirt and was last seen southeast of town in a wooded area.

Pausing, she reread the beginning, then started to write again, this time punching down her anger.

It is suspected that she lives with a group of people who may be responsible for recent outbreaks of lawlessness in Cedarton. In the past few days several children have been involved in stealing merchandise from various local stores. None have been caught. As of this writing, no statement could be obtained from acting sheriff Couch regarding the standing of the case. Anyone spotting unusual or suspicious activity involving young children should notify law enforcement.

A source at the sheriff's office stated that a search is underway for all the children involved.

Not much of an article, certainly lacking all the information for a well written piece, but if she knew Parker he would fill in some blanks, maybe even pry some facts out of that asshole temporarily holding down Mac's job. Her boss had a way of getting information when no one else could.

Itching to know what Dal had learned, she put the article in Parker's file on the computer and gathered up her things. Parker looked up when she stuck her head in his door.

"I'm going to catch up with Dal. He's on his way to try to find Lily and if he does it'll be one heck of a story. He thinks I'm online checking out local cults, just in case he calls."

Without looking up he nodded and waved her off. "Go ahead. Just get in here tomorrow to help finish up."

She drove home in a tizzy, as her grandma would've said. She would find Dal or die trying. Well, not that much, but it sounded good. No telling where he went, but she'd bet he was out around her cabin somewhere looking to pick up Lily's trail down below the logging road. And he'd sure be pissed when she caught up with him.

She fed the excited pit bull, changed into grubby jeans and walking shoes and a ratty old t-shirt. Armed with a flashlight, her cell phone, and some water, she started down the hill, following the animal trail to the logging road.

It was late afternoon when Dal's antenna led him to what he was looking for down in the valley far below Jessie's place. With care he made his way through a thick stand of cedar. An old road led to a dilapidated church, the remnants of which clung to the mountainside. Gray clapboards did the best they could to hang on to the sagging framework. All the window glass was long gone and the double doors hung precariously from rusted hinges. And nearby, clustered like chicks around a mother hen, were half a dozen RVs and a couple of trailers. What they were up to was anybody's guess. It was pretty quiet. He took up watch in the thick grove of cedar.

Bugs chewed on his flesh, sweat ran from under his hair and soaked the back of his shirt, and he wished he'd brought some water up from the car before anything happened. The sun hovered above the mountains to the west before an old beat-up Chevrolet pickup arrived down below, the bed crowded with several kids and tow-sacks that appeared to be stuffed full. Two men got out of the cab, went around back, and let the tailgate down, hollering and shoving the kids along toward the trailers.

Several men came out of a ratty RV, all carrying guns, and helped the arrivals lug the tow-sacks plus a lot of plastic bags from Walmart into the largest of the trailers. One of the girls wore overalls and had chopped brown hair. Chances were that was the missing Lily. None resembled the picture he'd seen of Rebecca.

For a long time after everyone disappeared inside the various trailers he sat propped against a scraggly tree. Shouldn't the kids be playing, laughing, teasing each other? It was so still, so damned still. Just what in hell was he gonna do now? Besides having no authority, he wasn't prepared to go up against all those armed men with women and kids in the mix.

Moving with a great deal of care, he made his way back toward the car. He couldn't radio any of the deputies for help and put their jobs in jeopardy. Had to figure out something for himself. Even letting Mac know was out of the question. The old man would find some way to help him, and frail as he was, could get hurt. Inside the unit, he dug a bottle of water from a small cooler Mac kept in his vehicle. Though the blue ice was pretty much melted, the water was cool and he drank half of it. It was way too hot in the car, but he leaned back a moment, gazing at the walkie in one hand.

Damn, he hated to leave those kids here, but one man couldn't go bulling into what appeared to be a well-fortified settlement. Movement in the rearview mirror caught his attention. His heart went into overdrive. Had they spotted him or the car? Prepared for the worst, he slinked down out of sight.

In the rearview mirror, Jessie's reflection crept out into the open, stood there for a moment as if mesmerized. She had to have seen the patrol car, though he'd driven it deep as it would go in the wooded area. He should be angry with her, but he wasn't. Didn't surprise him one bit that she was there.

Holy shit. She was about to walk right up on them. He shifted to the far side away from her approach, eased the door open, and slipped out. Working his way around to the rear of the car, he waited till she came closer, then hissed at her. Crossed his fingers she wouldn't react noisily. He had to make the hsst sound again before she heard him, slid her gaze in his direction, and stopped dead still.

Terrified she would reveal not only herself but his presence, he slapped his finger over his mouth. She nodded, hunched low, and made her way to him.

It was all he could do to keep from telling her off about following him. Instead he took her arm and guided her behind the thick stand of cedar trees where he motioned her to get down on the ground.

Mouth to her ear he whispered, "We're gonna have to get to some higher ground where we can better see what's going on. Follow me, and for God's sake be quiet."

He took her hand and led her up a rocky incline, both grabbing saplings to pull themselves up. Once in a while he stopped and made sure they weren't moving into the open where they might be spotted by a lookout. About ten feet above, a huge boulder offered good cover and he clambered up, then turned and helped her follow. Leaned against the cool, shaded slab, he kept its bulk between them and the trailers in the valley below.

Jessie leaned close to his cheek. "I thought you were in there with them. Didn't see you in the car. How did you drive in?"

"An old logging road."

She gestured off to her right. "From there?"

He nodded, gestured why?

"Let's drive out and get help. If they didn't hear you drive in, they won't hear us leave. Probably talking and playing music or whatever inside those awful trailers. Must be hotter than blue blazes in there."

"Hotter than that out here. Damn, I hate to leave the kids."

"We can get help, Dal. Ledger or maybe even Kimble. Couch has no say over them."

He squinted down through the thick woods. Had to do something. Couldn't just sit up here till hell froze over. She was right, there were some Couch couldn't threaten. Old Sam Watson was one.

Her lips moist against his cheek. Eyes squeezed shut, he slowly turned till his mouth covered hers. Like a feather's touch, like a man starved for something tasty, he took in her sweetness. Just a little bit, enough to savor her. Bits of electrical charges shot to the one place he needed to protect from her influence. Oh, God, he ached to hold her close, tell her things he'd so long held secret.

She breathed in and out inside his mouth, her taste exquisite. Was that a word a man should use? Maybe not, but he could think of no other. Her tongue crept around his and his resistance melted. One hand spread over the back of her head, he fed from her till his body trembled.

From down in her throat erupted a sound so entrancing he straddled her lap and eased her back onto the leaf-strewn ground. Just to lie with her a moment, hold her close and not think of anything else. Whispering to each other, her eyes wide open gazing up at him, glistening with tears. So like her to cry at a time like this.

Him saying her name, her murmuring his, their lips locking once more. Just to feel this much. Feeling an exchange of body heat, of gasping breath. Of her muscles rippling against his, the fabric of their jeans disguising the flesh.

He remembered every inch of her, the way she ran her hands over him, pausing to caress the best places. Every minute he grew harder against her, needed her to open to him.

Yet, they couldn't. Didn't dare.

Not here, not now. Coming together, they'd make too much noise. So they clung to each other, absorbing the pleasure.

From down below came a shout, gunfire, a child's scream. Dal leapt to his feet, she came to hers. A man down there dragged a crying child by one arm across the cleared spot between two trailers and threw her inside an open door, his cruel voice shouting.

"We have to do something. Clearly those kids are here against their will." Dal touched her cheek and she nodded.

"I can stay here while you go for help."

He shook his head. "And what would you do if they caught you, or if they took off? Follow them? No, I won't let you put yourself in danger. We both leave or we both stay."

The drive back to Cedarton seemed endless. She was unusually quiet. He hated to think what might happen to those kids if he didn't figure out a way to rescue them. He had to do this right with people who could handle the job.

He left Jessie at her cabin. "Please, let me know when you decide what to do. I want to go with you soon as you get everything arranged. Don't shut me out of this, please." She leaned into his window and kissed him under the ear.

Damn, that felt good. He drove off watching her walk up to the cabin in his rearview mirror.

It took all hands to get the paper ready to go to print the next day. During a quick lunch break sitting out back at the picnic table for ten minutes drinking a Pepsi, she called Ledger at the number in her phone. No luck. Determined, later that afternoon she asked Parker if he had a number for the marshal.

Hair rumpled by running his fingers through it, he glanced up from editing an article. "He left a card here somewhere last year, but...." He gestured toward the messy desk. "Probably in layer three, maybe four. Look if you'd like."

"I'll pass." She held up a hand and went back to work.

As usual, things got so busy after that she hardly had time to take a break. Still, she couldn't get the marshal and Dal's mission off her mind. Parker managed to get a release from Couch about the missing girl and a possible connection to the siege of shoplifting around town being carried out by youngsters.

He handed her the finished article for editing. As always his sarcasm bled through each paragraph till she was chuckling before she finished. Standing in his door, she waved the paper. "Do you really think people want you to get snarky about missing or kidnapped kids? Much as I appreciate your approach, I suggest you get serious."

"Just wanted to cheer you up. You look like you been sucking green persimmons. Do you think these kids really are being held against their will? Looks to me more like these families are teaching the little brats to steal for their supper and having very little trouble doing it."

"They're just kids. Whether they've been stolen or are just being taught to be little thieves, they need rescued."

"And put in a system already overcrowded with fosters, with not enough proper care?"

In many ways he was right, but what was the answer? Leaving them in that atmosphere or whatever it was should not even be an option.

He cocked an eyebrow. "For all we know they are already with foster parents. So what do we do with them then?"

"I don't know." She studied her boss, one of the smartest men she knew, though he chose to cover it with sarcasm. If he couldn't come up with the answer, who could? Sure as hell not the people in charge now. "So what do we do?"

"We? I don't know that there is anything we can do, Jessie. Maybe just bring it all out in the open and hope people will do something positive about the situation. It's worked before."

She wasn't convinced of that and was determined to be with Dal when he went in to rescue those kids. One way or the other. She called Mac and he told her that he and Dal were on their way to talk to Sheriff Kimble up in Nolton County. At least he was doing something. She finally dug up Ledger's number but he didn't answer.

Later that night, she tossed and turned in the bed, unable to get to sleep. Lightning bugs fluttered against the window screen, sending their messages. If Dal went off without her she was going to bop him one on the side of the head. Difficult to keep her mind off those brief moments behind the boulder, his hands, his mouth, his body caressing her. Somehow she would see that only good came from the way they felt about each other.

Dal and Mac met Sheriff Kimble at a café in Bee Rock. The meal turned out to be only a little productive. Dal allowed Mac and his friend to visit a while, getting up to date on their lives. By the time their meals were served, he was getting impatient.

In curt terms he explained why they were there. "You any idea what set those cult folks against you?" He eyed Kimble, a bald, freckled fellow.

"Can't say as I do. I've thought a lot about it. I figger I was getting too close to someone of importance while investigating a drug bust. Anyway, first thing I know I've been accused of taking bribes and am suspended."

"Just the same thing that happened to me, only mine is a medical leave." Mac gnawed on a fried chicken leg.

"Have you had a hearing yet?"

Kimble stared at Dal. "Nope, nothing like that. Just took to jail, suspended, and turned loose."

"Odd. Neither has Mac." He stared closely at the man. "He has been 'invited' to attend your preliminary hearing as a witness. Do you know anything about that?"

Kimble refused to meet Dal's gaze. Shook his head in silence.

"You haven't been notified?"

"Nope." It did no good to try to read him. The restaurant was filled with noise, both verbal and thoughts, but he didn't believe him.

"Well, it looks to me like someone just wants the two of you out of the way for a while. Someone with some clout. Makes me wonder." The man was clearly lying. It didn't take any special powers to see that, he was so bad at it. Damn all the noise.

Kimble raised his butt up to dig a handkerchief out of his pocket. Only when he got it out and spread it on the table it was a piece of purple cloth with a line embroidered.

"Now that makes me wonder some more. Looks kind of like a moon coming up, don't it? Where'd you get it?" Dal scratched behind his ear.

"Found it on my back porch this morning."

"Nobody broke in or anything?"

"Someone must've but my dog didn't even bark. And she's a good watchdog." Kimble stared out the window. "Got her for my wife before she died. Don't much care for a house dog, but can't bring myself to get rid of her now. She was locked up in the back bedroom when I got up, just laying there waiting for me to let her out. What do you think this means?" He poked at the cloth with one finger.

Dal shrugged. "I have no earthly idea."

Mac shot him a puzzled look, but said nothing.

In the car on the way back, Mac asked him why the reluctance to talk to Rob about the cult and their plans to rescue the kids.

"He's hiding something and I couldn't pry it out with all the noise in that place. We need to keep him out of this till I figure out just what it is.

"It's time we ran down these folks and see about getting those young'uns out of there. They might have freedom of religion or whatever, but putting those kids out to steal for them is something else. Couch has got his deputies tied up till their jobs are in danger. We'll need to go outside Grace County lawmen to do anything. Time to figure something out and to hell with Couch."

8
CHAPTER

It would be best not to let Mac know the vibes he felt around the Nolton County sheriff. Something was way off, but the guy had a way of letting his thoughts wander that was disconcerting. This was the first time Dal had run up against a mind with such blocks. Made him real suspicious of what the man was hiding.

Mac continued as if discussing the subject with himself. "Wish there was some way to prove those kids are being held there against their will. That Lily girl did appear to go back under her own steam."

Dal added to his suppositions. "But there is no question that one girl was trying to get away when we were there."

"Yeah, but kids'll do that when they're mad at their mom or dad. If we could find that even one of them, like Lily, has been took, then I wouldn't feel so nervous about going in to rescue them."

"Colby thinks we can get a warrant to go in and see about those kids. Judge Smith is pretty liberal, especially if he thinks a cult is involved, considering what's already gone on up in Nolton County. Jessie would have to tell him what Lily told her, but that's the next step. Leaving those kids out there isn't an option. You need to trust us to handle this and not go off on a tangent. Couch gets wind of this...."

"What makes you think I can't keep quiet?" The old man glared at Dal, eyes hard as silver stones.

"Oh, I don't know. Just a guess, I reckon."

"Might help if you told me who all is gonna be in on this plan, then that way I won't have to worry about who I can talk to."

"No one, dammit. You talk to no one. Safer that way."

Mac nodded, but he didn't look in the least happy.

Dal headed toward Cedarton.

"Where we going?"

"Taking you home, then I'm going up to talk to Nick Snow. He doesn't have a dog in this fight, so he can do as he pleases, no sweat."

"I'd as soon go with you. Besides, you could just call him."

"Nope. Don't trust the phones. Need you at your place for our contact in case something goes wrong. And you will answer your phone."

The old man grumbled.

Dal turned into the driveway at Mac's house. "It's because someone has to know where we are, who we are, and what we're doing. That someone is you. This backfires, no telling what might happen."

"I'll be in on everything?"

"You betcha. We won't be able to do this without you."

Mac didn't make a move to open the car door.

"Okay, what now?" Dal leaned back prepared to do some more persuading.

"Maybe we just ought to call in the staties and let them handle it. You could all get shot or failing that, go to jail. That Couch wouldn't hesitate."

"Couch is a statie. They already have their minds set that you and Kimble are guilty of letting this cult grow while you lived off the fat of their land. Soon as we get everything set, and we won't take long, we'll give you all the info you need to save our asses if we run into trouble."

Mac opened the door, walked bowlegged toward the house, discussing the foolhardiness of the plan under his breath.

Dal hollered at him. "Mac, don't you breathe a word of this to Jessie, you hear me?"

Mac waved a wrinkled hand over his shoulder and never looked back or said anything else.

After the door closed behind him, Dal backed out onto the street and headed for Red Rock to talk to Nick Snow. In his mind he went over who else would be safe to recruit. Sam Watson might still do his weekend stint at the jailhouse, and he was part-time and not under the purview of Couch. He also played around with the idea of Trey Ledger. That could be dangerous, for the man had his loyalties as a US Marshal, and might feel he had to report to them. Still, he'd be a good man to have on their side.

He headed northeast out of town. Within a mile the road changed from blacktop to gravel. Good God, what if this backfired and he got some women or kids hurt? Sure as hell didn't want something like Waco to deal with. Would be worse even if it was an official law-backed raid. One thing for sure. Even if they didn't get a warrant he was going in anyway. What choice did he have? Still, even if they pulled it off he could go to jail. Worth it if the kids came out unhurt.

Crushing the doubts, he accelerated up the mountain, leaving a boiling cloud of dust behind Mac's patrol car. Good thing they hadn't taken it from him when he was put on so-called medical leave. That was a joke too, but still fortunate for Dal and his plans.

Jessie drove to Mac's in the hopes that Dal might be there. He wasn't, but she knocked anyway, then went in to talk a while with the disgruntled sheriff.

He frowned when he let her in, stumped through the living room, and plopped down in his recliner.

"Glad to see you too. You seen Dal today?" She sank onto the slightly bedraggled couch.

"This morning, but not since."

"Did he say where he was going?"

Mac shrugged, refused to meet her gaze.

"What's going on, Mac?"

"Nothing. Not one blamed thing. And if there was I couldn't tell you."

She shrugged. "I'll bet he took off to round up those folks down in the valley. If he did I'll kick his butt up between his shoulders."

"Nah. That could be dangerous. If they're growing weed or doing anything illegal he could be in shit up to his earlobes. They'd as soon shoot him as look at him."

"I know, but you know Dal. I tried to get him to let me go with him."

Mac harrumphed. "What good would that do either one of you? Then you'd both be wading in it."

"Well, at least one of us could go for help when the other one got mired down, couldn't we?"

"Didn't say where he was gonna look, I don't suppose."

"I was hoping he'd told you where he was going. You'd think after last year, he'd learn to let someone know. He liked to have died, dammit. What's wrong with him? He's really messed up. I'd like to help him, but—"

"Well then, gal, what's stoppin you? That's what women are for, to stop men from doin foolish stuff."

A bitter chuckle escaped. "Impossible to do sometimes, though."

Mac tilted his head and glanced down at her backpack. "You got one of them fancy cameras in there? Not like one of them telephone dojiggers?"

So just what was he getting at? It appeared Mac might know something he wasn't revealing. "It's pretty fancy."

"Takes pictures from far off, like looking through them binoculars?"

"Mac, what is this all about? Are you suddenly taking a big interest in photography?"

"Well, not really. But if you were, say on a hilltop above something down in a valley, could you get good enough pictures to make IDs? Like they do on that CSI show on the TV?"

"I would say so. It would depend upon how far the hilltop was from the subject. Mac, what are you getting at?"

"You been where those folks are camped... with them kids? When Dal went down there?"

"Uh, yes. All right, this is enough beating around the blueberry bushes. Say what you mean."

"Cain't. Dal'd have my hide."

"I'm about to have your hide. You can tell him that, should he ask. Now speak. What's going on?"

"If you'll wait till later this evening, I can let you know something where that camera might come in mighty handy and save putting lots of folks in danger."

"Dammit, Mac."

"Don't you go cussin at me, young lady. I've said all I can say for now. Do I have your phone number in this fancy thing?" He pulled his smartphone out of his shirt pocket. "Where I can just punch your name and it'll call you? Dal charged the blamed thing up for me."

"I think so. Give it here." She checked the phone and nodded. "Yep, right here."

He leaned forward and she showed him the listing. "So you'll call me later, right?"

"Yep, I will. You be ready."

"Promise, no matter what he says?"

"Well, I ain't tellin him, if you're worried about that. And you can let him think you just figgered it out and not tattle on me. Now run on home and put some water an' crackers in that pack of yours."

"Speaking of home, I'm headed that way. You keep your phone on and answer it if it rings. Cause it could be Dal in trouble. You'll do that, won't you?"

"Course, gal. Keep my phone on, answer it if it rings. Will do. You let me know if you hear anything, would you?"

"Same from you." She gave him a kiss, studied his wrinkled face for a moment, then left. Clearly she'd get no more out of him. He could be stubborn and there was no use in badgering. His request regarding the camera puzzled her, but she'd have to wait and see what was up.

Instead of going straight home she went to the Red Bird to listen to gossip and eat one of their fabulous burgers. Trey Ledger's club cab truck was parked out front and she hurried in, found him at a table with Barton Clemmons, a rancher from over on Signal Hill. There were two empty chairs there and the place was crowded. She leaned on the back of one till Trey looked up and grinned.

"Hey, gal. Good to see you. Sit with us or you may never get to eat. Looks like everyone in town and then some's here today."

She slid into the chair and waited while Barton and Trey finished up a conversation about how many cuttings of hay the summer might bring. She was happy to see Barton demolishing a slab of pie. He would soon leave and maybe she could talk to Trey in private about the kids and that cult.

As soon as Norma took her order, Jessie gulped down some water, then drew her finger through the wet circle the glass left on the table. "I was wondering if you know anything about all this hullabaloo concerning these kids running all over town stealing stuff."

He stared at her for a minute. "Is this for a story for the paper or are you just curious?"

"I'm worried, to tell you the truth. These kids need some help and I'm not sure if anyone is going to do anything for them."

"Uh huh. What do you know about them?"

His earlier friendly demeanor had faded into a curtness she felt uncomfortable with. But she was in it now, and couldn't think of a way out. Still she hesitated. Should she just shut up or go on? He kept looking at her with eyes like glass marbles.

"I, uh, there's a bunch of them camped out down in Hooper Valley near the old Cold Springs church. They have RVs and beat up trailers and there are a lot of kids and women too."

"You've been down there? Seen this?"

"Well, uh, yes, but we were afraid to do anything for fear the kids could be hurt."

"We?" He watched her without blinking.

She opened her mouth to explain just as Norma brought his order and told Jessie hers would be along shortly.

He looked all around. "Go on, Jessie. We?"

149

Damn, she wished she hadn't said anything to him about this, especially about going down there. She could get Dal in trouble. "I don't think I want to tell you who was with me. Let's just say I was looking for a story. Someone needs to help those kids."

He waited for her burger to be delivered before picking his up, though she urged him to go ahead and eat.

While they polished off their meal, he kept studying her like she was some sort of specimen. Without a doubt she'd better be ready to answer some important questions when he swallowed that last bite, so she finished hers off too.

His gaze remained on her while he wiped his mouth, then his fingers, and drank the last of his iced tea.

"All right, spill. You came in here halfway looking for me for a reason. So here I am. What's going on?"

"Have you ever heard of a cult known as The Rising Moon?"

His irises flared. Even if he didn't tell her she already knew the answer.

"You have? They use this sort of flag with half a moon on the horizon, the image stitched against a background of purple. But I don't know what they believe other than that they have a leader known as Deacon. Trey, tell me more about them."

"Where'd you get your information?"

She laughed. "Silly. I googled cults, then moon. There's not much real information there. Just when the group was formed and where and that it went underground after an uprising in southern Missouri and the death of a trooper. Are these people them?"

He sighed. "You're a good investigator. I take it you've been up close."

"Well, not close enough to identify anyone but...." She snapped her fingers. "That's what Mac was hinting at."

"Okay, let's back up a bit. What does Mac have to do with this? I thought he was on sick leave."

"Well, he's a bit depressed, but mostly that's cause they took his job away from him, then said it was because he was depressed."

"Makes a hell of a lot of sense. That's the way politics works."

"Now you tell me the truth. Are you investigating these people?"

"Not officially. I don't know precisely what's going on, but someone has connections high up. High enough to shut down any official investigation, at least temporarily. I believe there are probably several fugitives hiding out with these crazy loonies and that makes it the business of the US Marshal's service. However, so far it's hands off. And I trust you, Jessie, to keep mum till I say different."

She touched a finger to her lips and nodded.

The bell tinkled, interrupting their conversation. Colby stood in the doorway a moment, then his glance landed on Trey and Jessie and he looked bewildered.

Finally, he made his way to them.

"What?" Jessie indicated a chair. "You look lost."

"Thought Dal would be here."

"Not yet, but you can talk to us. Is this about the kids?" She didn't want to say too much, but trusted Colby. It appeared there was more than one secret between them.

"Uh, well, will you see Dal?"

"I suppose, sooner or later. What is it?"

Colby's walkie went off. Jessie couldn't make out what was said, but he answered quickly. "I gotta go. Give this message to Dal, would you. Tell him the judge said no dice."

Before they could question him, he jumped up.

"Hurry back." Trey watched the deputy leave with a questioning look. He turned his gaze back to her. "Have any idea what he meant?"

"I can guess, but let's wait around here for a while."

Trey brooded and she stared out the window. Then she took up the conversation where it'd left off. "Those so-called loonies are sending children out to break the law. What could that be about?"

"Beats me. The minor things they steal aren't really worth enough to the cult to make sense that they'd take the chance of calling attention to themselves. Always stuff kids would want. Strangest thing."

"Trey, I think Dal is planning on raiding them as soon as he can get a posse put together."

"You're kidding."

"Nope. Deadly serious. If you knew Dal you'd believe that without question one."

"What do you mean?"

"He knows things no one else can know. Don't ask me how. It's a spiritual thing. But if he claims something nefarious is going on with these people, something dangerous and violent, then you'd better believe him."

Trey didn't say anything for a while. Probably thought she was as crazy as Dal sounded.

He tapped his fingers on the table. "You're going all woo-woo on me. Supernatural. Possession. Demon stuff? Come on."

The room had cleared out, only one couple remaining besides Trey and Jessie. The front door bell tinkled, the door opened, and Dal and Nick Snow strolled in as if they had an appointment with Jessie and Trey. At least it looked that way until Dal saw them.

Seeing Jessie and Trey at a back table, all Dal wanted was to turn around and run. But he stopped short and Nick plowed right into him with a mutual grunt.

"Oops, sorry. What's up?"

Dal turned, said quietly over his shoulder, "I think we're busted."

"Oh, shit. And I was looking forward to breaking the law."

Trey rose, ran his fingers through his hair. "We're done eating, but if you'd join us, I think we have something important to discuss. Don't you?"

"Well, hell." Dal glanced back at Nick. "Shall we make a run for it or surrender?"

"I for one would like to know what the two of them are hatching." Nick smiled and headed for Jessie and Trey. Dal raised his hands and followed suit.

"We give up, Mister Marshal. Don't shoot." This from Nick.

Dal simply made his way through the chairs and tables and laid a hand on Jessie's shoulder.

"What you up to, Jess?" He sounded amused, but his expression was far from it.

"Uh, well not much. You?"

"The same. Let's sit down, Nick. I think this will work better if we do."

"It definitely will." Trey lowered his lanky frame back into his chair. Nick sat across from Jess.

Jessie took a sip of tea, then aimed a stare at Dal. "Colby says to tell you the judge says no."

Norma came over. "You boys are later than normal tonight, but I can fix the usual if you want."

Dal raised two fingers. "Make it two and big glasses of sweet tea. This is going to take a while."

"I hope there won't be any fisticuffs, boys." She patted Dal's shoulder and he laid his hand over hers.

"I don't know about the cowboys here, but this Indian comes in peace."

She broke up with laughter and after a minute they all did.

Dal spoke through the merriment. "I was afraid he would. Colby asked for a warrant to go in to the encampment of the loonies. That message meant Judge Smith denied it. No surprise, just not enough to go on."

Dead silence for thirty seconds or longer, then Trey spoke.

"All right, it's this way. Taking part in your secret plan won't be the first time I've gone rogue. Why do you think I'm stuck here in Nowhere, Arkansas instead of DC or at least Chicago?"

What should have brought laughter only caused each of them to stare at the other in turn.

"Well, it's hard to tell who will be in charge of this gathering, since we have good representation from more than one branch of law enforcement." He nodded toward Nick. "Except I haven't been introduced to this fellow yet."

"Only one branch I see, Trey. The rest of us aren't showing rank. By the way, this is Nick Snow. Once a marine always a marine. Right Nick?"

Obviously he had surprised the quiet rescue climber, whose eyes shifted in his direction. An unblinking gaze. He hoped he hadn't gone too far, but Trey had to know this was serious business being planned by men who could carry it out.

"Good to meet you, Nick. Is this all of your gang, Dal, or will others be joining us?"

"We were on our way to find you and Sam Watson, a retired deputy. I put Mac in charge of communications." He leaned back and favored Trey then Jessie with a wide smile. "I'm not sure about her."

"Smartass," she murmured, and acted surprised when everyone heard her and chuckled.

Trey took a long sip of tea that Norma had delivered during their exchange. "Since I'm the only one with a job in law enforcement at the moment, does that put me in charge, or do I just take the blame when everything goes wrong?"

"Before you all get started whipping em out and measuring em, I have something to say." Jessie stared beyond the table.

"The only woman wants to speak." Dal used a mocking tone, but he gave her a long, admiring look.

"Mac had a good suggestion this afternoon when I dropped by to talk to him and we got on the subject of this very thing we're discussing which no one seems to want to give a name to. Not even Mac, and that's, uh, well, unusual." She reached down on the floor and pulled out her new Panasonic Lumix digital camera and set it on the table with reverence.

"This baby is mine. I saved up for her. She has a thirty-five millimeter equivalent magnification for an easy-to-view image that works real well in bright or dark conditions. Mac was the one who jarred me into thinking straight. He asked me if my camera would capture images from a good distance. Similar to binoculars, he said. Pretty smart of him. If we can sneak in there, get situated where this little jewel can start taking photos of anyone and everyone who shows their face, including the kids, then maybe we can identify some of these folks that belong in jail and the missing kids." She dragged in a deep breath and glanced around the table. Stopped at Dal. "And Mac couldn't know this, but she's way smarter than binoculars."

He replied. "You'd still be in there putting yourself in danger."

She smiled and shook her head. "Only long enough to set it up, though I'm not getting completely out of sight of this baby. She represents too many hours of toil."

"Explain." Trey appeared impatient.

"I can link it to a mobile device and it can be used to geotag imagery in-camera. We can plot to interactive maps and remotely monitor and control the camera's zoom, focus, and shutter release from a distance."

"Holy shit. Am I understanding this right? You can use, say your smartphone or tablet to control this camera from a distance? Without them knowing it and without putting them or ourselves in danger? That's one heck of a good idea."

She nodded. "And it'll tell us where our pictures were taken."

Dal glanced out the front window. "We still need someone to get in there and set up the camera. Right? Too late today. By the time we could get in place down there, being really quiet and going in slow, it'll be too dark to get around without revealing ourselves. That means being ready to set up when the sun rises in the valley tomorrow morning, which is way later than up here at Cedarton. And there's not much true daylight for more than a couple of hours a day deep down in there."

"I can get you some good identifiable photos using low light AF and the zoom."

"My God. Did you mortgage your first child to pay for this?" Dal gestured toward, but didn't touch, the camera sitting there like a chunk of gold. "But you could still get caught setting it up if they're keeping long distance watch and you can bet they are. Some of those men have guns, we saw that. It follows they'll be equipped with binoculars." He stopped short of saying she couldn't do it. He knew better than to make a comment like that. But he sure as hell wanted to. It was dangerous, what they were talking about, and he couldn't let anything happen to her.

Trey raised a finger. "Doesn't it need a signal to do all this fancy stuff? Back in that valley and all that wilderness, will she work?"

Jessie smiled. "There's something called a signal booster, the Verizon MiFi, that will help us there. There's a tower on top of Signal Mountain, and one day I'll tell you the history of that going back to the fifties, and if we're lucky we'll remain within its range using the MiFi."

Trey grinned at her. "You're way ahead of me, then. Continue." He turned to Nick, who was obviously anxious to speak.

"Jessie, I'll admit you'd have to set up the camera, but it's too dangerous for you to go in alone. Suppose you get caught? At least one of us needs to go with you." Nick said what Dal had been thinking, and he swiveled to see how she would take it.

She smiled cockily at him. "Oh, did I tell you it has a shit-kicking audio device too?" Hand on the camera, she studied each of the three men. "Do I get to pick who goes in with me?"

Dal let out a whoosh and everyone glanced at him. Nick chuckled. "Looks like he's worried we're going to hit on his woman. How do we do this?" He tapped Dal on the shoulder, a know-it-all smile.

"Not going to draw straws, that's for sure. Let her decide."

Without saying anything, she repacked the camera, then leaned back to study the men sitting around the table. Deliberately she went from face to face, taking her time with each one.

"Okay, let me tell you why first, then who. Why is we need someone out here who won't stop till he drags me out of there if I get in trouble. I know all of you are dedicated and would give it your all, but if I go in with Trey, who has a stake in the IDs, for his fugitive excuse, that'll leave Dal and Nick to rescue us if we're caught. Makes sense to me."

"Well, looks like she's made her choice." Trey reached over and patted her arm. "Ready whenever you are. Looks to me like we got enough right here to pull this off. More we drag into this, more danger there is we'll be found out and end up in jail. We can call this surveillance and I'm in charge. Looking for some specific fugitives I've reason to believe are hiding out in this cult. I've retained Jessie and her camera since the government can't afford one like it. Y'all are just on the outside in case something happens you can report it to my boss. That's the only connection you have to this situation. Does that work for you?"

Dal studied Trey for a while. He appeared to know what he was doing, but would he protect Jessie with his life? He wanted so damned bad to be the one who went up on the ridge with her, but in his gut knew Trey was right. The entire thing had to be under the legal auspices of the US Marshal services and he could make sure of that. But if anything happened to Jessie the man was toast. And she was right, he'd get her out or die trying. Simple as that.

So he remained quiet while Trey set it up. "Everyone get your shit took care of and come prepared. We'll meet down below Jessie's cabin at dawn. She and I will go in on foot. I'll bring my four-wheeler for you two just in case you have to come in." Trey indicated Dal and Nick. "Everyone put fresh batteries in your walkie. Bring water. Daylight in these hills is about six. Soon as we can see fairly well, Jessie and I will go in. Y'all can wait down on the logging road. Meet you down there first thing. See you later. I'm going home and grab some sleep."

Everyone stared at him, and when no one objected, he made his way through the tables and out the door.

Dal rose, scooped Jessie's backpack up off the floor. "It appears the law has spoken. You comin?" He didn't wait for a reply, just headed out the door without looking to see if she was following. She would.

Eyes tracking his broad back, Jessie went after Dal like a she-wolf on the prowl. He held open the door of Mac's unit and she climbed in. Without saying a word, he got in behind the wheel, set her pack on the floor at her feet, and drove across town and out the lane to her cabin.

The evening sky darkened, stars bloomed in thick clusters. A breeze drifted in the open window and cooled her neck under the veil of hair. She gripped her thighs to squelch a desire that overpowered her till she could scarcely breathe. Between her legs, a flutter like a heartbeat grew until she squirmed in an effort to sit still.

The headlights swept across the yard, already lit by the safety light. Brad waited on the porch, bouncing with each bark of greeting. Dal turned off the ignition, cut the lights, opened the door, and crawled out. She gnawed at her lip. What would she do if he took her to the door and turned to leave? Go inside and take care of her needs alone. Again. Damn him for doing this to her.

He opened her door, took her hand, reached inside, and picked up the backpack. At the porch steps he limped up ahead of her, then turned. He wasn't going to stay. She wanted to scream at him how much she'd missed him. How much she wanted him. Instead, she dug around in the pack for her keys, came up with them, and he took them from her fingers. Unlocked the door, stepped inside, and held the door open for her. Brad slithered in before he pushed the door shut.

A bar of light from outside touched one side of his face. He gazed down at her, rubbed a thumb along her jawline, bent, and touched his lips to hers. Like the softest of spring breezes against her flesh. She shivered with need. Deep down inside her grew a moan of desire that reached out to him. He bent, lips trailing down her throat and into the crevice between her breasts.

One arm curled behind her knees, the other under her arms, he carried her into the bedroom. Relief washed through her, sweet and warm and alive. He laid her on the bed and undressed her, taking a long time with buttons and the zipper, his mouth and tongue on her skin, slipping off her shoes so he could peel her from her jeans. When he had her completely naked and totally aroused he came to his feet and shed his clothes. Stood over her, a bronze warrior silhouetted by the outside light.

Kneeling, he cupped one of her breasts, flicked the nipple with his thumb. Good God, all he had to do was touch her and she was wet and ready. But he would take his time. He usually did, and that made the results all the more intense. For a moment she waited, one hand spread over his bare chest. In the dark she couldn't make out his features, just shadows and a gleam in his eyes.

It was like he'd barely breathed her name and goose bumps covered every inch of her body. His heat clothed her, the smell of him all leather and wildness, the feel huge and encompassing so that nothing else in this world mattered but what was about to happen between the two of them.

She ran a palm over his stomach, fingers trailing through the nest of hair to the swelling of his cock where they danced playfully. The breath he sucked in ended in a groan. She knelt, slowly slid both palms up the outer flesh of his thighs, bent forward, and kissed his hardness so tenderly she barely felt it rise to her lips. The skin, like velvet, hot, pulsing. Her tongue exploring, him making all sorts of noises down in his throat. Finally cupping the back of her head and pulling her forward to take him in.

But he would not want this to culminate in his coming too soon. This was playing, exploring, teasing. He would want to come long after their bodies locked, both of them shouting, screaming, roaring with a pleasure so supreme nothing else compared.

So he lifted her up and away, brushed her lips with his, then circled her waist, turned and tossed her across the mattress. Him laughing with delight sent joy all through her. On hands and knees, he loomed over her. Still teasing. Licking her nipples till both were tight nubs sending exquisite delight shooting through her like lightning.

She stared up at him. "I've missed you so much. Come here."

He nibbled his way up from her breasts, met her mouth with his, tasted her inside and out, planted kisses over her face, ears, throat.

"No one else, huh?" A whisper she barely heard.

"No one else."

Her insides throbbed until she squirmed. His hardness poked at her belly, slipped lower when he moved down to lick and suck at her skin. Time to entice him some more. With both legs she hugged his waist tightly, locking him in the near vicinity of where she wanted him.

"You about ready?" He nibbled the words into her ear.

"Whenever you are." She like to not got the three words spoken before he rolled onto his back, keeping her locked so close he slipped inside her in that one movement. Hands grasped her waist, seating her. Plunging deep, so deep that an orgasm shot through her in waves of heat and cold. Struck her temporarily blind and mute so only a small sound grew from her throat and escaped.

Gasping for air, she rose to her knees and jammed back down hard, trapping him fully inside, iron hard and throbbing. Both his arms pinned above his head, her knees tight on either side of his hips, him deep inside her, she leaned back till he touched her very depths. Remained there. Smiled down at him, even though it was too dark for him to see.

"You bout ready, Dal?" She mimicked his earlier tease, swung her butt up and rode him faster and faster. The movement ignited a fire that she fed with each thrust.

The noises he made told her how much he enjoyed their coupling and when he came, she did too, with one long glorious orgasm that met his with an ethereal rush into oblivion. He collapsed onto her limp body, held her there until she could scarcely breathe, rolled off with a low groan.

If she could've spoken, she wouldn't have, for it might ruin the total experience. Instead, she lay there next to him, clutching his hand in hers, holding on to the experience and doing her best to return to earth.

While they held hands between their bodies, his other arm crooked over his forehead. Hers sprawled out on the mattress.

It was quiet in the room for so long she glanced his way to make sure he was awake. He was, head turned so he gazed at her, deep green eyes reflecting a glow from beyond the window.

Their gazes met. Locked. "Welcome home, Dal." A whisper barely heard above the clatter of night critters through the open window.

"Come here." He let go her hand, wrapped that arm around her and pulled her over, rolled so they were belly to belly and sprawled his other hand over the back of her head. "Don't you ever let me leave you again."

"I won't, I promise."

But he could, he might. That's the way he was.

9
CHAPTER

It was that three in the morning wake-up. The one where the brain begins to find all sorts of shit to worry about. And no way will it settle down and go back to sleep where it belongs.

There were a lot of reasons for Dal to agree to Trey's plan, but he still didn't like Jessie going in there without him. He should go with her to keep her safe, but if they got caught, then he and Nick needed to be on hand to go in and bring them out. Damn. Was he getting so self-assured he thought he was the only one who could do anything right?

One thing for sure, though. If anyone in this world would face death to save Jessie, it was him. He'd failed to save one woman he loved, it would not happen again. Jessie was fearless, had no notion of danger. Just waded into situations, cocked and ready to explode. She would never realize that's what made her vulnerable. This kept him awake when the clock read three a.m.

All those months he'd spent at Frog Pond, he'd denied a need to be with her. Worked to drive her memory out of his mind when all he really wanted was her next to him. Being without her turned him into an empty shell. Who wants to live without love? Without happiness? Without self-worth and a purpose? He never thought he would ask himself those questions. Or answer them in the negative. But in the lateness of that night, he did just that.

After coffee and Honey Buns the next morning, he stuck a knife in his boot, took her .38 and a box of ammo from the drawer, and went with her down to the logging road, their fingers intertwined. The silvery morning cast a shimmer on her skin. Her face glowed with anticipation like a gorgeous horse ready to leap forward and win a race. He'd kiss her right there in front of everyone except for one thing. He wasn't sure he wanted to admit his feelings for all to see.

Not yet.

For a long moment he stood close enough to smell the wildflower scent in her hair, to touch the warm, velvety smooth skin of her arm. He adjusted the backpack on her shoulders to make it easier to carry. Waiting for her and Trey to return would be the hardest thing he'd ever done. He held her close, kissed her forehead, patted her butt, and stepped away before he made a complete fool of himself. By then everyone was making an effort not to stare at them. So much for secrecy.

In the first light of dawn Trey and Nick rode in to meet them on a four-wheeler. Shaking hands with Trey, he caught the man's gaze. "You take care of her, don't let anything happen."

The marshal nodded, an expression that did little to reassure Dal. "Let's make sure the walkies are working. Don't call us. The sound could carry. We'll call you."

They ran a quick test.

It would be better if they had the newer digital radios, but the department couldn't afford to outfit everyone, and their application for funding was bogged down somewhere. So they still carried the old analog units that worked most of the time. Cell phones were useless in the valley, which was a good thing. Their unexpected ringing couldn't call attention to their presence.

"We need to agree on how long we should wait before coming in if we don't hear from you." Nick appeared more eager to get going than the others, as if he itched for battle.

They all gazed at Jessie. Dal asked her what she thought being as how she was the one in the most danger.

She hooked a glance toward Trey and shrugged. "I'd hate to spend the night tied up in one of those RVs. Maybe give us the day to get plenty of pictures. We'll call in our location every thirty minutes or send back something through the camera. We're not back an hour before the sun goes down and you haven't heard from us, maybe you ought to come in like Rambo."

They all chuckled nervously. Trey looked at each one in turn. "Agreed?"

Silent nods. Jessie kissed Nick on the cheek, then gave Dal a hug and fast kiss.

You'd think they were on a black ops mission or something the way they were rigged out. Legs spread against the incline, Dal waited on the edge of the slope until Trey and Jessie moved off down the hillside and out of sight. It would be a long wait, that was for sure, so after a while he and Nick settled against the bank. Following a few minutes of silence, Nick pulled out a deck of cards. Grinned.

"Hearts or Texas Hold em?"

Dal tried to laugh with him, but came up short.

Because she knew where the cult was hiding, Jessie led the way along the animal trail Lily had followed when she bolted. After a while the path angled down the mountainside so steeply she had to cling to trees and saplings, feet slipping and sliding over rocks and exposed roots. It wasn't necessary to check and see if he followed. The clatter of his boots over the rough ground was enough to assure her he did.

The rugged descent dumped them onto an older logging road, so overgrown it was difficult to trace.

"Let's take a few minutes to rest and hydrate." She didn't wait for his agreement, but sank onto a flat rock leaving space for him. After calling Dal with an update he joined her where they sucked at the water bottles in silence. Neither of them spoke for some time, but her thoughts shouted at her. What if this didn't work? What if Couch got wind of their plans and punished Dal or Mac? Worse than all that, what if someone got hurt?

For herself, she didn't worry much. The false sheriff had no authority over her and couldn't cause her any trouble at all. Her story was going to bust this cult wide open. Might even end Couch's term as sheriff. It should hit the AP wire too. She could think of nothing they'd forgotten to do to insure everyone's safety. But something could always go wrong in such a situation.

Screwing the lid back on her water bottle, she pointed toward the lower edge. "See that broken limb? Dal bent that to mark where he lost Lily's tracks when it started to get dark."

Trey rose. "Well, let's get moving, then. Glad you've got a good sense of finding your way around in these woods. I'd hate to get lost in here. No one might ever find me."

"Well, there's the sun, and if we keep going down we'll be in Hooper Valley. It's only a matter of going north or south once we're there."

He cleared his throat. "I was a city boy till I started working this part of the country. I have to tell you, street signs would come in mighty handy."

"Maybe we can see about arranging that when we get back." She smiled and moved off down the treacherous slope. "I'll try not to leave you behind."

They'd been scrambling downhill for several minutes when something hit the backs of her legs. She stopped, latched onto a tree to steady herself, and angled her head to peer over her shoulder.

Trey stood above her, pointing off down the incline and then holding a finger over his lips. He might be a city boy, but he had a good eye and ear. Someone moved along the covering of leaves with barely a rustle. She remained where she was, bent down to see what he saw. Two men, visible through the trees, flashed in and out of sight as they strode crossways of her route. Each carried a rifle slung over his shoulder. One of the men said something, then they both laughed. Inching one eye out a bit past the rough bark of a tree, she caught sight of them. Both stopped and unzipped their pants.

She frowned at Trey. Mouthed, "Hunters?"

He shook his head. They waited some more for the rattle of footsteps to fade away.

Trey joined her, his voice low. "I think it was a couple of men we're searching for. I'd need a better look at them. Fugitives hiding out with loonies. Just like we thought."

"What do you suppose they were doing?"

He shrugged. "Besides pissing? Probably checking the perimeter. How far do you think we are from their camp?"

"It's way off down there. Can't see it yet. If they're keeping watch this far away, we may never get close enough to get the pictures we want."

"Let's wait here a while and see just how wide a circle they're making. Once they reach the far side, maybe we can set up the camera on this side. There's a bluff off yonder that might be ideal if we could get on top of it. Would that be close enough?"

She followed his pointing finger to the outcropping of flat rocks protruding over the valley like a table set by nature. "Doubt it. But from there we might spot a good place. We'd have to be careful not to show ourselves. One of them could have binoculars or a scope on their gun."

"It's worth a try. We ought to be able to climb up there in thirty minutes or so. It's up to you."

"Before we go better check in with Dal."

Trey nodded, called, then handed her the walkie. "Hi, we're okay." She kept her voice down. The static was intermittent and she didn't catch all he said. Just that she should be careful.

Too bad Nick Snow wasn't with them. He could scoot right up the shelf of rocks. Maybe it hadn't been such a good idea to leave him behind. Though she understood why Dal wanted him there. If they had to come in on a rescue mission involving the kids, the climber would be handy. Meanwhile she and Trey ought to be able to handle this in good time. Both of them were physically fit.

She checked her watch. Three minutes past seven. They'd been on the trail a bit over an hour. The sun hadn't cleared the peaks to the east, but the sky gleamed a tarnished silver to announce its arrival. Birdsong filled the morning air and high above a red hawk soared, screeing before diving to capture breakfast. She paused to watch the graceful bird swoop down into the valley.

If Dal were here he'd give them a short lecture on the hawk and her habits and habitat. She missed so many things about him. If only he'd decide to stay she'd take such good care of him he'd never have to worry about bad thoughts again. Mac was right. Most men needed tender loving care and Dal was well worth the effort because he returned it in kind. Except when he didn't. Even then it wasn't a shouting match or violence directed at her. He mostly settled for punishing himself with a brooding silence that never lasted long.

She reached the steep climb on the rocky escarpment and crabbed up on hands and feet. Loose rock tumbled down behind her. Hearing nothing from Trey, she braced against a small tree and peered over her shoulder. He wasn't in sight.

Where the heck had he got to? The silence told her nothing. How could he have fallen and not made a sound? Surely not possible. Bad idea to yell. Wait? Go on? Slide back down? Heart in her throat she leaned over, braced herself, and peered into the shadows.

When Dal had been pushed off the top of Red Rock mountain, he'd fallen almost all the way to the bottom and suffered a dangerous concussion, broken ribs, and skinned arms and legs. Yet he'd managed to claw halfway up before collapsing. His second brush with death, and it had broken something in him, as if he questioned his right to live. The rugged wilderness was a dangerous place.

Just as she was about to head back down, two hands appeared, clutching a thick vine that dangled from high in the limbs of a wild cherry tree. With a grunt, Trey pulled himself up till his head came in view. Covered in dirt and debris, with a good sized knot on his forehead, he managed to climb back onto the trail.

"Playing Tarzan?"

He grinned self-consciously. "Funny. A rock bounced down, hit me in the head, and I stepped on something, didn't want to holler so just skidded till this rope slapped me in the face and I grabbed it."

"Good going, but that's a vine. We need to look at that lump?"

"Nah. Let's get on to the top."

She nodded and finished the climb in fast measure. At the layered rocks she dropped to her butt. By the time he scrambled onto the hard surface she had finished off a bottle of water and had the first aid kit out.

"Sit here." She indicated a flat spot in front of her. He dropped down, legs crossed.

Ripping open a pack of gauze, she cleaned the knot and applied cortisone cream before bandaging it. The incident left her trembling, but she tried to keep him from seeing how frightened she'd been. He could've been badly hurt. As it was the knot was already turning black and blue and seeping blood.

"Does it hurt?"

Fingers feeling the lump he glanced up at her, eyes blue as a spring sky and reflecting her concern. "I'm okay, Jessie."

He knew about the incident when Dal had been hurt, appeared to understand her concern. To cover up she pulled the camera from her backpack and removed a 16x Leica DC Vario-Elmarit zoom lens.

Trey eyed the camera. "I know there's a lot of electronic gadgets I plain don't understand and I'm fine with that. But could you explain to me how that thing works?"

"Probably not. But I can give you an idea. You know when you take a photo on your smartphone and if you have the right apps, a copy is automatically sent to your computer or tablet or whatever?"

His nod was not convincing. "Sure, yeah… well, not really."

"I'm sure you know that when you take a photo with a digital camera it records where and when the picture was taken."

He gestured. "Okay, still not with you. Go on. I'll catch up."

"This camera actually maps a location, time and date, and when the camera is signaled from my smartphone to take a photo it does, then sends that information along with the photo not only back to my phone but to my iPad, which I left with Dal and Nick. It also takes a high-resolution four-k video recording if we want."

"A video? And Dal and Nick will know precisely where the picture was taken. Clever gadget. I guess I get it. Maybe not how it works but that it does, at least."

"Want to know a secret?"

"Hmm, love secrets."

"I haven't the foggiest how it works, either."

"Yeah, but you can make it work and I'd foul it up good."

"No you wouldn't. Like anything else it's easy once you know how to do it. It's a simple bridge-style point and shoot camera."

"Yeah, simple bridge-style. Gotcha." He grinned, gave up watching her set the camera to check the view through a small pair of binoculars. "I think I see them. Just the tops of a cluster of trailers, at any rate." He read her the directional setting from the binoculars and she adjusted the camera to match them.

"That's them all right. I didn't expect to find them this easy. You chose a good place for us. We need to be careful though with both the binocs and the camera. Once the sun is up a reflection could flash from the lens and if someone down there was watching they'd be mighty suspicious."

"Funny, I don't see any movement."

"When Dal and I were close in down there we didn't see much

either. Nor was there noise like you'd expect from normal kids playing or families listening to music."

She fiddled with the camera, setting the aperture for low light. The angle was amazingly accurate because the cliff was so high and on the opposite side of the valley from the camp. She snapped two or three photos, then moved into the shade to make it easier to check the results.

Unhappy results.

"Bad news."

He glanced up. "Real bad, or just average bad?"

"Bad enough. Come over here, you'll see right away."

He scooted on his butt to where she squatted and she showed him the screen on the camera. He squinted. "Can't make out much."

"Right. It's only showing us that they're there, but not much is real clear. We're not close enough. We're going to have to move if we want to see features clearly."

"I thought you could make it closer. They do on CSI."

"They do indeed. But in reality it pixelates once you try to get it too close up."

"Shit, yeah. Sounds dirty and we wouldn't want that."

She laughed and elbowed him. "You're having entirely too much fun with this."

"Okay, serious." He drew a hand down over his face and frowned at her. "Where to?"

"I'll bet you're a lot of fun at parties when your life's not at stake. Take a look around, but be careful with those binocs. Get some idea where we can set up, then check it out real quick. We don't want the sun in our eyes. We need to be high, but perhaps not so high as we are here, and closer."

Before she finished he scanned the panorama with his bare eyes. "Got a piece of paper and pencil?"

She dug them out of her backpack, watched him as he spread out the paper, weighed it down with some small rocks, and marked an X here and there till he had several possible locations.

"Give me that scarf you tie your hair back with."

She took it from the pack and he draped it over the lens of the binocs, then searched the area around each X on his map and penciled in notations.

"Clever, but can you see well enough?"

"Couldn't if it was a sniper shot. But for these purposes, it'll do. Just need to see the lay of the land. I'll let you take a look, soon as I see something. Okay?"

She jerked around to stare at him. A sniper shot? Hmm. A lot she didn't know about him. Or was he just speculating? He'd been pretty handy taking care of himself when he took that tumble. All his talk about city life.

"Okay come on over here so you can see and I'll show you what I've spotted that might work for our camera setup. I'm going to let you pick something out. If nothing will work, I'll do some more looking."

Jessie checked out his finds, using the scarf-covered binocs. Pointed. "One, there. It means crossing the valley, but it looks real good."

"Show me."

Shoulders touching they found the location, studied it, then moved back away from the edge till both were nestled under the canopy of trees surrounding the rock formation.

She keyed the walkie. "You there?" She could barely hear a reply.

"We're going to have to move. This isn't close enough."

"An …ound? …et too …ose." Static cut out most of the reply.

They'd agreed not to use the usual protocol, but just speak in the hopes if they were overheard they wouldn't sound official, but more like someone just messing around. They'd also agreed not to chit chat, for that would make it easier for a listener to happen across them.

She tried one more time. "Moving. Will let you know later. Out."

She had wanted to text back and forth, but they'd dropped that idea in case someone might be able to hack the texts. When they had the other site located and set up would be time enough to get in touch and send some photos.

"First we better get moving." Trey glanced into the bright rays of sunlight that had cleared the peaks to the east.

She repacked everything, he tucked away the binoculars, and they half-skidded, half-stumbled down the incline from the rock shelf, then headed on down the mountain into the valley.

Once on flat ground, they paused to check the terrain. It would be dangerous to try to cross in the open.

"I spotted a line of brush and trees yonder a ways." Trey pointed. "I think we can use them for cover to get to the spot you chose."

"We need to let Dal know. It's going to take a while."

"Only problem is, if he can't hear us any better than we can hear him, it won't do much good to radio him." He eyed the camera. "That gadget sends a picture when you take it. If I write a message on a piece of paper and you take a photo of it, can you send it to him?"

"Of course. Good idea. They'll see where we are and how we are."

"Let's do it before we start out. I'm a bit nervous about crossing the valley with these guys having lookouts on foot everywhere. It'd be good to let Dal and Nick know where to start if they don't hear from us again."

She nodded, took out the camera while he wrote a brief note on a piece of paper.

EVERYTHING OKAY, MOVING ACROSS THE SOUTH END OF THE VALLEY TO COME UP ON THE OTHER SIDE. WILL CONTACT YOU AGAIN WHEN WE GET THERE.

She took a photo, checked it for clarity, then sent it to her iPad and crossed her fingers. If she knew Dal he would scan each and every shot they sent, no matter what it was. The photo would show him precisely where she and Trey were at this specific time.

Trey pocketed the binoculars. "If it's okay with you, I'll take the lead. I think we can make it clear across with cover from what I saw earlier. Just do what I do."

"Fine with me, just don't run off and leave me."

"That'll never happen."

A man stepped out of the trees not twenty feet away on their flank, a rifle pointed straight at Trey. Hadn't even heard him coming. She glanced around, lowered the camera gently to the ground, the lens pointed in the direction of the man with the gun. Picked a likely escape route. She'd leave him if she had to. Get help and come back.

"Stay right there. Believe me, you do anything I don't tell you to do, I will shoot the both of you."

Dal kept an eye on the iPad Jessie had left. So far there'd only been mostly dim shadows. Then something moved into view that looked like a piece of paper. He read the words, the location, nodded, and relaxed a bit. Then something appeared to hover almost out of range of the camera. She must have it set on automatic and it was taking pictures, sending them.

He leaped up, leaned close to the screen. A man with a rifle loomed into view. Jessie stepped back far enough the guy had to do so too if he meant to keep her close. With a click, the camera captured a perfect photo of him.

"Son of a bitch. That's Kimble."

Nick leaned forward to peer at the man's face. "Who?"

"Sheriff fucking Kimble. Our innocent Nolton County sheriff." Under his breath, "Run, Jessie. Goddammit, run."

But she didn't. She was going to stay there, get her story, no matter the cost. Someone said something. She'd hit the video button. Kimble practically snarled a question.

"What you two doing off out here anyways? Meddling in our business." The question came through clear as a bell.

"Why doesn't she run? She's inches from that thatch of trees." This from Nick, who sounded stunned. Had he known this Kimble? Maybe suspected him? Nah, he hadn't even recognized the face.

Dal turned to Nick. "I can answer that with two words. The story. She'll risk her friggin life to get it. Stubborn damn woman, smart as a whip, sweet as honeysuckle, but determined to get her story even if she gets hurt."

Nick grimaced. "Tough to love a woman like that, but then she's got her work cut out for her if she feels the same about you, doesn't she?"

What the hell? This guy talked like he knew something no one else did. If he didn't like him so much he might've told him off and then some for saying something so personal.

"I don't think that's anyone's business."

"Hey, sorry. I have a bad habit of poking about when I like someone. You're right, it isn't any of my business. Now, let's gear up and get our butts in there to save this woman you don't give a hoot about and it wouldn't hurt either of us to save that US Marshal in the process. Might give us a get out of jail free card for the future. I'd bet we could both use that."

This guy was a smart aleck but he liked him. "You got any extra guns? All I have is this one and you almost have to be looking down someone's throat to stop em with it." He palmed Jessie's .38. "I prefer a forty or nine millimeter."

Nick hurried over to the four-wheeler, lifted the carrier cover, and pawed through a canvas bag. "Which?"

"Jesus Christ, man. You going to war?"

"Nope, been there already. Just kept some souvenirs." He patted the Colt Python holstered high on his leg.

Dal checked over the offering in the bag. "I'll take the nine." He pocketed a couple of magazines and Velcroed the holstered weapon to his thigh. "Let's get moving while that lying bastard is still thinking what he's going to do to them. You get the location?"

Nick produced a terrain map from the stash, tapped his head, climbed on the machine. "Yep. I can maneuver this little baby a bit closer, but then the going will be too rough."

Dal stuck the walkie in his breast pocket and climbed on. "Then let's get the hell out of here. He hurts her, they won't ever find him."

Nick didn't appear shocked a bit.

Wheels of the accelerating vehicle spit clods of earth and peppered rocks into low hanging branches, sounding like BB gun shots.

Dal hung on with hands and knees while Nick maneuvered between trees and around large boulders. He left the old logging road and followed a nearly invisible trail downhill. When he finally braked, the four-wheeler performed a half turn at the edge of a drop-off above a rock-strewn canyon. Dal sucked in a breath. This guy was fearless. Whatever he did before hiding out in the backwoods must've been classic warfare.

Nick produced a collection of ropes and handed Dal a pair of fingerless gloves. "Ever done any rappelling or climbing?"

Teeth gritted at the memory of climbing back up the mountain after being shoved off it. "In a way. All we have time for is a quick lesson and I'm good to go."

Nick tied off two ropes, tossed them over the edge, and demonstrated a sling and how the line looped under his butt and how to feed the rope. "Use your hands like this."

"Got it. Let's get down off this mountain."

"I'll go first to check out any outcrops of rocks you might smack into." He checked Dal's gear. "You slip, hang on, I'll have you from below. In and out, easy does it. You're just lowering yourself. Don't worry about what I'm doing. Object is to get to the bottom without cracking your head or body. Use your legs and arms. Just back off and don't hurry. Keep your feet on something solid much as you can. Run into trouble, stop where you are and yell to me. We want to get there in one piece so we can take care of business."

Impatient to the point of distraction, Dal waited till Nick disappeared below the rim and shouted go, then held on tight, let his butt hang off the edge, both feet planted firm on the rocky surface, took a deep breath, and kicked off. The rope slid through his gloves. Didn't take long to get the feel of it, but that didn't help soothe the underlying fear mixed with excitement. Might have to try this again when Jessie's life wasn't at stake.

More fun than being in a dark alley with gun-toting druggies on all sides. This was not at all what he'd expected when he fled Dallas to come here.

Tugs from below told him Nick was on the ground.

Don't look up or down, just keep doing your thing. Nick's words, 'Stay at a ninety-degree angle, use your legs,' helped him control a swing too far to one side.

A boulder off to his right. His swing brought him way too close.

Kicking out, he shoved his body away from the jagged surface and for a moment whirled out of control.

Deep breath, hang on, settle the damn thing down.

For a moment he halted, grip tight till his breathing slowed.

Stupid. He was using gear he wasn't familiar with, didn't know the terms or anything. Jessie was down there, her and Trey held at gunpoint by a maniac. Nothing mattered but getting to her, and he settled his mind on that one thought. Nick would get him off this bluff and they'd be on their way to her.

Eyes aimed straight ahead where lizards scrambled and tiny springs trickled through the moss-covered, rocky earth, he began the descent once more. Was surprised when the soles of his boots smacked onto a firm surface. The contact caused him to fast-step backwards and fall to his butt.

Holy shit, he'd done it.

Nick took his arm and gave him a hand up. "I'd give you a six."

"Any safe landing is a ten, buddy."

Nick chuckled, retrieved both lines, and tucked them into several saplings growing out of the rocky berm, doing their best to become full grown trees.

"We taking them out of here up that?" No way could he climb the sheer bluff. The guy was nuts.

Nick hauled his gear bag under the overhang. Dal hadn't noticed him bringing that down with him. "I'll come back and pick this all up later after we take them out the easy way. No sense weighing ourselves down with it. Let's get moving. I'll explain as we go. Leaping off that bluff was the quickest way to get down here. I'm hoping we can walk them out. There are easier ways to go."

Dal shuddered, "You mean if they can walk?"

"Have to consider that either Jessie or Trey might be hurt. I'll take them up to the top if they are. We'll get them out of here." Nick paused a moment, moved a low hanging limb back, and studied the valley floor. "I want to look at the map."

He scrambled deeper in the woods, found a large boulder and spread the thick paper, checked it with the tip of his finger. "We're about here." He traced an invisible line across the valley at an angle headed east. "They're about over here, at least that's where that photo was taken." He pulled out his water bottle, drank deeply.

Dal did the same. This man wouldn't make many more stops. "We bringing all three of them out?"

Nick stared at him for a spell. "Oh? I didn't realize we'd have more than two. We'll have to deal with Kimble and the rest. I'll leave you with the kids and bring a truck in to get them. There's an old road that comes out somewhere east of Red Rock Mountain." He pointed out the route, then folded the map and stuck it away.

"Why can't we go out that way? That's how we came in." Dal had to speak to Nick's back, for he was already on the move again.

"It's a hell of a long walk from here. Let's wait and see what condition they're in before we decide how to get them out."

Foolish of him to argue. Nick sure as hell knew what he was doing.

No sense in making an ego trip out of this. Tromping, stopping to look around, tromping some more, he followed.

"You sure know a lot about this place."

"I spend a lot of time hiking and climbing and rappelling all over this country. Keeps me sharp, just in case. Somehow my brain is good at recording the routes of trails and roads, even animal runs. I like the woods better than I do town, the animals better than people. And I like stepping off the edge of a bluff with only a line to keep me from falling."

"I got some of that, but there are a few folks I miss so much I'm torn between solitude and keeping them company." As far as stepping off a bluff, it had been more fun than he'd expected.

Nick gestured for him to halt and peered around a heavy growth of blackberry brambles. He squatted and Dal followed suit. The low rumble of conversation, men's voices, footsteps through last year's dried leaves.

Closer. Words more clear. "We'll have to move the camp. These two found us. That camera worries me."

"What'll we do with them?"

"Not up to me. Deacon's in charge. I don't like killing, but Deacon, he don't seem to mind. Wouldn't surprise me he don't shoot em and bury em so deep no one will ever find them."

The conversation continued but the men were out of their hearing.

"Guards?" Dal whispered.

"Yep."

"They're talking about killing Jessie and Trey."

"Fraid so."

"We'd better get in there and get them out. Now."

"Deacon is an unknown quantity. Reckon who he is?"

Nick didn't waste time wondering. "We'll find out and soon enough."

10
CHAPTER

Through a crack in the divider of the small bedroom in the tacky RV, Jessie gazed at several women in the next room. Robed in purple, they sat cross-legged, holding hands and chatting in low voices. Earlier they had averted their eyes when the men dragged her and Trey in.

What convinces women to follow men who do terrible things? What must they be promised? They might be afraid, but whether of her or the men with guns was a toss-up.

The place smelled like an unwashed public bathroom. Her stomach heaved and she swallowed several times to keep from adding further stink to the room.

The bastards slugged Trey hard on the side of the head with the butt of one of the rifles when he fought back. Then they tossed his limp body on a ratty couch and flung her hard against the wall. Her backpack went flying, landed in a pile of dirty clothing, and nestled there. Half stunned, she searched for the camera, couldn't see it. From outside someone shouted and their captors kicked their way out.

Calling them a bunch of dipshits, she gathered herself off the dirty floor, retrieved the pack, crawled to Trey, and checked his pulse. That big asshole had hit him way too hard. Could've killed him. His eyes appeared unfocused and she couldn't get him to talk to her. A rag hung over the edge of the sink. Not very clean. Better not to use it. The water bottle in her pack was half full and she poured some directly on his swollen bloody temple. He jerked and moaned. He probably had a concussion. Getting him out of here wasn't possible and she couldn't think of leaving him. Back against the wall, she sat on the floor and held his hand.

"It'll be okay, Trey. Hang in there. Dal will get us out of here."

Muffled conversation leaked through the thin wall. There were more people in the other room than when they'd tossed her and Trey in this one. There were children in the camp. They'd herded some of them into the big RV while dragging her and Trey here. Small faces peered from the windows. That meant more of them in there.

One way or another she would get word to Dal and Nick. They had to save those kids.

Trey groaned, his eyelids fluttered, and the muscles in his arm tensed so his hand squeezed hers. His head had stopped bleeding. He needed to be reassured. If he half knew what was going on he might try to fight back and injure himself worse.

She leaned down and whispered, "Hey, you in there?"

"Someone is. Not sure who." Weak, but definitely better.

What a relief. "Thank goodness. I thought you were hurt bad."

"Just a flesh wound."

"Tough guy. Don't move. You probably have a concussion."

"Yep, seeing double. Sometimes triple. Did they hurt you?" His voice remained vague and shaky.

"Nope. Just threw you in here and shoved me in beside you. I don't think they're much in the mood to do us any permanent damage as yet. That is, if we behave. I didn't want to try anything. I'm afraid they'll separate us."

"Wise, I'd say. But you need to get out." He shoved himself upright, covered his face with one hand. "Oh, hell."

"Lay back down."

"Don't mind if I do." A minute crawled by while she watched him closely. He squinted his eyes open. "Do you still have the camera?"

"I don't know. I dropped it when they tossed us in here, but one of them may have taken it. I don't see it in this mess. I managed to take a few shots and my backpack's here. If Dal and Nick still have my iPad that'll give them our location. They dragged us a good long way."

"So you have some water?"

She scrambled to get him some. "Yes, I'm sorry, not thinking."

He raised his head and she tilted the bottle to his lips. He drank deeply. Squinted up at her. "You need to get out of here, go for help."

She took his hand. "I won't leave you here, not hurt like you are."

"Jess, that doesn't matter as much as getting the law on these assholes before they move on. That's Sheriff Kimble leading them around. We know him. He's not going to let us go. He'll kill us. Don't know why he hasn't already."

"That wouldn't be too smart. Why would he do that?"

"Because we can identify him. You have to get away, get some help. I'm afraid for these women and kids."

"I leave when you can leave."

His hand went limp in hers. He'd passed out again. That man had hit him really hard, and only because he knew he was a lawman. The bastard.

She crept back to the crack in the door and stuck her fingers through it. The wood was so thin it bent when she tugged on it. Four or five women in purple robes still sat in a circle, holding hands. The others whose voices she'd heard were gone. They might have been praying, but she couldn't make out the words.

The huge man who'd hit Trey dragged open the outer door and lurched inside. Pointed at a small blonde whose hair hung in knots. "Go in there. Fetch me the bitch."

Her heart slammed against her chest. No telling what they'd do to her. Then she couldn't help Trey, or anyone else for that matter. He was right. She had to get out while she still could. No more thinking. Just do it. Rolling onto her back, she bent her knees to her chest, then kicked the flimsy door with both feet. The boards splintered in all directions, making a godawful noise, and she scrabbled through on the floor, squeezed between the man's legs, and tumbled down the few steps into the dirt.

Knees raw and burning, she staggered upright and took off toward the nearest woods. Shouts close behind but she didn't look. Just ran. Bullets zinged through the air.

Darting behind boulders and into a ditch, she rolled into the narrow gulley. A bullet cut dirt overhead, sprayed her hair with grit.

On hands and knees she clambered behind a good-sized rock. Bullets cut shards from the sandstone, biting into her cheek. Warm blood dripped from her jaw.

Gasping for air. Had to get going. They'd move in on her and quick.

Dammit, Trey, I'm sorry. I'll bring help. I promise. If she gave herself up neither of them had a chance in hell. Dear God, don't let them kill him. Are you listening?

A lull in the shooting and she scurried into a thick growth of brush off to the right. Keeping it between herself and the shooters, she crawled into the woods on hands and feet while they shouted and ran around in circles. No doubt looking for their own asses.

Under thick cover she blindly stumbled forward. Sucking air, she shoved aside branches that tore at her skin. The ground dropped from under her and she tumbled head over heels. Landed with a thud that knocked the breath out of her.

Pawing dried debris off her face, she checked to see if she'd broken anything. Everything hurt, yet it all worked. She was in a dark hole. Long, gnarly fingers clawed toward the sky like a huge monster's hand.

After her.

Panic squeezed at her heart, choked her. A throbbing pain in her chest till she couldn't breathe. Childish fears.

Stop. Stop it. Ride it out. Take deep breaths. Calm the hell down. It was only the ripped out roots of a giant tree.

Both fists pressed into her abdomen. To slow her breathing, she counted to twelve. Took in her surroundings. A dozen or more of those ragged fingers guarded what looked like a cave and she went for it, her skin crawling with another kind of fear. More real. Snakes, spiders, unknown creatures lurking in wait. Inside she hugged herself tight and waited. Shaking. Afraid to open her eyes, terrified to keep them closed. Her heart slammed around like it would flail itself to death.

The smell of wet earth and rotting wood crawled into her nose. Hairy strings hung in her hair and on her shoulders, blocking her view.

Okay, you're a big girl.

Squinting one eye open, she glanced around. Couldn't see much. She dared not move. The real danger was outside her hidey-hole, for soon those chasing her would search the woods. When they came for her she would hear them running through the dried leaves on the forest floor. She had to stay right where she was. Run and they'd have her. They would kill her if they found her. Maybe had already killed Trey. Uncontrolled tears wet her cheeks.

She should never have left him.

When Nick put the map in his pocket, the iPad signaled it was receiving a message. Dal pulled it from the bag tucked under his arm and they held it between them. Three new photos appeared. Jumbled, unfocused, but with the geotag, just like Jessie had said they would.

His throat constricted. The bastards had her and Trey. Both fists clenched and he stared through the trees. Nick took the map back out, located the GPS coordinates, and pointed into the valley. Before they could move gunshots cut the still air. The noise crashed into the surrounding hills and echoed back till it was hard to tell where they came from. Far off, that was for sure.

Hunters? Could be, but more than likely not, since there was no hunting season open. But some of these wilderness residents paid no attention to that.

Dal crouched behind a huge oak tree, glanced over to see Nick doing the same nearby. He had to keep it together. The only way they could bring her out was not panic. How many times he'd thanked everything that was holy that Nick had come with him. The man had an innate sense of self-preservation. Not only that, he communicated well without saying anything. Probably whatever military training he had. If anyone would be able to help him find and rescue Jessie and the kids it was Nick.

The shots worried him, for they had stopped abruptly, which could mean someone had been cut down.

Nick sidled closer. "We come up on these guys, you got any problems taking care of business?"

Dal patted his holstered pistol. "None at all. But they'd better not have hurt her. Or none of them will walk out of here. You with that? You still got that beautiful piece?"

"Yep. And I'm with you. They're armed and shooting, we take em down. No questions." He rubbed a palm over the revolver. "Never let it out of my sight. Special issue."

"I figured." Probably not the first men it would shoot, either

Shoot to kill.

He didn't ask from where or who. None of his business. Snow was a man of many layers and would be mighty useful. Engraved pearl handled revolvers like that. Only given to certain men on rare occasions and for actions beyond the call of duty. It was all he needed to know. It gave him confidence in this guy at his side.

Nick gave him the high sign. "Hey buddy, right now, it's the mission. Go in and get them out. Don't think of anything else."

In the silence that followed, Nick signaled him to go right, then he went left. Both nodded. Nick disappeared into the shadows off to the left and Dal melted into the thick woods to the right. All alone the two of them would surround the encampment. The hunt was on. Nothing else mattered.

Deep in the hole dried leaves would disguise Jessie's presence. Or so she

hoped. All around her there were only birds singing and ground critters skittering. Weary to the bone, she eased upward to peer out between the gigantic tree roots. Something moved across her foot. Heavy enough to be felt through her Keds. Frozen, she glanced down into the shadowy hole, didn't have to see what it was to know. The telltale feel of a slithery body working its way across the top of her foot could only be one thing.

Snake.

Fear tightened the muscles in her leg. The question was, friend or foe? Best to just wait it out. Let him go on his way. Or not. Sucker was long, fat. Took him a while. The brush of a tongue tasting her bare skin sent rivers of terror up her spine. Still she remained absolutely still. There were much worse things in this world than snakes. In her life she had faced them. Many slithering around on two legs. The rustle of dry leaves faded and the belly crawler went on his way, having decided she was neither prey nor predator.

Her breath escaped slowly. She'd almost wet herself from fear. Darkness danced over her eyes. She lowered her head between her legs to get the blood flowing through her brain.

Damn, that was a close one.

Have a great day, sir snake, and thank you very much.

With slow deliberation she worked her way from the deep hole where once a great tree had rooted itself. In the distant past a storm had uprooted the half-dead giant and created that hole for her to hide in. Another whispered thank you to Mother Nature.

Hunkered down. Breathing controlled. Off to her right beyond the edge of the woods the enemy waited.

Decision time. Hightail it through the thick growth of timber and up the mountain. Try to find Nick and Dal, or stay put and let them find her.

Either choice was iffy. No way could she escape if she tried to run out in the open. Guards watched the valley and they'd be on her in no time.

If only she had brought her camera. Everything would be much easier. If the last pictures had been sent, they knew about where she was and were on their way.

Low hanging branches of a pine tree hung against her shoulders, its scent reminiscent of other times. The high Rockies, camping with her family. An eternity, another life ago. From her memory she traced the route back to the camp from which she'd escaped in the dried, aromatic needles covering the ground. They would never expect her to return. Never ever, but they'd be watching all the escape routes. She'd have to forge another way in.

Damn it, Dal where *are* you guys?

If she were lucky they too were headed for the camp. She could find her camera, get some pictures, then hide out till the men showed up to rescue Trey and the kids. No question, she was going back. Not as a prisoner but as a predator.

She'd move in close, keep an eye on the place, wait till dark after they all went to sleep, then sneak in and recover the camera. If luck was with her, it still lay where they'd tossed it when they grabbed her and Trey. If he could walk she'd get him out of there as well. If he were alive. He'd have a conniption fit to see her back, but at this point it was the best of worse choices.

The woods offered the safest route back to the parked RVs and trailers. Even so it was by far the toughest. Thick brambles alternated with wild blackberry bushes to block her way at every turn. Sometimes she found a trampled deer trail, but mostly the animals headed for water or browsing, so she had to strike out on her own. Her jeans and the skin of her legs were ripped and bloody. Sweat burned the scratches. Her throat begged for water. The best she could do was stop and eat juicy blackberries to soothe her dry throat or sip from an occasional meager spring.

The sun dropped slowly behind the ridge, flares of gold and orange setting treetops on fire. A pine-scented breeze lifted a few leaves, dried the sweat on her brow. Birds, hidden from the heat all day, ventured out to sing lullabies.

Darkness stopped her in her tracks. As if someone tossed a huge blanket over the peaks, rendering her blind until her eyes grew accustomed to it. Soon she should see lights in the trailers unless she'd overshot them. Or if they'd pulled out for hidden pastures. Too much to believe she'd walk up on Nick and Dal reconnoitering the target. But she had hopes. They must be somewhere near.

Her eyes burned searching the blackened landscape. Yet they'd never see each other. Talk about the belly of the beast. Even moving slowly she stumbled over downed tree limbs and bramble vines tangled around her ankles. Still she persevered, feeling her way step by step.

Across the valley something glimmered. What was that? A lantern or candle in a window? Some of them had generators. She'd heard them running. Dark as it was, she might venture from the woods without being seen. Get a closer look. If she didn't fall off a cliff or into a creek.

Okay, she had to go out into the open or just hide like a scared rabbit. Step by step, she made her cautious way closer to what must be a light in a trailer. Another came in sight, then another. They were pretty sure of themselves. Clearly they did not expect her to return, and didn't feel threatened by anyone else. At least not yet. They'd probably move out come morning. And what would they do with Trey?

She dared venture no closer till an idea or a plan offered itself. With a sigh she sank to her butt in a patch of dew-dampened knee-high grass. At least she hadn't fallen. Now what? Close but not close enough. She'd made no plans for rescuing her camera or Trey, cause she hadn't thought she'd make it this far.

Now here she was within sight of the RVs and trailers with no plan A or B. She settled down in her hidden spot. Watch and wait for the right opportunity or enough courage or a brilliant idea. She had to do something before daylight.

It had been hours since she'd sent the last photo to the iPad. Surely Nick and Dal would have seen it and were somewhere near by now. That is, if they got the last photos she'd managed to send. She didn't trust a reliable Internet signal and had long ago learned to carry a MiFi in her backpack for a constant signal. But even that could fail if they wandered too far from the cell towers.

What if they didn't come? It would take something drastic to keep Dal from barrel-assing in when they didn't receive any more messages. But something could've happened to them. They could be in jail right now, guarded by that prick who called himself sheriff. Couch and Kimble. Quite a partnership. But who was Deacon?

She'd wait till things quieted down and the lights went out in the camp. There'd be a moon later. She could only hope they would all finally sleep and she could sneak in then, find her camera, get Trey, and boogie out of there. No sense trusting that Dal and Nick could find them. No sense at all.

Off to her right a shadow crept toward the encampment. Almost upright. Surely not a bear. She eased grasses aside to get a better look. The shadow melted into some trees. In a while another joined it.

Someone sneaking up on the camp. Her heart thundered. It had to be Dal and Nick. What were the odds of someone else being out here poking around? Sneaking up on the caravan? Did she dare reveal herself to find out? Maybe wait a bit and see what they did next. She wanted so badly to go racing across the space and throw herself at them.

But what if it wasn't them but some hunters or... hell, who knew?

Keeping her gaze glued to the spot for fear of losing them, she rested on her haunches. Okay. Enough of this messing around. Make up your mind. She picked up a small pebble from under her palm and tossed it toward the shadows.

Soon one came back landing practically at her feet. It was them. Scooting forward without standing, she tossed another. Got one back. Only able to see the outline of rolling peaks against the silvery sky, she leaped up and ran toward the last place she'd spotted the shadow, stumbled and fell, landed face down with a whoof.

"Damn it all." Under her breath. She couldn't help it.

"Jessie?"

"Dal?" She'd landed right at his feet.

He hauled her to her feet, arms wrapped around her. Heart thundering in her ears, she relaxed and sucked in air with a hiss that sounded much too loud.

She hugged him so tight he gasped.

"Jessie? Be quiet." Lips against her ear. "You okay? Not hurt?" He went silent. Held her close.

A vigorous nod. That had definitely been her plan. Sweet relief. Dal. Oh, God, it *was* Dal. Her breath huffed out and she tightened her arms around his neck. A nearly full moon slipped from behind the distant mountains and someone dragged them both to the ground.

A whispered command. "Yonder, in those trees. Now and stay low."

Nick's demand obeyed instantly. Hunched forward, she ran, holding tight to Dal's hand.

Even as moonlight crept into the valley they gathered under the safety of huge oaks, low hanging sycamore branches with leaves the size of dinner plates, and scraggly barked hickory, the nuts thick on the ground. As if he couldn't let her go, Dal kept her close, his breath hot and damp against her throat. The release of fear left her limp in his arms.

"I love you. Oh, God I love you." Careful to only whisper it in his ear. Sometimes she needed to think before acting. He wouldn't like that one little bit. It was too late to take it back though.

At last, some softly spoken words from him. "Where did you come from? Where's Trey?" Maybe he hadn't heard her, maybe she'd imagined that she said it.

"Jess?"

She shook her head. "They got him. He's hurt bad. I didn't want to leave him, but he said... he...." Tears rolled down her cheeks and she snuffled, drew in a wet gasp.

"Hush, settle down. They'll hear us." Nick gripped her shoulder. "We're right on top of them."

Out of the moon-speckled darkness a thumb wiped away her tears. Dal. "It's okay. You did right. Why didn't you keep going?"

"The camera. I lost it and I didn't know where to go. Besides, I couldn't just leave him there. He could die. So I was going back as soon as it got dark, sneak in and find the camera, and send you some pictures so you could find us."

"And we did. Find you, that is."

"You came. I hoped you would. I knew you would." Words babbled out and she stopped. Pressed her face into Dal's shoulder to muffle them.

"That was smart, sending a picture of a written message. Nick, here, he had to teach me how to be a mountain climber or we'd've come sooner." Once more he held her close, trembling against her. The reaction reassured her about his feelings.

She put her fingertips over his mouth, gazed up into eyes she could barely make out in the spattering of moonlight through the leaves, and released a long sigh.

He curled an arm around her waist and lifted her, bent down, and kissed her so thoroughly she lost her breath. Forehead to forehead neither moved for a long moment. His familiar touch, their bodies fitting together. She had missed him so very much. Way more than she thought she ever would. Best not to say anymore though.

"You two guys go right ahead with what you're doing. I'll just hang here till you finish. Just keep it down, would you?"

Dal ignored Nick. "You okay? Did they hurt you or anything?" He paused a minute and when she didn't reply, asked again, grit in his voice. "They didn't hurt you, did they?"

"Calm down, warrior. I'm fine. But we have to get Trey. And those kids. I think they're stealing children somehow. Those kids don't belong to any of them. They keep them all locked up in the bigger RV."

"What for? And where are they getting them?" Nick's words came harsh and unforgiving.

"I'm not sure. I'm not sure of anything. It doesn't make sense."

Dal seated Jessie against a large tree trunk and slid down next to her. She was right. None of this made sense. Why not stay hidden, not let anyone in town see the kids? Nick remained at the edge of the tree line, alert and watchful. She shifted and leaned back against Dal, folding his arm under her breast. Content, he left it there for a bit, then squirmed away to join Nick.

"We need to get in there. Now, tonight, before they do something to Trey. What do you think?"

"Only two of us. We can't surround them. We have to figure out a way to get in and out. Jess, are all the kids together? If so, which RV are they in? One with a motor, or is it one of the trailers?"

"'There's three of us, not two." With the tone of voice she made it very clear she could help.

"Okay, three of us. I apologize. Where are the kids?"

She pointed. "See that one glowing white in the moonlight, right in the middle? They've circled all around it like in one of those westerns when the Indians attack. If there are more I didn't see them."

"Yeah, like they're guarding it. Okay, it's one of those old RVs. Probably hard to start. Did you see any adults in there with them?"

She nodded. "A couple of men with rifles like guards. Wait, I have an idea. What if I let them catch me sneaking in? Maybe they'd even throw me back in with Trey. Then you'd have me on the inside. We could figure out something."

"No, definitely not." Dal wasn't about to agree with that. "Maybe one of us could cause a disturbance while the other two drove that monster right out of there."

"Leaving behind Trey and the one who caused the disturbance? No."

"Okay, not good. So where's Trey?"

"When I left he was in that old red and white snub-nosed one." She pointed it out. "There are several women and a couple of armed men in there too. Since I kicked my way out of there, he's probably pretty well guarded."

"How come you got out and he couldn't?"

"I hadn't been hit upside of the head with a rifle butt. I surprised them. Kicked out a wall and ran between their legs when they came in to see what the commotion was. Both had rifles."

Dal held her tighter. "You could've been killed."

She ignored him. "Did you notice in the pictures? The guys with guns all have a shoulder patch, purple with a rising moon. Flags everywhere with the same symbol."

Dal frowned. "Wasn't there something about the kids having tattoos like that? Weird as all get out. What about the women? Do they seem to be members of this cult thing, or are they prisoners too?"

"Wearing purple robes, but it's hard to tell. I suppose they could be prisoners." She stared across the way. "They didn't try to help me but they didn't try to stop me either."

"Do you suppose Trey is still out of it? We might have to carry him." Nick peered toward the trailers.

Dal nodded. "The main thing we need to do is get him and the kids out. If we have to we can come back better armed to rescue any women being held here."

"You're right. So, we've got two weapons—"

"Three, counting her thirty-eight. I kept it when you gave me the nine."

Nick eyed her. "Okay, we use it for close-up. Can she shoot?"

Dal glanced at Jessie who managed a harsh whisper. "*She* is right here."

"Sorry. Of course. I'll ask her." Nick waited a beat. "Well, can you?"

"I shot someone. Once." Her throat clicked. "Swore I wouldn't do it again, but I'm about to make an exception."

Dal cleared his throat.

"You go in there with a gun, you'd better make an exception or someone will shoot you." No longer a soft-spoken introvert, Nick became the man Dal had only caught glimpses of. "Give her the thirty-eight. I forgot you had it." Nick stepped into a patch of moonlight to regard her. "Show me."

She held the revolver, finger alongside the trigger, barrel pointed toward the ground. "I hold it like this, aim at his middle, pull the hammer back, squeeze the trigger, and shoot. He keeps coming, I keep shooting. What's to show you?"

"Jessie, I apologize. But there's no time for soothing hurt feelings here. We're going in there, it's serious business and if you can't pull the trigger you will most likely die." He dug in his pocket, held out a hand. "Here, you'll need these."

She took the cartridges, dropped them in her jeans pocket. "You know, I was shot once. I don't intend for it to happen again."

Dal shuddered, remembering the blood and holding her, thinking she was dead. Sitting on the floor in her cabin waiting for the responders, both arms locked around her as if he could keep her life trapped there.

He glanced at Nick. These two were toeing around in the sand drawing lines and he'd stay out of it. Jessie was way tougher than she looked and Nick would soon learn that.

"Sorry, I didn't know that." Nick knelt and cleared a patch in the dirt. The bright moonlight allowed his efforts to be seen. He picked up a few rocks and spread them out in a pattern like the trailers and campers were parked, put the stick on the center one. "This is the white one, where Trey and the women are. Is there a back door?"

He waited for Jessie to answer. "Oh, sorry, me?"

He just kept looking at her.

She caved. "No, the back room where he was laying on a rotting old couch does have windows, though. Maybe it'd be possible to get in one if we could take him out that way. Or in the door. Like I said, the women were pretty calm." Shivering, she hugged herself. "They've got those flags up on the walls. Handmade. Purple. Downright scary."

Dal took her hand. "Good God. Sounds creepy. Did you recognize any of the women?"

She shook her head.

Nick went on as if he hadn't heard them. "Good idea about the window. We'll go in silent first and check that out. Once we're in there looking around, we'll use hand signals and not speak. Soon as we figure if we have a way to get him out, I'll carry him over here and come back to see if we can get the kids. While I'm gone you two surround the camper where they're being held. If you can, just climb in the thing, start it, and drive out. If there are armed guards, wait for me and we'll take them out silently. Might be we're not getting those kids without shooting someone. How do the two of you feel about that?"

"Someone has a gun shooting at me I can shoot back." Jessie's voice held a tremble, but she was brave enough. She would do the right thing.

"Those old boys don't carry those rifles to use them for clubs."

Jessie shuddered. "Trey said two of them are fugitives. He recognized them. I guess it's pretty smart of them to infiltrate this cult to hide out."

"Don't give them credit for being smart. They're psychopaths who would kill all these people if necessary. We need to make sure that doesn't happen." Nick pointed at the rock representing the red and white camper. "The kids are in there and shooting could get them killed. One of us should go in and make sure they're all hunkered down before we start a firefight."

Jessie raised her hand, then pulled it down as if embarrassed. "Sorry. I can do that if you want. I think I can get in and keep them calm. You guys, well, you might scare them, and they'd start hollering or something."

"If there's a guard with them, you'll have to take him out." Nick again. "And if he's bigger than you, it means using that." He pointed at her .38.

"Huh-uh, no way am I letting her go in there by herself. Sorry, you'll—hey, guys. There's lights coming our way." Dal pointed up the valley beyond where the clan had settled. "Looks like a motorcycle."

"We'd better get back a ways. In this moonlight, someone might spot us." Nick scooted down into the shadows.

She slid onto the ground, Dal right next to her, and they all crawled under some bushes.

"Reckon what they're doing?" Dal pushed back some dusty limbs to make a bit more room.

"Don't think that's a bike. I believe it's a car with just one headlight."

Dal agreed. "Let's just sit tight. See what happens. I'd hate to get shot."

The one-eyed car passed on by followed by two RVs that rattled and roared. Hard to tell, but it looked like two people inside the car. No telling how many in the RVs. This didn't look good at all. Nick pointed out more headlights approaching from the south. It wasn't too long before more came from the north.

"Looks like we're having an assembly of some sort." Dal scooted deeper under the brush to get out of the sweep of the lights. "Where the hell are they all coming from? And why?"

"Looks like we waited too long. We'll not be able to get those kids out, or Trey either. What do you want to bet they're going to look for themselves a new hidey-hole where we can't find them? Dammit." Nick was still for a few minutes, and Dal let him think. Finally he came up with an idea. "Dal, I can make it to town on foot fast. You and Jessie stay here, keep an eye on these guys till I get back with a posse."

"You can't convince Couch or anyone else to come out here on your word. They don't even know you. And he won't listen to me either."

"They've got kids in there who don't belong to them. Looks like that'd be enough to throw their hides in jail till we can get things sorted out. If Couch won't do something I'll get the Feds on it."

"What we gonna do if they take off?" Jessie didn't sound too happy, but come to think of it, who was?

"Follow em. Didn't you say your camera is in there somewhere? We've already had pictures from it. You can figure something out. Just do not let them get away. Leave a trail we can follow and we'll track you down."

Jessie grabbed Dal's hand. "We can do that, can't we?" She didn't really sound convinced, but she would hang in there. Of that Dal was sure. He'd seen her do just that.

"Yep, we can do that." He held on to her tight. All sorts of crazy vibes floated from those trailers. He didn't even like to think what some of them meant.

11

CHAPTER

The discussion went on while all the trailers and campers lined up and the windows went dark. Several times the two men came close to blows while they talked about what would be the best idea for dealing with the situation.

Jessie finally had enough of it.

"Would you two let it be, please? What we ought to do is get some sleep. Come morning they're liable to move out and we'll need to be ready. Do I have to settle this, or maybe you could settle it with your fists?

Ignoring her, Nick demonstrated by reaching into a patch of moonlight. "Look, I know this valley like the back of my hand. And it's clear the two of you want to stay together. So I'll go. I can run all the way to Cedarton. I've done it before just to see if I could. I'll be back before dark tomorrow with the cavalry."

Dal hung an arm around Jessie's shoulder. "I give up. That's probably the best idea."

At last, they agreed on something. "Now, could we get some sleep?"

She laid her head against Dal's shoulder. But what if no one would come? They had forgotten one thing. She raised up. "Wait."

"What?" Nick turned to Dal. "I think she wants to see us fight."

"Wouldn't surprise me. That right, Jess?" He held his fists under his nose.

"No. Don't be silly. I just thought of something. We don't know that these people are doing anything illegal. What reason can Nick use to get the deputies to come here with him? Couch will certainly never go for it. And that means the others can't either."

Silence while they thought about it.

"Hey, that's easy." Dal chuckled. "We can get not only Grace County Deputies but another bunch of law enforcement guys who will be happy to come storming in here."

"Who?"

It was like talking between invisible beings, for everyone was hunkered down on the ground ready to go to sleep. And it was dark, though moonlight lay all around them.

"The US Marshals. Hell, these people have gone and assaulted and kidnapped them a marshal. That's a Federal crime. *Federal.* And Nick can bring them back in here in vehicles storming the place like SWAT without all the detours we've taken. Sorry I was being so damn stubborn earlier."

She punched his shoulder. "First time I ever heard a man admit that. Glad we finally agreed on something. Now, I'm going to sleep."

She curled up on a bed of leaves and smiled when Dal coiled himself around her backside. Tomorrow could be a frightening day. No telling what might happen, but tonight she would sleep in his arms.

A noise startled her awake. The sky was streaked with silver. What had she heard? Dal continued to sleep wrapped around her and the dark lump that was Nick didn't move either. Again a muffled sound echoed off the surrounding mountains. A gunshot.

She struggled from Dal's arms, shook his shoulder. "I heard a shot."

He mumbled something, but nothing else, so she shook him harder till he sat up.

"What, Jessie? You okay?"

"I said I heard a shot, maybe two."

"Sure you're not dreaming?"

"Pretty sure with the first, darn sure with the second."

They both waited what seemed like several minutes, but all remained quiet. He wrapped her up in his arms, lay them down. "Go back to sleep, it was nothing. Someone out hunting squirrel for breakfast."

Not convinced, she stayed awake while the sky turned lavender and pink. Then she had to pee. Couldn't wait another minute. Gently she unwrapped Dal's arms and slipped away, creeping behind a growth of sumac. Just as she rose to pull up her jeans a woman screamed, the sound cutting through her.

"What the hell?" Dal came to his feet. "Jessie, where are you?"

She hurried back, grabbed him around the waist before he could bolt out into the clearing. "Did you hear that or am I still dreaming?"

Leaves clung to Nick's jeans when he leaped to his feet, that fancy revolver of his in one hand. "What? What?"

Dal clung to her. "Damn, I sure did and you weren't here. I thought it was you. Scared me. Could you tell where it came from?" He bent to peer through the low-hanging limbs.

"You two have any idea what's going on?"

"I think it came from over there." She pointed at the caravan. "But these hills, the echoes."

"Good bet it came from there. Shit, I hope they aren't killing each other." Nick moved to the edge of the woods, put the binocs to his eyes.

Jessie and Dal joined him.

"Anything?" She was so scared her throat closed over the words.

"Nope. Nobody around I can see."

Jessie found her voice again. "What if they killed Trey?"

"We can't do anything about that right now." While he talked Nick swept the caravan with the glasses. "These people have existed without our help for God knows how long. Until we can get some law out here to rescue Trey, and that's gonna be the only reason they're here." He glanced toward Dal. "Thanks to your smart reasoning. We can't interfere if they cry freedom of religion, and they will. But we can go in and get our man out. And the two fugitives, if he can identify them. Then we'll get someone to investigate where the kids came from and what might be going on there. We've got to keep it cool or we could scare them into hiding so deep those kids wouldn't have a chance, no matter why they're here."

Reality set in. If things went wrong they could all end up like Trey. Dal studied Jessie. She shouldn't be out here like this. What if someone spotted them and those old boys over there decided to take care of business using their guns? Jessie could get hurt.

"Nick, do you have any thoughts on what they've got going on here?"

"Not truly, but I think it's serious enough we need to follow through."

"I can't quite figure out what your stake is in this. I mean, we brought you to help get the kids out if necessary. I realize that. But you could walk out of here any time. You have no reason to stay."

Nick wouldn't look at Dal for a minute. Then he spoke softly. "Guess I just want to get back into the fray one more time. This sort of life is addictive and maybe I retired too early. At the time it seemed the best thing to do. I'd been involved in some stuff that... well, carried some ghosts with it. But I sorta been missing the excitement. This'll be my last go at it, though." He turned his gaze on Dal. "If you're worried I may not come back, that I'll just walk away, don't be. I *do* have a sense of honor."

Thinking about it, Dal had no worries about Nick returning. It was all he could do not to pick around in his mind. But that carried more trouble than he wanted. Suppose he did learn something about him that was best kept quiet? He sensed a horrible death, something that had scarred Nick badly. Even though he sensed a reluctance in Nick, maybe like he'd been out of the life a bit too long, he still handled himself like he might've been involved in military special ops or undercover work of some sort that he couldn't talk about, which could explain a lot. It was none of Dal's business but he itched to learn more. The right way. Asking.

"Because we can dig out secrets doesn't mean we should." Grandfather hovered beyond Nick's shoulder, gazing somberly at him.

Dal squinted back, resisted the compulsion to tell the old man to get out of his head and go back where he belonged.

Instead, he continued the conversation with Nick and tried to ignore the shimmering figure of Bear That Stands. "I'm glad you're up for going out for backup."

Nick lifted the revolver. "Makes better sense than going in guns blazing. Kids could get hurt. I'm thinking I might ought to go on to Cedarton. Whether they remain here or take off, it'll give me a head start. Let me show you a quick way you can leave a trail in case they decide to follow creek beds where I can't easily track."

Nick showed him how to bend small limbs so they pointed in the way they had gone. "Anytime they change direction just leave me good signs whether it looks like I could follow or not."

Dal resisted telling Nick he understood tracking. No point to it. "I got it. You be careful, you hear?"

Yeah, be careful. Nick had been dragged into something he had no stake in. But he could take care of himself. Take Jessie, though. She put up a good front. Being brave and all that. She'd waded in with both eyes open. Why did she have to say she loved him, in the midst of all the danger? Maybe it was fear.

Besides, he didn't deserve her love. He treated her like a prostitute. Someone he went to when he needed to scratch an itch, then pushing her away. Each time he hurt her more and still she came back. So here he was, right back where he'd left things with her when he turned tail and ran. And he blamed himself for her being here in danger. He was a coward, pure and simple. Running from a pretty woman who might work her way into his heart. Put him in the same dark place he'd been in with Leanne when he lost her.

He must've been way off somewhere, cause Nick prodded him. "Hey, buddy. I asked if you have Jessie's cell phone? She thought it was in your backpack, but can't find it. I need to take it out with me so we can keep track of each other. The tablet's in there."

Dal dug around in his pockets with no results. "Last time I saw it, she had it."

"So it's around here somewhere."

Jessie finally came up with the phone, lying in the leaves where she and Dal had slept the night before. Nick grinned right big.

"Don't celebrate so fast. The battery is dead."

"Wasn't exactly why I was grinning. You two must've rolled around together pretty rowdy. At least someone's having some fun in all this mess."

Dal glared at Nick and Jessie huffed.

"So, where can I go to get it charged?" Nick asked, looking innocent.

"At *The Observer*. There's a charger in my desk drawer. Ask Parker, and tell him what's going on here too. He can be of help convincing Couch or getting in touch with the marshal's office. Just remind him that you're the guy who hauled Dal and me off the side of that mountain last year. He'll believe what you tell him about what's going on out here."

"When they see these pictures that'll help."

"They may move while you're gone." Dal nodded toward the caravan that had tripled in size since the day before.

"So go after them. Just don't let them go somewhere without leaving me sign of some sort, like bent limbs. Something I can read." Nick stared at the ground and grinned. "Remember, I'm bringing the cavalry and they're bound to make some noise. All hell could break loose." He rubbed his nose. "Wish I had my old unit." He glanced up as if afraid they'd heard.

From the look he gave him, Dal read that thought loud and clear.

"Well, I'd best be on my way. You two will be okay. Water. There are springs all in these woods. Animals drink the water, you can too. We're way too isolated for it to be contaminated by people."

"Go, Nick. We'll be okay. Trust me, I can handle this."

Nick clapped him on the shoulder. "I know you can buddy. Jessie, if he fouls up, you can take over."

She laughed and hugged Nick. "Be careful. See you soon, huh?" Sounding a little afraid.

"You too. Don't panic, and see our Indian friend here doesn't decide to attack them, okay?"

For a long time after Nick made his way through the trees and out of sight, she hung on to Dal's hand and watched the shadows where he'd disappeared.

"Hey, he'll be okay." He squeezed her up tight.

"I can't help being scared. So many terrible things can happen to any one of us out here alone. Snakes, widow-makers, a marijuana farmer guarding his crop, a fall that breaks a leg or neck."

"Your imagination is on full alert." He ruffled her hair.

"I'll try to tamp it down, but I have this awful dark feeling that something is going to happen and it won't be fun."

"Well, we didn't exactly expect this to be an enjoyable adventure." He kept an arm around her shoulders, grinned when Nick sprinted right past Grandfather, who waved at the departing man as if he too were still among the living.

Perhaps it was a good thing that Grandfather was there. Dal might need his help before this was over. The thought darkened his mind. Jessie wasn't the only one with fears of what could happen.

Keeping an eye on the cluster of trailers, he pulled her down to the ground, his back against a huge tree trunk and her settled between his legs so she was cradled in his lap. Recalling the earlier gunshots and screaming, he unfastened the holster on his thigh and loosened the nine so he could get to it quicker.

Her back snuggled to his front all warm and soft in the right places.

Goddammit that felt good. Better than anything had since leaving her last year. Relaxing there, one eye on the parked vehicles and her in his arms felt, if not perfect, at least right. Like they were working together again. Why in the world had he ever wanted to leave her? Everything about the way they fit together was so good. She must have sensed his feelings, cause she relaxed and let her head roll into the curve of his shoulder.

"Feels right, doesn't it?" He whispered the words and she nodded.

"You leave me again, I'm coming after you. You got that?"

He choked back the urge to laugh. A chattering squirrel startled him. The little gray fella sat on a limb above them, tail slapping up and down, front feet under his chin.

He pointed. "Look. Did you know there are black squirrels and white squirrels? Black squirrels are becoming common. It's a genetic mutation that stops their fur turning to grey. Scientists have found it could make them more immune to diseases."

"Oh, is that right? Can they mate with each other?"

"Yep. Blacks are no threat at all to the grey squirrel either. The mutation is inherited from both parents. There's a piece missing that helps produce pigment."

"And here I thought there were only red and gray. This is something I'll definitely remember. I can bring it up at cocktail parties."

"Okay, okay. So when was the last time you went to a cocktail party? Just thought you'd like to know." He tickled her and kissed her neck.

Still nothing moved over there. Why were they just sitting there? Like they were waiting to be discovered. He struggled to sit up, pushing her forward with a grunt. The squirrel scolded and bounded away.

"I want to take a closer look." Nick had left the binocs and he propped himself upright against the tree and swept the glasses slowly over the caravan. One by one he studied windows, doors, gaps between the vehicles.

A tiny face stared out and he adjusted the glasses to make sure of what he was seeing. "Psst, Jessie—here, check this out. Tell me who that looks like."

She took the glasses and gazed where he directed. "That's Lily."

Even as they took a second look, the face was yanked away, the curtain swinging back and forth.

"Poor little thing. Makes me want to go get her. Drag her out and dare anyone to stop me."

"Be patient. We can handle all this when Nick gets back with the cavalry. Let's just keep an eye out for now."

His stomach rumbled and Jessie snickered under her breath. "I saw some blackberries back in there earlier. I could go get us some."

He nodded. "But be careful. Snakes love those thick brambles. Take something to gather them in. Sure wish we had some Honey Buns."

She dug around in his backpack, came up with a bandana, and kissed him on the cheek before disappearing into the shadows.

He kept the binoculars trained on one or the other of the RVs all the while she was gone. Which was too long, but he finally heard the crackle of leaves. She came out of a thicket carrying a bundle tied in a knot.

"Took some time to get the juiciest ones. I think animals must like them cause the best ones are way in the middle of the thick brambles." She sank to the ground beside him, forearms scratched from the thorns. "Here, sit. Anything going on over there?"

"Nope. If I didn't know better I'd think those vehicles were every one empty." He lowered himself to the ground, keeping his eyes on the caravan. "Can you imagine how hot it must be inside there?"

"I'm worried about Trey and those kids. The rest of them deserve whatever they get. I wish we could do something."

Not sure what to say Jessie glanced at him. The filtered sunlight silhouetted his features, the sharp cheekbones, finely drawn nose, and a chin writers of romances called chiseled. For a long moment she studied his body language. The way he always looked as if he was poised to face some hidden danger. Even when they made love. Though she knew his background in law enforcement on the dangerous streets of Dallas, there were secrets he kept hidden behind that calm façade. He ate the blackberries two and three at a time, pausing to glance across the valley.

She laid her hand on his arm. "What is it?"

Muscles tensing under her touch, he nodded. "I was thinking what a shame it is that pure evil lurks in such a beautiful place. I thought I'd left it behind in Dallas, but it's everywhere, isn't it?

Stretching sideways she kissed the line of his chin, leaned into him so the warmth of his body flowed into hers. "Is that why you left? Of course there's evil everywhere, a lot less here than in some places. I've missed you so much. Stay."

"I'm trying very hard here. There are things I need to sort out. Reasons to be with you, reasons to go." He turned ever so slowly and she met his movement with one of her own, so they united. He held her in place for a minute, gazing down into her eyes. "Jessie, what you said back there last night."

She laughed against his throat. He *had* heard her declare her love after all. Now he wanted it out in the open and she was afraid she'd scare him off. The story of their life together. "I was just glad to see you, Dal. So glad to see you."

A morning breeze caught long strands of his unbound hair, and he shoved it back off his face. "Yeah, sure. And cows give chocolate milk."

She laughed under her breath. He didn't want serious then he'd wouldn't get it, though every inch of her yearned to hold him close and whisper words only the two of them would comprehend. To drag him into the bushes and make love till the universe wobbled, cause he was the only man who could do that for her. But she let him have his joke anyway and casually brushed his arm with her breasts so the nipples puckered.

He tilted a quick glance where she'd touched him. "Better be good. For two cents I'll get a hold of those, show you who's glad to see who."

"Go ahead if you think you can. We'd better be quiet or someone over there will hear us." As if by accident, she let her arm drag down over the front of his pants. His jeans tightened and she pulled away, gathered a handful of berries, and made a big show of eating them one by one.

There, mister.

Served him right.

A door slammed in the distance. Several men gathered in a group, all of them well armed. If Trey was on his feet and okay, she didn't see him anywhere. He'd taken an awful blow to his head. What if he'd died? Those people wouldn't care. They'd just toss him off into the woods.

And wasn't it odd, as many children as were there—and she'd seen at least a dozen at different times while they had her trussed up—none were outside playing, or shouting, or laughing. Mostly it was men who wandered about, every one carrying some kind of rifle or handgun. Good thing Nick and Dal decided not to rush in. The group had tripled in size with the arrivals last night. Could be some more kids as well.

Something beeped and her shoulders jerked. "What the hell is that?"

"Shit, I must've accidentally turned on the iPad when I took off my backpack a while ago." He opened the flap and pulled out the pad. On the screen was a blurred face with a time, date stamp, and a Kelley Creek locale in the corner.

"That's got to be Trey. He's got my camera."

Another photo popped onto the screen. A small, badly lit room crowded with kids. Sitting on the floor, on a couple of couches, one holding a little girl who couldn't be more than three.

"Dear God." Jessie pointed but couldn't say anything else.

"They brought in a whole load of kids last night. From two different directions. That's what was going on. And this proves Trey is alive."

"Thank God, but those poor babies. What are we going to do?"

"Turn off the iPad to conserve the battery." He glanced at Jessie. "Is this on your iPhone too?"

"Would be. Stupid, stupid. I turned off the iPad to save the battery but forgot about my phone. But Nick will get it charged when he gets to town. Then they can see those."

"What did you learn about them with your research? Any possibilities they've killed or hurt anyone?" He gestured toward the caravan of campers.

"The Rising Moon is fashioned a bit after the Moonies from the seventies and the Alamos, who were so popular in Arkansas during that time. Except for one thing. The cult masks something much more evil. Those kids are not there to entertain or help them. Only one reason they're gathering them and coming together. They're going to sell them."

His face reflected disgust. "Are you sure?"

"Can't prove it yet, but I'd bet that the feds can. The Internet is filled with information on missing children and trafficking. What else could it be? Don't have much of an idea where they're getting them or how, but it figures they're not adopting them. It makes me sick to my stomach."

"They could be sexually abusing them."

"Well, it would be unusual for an entire cult to be doing that. Could be one or two people, but all of them, men and women alike? I doubt it."

"Then they are a cult?"

"They refuse to call themselves that, but rather refer to themselves as a New Age religion linked to nature. There's not much online about them. They keep a low profile, like they're not exactly recruiting or proud of their beliefs." She frowned. "I don't think they know how to get hits on Google yet. Or maybe they're just secretive."

"Oh, they've sure developed a new concept with that nature thing." He let the sarcasm show.

"They stole part of the name from a story by Edgar Allan Poe titled 'Masque of the Red Death.' Why a religious organization would choose Poe to emulate is beyond me."

"Perhaps they're letting everyone know they have an underlying credo."

She parted some limbs, peered through. "Something darker, hidden, and a bit vicious? Sort of proves my supposition. If this can be proven, the feds can do it. We'll just deliver them and be done with it."

"I didn't know you liked to read Poe."

"Some, mostly his more romantic stories."

"They used to claim he was crazy, on drugs, stuff like that. But now doctors say from the symptoms he presented, he probably was a victim of some undiagnosed disease."

"Wow." She stared at him. "All the time I've known you it never occurred to me that you liked to read, especially not Poe."

"Well, we all have our secrets. I read a lot. Mostly weird stuff, but I like mysteries that have something else to say. Like Parker or Burke."

"He's my favorite author. Burke."

"Yeah? See, we do have more in common than sex."

She laughed softly. All the while they'd chatted he hadn't looked at her, but rather kept an eye on the goings-on across the valley.

Her laugh faded into what might be a sob. What the hell? He couldn't have said something that made her cry. But sure enough. She covered her face in both hands. He crawled over to her and wrapped both arms around her shoulders.

"Hey? What's wrong?"

She took a deep breath and rubbed away the tears with her fingertips. "Sorry, it's just... I guess all that's going on. Sad thinking about those poor babies. Then all that's going on between us. I learned to get along without you. A little. I really learned to be alone, I guess. Tink doesn't have time for much girl stuff anymore, what with her job and her marriage. Don't get me wrong, I'm happy for her. And ever since... well, of late, Parker and I don't do the friend stuff like we used to. I missed us."

She collapsed into his arms. He muffled her sobs against his chest so they wouldn't travel across the way. What had he done to her, coming back and turning her whole world upside down?

She snuffled. "Enough of this pity party. Crying's never been my thing."

He barely understood the words muttered into his shirt front. "I'm sorry. I really am."

Was he sorry for leaving or for coming back, and which had made her cry? He had no idea, but when a man had no idea why a woman was upset, it was best just to tell her he was sorry and hold her till she got over it. He might want to consider what he really was sorry for, though, just in case.

Before he could discuss it with her men's voices shouted, a kid screamed, the noise coming from the encampment. Someone was running across the pasture. He pulled out the binocs and zoomed in on the figure. Holy Hell. A child being pursued by two women, who in turn were being chased by two men. The men had guns, but so far weren't trying to fire them.

Jessie pulled at his arm and he handed the glasses to her. "Oh no. Can't we do something?"

"We do, they'll have us as well. Let it play out." In spite of his words, he pulled the nine, jacked a shell into the chamber. One of those fuckers tried to shoot any of the runners, he'd drop him. And start a war he couldn't win. No matter the outcome of this, he and Jessie were in deep shit.

"Honey, reach in my pocket and get your thirty-eight."

She did without asking questions. Goddammit, the kid and the women were headed right toward them.

"Jessie, I want you to go. Run and hide."

"I can't leave you. I won't."

And he knew that to be true, just like he wouldn't leave her. "Then be prepared to grab that kid. I'll take care of the two men and I'll be right behind you." He'd gotten her into this, he'd get her out. Should've tied her to a chair or something, back when he had the chance.

"Promise. Please promise you'll come too."

"I promise. Listen, if one of the women tries to get the kid, then you need to shoot her. You got that? We don't know which side they're on yet. Run like hell and I'll be with you."

Her swallow was so loud he heard it. "Yes. Yes." The knuckles on her hand turned white from her frantic grip on the gun.

The figure grew closer, still running right at Dal and Jessie. The women, wearing long purple robes, couldn't keep up with the kid, whose legs literally flew over the ground. Hurry, hurry, hurry. He must've said the words aloud, but didn't hear them come out of his mouth.

Just before the boy burst into the woods where he and Jessie waited, he veered and crashed into the trees maybe a hundred yards off to their right. One of the women disappeared after the kid but the man grabbed the other. She screamed and kicked and he carried her off toward the caravan. The other man stomped around in the woods for a long time, then came out and followed his companion back to the trailers.

"Should we see if we can find them?" The question a querulous whisper.

"A good idea. Yes. No. Hell, I don't want to leave you here and I don't want you to go looking. Either way is too dangerous for you." He couldn't let this go on.

"We got a problem then. Cause to me either way is too dangerous for you. Maybe we ought to stop thinking of each other and trust that we can each take care of ourselves."

He touched her cheek with his fingertips. "But that hasn't always proved true, has it?"

"Let's both go see if we can find them. Even if the cultists decide to leave, it'll take them a long time. We can be back in time to follow them, and mark a trail for Nick."

"Seems to be the only solution." He thumbed on the safety and tucked the nine back into the thigh holster. "You want to keep that or let me carry it?"

"You keep it. I don't have a pocket to put it in." She handed him the .38 and they moved off together in the direction the woman and child had disappeared.

Chances were good the loonies would send a search party to grab the woman and kid, but he refused to think about that. Would handle it when and if it happened.

12
CHAPTER

Chasing after the fleeing escapees, fighting brush and brambles sapped Jessie's energy. Hot and getting hotter every minute. Entire body covered with stinging scratches. Sweat soaked what was left of the tattered jeans and torn t-shirt. Why wasn't she tougher? Dal seemed to be hanging in there. Almost impossible to keep up with the woman and kid. Running for their lives no doubt added to their strength. Something purple fluttered from a growth of brambles. The woman's robe, whether discarded or torn off. Hard to tell.

A flutter of breeze helped cool her some but with the high humidity it didn't do much good. Every step sent lizards and other critters scattering from underfoot and made her leery about snakes. Ahead, he stopped and she stumbled into him. He was barely breathing hard, his t-shirt soaking wet.

Tough as an old leather knot, Mac had once said of Dal.

He steadied her. "Listen for a minute."

The rattle of feet running through dried leaves came from off to the right. They were heading upward toward the logging roads. Panting hard she bent forward, rested both hands on her knees.

"Maybe we ought to let them go. It sounds like they're making good time." She took several breaths. "The woman can surely take care of the young'un. No one is chasing them but us. What do we do if we catch them and they start howling so loud those men come back?" She swiped sweat from her eyes, looked up at him.

He stared in the direction of their prey. It was evident he was having a hard time deciding what to do about the runaways. If they caught the two of them they could pose more of a threat than the people in the caravan. Especially if they fought, which they would because they were so frightened. There'd be enough noise to attract attention.

His muscles tensed when she grasped his sweat-slick arm. "They'll be okay. You said it yourself. They're going in the right direction."

He finally gave in, halted, and leaned against a tree. "Let's go back. Those two are headed toward Cedarton. They'll come out on one of the roads into town and someone will help them. We're getting too far from the caravan."

Pain jagged through her ribs and she agreed. "Gotta rest a minute." She joined him, arm folded against the tree. Following the caravan was more important and if they were gone too long it could disappear. They'd never find it in this rugged wilderness. Even with a good tracker like Nick, there were ways to cover tracks. Places where the entire bunch could hide from even Google Earth. The wilderness was vast and wild dotted with caves and overhangs. She chuckled. Good reason to call it wilderness.

"I know you're right. I just hate to give up and leave them in here." He pushed away from the rough bark and started back, wading through thick brush and disturbing a cloud of insects.

"I'm dry as a bone." She caught up with him. "I remember a spring we passed a while ago." Sure enough, the burble of falling water and the air came alive with the aroma of wet earth. They almost stepped into the overflow of a falls that tumbled over a bluff about ten or twelve feet high. A rainbow-colored mist took her breath away.

For a moment she faced into the wet air. "You kept an empty water bottle, didn't you?"

She dropped to her knees, bent forward, and drank from the spring like an animal. After splashing her face and neck she, filled the bottle he handed her and screwed down the cap.

Rising, she wiped her dripping chin and smiled at him. "Good and cold. Drink. You are way overheated."

He followed suit, mimicking her movements before rising. "God, that feels good."

"Sit for a minute." She ran her fingers through his long hair, took the bandana from his backpack, and tied the damp strands at the nape of his neck.

He grinned at her. "Have you always been so motherly?"

"What?"

"It's like you have this need to take care of everyone."

"Well, I guess I could just stop caring."

"No, that's not what I mean. You saved my life on that mountain and to thank you I packed up and ran off. Left you to wonder what you'd done wrong. I'll always regret deserting you. And now you're fixing my hair." He plucked at green moss growing on a rock near the spring, like he couldn't say these words while looking at her. "It's touching." He whispered as if he wasn't sure he wanted to reveal how he felt.

His admission brought a knot to her throat and her eyes burned. It was so hard understanding someone who hid his emotions so deep. "I thought you were ashamed that you needed help. You've always been so independent. Pushing me away anytime I came too close to caring about you. I'll admit it hurt me deeply. I'd been so frightened that you were badly injured and then you brushed me off as if it were nothing."

"And I didn't mean to hurt you. I guess I didn't know my actions could affect you like that."

She splashed handfuls of water on her face and neck. "That feels so good. I don't know, maybe you just can't let me in. Can't let me become a part of your life. I'm sorry if you don't feel the same about me as I do about you. Neither one of us can help how we feel."

"Come here." He reached for her and she moved to sit beside him, the wet moss soaking the seat of her britches. His holding her was all she cared about and she relaxed against him. The danger and their situation disappeared surrounded by the song of the falling water, a bird on a branch tweeting its heart out, his lips against her forehead. She closed her eyes in contentment. Here in this exotic place it was easy to believe he cared for her in the way she'd always wanted. Maybe it wouldn't last, would disappear back in the real world. She'd take it where she could get it.

He stood and pulled her to her feet, led her by the hand back down to their hiding place where the caravan remained. Removing the backpack, he pulled out the iPad and turned it on but only the last two pictures Trey had sent came up. For a while he stared at the thing.

"If only he could send us some more pictures. Prove he's still alive. What if they've killed him by now? One of those shots we heard. Something. *Dammit.*"

She nudged him. "It looks like they're getting ready to leave."

The men guarding the trailers climbed one by one into an RV or trailer. Somewhere an engine powered up, then another. They must have given up on following the two escapees. Some of the women gathered chairs, yanked clothing from where it hung on low hanging tree branches, carried belongings to various trailers. Probably afraid that the fleeing woman would lead the authorities to them or maybe they'd received word to move out. Still no sign of children among those who hurried about. How did they keep them locked up? And why?

She and Dal had returned just in time to keep an eye on them.

"What do we do if they take off so fast we can't keep up? Or they decide to get rid of the kids and just run?"

"Jess, don't go making trouble we don't need. They're keeping those kids with them. They've gone to a lot of trouble to round them up. God knows what all they plan to do. Probably no good at all. Sad to say, kids are a valuable commodity. I just never thought I'd see trafficking here in the Ozarks." He turned a circle, cursing under his breath.

So he'd bought her theory about the kids. "Hush, they'll hear you. We don't want to get caught."

"Shit, I'd like to line their asses up against a wall and shoot them, one by one. No telling what's going on with those kids besides sending them out to steal. There's got to be a hell of a lot more to this than that. That backwoods sheriff can't be the head honcho if that's what it is. He hasn't got the connections. Selling kids is lucrative, just plain dirty business. Thing is, people don't expect child trafficking in the United States. We catch who's running this, they won't make it to trial."

"You don't mean that. Please, settle down. They're going to hear or see us." She touched his arm and he jerked away, stared back toward the targets of his anger.

After two or three deep breaths he nodded. "You're right. It's just that so much of this filth goes on it seems like no matter what we do we can't put an end to it."

"Well, we can end this, and that's all we can hope for."

Easy to see why he'd left Dallas and his involvement in the drug wars. Anger at a failure to stop the violence and drug-related crimes had finally gotten the better of him. Especially when his wife died as a direct result of what he fought so hard to stop. Guilt was a dreadful human emotion. He needed peace and she so wanted to give it to him. But that wouldn't happen until he accepted it for himself.

She moved close, coiled an arm around his waist so their bodies touched. Head tucked against his shoulder, she didn't say a word. It wasn't long before he calmed down, kissed the top of her head.

"Hate to say so, but you're good for me." Hugging each other, they waited while the cult members slowly formed a line of the ragged vehicles and snaked off into the woods.

This would all be over sooner or later. Would he leave then? Go back wherever he'd been hiding out? Or could she convince him that life in Cedarton was much better for the both of them than living apart and lonely? Time would tell. Meanwhile, they'd work together to get this strange case solved. And right now that meant trailing the caravan and making sure Nick and the cavalry could follow them when they came to the rescue.

By midafternoon Nick jogged into Cedarton. The sun hurried toward the peaks to the west, the hottest part of the day. Soon the heated air would cool down some and a soft breeze would drift over the mountaintops and through town. Heeding Jessie's suggestion, he cut across the square toward the office of *The Observer*. Here and there people stopped to stare. He must look a sight, covered in sweat, clothes ripped by brambles. A black Land Rover sat outside and he let out a sigh of relief. Unless some foot traffic had dropped in it looked like Parker was there alone.

Nick had drank the last of his water long before he hit the outskirts of town. His tongue stuck to the roof of his dry mouth. There'd be something cold to drink inside. He twisted the knob, but the door was locked. Frantic barking. Must be Jessie's little pit bull. She'd be happy he was being taken care of. No one came to the door. Odd, but maybe the publisher was busy and didn't want to be disturbed. Looked like all that noise from the dog would be worse than a visitor. He had to hear this. Nick rapped sharply on the window pane, waited a while, then did it again. The dog went wild.

The door swung open before he lifted his knuckles from the glass. The frowning man in the doorway spoke to the pooch. "Okay, okay. Hush, you little mutt 'fore I send you home."

He turned his gaze toward Nick. This had to be Parker. "Locked door means I'm working. Everyone knows that."

Though Nick had seen him around town or at the Red Bird a few times, they never actually met face to face to be introduced.

The dog continued to run in circles but at least he'd shut up. "Lay down and stop that now, you disrespectful canine." The ugly little pit snuck under one of the desks and continued to peer out at Nick. Parker did his own peering over dark-rimmed glasses.

"Sorry, sir. This is important or I wouldn't have bothered you. Name's

Nick Snow, and I have an emergency to talk to you about. Has to do with Jessie and Dal. Could I come in and get something cold to drink? It's a long run up out of Hooper Valley."

"Good God, man. Come on in here. You ran all the way here? Must be six or seven miles, mostly uphill. Have to be a matter of life or death for me to even try something like that. That's a hell of a message to hit a man with. What about Dal and Jessie? What's happened?"

"They're okay, but it is an emergency. If I could just get that drink, then we can talk."

"Course, I'm sorry. There's cold pop in the fridge in the back, or some bottles of water. Get whichever you want."

While he talked he led Nick through a room filled with long tables and a scattering of desks, many of which were littered with stacks of colored paper. "You mentioned Jessie and Dal. We all wondered where they'd got to. Here one day and gone the next. Used to such shenanigans from Dal, but Jessie's always here on Mondays when we start working on the paper. Have to admit I've been a mite worried about her. Not like her, not at all."

He swung the fridge door open and let Nick pull out a bottle of water and a can of Coke. Nick screwed the cap off the water and guzzled most of it, then popped the tab on the Coke and swigged some of it down.

"Ran all the way up out of Hooper Valley? Why in the hell would you do that? Even one so young and... well, you do look like a runner. Is Jessie in danger? You say she's with Dal? The two of them can get in more trouble together than most of us can imagine."

Parker watched till he pulled the bottle from his mouth. "Has something happened to them? I've been patient enough. Tell you the truth I figured they ran off together for a private getaway, the way they feel about each other and him being gone so long. I just figured that's what'd happened."

Nick took another long swig, then sucked in some deep breaths. If the man would stop talking he could get a word in edgewise. But he was at it again.

"Okay, son. I've waited all I can. Tell me what's so important you have to tease a heart attack just to get the word to me. What is that Jessie up to? Chasing the best story in the state?"

"Could be, sir. I think we'd better sit down. This will be long in the telling and I may be in good shape, but I could use a bit of a rest."

By the time he finished his tale, Parker was walking the floor and running fingers through his thick black hair. "For all that's holy, son. You sure it's Sheriff Kimble leading these misguided souls?"

"They've got them a preacher called Deacon. We didn't see him, but we supposed Kimble is protecting them from the local law. We saw him with them. He was out in the valley with some of the men. What's worse, we think they're set to go deeper in the wilderness with all those kids. Can't figure out where they got so many, or what they intend to do with them, but several caravans came in late yesterday from the north and the south and they had kids with them. They're getting em from somewhere and it can't be from here. There are those two we know of, Lily and the Bainbridge girl, but no others been reported missing that I know of. Jessie thinks they're selling em but we couldn't figure to who."

"Odd they'd drag them off into the wilderness if that's the case. And not smart to send them out to shoplift and get seen and nearly caught." Parker moved his glasses to the top of his head.

"Well, there are some strange things going on with this. I left Jessie and Dal down there to follow them if they take off. Dal's going to make sure we can pick up their trail. Oh, and one more thing. They assaulted Trey Ledger and have kidnapped him. He may have a concussion. They had Jessie too but she got away."

Parker whirled from his pacing. "Don't you think that should've been the first thing you told me about, not the last? Good God, man. We need to notify the sheriff and someone from the US Marshal's office. Now."

Parker went to the closest desk and picked up the phone, dialed. Asked for the sheriff.

Nick leaned on the corner of the littered desk and finished the Coke while Parker told Couch what was going on. He answered a few questions with yes or no or I'm not sure, then hung up.

"He's notifying the marshal's local office in Fayetteville and calling in his deputies. Says for us to meet him at his office. Good God, what's happening to this peaceful place? Sort of makes me want to go live in a cave." He glanced at Nick. "Well, come on, let's high tail it over there."

Nick set down the can, followed Parker out to the Rover. Brad scooted between their feet and claimed shotgun. Parker glowered at the dog. "Just put him in the back."

Nick wasn't sure he wanted to do that. "He won't bite me, will he?"

"Him? No, all he is is a troublemaker."

"Sort of like his mistress, huh?" Nick carefully transferred Brad into the back seat, then climbed in. He hadn't shut the door before Parker keyed the ignition and they were off, spitting gravel from under the tires.

Down in Hooper Valley black clouds chased the sun, finally swallowing up the light. Thunder followed, so distant at first Dal could barely hear it. The caravan had formed a slow moving line, the leader driving the big RV where Jessie had said all the kids were. Some of the others were still packing up. He counted sixteen different vehicles of various types and sizes. Wished he knew where Trey could be, thinking after dark tonight he might try a rescue attempt of the injured marshal. Unless they'd moved him he'd be in the ratty red and white one.

Tailing a contingent of campers through the wilderness was going to be different than following a suspect through dark, litter-strewn alleys. And hopefully not as dangerous.

He checked out the storm clouds and crouched beside Jessie. "Looks like we're going to get wet. Good thing it's not cold."

Still nothing on the iPad, nothing from the iPhone Nick had taken with him either. Wouldn't surprise him if that prick Couch refused to do anything. So there they'd be somewhere out in the wilds keeping an eye on a bunch of kooks for the rest of their lives. Dal snorted under his breath. A tad of an exaggeration there, buddy, but seriously, what would he do and how long should they wait before they did something? It was a valid consideration.

By his watch it took almost twenty minutes for the last of the RVs to move out. While they did fat raindrops splatted loudly on the canopy, water dripping through to sprinkle both of them. Because the valley was rather narrow with woods on both sides, they could remain under the trees out of sight and should have no trouble following the slow-moving caravan.

Walking in the rain wasn't bad at first. It felt good, cool to sweaty skin, but soon long, jagged fingers of lightning split the sky. Once a strike came so close it jarred the ground underfoot and cracked open the silence. His ears popped.

He grabbed her hand and crouched low. "We're going to get struck if we stay under these trees. We've got to find shelter."

"But if we stop they'll get away."

"They're moving slow as the seven-year itch. Looks like they may be gonna stop and wait out the worst of the storm. They've no place to go but straight ahead anyway. Come on, there's an overhang just over there. Let's get under it till the storm passes. If they do move on, we'll be able to catch up."

She followed him without a word, slid down beside him, and leaned against the wall of rocks under the sheltering bluff.

The heat of her body poured through him. An arm against his, the touch of her flesh awakening a long tamped-down passion. Recalling the other night, he wanted more and wanted it with a heated desire that ignited fires in his gut. She did too. His mind opened and embraced her thoughts, an imagining of the two of them naked in the rain. He turned and she was staring at him as if she'd read his mind too. He smiled at the irony of that possibility, cupped her chin and kissed her. Taking her lips with his gently. She offered all she had. So soft and sweet. A passion took root in his groin, a need as wild as the storm so intense it made him dizzy. Her tongue outlined his mouth slowly and desire exploded in his gut. Filled him with a hunger so desperate he feared the consequences.

The sweetness of her lips, her hand moving under the hem of his shirt, fingers playing over his skin, added fuel to that fire. A fire fanned by the danger they were in. He could no longer resist and gave in with a low moan. Taking her shoulders in both hands he laid her on the smooth dark earth.

Here for centuries man had taken his woman in an age-old ritual no one could teach and everyone was born with. Those memories played through his mind. The spirits had left their mark in the rock and the soil, even the air held memories of lives in this place where once Indians made their homes. The emotions of those primitive people added to the adrenaline pouring through him to set his world ablaze.

The caress of his hands on the flesh of her arms, urging them above her head. Slowly peeling off her shirt, bending to kiss her breasts one at a time as if worshiping them. Lifting her butt to skin her jeans down slowly. Shoes and clothing lay in a pile, as did his shirt and britches. His body yearned to have her. To pounce on her and take her in a frenzy. Yet free of clothing, hands spread under her hips, he took his time to relish the touch of this lovely woman.

He brushed hair from her cheek, stared into her eyes, ran the tips of his fingers along her jawline and over her lips. An expression passed through her solemn gaze, something so touching he caught his breath. Whispered her name. Opened his mind to hers and embraced her thoughts, her longings, her passion. What he sensed jarred him to the core.

"Oh, dear God, Jessie."

She knew he was inside her mind again and smiled. "It's all true, every bit of it."

He spread one hand over her heart. Counted the beats until his own heart matched the rhythm of hers. Waiting, feeling, enjoying their bodies embracing each other. So slow he ached all over. Drank in the desire that sent pain through him. Her fingers fisted in his hair when he trailed kisses to her belly.

Without taking his gaze from hers he straddled her, one knee on either side of her bare body. She arched upward, eyes begging him to take her. Not yet, though. He needed more, of what he wasn't sure. She was ready and accepting.

What the hell was wrong with him? Every inch of him yearned for her. Still he remained above her, outlined her jaw and chin, the other jaw with the tip of a finger. Leaned down and kissed each eye, her nose, her mouth, and chin. Slow moist kisses that had her whimpering deep in her throat. What more did he want?

Enough. He'd tortured himself enough. And her too. Couldn't wait another moment. Teeth grinding, a low moan building in his throat, he entered her so slowly he could hardly bear the pain that shot through him. And when he was fully enclosed within her sweet warmth he spread his palms under her bottom and lifted her, leaned back on his heels so that her legs were locked behind him, her weight fully on him. Going deep, so deep he feared hurting her, made sure he didn't by moving about in her mind. Arms fastened around her he rocked back and forth, passion rising like red hot flames spurting from a bed of glowing coals.

Around them lightning split the darkening sky. Trees swayed, limbs cracked and fell, the ground trembled. Water poured off the bluff's edge in sheets.

The rain-soaked breeze kissed his bare wet skin where she'd licked. Her nipples were hard against his chest. His movement begun so slow, increased. Her body convulsed with an orgasm and she hung on tight, making little *huh* sounds till he lost his breath.

His cupped hands around her firm ass, flipped them over so she was on top astraddle of him, bringing a healthy squeal from her. Men didn't squeal, but if they did, his would have been the roar of a bull elk. The idea tickled him and they coupled with great abandon, her laughter joining his.

Damn good thing it was storming or someone would've heard them. Strange, but it was the thunder and lightning that had driven him and now it shielded them. So they could continue this weird rain dance.

It was all he could do to hold back, but if he came now it would be done and he wanted this to last. Make up for the months they'd been apart. It appeared she wasn't finished either. She grabbed his wrists, held his arms above his head, and rode him in a slow, graceful waltz.

At last he gave up to the passion and when he could hold back no longer he flipped her onto her back and with one final plunge came inside her with such glory he curled around her in a feral ecstasy, clung so tight she gasped. Was it for air or for the wonder of their mutual coming?

After having her like this he could hardly manage to think straight, or recall just what it was about her that brought him to the brink of immortality. Nothing left of the body but the spirit, spiraling up and away into a cloudless, soundless, colorless space. Like eagles that soared on high and came together in midair to fuck like no other creature could.

He had no breath, no heartbeat, no blood rushing through his veins. Absolute lifeless tranquility. Beyond their cave, the storm passed. Silence descended with a roar. Only the rain, falling soft upon the land. She lay on him, over him, around him. And then she took a breath and he did too. She crawled off, put a finger over her lips. Shushed him.

He laughed, reached up to her and she took his hand. The ethereal surroundings hung over them. She led him into the open, found a spot where the rain poured through the canopy and coaxed him to be with her there. Bare belly to bare belly she washed him and he reciprocated. The two of them stood in the rain scrubbing each other's bodies.

Somewhere in his memory might lie a time that gave him such peace and enjoyment, but if it was there he couldn't find it. This he would never forget, the experience forged in his mind like a brand.

Hands rubbing between his legs, she laughed at his immediate reaction. He covered her mouth with his, pointed toward the trail where the last of the line of RVs sat waiting for the harsh rain to pass. "You'd better stop that."

"Just washing you off."

"Uh-huh. We'll see." He did the same for her and reveled in her expression when he paused to slip his fingers deep inside.

She tightened her thighs and closed her eyes, turning her face upward into the rain. He flicked her tiny heart until she came, then placed his lips over hers to inhale her breath.

Rain poured over them. Locked together he couldn't bear to part from her. Whispered in her ear. "I'm so sorry I hurt you." Then wondered if she'd misunderstood.

"I know, I do know. Don't do it again." She understood what he meant.

Could he promise her that? Probably not. He was such an ass.

"Well then, we'd better get dressed and catch up with those idiots. Looks like they're moving out."

"I suppose." But he didn't want to let her go. It was such a euphoric feeling, standing naked in the rain with this glorious woman in his arms.

She slithered from his grasp so he had to follow her to where their clothes were piled. "I wish we had clean ones." She shook the clothing, put on the underpants and ripped jeans, then sat to slip her feet into the Keds.

Watching her dress was almost as enjoyable as watching her undress, so he did so, then climbed into his own clothes. Hand in hand they crept through the woods where the caravan curled off like a snake. By the time they caught sight of the white RV it was almost dark.

"I'm starving," he muttered.

"Me too. They're not going to get here tonight, are they?"

"Nope."

"Well, at least the rain has let up."

A noise nearby and someone emerged from the darkest shadows of the woods. "You folks lost?"

Dal swung around, pushed Jessie behind him. The man held a gun pointed casually at them. There was no time to draw his nine, so he shrugged and held his hands out to show he wasn't going to fight back.

Unlike Jessie, who tensed behind him, then was gone. Running into the darkness.

No, Jessie. Don't. Don't. But she kept going.

The guy aimed his rifle in her direction and Dal leaped, knocking him aside so the rifle went off into the sky. He chased after her. Probably never find her in the dark. What was she thinking? So wild and crazy.

Amazing how much influence Mac had in this town. Looking around, Nick couldn't believe how quickly the deputies and others connected to law enforcement in Cedarton gathered in Mac's small house. They turned up in the pouring rain, shaking water off their rain gear and stomping into the house. They were literally falling out the windows. A retired deputy everyone called Sam, a guy in his late sixties. Then someone named Doc who had been an honorary deputy during the Fourth of July parade, plus all the deputies either not on duty or patrolling nearby. EMTs and volunteer firemen showed up. Everyone but Sheriff Couch.

It was so noisy he couldn't hear himself think, but he needed it quiet and quick. They had to move on this. Mac beat on the table with an empty beer bottle and everyone came to attention.

"I appreciate y'all's concern. I'm gonna let Nick tell you what's going on, then we'll come up with a plan. This here, for those of you who don't know him, is Nick Snow. He's originally from up to Red Rock, but has been away most of his grown-up life. Professionally, he's a mountain climber with search and rescue—or was till he retired. You remember he went down to bring Dal and Jessie up off the mountainside last year."

A murmur went through the crowd until Mac held up his hand. Nick rose from where he'd hunkered just inside the door. Not accustomed to speaking before a crowd, he first cleared his throat and found a target to concentrate on. A young woman deputy who sat near Mac. He tried to make his story as short as possible, but didn't want to have a delay with a thousand questions, so he told it as thoroughly as he could. Then finally finished.

"And so I left Jessie and Dal there along with a caravan of almost two dozen vehicles and a lot of kids. We need to organize something legal, so I figure we focus on the kidnapping of Trey Ledger." He glanced at Mac. "Did you contact the marshal's office and what did they say?"

Mac nodded. "I talked to a Scott Remington" —everyone chuckled— "and he's on his way with three other deputy marshals and probably some FBI agents as well. Said I need to get the acting sheriff to authorize several deputies here to go down there with them."

"Mac, you know good and well that prick Couch will bristle up and refuse to let any of us go. He'll just call young Nick there a liar. Hell, he hasn't even shown up." Colby had kept quiet up to this point.

"Then we'll do it without him. If he does try to stop us he's liable to find himself back home sitting out his retirement. You don't tell the feds no. Nick here says he has pictures to prove what he says."

Nick glanced at Jessie's phone, plugged in and lying on the kitchen cabinet. Hopefully he'd have even more photos if Trey had managed to take some more and get them sent.

He glanced out the front window in time to see two black Tahoe SUVs park under the maple trees along the street. Men erupted out all four doors, some dressed in BDUs carrying weapons, others in jackets with FBI across the back. Holy shit. He expected men in black and that's what he gets.

He hurried to let them in before they decided to knock down the door. The lead guy introduced himself. "Deputy Marshal Scott Remington, sir. Is Sheriff Couch here?"

"The *acting* sheriff is not here today. But Sheriff Mac Richards is, sir."

Nick stepped back and looked at Mac with a smile. Neglecting to mention Mac's enforced retirement would get the deputies in trouble, but Nick wasn't too concerned for himself.

The marshal looked around. "Looks like you've got quite a crew here."

Mac stood. "Ready to go when you are, sir. Our vehicles are parked up the hill." He turned and pointed. "Sample, Colby, Duggan, and Watson are ready to go. Snow here will take you down. He knows how to get to them. The rest of these men are prepared to follow your directions. So if you don't mind I'd like to get them organized and on their way into the valley."

"Long as everyone understands this is a federal operation. Could we see those pictures, Snow?" Remington turned to face Nick.

Nick fetched the phone, found the photo gallery, and handed it to Remington. He stretched to peer over the men looking at it. Remington slid the photos across the screen on past the last ones Nick had seen to one showing Trey Ledger, face swollen and eyes black. Must've shaken off that concussion pretty well to realize if anyone was looking for him, this would turn the trick. He'd taken a selfie.

"Goddamn," Remington said. "Let's get these men on the road."

"Four of us have a Jeep. Four more a four-wheeler. Then there's the responder vehicle. Everyone can follow me. There's no road as such. Sure you want to get those shiny black vehicles all scratched up and covered in mud?"

"Hell yes." The feds spoke all at once.

"Well, they'd better be four-wheel drive." This from Colby walking past them and following Nick. Sample and Duggan trailed them. Watson had a four-wheeler that he ran all over town on, even though technically he wasn't supposed to take it on a highway. Everyone pretty well ignored that. He also had a case of bottled water strapped to the back. Nick had a carton of nature bars. That ought to do them till they rounded up those folks and took them to Fayetteville. The EMTs and firemen were in one of the first responder trucks and they fell in behind the Jeep before the marshals could nose their Tahoes in. It was certainly a caravan all its own.

This could turn out to be a longer hunt and chase than those feds figured on, but Nick would go prepared, no matter what they did. Just for the fun of it he took a couple pictures of the Tahoes and the camouflage-attired feds loading up. He sent that to the iPad, turned off the phone, and stuck it in his pocket. No sense in running it down, and everyone had walkies anyway. The feds probably had satellite phones.

Remington had pretty well let it be known he was in charge, and Nick could understand that. It was one of his men down there in danger. All the rest took a backseat till the law could get it all sorted out. He wasn't worried in the least about that part. But those kids were not going anywhere with those so-called moonies if he had to steal them himself. The rain let up to a drizzle by the time they reached the Jeep.

Those children down there might not be his responsibility. A memory eased into his head. The only one he could allow. His daughter Corrie dancing through a field of white daisies, hair flying, her laughter touching his soul. He couldn't bear to recall the true, brutal end of his daughter's life. She didn't get to go home, but those children down in the valley were going home. He would see to that.

13
CHAPTER

Darker than the belly of a cow doesn't quite describe a country night when there's no moon. Since Jessie was fleeing for her life that was a blessing. Except it made it too easy to fall, exactly what she did. Stepped right in a sinkhole that was little more than a yard across. Both knees tucked under her chin, she scooped leaves over herself, in the process determined nothing was broken or bent, and lay still, afraid to breathe for fear she'd cough or sneeze and they'd find her.

Making lots of noise running meant getting caught. Hiding was her best bet. Not even a minute later the men chasing her stumbled past. What kept them from hearing her heart banging around in her chest she'd never know, unless they were making so much blamed noise themselves. The only way they'd find her was if one of them tripped and fell on top of her.

Time dragged waiting for them to double back and find her, maybe kill her. How long should she stay here? Would they return this way when they gave up? No matter. She had to remain right where she was.

The hardest thing she could do because Dal was out there and if they got him, they'd do to him what they'd already done to Trey.

But he was tough and knew how to handle himself. He had to be. It would not help him for her to leap up and yell "Here I am" just because she feared for him. Then they'd have them both. While her mind raced a mile a minute the hole she lay in was filling with run-off from the rain.

Hand on the backpack. Mind somewhere else. Returned. It would shed rainwater, but lying in this hole of water it would soon leak. The iPad would be ruined. She had to keep it dry. She needed to find a place to put it. Nearly blind in the darkness, but her hands found a large tree. About head high a fork formed a good resting place. Strong enough? She balanced the leather pack holding the precious iPad across the forks. Tilted at it but it stayed put. Looked okay for now. Out of the wet.

Eyes closed. Mouth clenched. Nestle back down in the bed of leaves. Don't make a sound, just breathe through the covering. She hugged her knees to keep from shaking too much.

What a story this would make. If only she had a recorder she could begin to write it now. In reality she could do that in her mind. Yes. Begin with a line that would catch everyone's imagination.

"It was a beautiful night to die." Don't be stupid. "I never thought this would be the way my life would end. Huddled in the woods covered in leaves." Better. Catchy, but it didn't make the promise of the specific story she had to tell.

Water gushed down the mountainside, rose in a pool around her.

Ignore it.

Okay. Start over. First lines were difficult. Almost impossible to write until the story was finished. So the story. About stolen children? Or the cult? Or the kidnapping of a US Marshal? This was going to challenge her. The cult. It had to be the focal point, for without it there wouldn't have been the stolen children or the kidnapping.

First, information about cults in America. Maybe in a sidebar. Yeah, that's it. The main story, the Rising Moon, how they came here. Interview one of the members, learn what they believe, then move on to why they took the children and kidnapped Trey, how their existence affected people in Grace County. Then tell the story of the chase, who took part and the outcome.

Still, didn't it all come down to the children? If they were indeed the victims of human trafficking, wasn't that then the real story? Something to be researched and written about.

Sounded pretty good. She'd play around with it a lot, though, then Parker would put his blue pencil to work, discuss her approach, she would rewrite it and do a follow-up on the kids and how they were reunited with their families.

Water lapped around her shoulders. Crap. If she didn't get out of here soon she'd be breathing water. Shoes, jeans, and shirt soaking wet. Time to leave whether she dared or not. Try to find Dal? Much as that's what she wanted, what she needed was to locate that damned caravan and send a text to Nick, something to let him know where the kids were, where Trey was. Then she could look for Dal.

How long had it been since anyone stomped past her hideout? It seemed hours, but she knew better. Turning her face toward the sky she rubbed away some of the debris and opened her eyes. Up to her ears in water. The sky gleamed. An odd phenomenon of clouds that lit the night, made it easier to see. She peered above the rim of her hole. It was hard to get oriented. First find the RVs. Tilting her head she stuck a finger in one ear then the other. The water ran out with a popping sound. She strained to hear even the slightest noise, slid the iPad off its resting place. Nothing but creatures of the night and something else. Faint, but regular. The movement of tires slowly rolling through leaves, the purr of engines.

Off down the incline a ways. She would crawl in that direction. On her hands and knees, clothes a soggy mess. The sound, so close she could smell the exhaust held down by the heavy air. Weight of the .38 in her pocket reassured her. Yes, guns could shoot after being wet. Unless, of course, they'd been in the bottom of the river for six months and rusted shut.

Could she shoot someone? Better, *would* she?

If there was a good reason she would.

That settled, she crawled toward the sound and smell of moving vehicles. Not to shoot anyone but to find them and let the guys who were used to shooting at people take over. Surely they'd be here soon.

Ozark hills are littered with rocks, small and large. It's almost as if they grow from the earth like trees. That can make crawling slow and painful, especially on the knees. So it took a long, uncomfortable while to finally locate the caravan. As soon as she did, she snapped a picture. In the dark not much would show, but the time and location would.

Behind the shelter of a large oak she tapped the app that allowed transference to the iPhone for Nick and posted the photo. The light from the iPad rendered her temporarily blind.

Dummy. What if they saw?

Sheltering it with her body, she gazed at the gallery of pictures. Trey stared back, his poor face battered. He was definitely alive and taking pictures with the camera the men at Rising Moon had grabbed away from her. The marshal had taken a selfie.

She smiled at him as if he might take heart from seeing her. While the phone and pad could send and accept photos the camera could only send them. There was no way she could let him know they were coming for him and soon. Very soon. She slipped the pad back in its leather case.

Dear God, how badly she wanted to walk up to one of those RVs and surrender. Get herself locked up with either Trey or the kids so she could see how they were, maybe do something. Anything. Boy what a story that would make. But there was no guarantee that would happen. For all she knew they would shoot her on the spot, or toss her in with a bunch of men with guns and peckers. Not a very happy prospect.

Someone from way to the front of the long line hollered and one by one the RVs circled up and rolled to a halt in a clearing. Under the silver sky they looked like a herd of giant turtles. Odd that they'd traveled this long without stopping to sleep, first in the rain, then in the dark. Must be a deadline of some sort for arriving at their destination. Since she had no idea where Dal was or if he was leaving a trail for Nick to follow, she would make sure to mark the way when and if they changed direction.

The huge question now was had Nick succeeded, with Parker's help, to round up some lawmen? And if he had would they set out in the storm or wait till it abated? Damn, she so hated being left in the dark about what was going on. Maybe he'd taken a photo with the phone after he charged it. The iPad. She pulled it out, opened the gallery.

Yes, there after Trey's selfie were two shots of men gathered in Mac's house. Nick had made it. If he had his way they'd start out storm or no. A waste of time to second guess that.

Once the RVs circled up and the lanterns were lit it was easier for her to identify each one.

Wait, something moved. A guard?

No, someone was sneaking around the outside perimeter of the circle. Too furtive to be a guard.

Could be Dal?

Enough was enough and she couldn't stand it a moment longer. Darting between large trees, she worked her way closer. With no more trees to hide behind, she snuck from one dark place to another. Light beams reached from windows into the night. There would be guards. A couple of times she held her breath while an armed guard walked from one RV to another, so close she could've reached out and touched him before he faded out of sight.

She shook all over. Not from being cold or wet, but from fear. That shadow was Dal, it had to be, and his form disappeared each time a guard rounded one of the vehicles. Almost as if by magic. If she dared approach him, it would be one of the moon people, or it would be Dal and he would make a noise when she surprised him.

Time to move in, take a chance. She could stand it no longer. Gaze pinned to the hovering form, she crept slow as a snail till she could hear him breathing.

"Quiet." A whisper from the ghostly figure. Of course he knew she was there. All he had to do was tune in to her mind.

Hand gripped over her mouth, she froze in her tracks. An armed guard circled around the end of the adjacent trailer. For long moments she waited for Dal to signal something, but he didn't. Time for her to move, but his hand gripped her upper arm.

"Wait." Another whispered command.

So she waited.

Movement from the other direction. They were like ants around a damn ant hill.

Dal's grip tightened. "Go left. Now."

He moved on the command and dragged her with him. Into the

trees, stumbling deeper until the woods enclosed them. At last he stopped. Wrapped his arms around her. Held her for the longest time saying nothing, just breathing warm and moist against her neck. Oh, God it felt so good to be safe in his arms.

"I thought you were—"

"Hush." Lips against her ear. "Down."

He lowered her next to him in the wet leaves. Touched her forehead with the flat of one palm. "You're safe. I thought they had you." The fear spoken against her throat. Arms around him she relaxed as if the leaves, wet from the rain, were the most comfortable mattress ever.

"Shhh. Close your eyes and go to sleep."

After a while she did because he held her.

It took right at two hours to arrive in Hooper Valley where the caravan had been when Nick left to fetch the law. Access roads were far apart, some mere single trails that challenged forward movement of the Tahoes. The first hour was spent fighting their way through the storm without getting lost. As they drew nearer their destination Nick advised lights out and slow going so if the trailers were still camped where he'd left them they wouldn't hear or see them coming.

By then the rain stopped, the storm moving on. Once they arrived at the spot where the trailers had camped, he went to reconnoiter the area on foot by himself. When they left Cedarton Mac had caught him going out the door and handed him an Enfield .303, which he carried strapped over his shoulder. A rifle would come in handy, so Nick didn't argue that he was already armed.

The ground was plastered with churned up wet leaves. No specific signs of the departure of the RVs. The heavy rains had washed away any tire tracks. Finding nothing, he returned to tell the lawmen that they would have to wait till daylight so they might as well get some rest.

The bivouac carried Nick far away to another time and place. Men sleeping anywhere on the ground they could lay their bodies. Waiting for something, anything, to come at them out of the dark.

Here Sam passed out bottles of water and Nick tossed an energy bar to each man. It wasn't long before all were sleeping. Men like these could sleep anywhere anytime, including leaned up against a tree. They could exist on water alone for days, and when it came time to do the job they were there for, they were in total and calm control. Ready to kick ass. Memories of that life came back to him as if in a dream.

Rays of early morning sunlight drifted through the trees and the men stirred. Going into the woods to relieve themselves, drinking more water, munching on energy bars. Speaking in low murmurs. Nick conducted a quick search of their surroundings, especially checking low hanging limbs and branches.

There were only a few ways a caravan with vehicles that size could go, so he spent plenty of time until he found, not broken limbs, but a place wallowed out next to a faint old logging road. Head down, he searched the ground. Here and there a moving wheel had dropped into a muddy spot. Faint, but there. Then a sapling bent over, the bark scraped off by a passing vehicle. Dal and Jessie might be in trouble, and unable to leave signs, but there were these to follow and he had to keep moving. No choice at this point.

He summoned the men. Pointed off through the trees at the occasional sapling scraped as if something had been dragged over it. The road was old and overgrown almost to invisibility, but it was there and the caravan had taken it, leaving the valley in favor of the wilderness.

But where were Dal's promised bread crumbs marking the way? Had the people somehow captured him and Jessie?

Nick motioned to one of the feds. "This is going to get rough going for those fancy black vehicles of yours. Want to leave them?"

"Hell no. They can get through same as RVs and trailers. Besides, they're almost a year old. Time to replace them anyway."

Nick didn't give a shit one way or the other. "Okay, then. Let's mount up. Once more, I want to remind you that there are kids in those vehicles. No cowboying."

"Yes sir." The fed gave him a mock salute, a reminder that they were running this op.

Christ. Nick turned away to keep from laughing in the guy's face. For all he cared they could drive off a cliff. And they might well do just that. He had four deputies with him who he trusted in these woods plus a truck full of good ole boys who knew how to handle themselves. He put more faith in them than he did those feds, even if they did dress and act like experts.

He went over to speak to Sam. "It'd be best if you lead the way on that four-wheeler. We'll follow in the Jeep, and then those guys can bring up the rear."

Sam snorted. "You actually talked them into that?"

"I didn't exactly talk them into it, I told them. I don't figure any of them could follow sign of any kind, but once we spot these people, I look for them to take the lead in what's done. So stay alert."

The old man had worked for the sheriff's department of Grace County for almost thirty years, and though he was getting up there in age, he was smart and knowledgeable. Still, hopefully they'd run up on that Cherokee before long. Something must've happened to him and Jessie. Nick hoped to God those loony tunes hadn't caught the two of them.

The damn phone. He wasn't used to carrying one and he'd forgotten he had it. He pulled it out. There were two messages. He climbed in the Jeep and stared at the screen. Looking back at him was Trey Ledger's battered face. With a finger he moved past his photos at Mac's to the image of several RVs. In the corner the words Bailey Creek. The GPS location of the caravan the previous night.

"Well, hell. That didn't help much," he told the phone. Bailey Creek ran alongside Hooper Valley south for several miles, then crossed over to hug the mountains on the other side. Best guess would be where the creek cut across the valley. An old road forded the rushing water over some flat slabs of rock. They'd probably cross there if they didn't want those hulking vehicles lying on their sides in water. But he wouldn't count on it. Better to watch for signs from Dal Starr that he was still on the right trail.

Dal pulled Jessie to her feet before sunrise. Something had woken him and he snuck close enough to see the caravan moving out. Leaving the old road. One by one each vehicle made to cross the creek, but instead stayed in the rocky bed and headed upstream around the curve and out of sight in the protection of the woods.

Where in God's name were they going?

Huddled under low hanging branches where he'd already marked the movement for Nick, he waited till the last RV waddled and rattled into the creek and out to disappear in the thick growth of sycamore, oak, cedar, and shaggy bark hickory hanging solid over the water.

"Where are they going?" Jessie halted against him.

"Leaving the road. Maybe they're trying to shake any trail by following the water. I don't know. But let's wait a while before heading in there."

In a few minutes they waded across the chattering stream, shoes slipping on the slick rocks, and made their way along the rocky bank, sticking close to the wandering creek bed. Once in a while Dal left a broken tree limb as deeper and deeper into the wilderness they went. Soon trees so large they had to be virgin timber surrounded the creek. Doubtful many men had ever walked in here. It was like another world. No beer cans or plastic bags, nothing to leave the mark of man.

He stuck out his arm to stop Jessie. "Look, there." He pointed at an enormous bird perched in an ancient oak. Whispered close to her ear. "It's a *campephilus*, a genus of woodpecker sometimes called the ivory-billed woodpecker. I'll be damned. It's true then, they are on the comeback."

"It's so big." She framed the bird in her iPad and snapped several shots. "Isn't it beautiful?"

The huge black and white bird tilted its head as if listening to their conversation, then took flight, turning onto one wing to sail between two enormous trees and up toward the blue sky. It was like being in some prehistoric movie.

Some more shots of the bird, though iPad cameras didn't capture good action photos. Her eyes teared at the beauty and gracefulness.

"There were some wood hens nested down below the cabin one year, and I thought they were huge. Pileated woodpeckers, someone told me they were called. But that one."

"He's the largest of the woodpeckers. Too much logging of virgin forests drove them out back in the late eighteen hundreds, then one was spotted in two thousand five in southeastern Arkansas. But none have ever been seen this far north. Till now."

She tilted a look up at him. "Well, I'm not surprised. I don't think a human has been in these parts, not for a good long while."

"No doubt you're right. Not even a Coke tab or beer can to be seen. And surely no Walmart tumbleweeds."

They both chuckled at the idea of plastic bags in the wilderness.

He led the way for a while, enamored of the rare bird.

She caught up with him. "Where are these people taking us?"

"Beats the hell out of me."

Up ahead the last of the RVs left the creek where it swung out into the open to cross Hooper Valley. The caravan headed once more into the wilderness, shoving aside saplings and low hanging branches. They were going toward a distant towering bluff. He left several broken branches then led her deeper into the thick growth of virgin forest. Nick would have no trouble after they left the creek bed, but he wanted to make sure to mark the exit well.

The sun climbed the sky, sometimes barely visible through the thick canopy under which they walked. They scared up deer herds, a twelve-point buck with his family of does and yearlings. Startled a flock of turkeys. She laughed when he told her they were called a rafter not a flock. A small red fox skittered into the underbrush. And so she took more pictures.

"No one really knows why, except that wild turkeys were discovered long after other birds like geese and ducks, so they ran out of terms."

"You're just a barrel of information, aren't you?"

"Very good, you just applied a new term to accumulation." He held back a branch that threatened to slap her in the face.

Nervous about being seen or heard, he left plenty of room between them and the RVs. Their trail was easy to follow, though it wasn't clear where they were headed. Worse, where were the deputies?

A sudden outburst of men shouting and children crying drew him up short. He left Jessie, told her to wait, and crept toward the noise. The entire caravan had stopped in a small pasture, drawn together till they resembled a trailer park. A crowded one. Men and women he'd never seen before emerged and wandered about.

Where were the kids? Good God. They were on the steep incline where two men worked tying them together by the wrists. There were at least a couple dozen. Boys and girls, looked to be mostly ten to twelve, trudged along between two armed men. He spotted Lily, but where was the little one? The one shown in one of the photos Trey sent.

And where was Trey?

A familiar figure strode into view and Dal put his hand on the pistol holstered on his thigh. Robert Kimble, ex sheriff, in all his glory, walked among the crowd.

How many of those bastards could he shoot before they shot him? Or some of the kids. He let his hand drop away from the butt of the gun. What were they going to do with them up there? And where was the cavalry?

Some of the kids were crying, but all were obeying, stumbling along, some holding on to each other. One man walked on each side of them and another brought up the rear, all carrying guns. In front of them the mountain rose and halfway up stood a rock wall. Above that a bluff sheltered what appeared to be a cave. From one side water cascaded, splashed its way down to a pond. A rainbow arced through the mist. They appeared to be taking them up to that cave. What in hell for?

Dear God, it was like a poor man's Shangri La. But for the life of him he couldn't figure out what these loony tunes were up to. And he couldn't do much about whatever it was. He needed backup. Where in hell were Nick and the deputies?

He returned to where he'd left Jessie but it took a while cause he didn't want to be spotted or heard. She was gone. Probably in the woods peeing. Turning circles, his heartbeat crawled up his throat.

Don't panic.

Not yet.

Frantic, he searched the ground around where he'd left her. Nothing unusual. Her footprints went off toward an undergrowth and he trailed her. They disappeared, almost as if she'd flown away. Leaves looked as if they'd been scattered around. He circled the area. No more footprints just a random mixing of leaves.

He would kill every last one of them if they touched her, hurt her in any way.

A noise off in the distance, so brief he almost didn't catch it. An engine that sounded more like a chain saw. Maybe someone was out there cutting down trees, but he didn't think so. There then gone, replaced by words echoing in his mind, bits and pieces of military jargon. The cavalry had arrived. Now if they just didn't shoot those kids in their enthusiasm.

And Jessie.

Goddammit Jessie, where *are* you?

Nick and the four deputies darted behind one large tree trunk after another to cover their advance upon the caravan. The four feds fanned out wide on either side, using hand signals to approach their quarry while the responders held back to catch anyone running away.

"Let's not have another Waco," one reminded the others before they left Nick and the deputies.

Good God. Nick gripped his revolver in one hand, the rifle still strapped over his shoulder. The plan. To get as close as possible without being spotted or heard, move apart to encircle the camp. Disarm them without firing a shot. Something rustled near his position. He used the tree for protection, couldn't see anything through the binocs. A hand on his arm and the big Cherokee stepped out. He couldn't help taking a deep sigh of relief, then Nick gave him a thumbs up.

Dal returned the gesture. "Thought you guys would never get here. Have you seen Jessie anywhere?"

"No, what happened? Sorry we were delayed. What's going on?"

"I think we need to speed things up. They're fixing to take a bunch of kids up there." He pointed at the bluff visible between two huge pine trees. Shoulders hunched, he turned to Nick. "And I can't find Jessie. She was here one minute, gone the next. All I did was turn my back for a second."

This was what happened when people in love walked into danger together. Focus left the target. It wasn't a good idea. "Listen, Buddy. We'll find Jessie. You know her. She's probably hid out somewhere furiously writing a story. Coming apart isn't an option. What about the kids? Why are they taking them up there?"

"I didn't get close enough to find out. I heard you guys roll up and that's when they left with the kids."

"You heard us? Damn, and I was real careful, too. You must have special hearing."

"You could say that. Old Injun trick." Dal chuckled. "Can we get them down off that mountain?"

"Looks like we have to. Be damned if I'll stand around while they drag them up it."

"Where are the feds?"

"Surrounding the enemy, organizing for a blitz attack. They think they can rescue the kids and round everyone else up, all in one fell swoop."

"Hell, maybe they could, except for one thing." He pointed between the pine trees at the long line of kids climbing toward the bluff.

Nick shuddered. Above the kids loomed a sheer rock face, perhaps forty or fifty feet high. Best deal would be to stop them before they dragged those kids up it. Once they managed to get them up there, which looked like was their intent, how could he possibly get them back down? And why were they taking them up there in the first place?

Four men, twenty or so kids, roped together. A sheer rock face, and all he had were a half dozen carabiners. The rest of his climbing equipment he'd left back where he and Dal descended into the valley. Could he and several inexperienced men bring those kids back down here without anyone getting hurt?

"Dal, how many men are left on the ground with the RVs?"

"No way to tell. They've never all shown themselves, but I'd say near a dozen or more. They always had plenty of guards during the night."

"Okay, look. What we're gonna need to do is disarm everyone down here while those folks are still up on the mountain. Are the women—?"

Dal's pointing interrupted him. The women, dressed in purple robes, were arranging chairs in an open spot near the parked RVs. A man carried something that resembled a podium and placed it up front of the rows of chairs. The flag with a rising moon covered the front.

"What the hell?"

"I think we're fixing to have a sermon of some sort. Best if we wait till they're all involved in that before we rush them. How do you get in touch with your super cops?"

Gunfire broke out on the opposite side of the arena. "Gotta be the feds. Our men were told to close in, no shots fired."

Nick crouched, led the way toward the shots with Dal on his heels. Sam burst from hiding to join them as did Colby.

"They've stopped shooting. Let's go round up these fuckheads." Nick grinned and signaled to advance.

All around the cluster of RVs men emerged, darting between trees, rifles and guns pointed. Nick using hand signals to keep them moving, closing in.

Dal carried the semi-auto pistol, Nick opted for the Enfield, while Colby and Sam had chosen rifles. Who they would shoot at was anyone's guess. Nick led them like a platoon of marines, yet not a shot was fired.

"Jessie is out there somewhere. At this point I'm almost hoping they did get her. At least she'll be safe inside, maybe with Trey. Has anyone seen him?" No one had seen the marshal. All they knew was he had been alive enough to take a selfie the day before.

A few more shots from the feds and the women who had paid little attention to the first ones ran to the largest RV and clambered inside. That left the men. Four had gone up the mountain with the kids, and the remaining eight or nine took scattered shots at the deputies and feds from behind various trailers and RVs. The four camouflaged feds poured into the encampment firing semi-automatic rifles in short bursts that appeared to be warning shots, for they hit nothing.

Outgunned and outmanned, it didn't take long for the men from the cult to give up. Two loonies fired back and were taken down, but rolling around and definitely alive. Six more threw their guns down and raised their hands. Mike, one of the EMTs, came out of the woods shoving along a stray who had obviously tried to run away.

Subdued, the men gathered to grumble. Nick, who had led the assault, moved around shaking hands with each of the men under his temporary command. He was damned proud of the way they'd handled themselves and told them so.

He eyed Dal, motioned him to follow, and led him to the RV where the women had hidden. Having seen his share of women gun toters, he stood to the side and yanked open the door. Dal jumped inside, yelled "Clear," and drove seven frightened women into the open.

Nick didn't go easy on them, shoving them to where they had put out chairs earlier. "Sit. Now. Where's your leader?"

The women stared at each other. They all wore long dresses of a deep purple and their hair was pinned in a loose bun at the back of their necks. He didn't like scaring them. They reminded him of the women who'd attended his grandmother's church when he was a kid. She took him once, and when everyone began to fall on the floor and gabble like they were crazy it'd scared the bejesus out of him.

"Deacon. Where is he?" Nick tried a harsh glare on each of the frightened women, but they just shook their heads as if they didn't understand him.

Shit.

They weren't going to give the bastard up. The feds handcuffed the men and sat them on the ground a good distance from the women. All of them appeared irritated, but remained quiet.

All in all, considering what he expected, it went pretty well. Except for Trey and Jessie still missing and the kids crawling up that rock wall, from here looking like ants. What the hell was that all about?

The women would know. Whether they'd talk or not was something else. But he intended to get to the bottom of this before going up there to bring those kids down off that bluff.

Headed his way was a very agitated Cherokee. "I still can't find Jessie or Trey anywhere. I'm going to look for them since you've got things well in hand here. She was so worried about him she may have gone in and grabbed him out of danger when the firing started. It'd be just like her."

"Take some of the guys and search for them. I have to see what's going on with the kids and that fucking rock."

Dal nodded and trotted off to round up a couple of deputies.

Nick raised the binoculars and studied the kids on the bluff. "What the hell? Colby, would you take a look at this? Tell me what you see."

Colby put the glasses to his eyes. "What the fuck? They're climbing a rope ladder. A damned ladder fastened at the top. What in hell is going on? Who hangs a ladder on a cliff and puts a bunch of kids on it? And why?"

Nick shrugged. "I reckon it's time we found out. Who's with me?"

14

CHAPTER

When sporadic gunfire broke out Jessie skinned around the corner of the red and white RV where she'd hidden for some time. The occasional shots were concentrated more on the other side of the encampment. A couple of men hanging around near the rattletrap RV took off. One quick look and she opened the door and slipped in, pulling it closed behind her. Trey had been in here when she made her escape. He was tied up, injured and unarmed. It was time someone got him out. Dal would no doubt be pissed at her for taking off without saying anything but she couldn't help it. He'd just have to get over it. Those feds were supposed to be here to rescue Trey. Instead they were out there pounding their chests and taking pot shots at nothing.

From what she'd seen of the men and women in this so-called cult, it wasn't in them to do any serious shooting. A couple of the guys who carried rifles over their shoulders looked like real hard cases, but the rest were just ordinary looking men. What they intended for the kids she still didn't know, but right now freeing Trey was her goal.

The inside smelled bad, was dark and quiet. Her heart hammered and she crept through the mess of bedding toward the wall she'd kicked earlier.

"Trey? You in here?"

A muffled sound. A duct-tape-over-the-mouth reply.

She leaned down to peer through the busted door. There he was, trussed up, no doubt thirsty and badly in need of a bathroom break and first aid. Thank goodness he was alive. An unopened bottle of water sat on the countertop and she grabbed it. He lay on his side on a mattress in the light coming through the window, mouth, wrists, and ankles taped.

Kneeling, she removed the tape from his mouth and opened the bottle. One hand raising his head, she let him drink a few sips before pulling it away. His eyes were bloodshot, the pupils normal. The tape peeled easily off his wrists and ankles.

"Hey, hi. Thanks for stopping by." He rubbed his skin where the tape had been.

"Can you sit up?"

"Yeah. Head hurts, otherwise I'm alive. More water, please."

He gulped down half the bottle and she pulled it away. "Not too much now."

"Where is everyone, or are you the cavalry?"

"Everyone is conquered and they're watching kids climb a rock and trying to decide why they're doing it and what to do about getting them down. A bunch of idiots."

He chuckled, then groaned.

"You hurt anywhere besides your head?"

"My ribs are sore, but I'm fine. Don't forget your camera. I was afraid it was broken when they threw it down, but it had ended nested in a pile of blankets. I guess they never saw it."

"That's a darn good thing. I sure couldn't afford to replace it." Strapping the camera strap across her chest, she took his arm and pulled him to his feet, providing a shoulder when he staggered.

"What do you say we go out there and join the fun? We might get a pool up on the reason for the rock climb and who's going to bring them back down and how."

She supported him through the litter. Outside the door he took a deep breath. "Oh, man, that smells good. Things were getting pretty ripe in there."

Better not to mention how smelly he was. He'd probably have to ride back with Sam on the four-wheeler before he could get a shower and proper medical care. Some of these fancier campers came equipped with showers if only they had a full water tank, but he'd probably want to wait till he got back to Cedarton.

The deputies, eight feds, five first responders, seven trussed-up men, and a bunch of women in purple dresses were gathered out in the open, all staring across the way at the rock climb as if it were entertainment. Looked like all but a couple of kids had made it to the cave entrance at the top. She and Trey stood there for a while without anyone noticing them. It looked as if everyone had survived the shoot-out.

Then she tugged on Dal's arm. "Figure out how to rescue them yet?"

He whirled, his features going from happy surprise to anger. "Where the hell have you been? I was so worried about you I almost sent a search party out."

Looking all around, she laughed. "Yeah, I see that. I was completing our objective while you guys played heroes. In case you don't recognize him, this is Trey Ledger, US Marshal Trey Ledger. The guy who was kidnapped. The guy everyone is here to rescue."

Dal glowered. The rest of the men turned in her direction.

"He's a bit the worse for wear, but I believe he's okay. I see you captured our kidnappers. Congratulations. They look like a frickin rowdy bunch. Anyone tell you what is up with those kids?"

"Not yet." Nick was the first to answer, but the rest shook their heads.

She gave them a fierce look, then supported Trey toward the gathering of chairs. "Come on, you need to sit down."

A couple of the marshals followed, finally taking some notice of their rescued colleague.

Two women sat in the front row, as if expecting at any moment for someone to walk out and start preaching. She put Trey next to them, sat on the opposite side.

Watched the show up on the mountain for a while. The last kid stepped onto the rock off the ladder and all disappeared into the black mouth of the cave. The two marshals sitting near Trey rose to their feet and joined the staring crowd.

She turned to the woman next to her who had eyes that bugged like a frog. "Where are they going?"

Frog Eyes clamped her lips shut.

"Aren't you afraid they'll fall? They're awfully little to be climbing around like that."

That remark earned her a glower from Frog Eyes, who couldn't be much older than her.

"Any of them yours?"

A shake of the head.

"Well, all the same, I wouldn't want to put kids in such danger."

"They're in no danger. The angels protect them. They will be cleansed before being sent to the joining."

"Uh, cleansed how? Given a bath? Joined to what?"

With another of those dark looks, the woman turned away to go back to staring at what was now an empty black hole.

"If this is such an important ceremony, why aren't you all up there with them?"

The other woman, maybe eighteen or nineteen, spat. "You would *not* understand. This is a secret rite, bringing us all together. It is only witnessed by our most revered—"

Frog Eyes stomped a foot. "Be quiet. We do not speak of secrets to outsiders." If looks could kill....

The spitter blushed and returned the look. Any minute there might be a cat fight.

Jessie touched Spitter's arm and smiled at her. She'd get something out of her before this was over, she was certain. Trey slumped against her, dragging her attention away from the two goofy women. The marshal wasn't doing well at all.

She gestured to Nick. Dal had refused to look at her since she'd shown up. Maybe she was supposed to have hung onto his arm whining and screaming help during the fray. Well, he could get bent.

Nick trotted to her side. "He okay?"

"Not really. Someone needs to get him out of here. He's not doing well and could use a doctor. How far are the vehicles from here?"

"Maybe half a mile or so. Those marshals are just wandering around. They can take him out and let us finish this up, since it's more a deputy's business than anything now he's safe."

He trotted off, and soon had the marshals gathered around him, arguing and gesturing. Finally the same two from earlier came and fetched Trey. Without even saying boo to her, they took his arms, and one on either side of him, disappeared through the trees. The other four resumed guarding the vicious kidnappers who sat around enamored of the black cave like they saw something going on up there no one else could. Surely they were going to arrest the whole bunch of them.

Determined to get more information out of the women, Jessie went back to the young one and offered her a nature bar.

Dal would say something to Jessie, but her disappearing act had frightened him so much he was afraid what it might be. Just as he decided that he wanted back in her life she pulled a stunt like that. One of the reasons he'd left was because of the possibility he had grown to care for her too much.

Fuck em, play with em, but don't love em. That had been his motto since he recovered from the gunshots that had nearly taken his life in Dallas. Then he arrived here and along came Jessie. And it's like he couldn't be in the same room with her without wanting to fuck her.

Well, fuck her.

He chuckled bitterly.

Nick approached and Dal let go thoughts about his love life—or lack thereof. Time to focus.

"I need someone to go with me up on that rock and get those kids down here."

Dal laughed. "You really think I'm the one for that?"

"I know you are. Fear motivates you and makes you so damned angry you vow to do whatever it is that scares you."

Nick's remark dug deep. "What are you? My shrink?"

But Nick was right. Pretty clever too, seeing through him like that. One might think he could read minds which was funny if you really thought about it.

"So you'll go up there with me?"

"Sure, why not? I'm curious what's going on in that cave." He had some notion, from thoughts that touched his mind when he studied the women in purple. Made him believe he wasn't going to like it. Something about cleansing those kids and getting them ready for an important event called the joining. Too many minds chattering at once to make much more out of it than that.

"Good. What do you know about Colby? I figure it'll take at least three of us to handle this and Sam's too old to go clambering around on a rope ladder."

Dal grinned. "Well, Colby *is* a jarhead, if that tells you anything."

"Enough said. Let's go talk to him. Need you along. I don't think he cottons too well to talking to strangers."

With a nod, he followed Nick to where Colby stood talking to Duggan, the youngest of the deputies. He hadn't been in the field too often. Mac had started him on night shift on the desk and phones. Probably a good call to leave him down here with the others. More and more Dal was impressed with Nick's common sense and ability to perform under pressure. What was a man like him doing living in the backwoods?

While they spoke to Colby about the job at hand, he sensed Jessie watching him. She resented that he was ignoring her. That much was clear from what little he allowed to filter in. He shut down the part of his brain that picked up on shit like that. Wished he could carve that ability right out of himself. Grandfather chuckled and he glanced toward the sound to see Lone Bear Stands studying him from the nearby woods.

Why the old man couldn't just leave him be was beyond him. Grandfather was dead—had been for over a dozen years now, yet his spirit seemed attached permanently to Dal's. He just wouldn't journey on to the land in the sky.

Ah, well. Just another cross to bear. He did love the old fart.

"You about ready to go?"

"Huh?" He met Nick's gaze. He'd missed something. "Oh, yeah. Sorry. You got a plan?"

"Sort of like I said. We'll climb up there and see what the hell is going on. Find out from the kids how they came to be with this motley crew, then go from there. Just hope they don't fight us. From the way I figure it, they'll be glad to be rescued. You with us?"

"Sure. Sounds like a good idea. Playing stuff by ear usually works out best anyway."

Colby laughed. "Especially when you don't have the slightest notion what's going on. What about this Deacon guy? No one will say where or who he is."

"Well, only one person I know of is missing, and that's Sheriff Kimble, who was spotted riding with this bunch back a ways. I saw him when they first circled up here. I'd bet he's this Deacon."

"We get back to Cedarton, maybe the sheriff will put out a BOLO on him."

Dal chuckled. "I wouldn't count on it."

Nick gave him a curious look, but before he could say anything, Jessie approached. "Could I talk to you guys a minute?"

Dal stared at the ground. That traitor Nick smiled at her. "Sure, what you need?"

"You going up there?" She brushed a strand of hair from her eyes.

"Thought we would. Sure. Why?"

"I'd like to go with you."

"No." Dal glanced at Nick and shook his head.

She sent him a look that would've singed bristles off a hog.

He ignored her.

Nick dug in his backpack for the carabiners. "You ever do any climbing, Jessie?"

Dal's stare turned stony.

Ignoring him, she nodded. "A little. When my cousins were teenagers they talked me into spending the summer learning to climb. I enjoyed it, but haven't done it in a lot of years."

"Why do you want to go?" He clipped the biners to his belt loop.

This yard bird was actually going to let her do this. A trickle of sweat ran down Dal's back. He thought about saying something, but Jessie replied to Nick's question before he could.

"I have a feeling what's going on will tell us a lot about why they've taken these kids. And I have a story to write."

"And that's what's important. Your story."

Jessie opened her mouth to reply to Dal's remark.

Nick swung an arm toward the rock face. "Can you see that ladder hanging there? Here, look through these." He handed her the binocs.

"You're surely not considering letting her go, are you?"

She turned her back on Dal, peered through the glasses. "Okay, so?"

"We'll be climbing that rope ladder with nothing hooked to us. I don't have any line with me. Someone freezes we could all be in trouble. I can fasten the ladder to the rock with these." He fingered the biners hanging on his belt. "Keep it steadier."

Dal peered at the sky. Tried not to think about taking a header off that mountain last year. Were the both of them crazy? What if she fell? He couldn't let this happen.

Jessie's voice interrupted his thoughts. "I've never had any trouble with heights. I enjoyed that summer with my cousins."

"Did anyone ever fall?"

"Nope."

"You're an adult and I'm not your trainer. You think you can handle it, I see no reason why you can't go along. It might help to have a woman with us anyway. Those kids could be afraid of three men."

"Jesus," Dal said under his breath. "All for a damned story."

She pivoted on one foot, glared at him. "That's what's really galling you, isn't it?"

Nick straightened his shoulders. "You two need to take this somewhere else. I'd rather neither one of you go as to have you at each other's throats. I don't know what the problem is, and I don't really give a damn. But I'm not climbing with two people who can't put their personal problems aside."

The man was right, but damn Dal hated to apologize. Made him feel like a fool. Still, it was that or back off completely and he had to see this to the end. "Look, I'm sorry. I apologize to both of you. Guess it's just been a bad day."

Nick looked at Jessie. "You okay with that?"

"Sure, no problem here. I've got a job and I want to thank you for allowing me to go along. You won't have any trouble from me."

Dal pretty much felt stupid. They'd both acted like teenagers having a squabble. But damn it, she'd do anything for a story and that's what really upset him. He'd had it long ago with reporters and the lengths they'd go to, especially downright lying. But he needed to distance himself from her and the way they felt about each other till this was over. They'd sort it all out once they were down off that mountain. They had to get down in one piece. Nick was right. This was something that needed total concentration or someone could get hurt.

Meanwhile Nick had fetched Colby. "Could you go through those campers over there and see if you can find any rope? I'll check these. It would help a lot if we could tie those kids off before we start down with them. We need enough rope to tie them off up top for some control if one or more should fall. I'd rather not risk getting them down here like they took them up."

Dal rose. "I'll see if there's any in those right there." He indicated a couple of nearby RVs.

"Thanks."

Jessica went back to where the young woman sat. "If there's anything you'd like to tell me that would help us deal with those kids, now's the time to do it."

"You can't do anything for them, no use in you trying. It's too late."

Dal glanced back at the two of them. No use in trying, huh? Too late? Good God, what if they were going to drink the Kool Aid? What in the world could they be up to in that cave with those kids? He feared abuse of some sort, but it didn't quite fit with what the woman said. Besides these women didn't seem the type to allow that.

He opened the door of the nearest camper and stepped inside. They'd know soon enough. He sure didn't relish going up there, but it would be good for him to face the fear he'd developed and get it the hell out of the way. As long as he didn't cause a delay.

The men returned with a few coils of rope. Looked more like clothesline than rope, but Nick said it would do. He, Colby, and Dal each looped a coil of line over their heads and across their bodies before starting up. Because Jessie had her camera, he didn't give her any.

She tagged along behind the three men. One of the women yelled something that sounded like help them, but she couldn't be sure. The uphill climb winded her and she swallowed half a bottle of water. At the bottom of the sheer rock face, Nick turned toward them.

"It's easiest to rely more on your feet and legs than your arms and hands. Set each foot on the wooden rung, find a place to brace your toe firmly against the rock, and use the muscles in your leg to raise your body. Once you're set take the step. Don't try to move your foot around and don't try to pull yourself up with your arms. Just hang on to the ladder rope and stand using your leg muscles. Slow and steady and try to keep moving without looking down or up. I'm going first to stabilize the ladder where I can. If you get in trouble I can come back down and get you."

A collective sigh went through the group and Jessica added hers.

Nick chuckled. "Try not to get in trouble. Looking at this ladder, I'd suggest only two of us on it at once. Colby why don't you bring up the rear? Let Jessie follow me, then Dal, then you.

"And before someone asks, I have no frickin idea how we're going to get them down. We'll figure that out when the time comes."

Dal touched Nick's arm. "Two men went up with these kids and they had rifles on their backs. I'd hate to think there'd be any shooting. If we don't take guns maybe they'll refrain. I don't think they're too keen to shoot one of us anyway. I wouldn't be surprised if those kids are used to making the climb. Kids can sometimes be like little monkeys. If they've been going up they've been coming down."

"Yeah, you're right. And these people haven't shot at us yet. I'm not saying they won't, but let's presume they're not killers."

Colby laughed heartily. "If it'll make you feel better."

Men, being like they were, could joke around when they were frightened or nervous. Jessie's stomach turned over looking straight up the rock face. Why in God's name had she asked to go along on this? Dal was right. She'd do anything for a story, even risk her life. At least she wasn't risking anyone else's this time. Well, she hoped not anyway.

"Remember, find a good toehold even though the ladder has wood rungs. It'll help you make the climb easier. And the ladder will be more stable." Nick announced this after he'd taken four steps that looked so simple and easy she even relaxed a bit. "Let me get about halfway up before you start, Jessie. I'll be finding places for these, so don't get in a hurry. If you change your mind, kindly do it while you're still on the ground."

Don't get in a hurry? She snickered.

He appeared to walk up the face of the rock, only pausing long enough to hook the ladder to the rock with a carabiner here and there.

Hands trembling, she tried out the first step, sticking the toe of her Keds firmly into an indentation and rising, the next place a small hole just big enough for her toe, then tense leg muscles and stand. It wasn't as easy as Nick made it look, but not as difficult as she'd expected. Hold on to the ladder, don't pull with your arms but step up. Doing just fine. For a while. Froze.

For some reason she could not make the next step. Saw herself sailing through the air backward.

Took a deep breath. Use the muscles of the legs. One step at a time. And it began to work for her.

Don't look down, don't look up, don't look down. The wooden

crosspieces and the 'biners kept the dangling ladder steady. Not what she'd expected at all.

Surely she was almost to the top. She steadied herself and glanced up. Froze.

Oh God, no.

No, find the next jag in the rock put there especially for her toe. Taking two deep breaths.

Up top, Nick's gentle persuasion guiding her upward. Interesting pattern in the rock in front of her nose.

Move, move on up to the top.

Terror faded when Nick took her hand and she stepped onto the flat surface, but her knees continued to tremble for several minutes. Don't even think about going back down. Push it to the back of your mind.

"You did good, Jessie. Just fine. I'm going to go talk Dal up. I understand he's dealing with some issues after his accident last year but I'm sure he's tougher than he thinks he is. You stay here. Okay?"

She nodded. Only a man would refer to fear as an issue. No way did she want to watch Dal come up the ladder. If he fell she would come totally apart. And she sure didn't want to see it happen.

Grandfather hung back in the shadows, a solemn expression on his face. The contentious old fart. If he ever wanted to help Dal get through something, now was the time. Knowing him, he'd sit back and enjoy the show and not offer one iota of support.

You can do this without my help, Grandson. You are strong. Stubborn but strong. So just go up the ladder and don't think about it.

Good thing he wore his walking shoes rather than the moccasins he'd grown used to back in Frog Pond. Heart in his mouth he waited until Jessie was halfway up, then planted his right toe in the same indentation she'd used. On the next one, he couldn't find a toehold and hung there for a long while poking around with his toe, getting more and more nervous. Maybe he'd used the wrong foot. What if there wasn't a place to step?

Stop thinking it to death. The ladder rung was there, use it.

"Move on, Dal. Take that second step, sir." Colby, with his marine voice, that positive a-man-can-do-anything-if-he-puts-his-mind-to-it tone. Waiting on the ground for Dal to shimmy up like a damned snake climbs a tree. He should've moved to Kansas if he'd wanted to stay on flat land. But he could stay away from the edge of bluffs, and he had. Till now. So here he was climbing a damned rope ladder up fifty feet of sheer rock.

He'd done three steps in the time it took him to think about something else besides climbing this fucking ladder. So maybe that was a good idea. But suppose he let his mind wander and forgot to follow Nick's instructions? Better pay closer attention.

It was amazing how a rock face like this that looked so smooth had so many nooks and crannies to place toes. Almost to the top. He obeyed Nick's command not to look up or down, when he reached for a toehold and there was none to be found.

He rubbed the toe of his shoe around for a spell and panic set in. He actually saw stars and believed he had let go and was falling backwards. All he could think of was the day he rolled head over heels to the bottom of a rock-strewn, tree-covered mountainside and almost killed himself.

He gripped the ladder, taking in air too fast. Hyperventilating. Goddammit, he couldn't wimp out now. He surely only had two or three steps to go.

"Reach over to your right just a hair with that toe. There's a bit of a ledge there. Get a good hold on it, hang on, and come up. Right above you can put your left foot."

Nick's calm voice, speaking slow, was what saved him from freezing right there. The man sounded like it was so simple, and when he calmed his breathing and reached for that ledge it was there and the next one was easy. When he raised up in it his eyes came above the top and he scrambled onto the flat surface.

On his feet, he stared out across the peaks spread to the horizon, then looked down at the small group of people beside their campers. He would have pounded his chest with both fists, but that might be a little much, so he laughed, stepped back, and dropped to sit cross-legged while Colby scaled the rock. Jessie raised her camera and snapped off several pictures of each of the three men.

Damn, she was something. He'd always admired people who loved their jobs, women especially. Why did he not respect her for liking hers? She was good at it. Her stories were right on, without using supposition.

Colby practically skinned up the rock and Nick told him he was a natural. The deputy laughed. "Not any different from climbing a rope hanging from a helicopter."

Nick pounded his back, but they had little time to celebrate before one of the men who'd brought the children up appeared in the yawning mouth of the cave.

"You aren't allowed inside." He sounded authoritative, but left the gun slung over his shoulder.

Colby stepped forward and rested his thumb on his waistband above his badge. "Please move aside sir, or we'll have to arrest you."

"For what?" The guy tried to get in Colby's face, but the former

Marine brooked no nonsense and reached for his handcuffs. "For hindering an investigation. Now unless you want me to cuff you right here you'll lead us to those kids."

The man glared at Colby for a minute, but must not've been willing to take a shot at a deputy, for he didn't even make a move for the rifle. Dal and Jessie trailed the three men into the darkness. The man with the gun had a flashlight and he turned it on. After a few steps, light appeared ahead of them.

The guy stopped. "You'll need to be quiet, please. Cleansing is an important ritual for these children and it would upset them if you disturbed it. Once they're finished then they will be ready to go back down. It really wasn't necessary for you to come up here. We aren't going to hurt them."

"Yeah, right." Jessie snapped more photos.

"Will you please not take pictures?"

Before she could react to that request they broke out into what appeared to be a cathedral. Stalactites and stalagmites streaked in purples and pinks stretched from floor and ceiling around an arc along a pool of water that reflected their majestic beauty. The children, dressed in white robes and wearing full face masks, stood in a circle along its bank holding hands. A man in a white robe and also wearing a mask waited thigh-deep in the crystalline water, his reflection rippling. He appeared not to be aware of their presence.

A group of men and women, all in purple robes with a gold rising moon on the back, sat nearby. Where they came from Dal couldn't figure out. They either went up during the night or there was another way into the cave. They didn't seem to notice Dal's group but gazed mesmerized at the pool.

The rite began with the white-robed man praying over each child, calling on an angel or goddess called Sarpandit the Goddess of Moonrise to enter their bodies to prepare and protect them for what was coming. Once that was finished, he chose one boy and one girl and repeated over them a vow that appeared to be a bonding ceremony of some sort until each couple had been joined in the strange rite. They were then led into the water, separated and their masks removed before a rite that resembled a Christian baptizing.

What was that all about?

During all this the purple-robed people shouted and praised Sarpandit on cue from the white-robed priest, or whatever he was. He looked real familiar, but the backlight cast his face in shadow. The asshole was baptizing these kids after a ceremony that seemed to bond them together in some way. Almost like a marriage ceremony.

"Wait just a minute, sir." That was Nick's voice and Dal stepped forward with Colby to support him. "I think you need to come up here out of the water."

Another man appeared from the shadows and pointed his rifle at Colby, Dal, and Nick. "This is a private religious ceremony. Back off now or I'll shoot."

The man in the water raised a hand. "Hold on, Brother Bracken. No need to get violent. I'm sure there's just been a misunderstanding. We have the right to do this. It's a part of our religion. I know you understand that."

"I sure as hell don't." Dal had let the others handle things long enough. "These kids don't belong to you, so you can't drag them into whatever sick religion you have going. Unless you want to go to prison for a long time, you'll turn them over to us. Right now."

The man in the water took a couple of steps up the sloping floor and looked up at Dal. "You don't know that. And just what is your authority in this matter? You're not even a lawman in this county, Mister Starr."

"Couch?" The stand-in sheriff Arthur Couch? The nut running this freaked out cult? Unbelievable. Him and Kimble together? Funny, Nolton County's sheriff seemed to have vanished.

"That would be Sheriff Couch to you, sir. And I believe I can practice any religion I wish. Now if you would kindly step back while we finish. Our religion allows us to promise these children to Sarpandit the Goddess of Moonrise for their lifetime. They must culminate their joining tonight by the time the moon rises." He pointed toward the opening in the cave. "Yonder in the heavens."

"My God, you're out of your fucking mind," Colby shouted.

They were actually going to force these kids to join their crazy cult? Dal might just start banging heads together. It appeared Colby would gladly join him.

A shot sounded, the noise slamming around through the cavern and Colby dropped to the floor. Nick got to him first, knelt beside him. Dal leaped into the water and grabbed a couple of kids, tucked them under his arms and sloshed out, dropped them on the cave floor and waded back in.

Couch chased after him, waving his arms and yelling at his men. "Don't shoot. You'll hit one of ours. Don't shoot."

He grappled with Dal, who tossed him off as if he were a fly. He landed butt first in the water and splashed about. Before he could stop flopping around Dal gathered up the crying children and deposited them near Jessie, where they huddled together.

"You ignorant son of a bitch. You can't baptize these kids just because you holler freedom of religion. Where'd you get them, anyway? They aren't yours." He laid Couch out with a solid punch to the jaw, then dragged him out of the water so he wouldn't drown, though he considered the idea for a minute or two.

Soaking wet, he went to Colby's side. The former Marine was sitting up holding his shoulder. "It's just a—"

"Flesh wound," Dal finished for him. "You crazy jarhead. Does anyone have any idea who fired the shot? Or what we ought to do about this?"

"Throw him off the bluff." This suggestion came from Nick, who had ripped a piece of material off the tail of his shirt and tied it around Colby's wound.

Dal chuckled. "Well that's a start. How we gonna get these kids down off here with Colby shot and shit-face over there fighting us all the way? If it's unanimous I'll take Nick's suggestion. Be glad to carry it out myself. Solve one problem."

To demonstrate his willingness, he picked Couch up under both arms and dragged him all the way out of the cave and over to the edge of the bluff. Couch bleated like a tethered goat and kicked his heels.

"You'd probably better not," Nick said in his calm tone.

Dal shrugged and dropped the struggling man so close to the drop-off he scrabbled backwards. Someone tugged on Dal's shirt and he looked down into the big brown eyes of a little girl. "Do you know where my daddy is, mister?"

He squatted down and tucked a lock of sandy hair off her face. "We're going to find him, sweetheart. Real soon."

Something flashed and he glanced up. A smiling Jessie with camera in hand. Just doing her job.

Something inside him swelled with pride.

15
CHAPTER

Jessie wandered about taking pictures. Kids played on the bluff like a bunch of little mountain goats. No fear at all. Knelt on one knee to catch a good angle for shots of the children close-up. In the lens a pair of familiar eyes. It was the boy who'd run out of Walmart knocking her down. She'd know those pleading dark eyes and white hair anywhere. He held a smaller girl's hand in his. She wore a pink dress. They looked enough alike to be brother and sister. Of course, he had stolen the little pink dress for her. The camera clicked over and over, catching them in several poses. When she rose the pair disappeared in the crowd.

How would they ever get these kids back where they belonged? It might not be her problem, but worry about it she would. The brutal sun beat down while a few adults struggled to corral the children. The little girl who asked about her daddy wrapped herself around one of Dal's legs, throwing a screaming fit when she was pulled away. He finally picked her up and placed her on his back where Nick tied her securely then fastened a line around Dal's waist.

"Now hang on, *uganasdv ayoli* and don't worry about a thing. We'll have you down before you know it."

A rare shot of Dal with the child, so she snapped several.

He leaned down where Nick worked tying lines for the rest of the girls. "She's pretty upset. Let me get her off this rock now. I'll come back up if you need more help."

"You sure about this, Buddy?"

"Damn right I am."

Nick laughed. "They went and got the big Indian mad, no telling what he'll do." The remark aroused a few chuckles.

"You just think this is all a joke." Couch fumed till his face turned red.

Another terrific picture, this time indignation and humiliation. She kept the camera always at the ready for fear of missing something candid. Like maybe one of the men popping that smartass in the jaw.

The idiot continued his rant like he didn't know what a fool he was making of himself. "I'm gonna see those deputies never work in law enforcement in this county again. Especially that mouthy Injun. You've no right to disturb a religious ceremony."

Ignoring him, Nick rose and secured the line before gripping Dal's shoulder. "Just go easy, don't look down. Same deal with placing your feet."

As if the prick didn't exist or hadn't insulted him, Dal lowered himself carefully with the girl on his back and found a wooden rung with one foot, then another. Nick steadied him till he had a good hold on the ladder, after which he glanced up and sent a parting shot at Couch.

"You're just not very bright are you? I'd be surprised if you even draw a pension once you get out of jail, if you ever do."

Couch made a lunge but Nick tripped him with a neat stab of his foot between the man's legs. "You'd be wise to get your ass on down there.

There's someone waiting to haul you to town and plant you behind bars. And you can take your chances. There's not enough line to tie you off."

Jessie kept the camera busy. Parker wanted people in her photos, she'd give them to him. She was getting more action shots than they'd ever be able to use. Maybe she could do a magazine article once this was all said and done.

"Good move, Nick." Dal's head disappeared below the edge of the flat rock.

Nick finished tying lines around the girls' waists, securing them to himself. The little girl holding her brother's hand refused to let go, so they let him go down with her.

Jessie looped the camera across her chest and prepared to go with them. They were probably less jittery than she was. To kids stuff like this was all a big adventure. Till they got old enough to realize they could be hurt or killed.

"I'll lower you, just go slow and easy. You've all done this before." The little girls nodded yes to Nick and moved to scamper, one after the other, onto the wooden rungs with Nick and Jessie following.

Her nerves jumped around when Nick whispered in her ear. "One of em loses her footing, just hang on tight till I can get down to help you out. They're secured."

Don't look down, don't look up. A mantra she kept repeating, her eyes aimed straight ahead. It took forever to reach the bottom.

When they did she searched for the tow-headed boy and his sister, but couldn't find them. Some of the women of the cult rounded the group up and put them in a trailer. Maybe they thought somehow they could spirit them away, but two of the responders stood nearby keeping an eye on them.

Despite his gunshot wound, Colby went down with the boys and assured them that they would all make good Marines one day. One little boy said he didn't want to be a Marine, he wanted to be Spider-Man. The boys insisted they knew how to descend the ladder and didn't need to be hogtied like the girls.

Her grandfather had once told her that little honyocks had no respect for danger at all. This certainly proved it.

Nick untied himself and scaled back up to the top. She tilted her head till he disappeared out of sight. It wasn't long before he rappelled back down. "Damndest thing. No one is up there. Not Couch or his henchmen nor nary a one of the purple-robed group. Place is empty as a tomb."

"Any idea where they went? I had a feeling all along there was another entrance. Probably leads to that cave Lily told us about." Dal gazed upward as if he might spot someone Nick had missed.

"They vanished the same way they got there. And you're probably right. I'm going to organize a group of volunteers to go up with flashlights and see if we can find an exit in the back of that cavern."

"Couch is gone too?" Jessie could hardly believe this. "Bet he shows up with some cock-and-bull story soon as he gets his lies straight."

"No one has seen Kimble since he was spotted riding with the group early on." Dal stopped looking up at the cave. "So we've got two lawmen missing who probably kept this trafficking moving. But I don't think either of them has enough sense or connections to have organized it. Someone else is responsible for that."

The temperature remained high and only the older boys left to play outside didn't seem to mind. Jessie continued to wander about speaking to those who would talk to her and taking pictures. Some of the women shed their purple robes, piling them high in a chair outside one of the campers, then huddled together crying because the rites had not been completed. Nick appeared to take great satisfaction in announcing that the Department of Human Services in Fayetteville would be notified about the children as soon as they were taken back to town.

"They'll sort this mess all out. If any of them belong to any of you, you'd best be prepared to prove it."

The women could not be consoled. As one they threw their arms above their heads and began to pray to their goddess in loud jumbled words. Surely even they couldn't understand their meaning.

The mysterious crowd from up top, still dressed in their flowing purple robes, emerged out of the woods near the waterfall and joined the shouting crowd. If only someone would take a shot over their heads to shut them up, let peace and quiet reign. But nobody did. They milled around like a bunch of lost sheep. And Jessie only wanted to go home where it was peaceful.

Deep in conversation, Dal and Nick appeared to ignore the noise. She wandered over and eavesdropped without shame when Dal eyed the new arrivals.

"I knew there was an easier way down off that bluff. We need a map, but I'll bet one of the old roads into Hooper Valley goes right by the cave entrance on the far side of that rock up there."

Leaving the two men to discuss the situation, Jessie cornered Spitter, who sat alone glaring at everyone. "Want to talk to me now? Maybe you could tell me just where those kids came from and what the idea was in carrying out that ritual."

The angry young girl tucked her feet up on the edge of the chair. "I ain't gone to talk to anyone. Just go away."

"No one is going away. Don't you realize that you're all going to be the center of attention for a long time when this story breaks? You might as well get used to it."

"People are going to see our pictures and everything?" Her eyes bugged.

Jessie nodded. The girl didn't look so tough anymore. Just scared.

"Why don't you tell me about it? Where do all the kids come from?"

At last frightened into speaking, words poured out of her. "I ain't sure, but I was in a foster home when Reverend Arthur and Bea, that woman over there" —she pointed at one of the wailing ladies— "come and got me. Fostered me, they said. My folks went to jail for selling dope and see, I didn't have no other place to go. A couple of kids were already with them. I remember we stayed in Saint Louis for a while, till there were six of us kids. People from the home kept coming and yelling at them for finding us dirty, so we left in the middle of the night and come here in a camper. There was already some people waiting. They had kids with them too."

What an outrageous way to steal children. Did she dare believe this? Certainly couldn't write about it without proof, but what a story if it were true. Almost twenty kids all obtained by couples posing as foster parents. Was this possible?

The girl stared at the kids squealing and chasing each other around. "I ain't never seen them play like that. They're always kept shut up except when they are taken to town to get stuff."

"About taking stuff from stores. I don't understand why. Looks like they would want you all kept out of sight. Everyone chasing around after you when you shoplifted only made people aware there were kids in town who didn't belong to anyone."

"Oh, Deacon's real mad when we get seen or caught. Sometimes wails us with a belt. We're supposed to find stuff we need like clothes and shoes, and stick em under our clothes. We'd take toys an stuff too, but he'd get real mad about that. He kept sayin it costs too much to keep all of us if we don't steal things. But we're supposed to sneak away and not get seen. He claims it's bad enough they have to buy food for so many hungry mouths. But they don't buy much food. We're always hungry."

Jessie studied the gaunt young woman for a long time. Something was really screwy about this entire thing. Usually a cult like this counted on converting people to their beliefs and conning them into turning over all their assets in order to join. But this. If they were trafficking these stolen children they could at least spend some of the money on food for them.

"Honey, what's your name? And what are you doing here now?" The girl chewed a thumbnail for a while. "If you tell me your side of the story and how you got mixed up in this, things will go easier for you."

The dark eyes snapped. "My name is Rose and you can't put us in jail. Reverend Arthur says so. He says it's our religion. We worship Sarpandit, the goddess of moonrise."

Something was wrong here. "But Rose, I don't understand. Where are the foster children Reverend Arthur and Bea brought here to begin with?"

The girl folded and unfolded the hem of her dress before continuing.

"They took me when I was nine. I was little for my age and so had to wait till the next year for the cleansing and the joining. The older ones went through the rites then they went away one night and I never saw them again. We were hiding out in some caves up in Missouri. But then the law got hot on our trail and so we came down here."

"But you were never sent away. How did that happen?"

"Mama Bea, she threw a hissy fit and begged Father Arthur to let her keep me. Cause I was such a help with housework and caring for the younger ones till they were sent away."

"So you are a member of the cult."

The girl nodded and gnawed her nail some more, rolling her eyes downward and refusing to meet Jessie's gaze. She was not telling everything.

One of the women in purple strode purposefully to where Rose and Jessie sat, grabbed the girl by one arm. "This one you cannot take. She is of age to remain."

Jessie reached out and fisted one hand around the woman's wrist. "Where are all the children taken?"

The woman tightened her lips and jerked out of Jessie's reach. "That you will never know. The goddess protects them from your prying ways."

She dragged Rose off, speaking harshly to her all the way back to where the other women were gathered.

Total and utter nonsense. Somehow the cult masked the real reason for all these children being here. Searching the crowd, she spotted Dal, but rather than going to him, she found a shady spot under a tree, slid down onto her butt, and sorted through the images in her camera. Let him come to her when he was ready.

It wasn't long before he moved away from a cluster of children and came to sit next to her.

She leaned against him. His arm eased around her shoulder. For a while neither spoke. Then he pointed at the camera.

"Did you get any pictures of Lily or Rebecca? I couldn't find them anywhere, but everything's been so crazy."

"No. I didn't see them. You're right, I hadn't even thought of either of them in all this confusion. Where do you suppose they are? You don't think something awful happened to them, do you?"

"I don't know. I've been wondering just what kind of laws are being broken here and what we can prove. Maybe the two of them got away or maybe Rebecca truly did run away and was never here. I thought I saw Lily earlier. Wonder what could've happened to her?" He peered back toward where the other men were gathered.

"I guess what's planned right now is two of the marshals will take the children back to Fayetteville DHS in those two honker SUVs. They'll be checked to see if they're runaways and returned home. If they're foster children, then they'll go back into the system and hopefully find a decent home. I have no idea what will happen with all these people. They've sent for a wagon to haul them all in. Some freaking lawyer or judge may get them all set free. It will take months to clear up. But let the FBI or ICE or whoever's in charge do that. They've got the manpower and the laws." He laid his head on her shoulder. "I feel like I could sleep a hundred years."

That felt so good, his head resting there in such a familiar way. She closed her eyes and enjoyed it for a long moment. "Me too, but I've got a story to write."

"Well, it'll be a while before it plays out enough for a story. Be okay if I crash at your cabin? It's just off up yonder. We could take the Jeep and be there in an hour or so. I think two of the marshals are remaining down here till they can get some backup down from the FBI and ICE. No need in us staying here. I don't know what the US Marshals will do. Ledger and Colby will probably go out with the kids. They both need a hospital."

She glanced at him. "You want to go home with me?"

He grinned. "Well, I could always sleep on the couch. Lord knows I've done it often enough. Then we could get a good start first thing in the morning."

Much as she wanted their relationship to come to something, the two of them had a lot to work out before she was going to fall in bed with him. The thing was, could she stay away from him if he came to the cabin with her? He looked so exhausted. It'd been two or three nights since he'd slept. And like he always said, she couldn't resist a big, strong, handsome man who needed care.

"Okay, but first thing in the morning I have to start putting this together. It'll probably run for weeks before it's all told."

"Do I really have to sleep on the couch?"

"Well, we'll see, won't we?"

He rose, pulled her to her feet, and led her through the throngs milling about, voices raised in arguments. On the way he stopped to tell Nick where they were going. "You've got our cell numbers, but no one may answer. We're both beat."

"Yeah. But not too beat for what you've got in mind, huh?"

Laughter followed them to the Jeep. Sometimes it took laughter to get the bad taste out of your mouth.

Dal held tight to the steering wheel and crabbed the Jeep through the woods to an old logging road. Noise from the encampment faded and stillness embraced them. Only the sound of the engine disturbed the lull of evening birdsong. The forlorn call of a whippoorwill floated in the springtime air. Shadows hung beneath the trees, the sky above gleamed like polished steel. Once on the flat stretch he relaxed a bit. Next to him, Jessie leaned her head back against the seat. A light breeze blew a lock of streaked hair across her face, the skin tanned from the sun. And he wanted her desperately. Yearned to reach out and hold her right there. Odd how making love often helped humans recover from dreadful experiences.

"Oh, God." He groaned and rubbed his face vigorously with the flat of one hand. She peered at him from under her lids. He shrugged and grinned. Grown men should be able to control their passions. But not him, and sure as hell not her. He met her glance with one of his own.

"I know what you're thinking." She looked away.

"That's supposed to be my line. I truly know what you're thinking, but I'm trying to be polite and not listen in."

"You staying?" The question curt.

"Thinking on it. That is if you'll let me."

"You bastard."

He laughed. "I know, darlin' I damn well know it. And you're a bitch, in the kindest sense of the word."

"Well, I guess we are two of a kind then."

A rear wheel climbed over a large rock and bounced them off the seat and back down. "Don't get any ideas, Jess."

"Oh, don't worry, I won't. And don't you either. I need to think on this some more."

"Me too."

For the next few miles both were quiet. The Jeep growled its way from one flat weed-infested road to another, consistently climbing the side of the mountain. He did his best to think of something else to say, worked hard at not touching her thoughts, even briefly. Caught words he couldn't help but hear. Choked them down and got that damn vehicle out to the road to Jessie's without further complaint.

Parked near her cabin, he leaned back and closed his eyes.

She sighed, then her hand moved over his lying on the seat between them and she pulled it up against her chest. "Come on, let's go inside. I'm dry as a bone and so tired. Let's just shower and not spend too much time thinking about anything. We can just do what we feel like doing. No strings. Okay?"

In the shower, they scrubbed in silence, washed each other's backs, and padded into the bedroom. Lingering heat of the day dried their skin and they crawled onto the bed. Flat on their backs, they clasped hands.

Dal stared at the window where fireflies signaled each other in the falling darkness till her breathing gentled, then he closed his eyes and went to sleep.

The moment she stirred the day snapped her awake. Hundreds of things to do and little time to do it. The bed was empty. The scent of coffee filled the room. Low conversation from the kitchen, so he was still there. On the phone or else he'd gone nuts and was talking to himself. After the bathroom and brushing her teeth, she dressed in shorts and a t-shirt with the original Spock on the front. Bare feet squeaked on the polished wooden floors.

He stood at the table pouring her coffee. Barefoot too, in an old pair of shorts from some time in the past when he'd spent the night, and no shirt. Damn, he was one hell of a good looking guy. Especially when he smiled, showing white teeth against bronze skin. Sunlight slanted through the windows, his black hair shimmered.

"Smells good." It seemed only natural to go to him and raise her lips for a kiss. A nice one, warm and soft. "How long you been up?"

"Only long enough to brew this." He held up his cup, half full.

Sugar, creamer, and she took a long sip. "Oh, man. That's as good as it smells."

"Parker called."

"Hmm. Didn't hear the phone ring. What'd he want?"

"Just to make sure we got back okay. Said the long black SUVs parading around the square late last night had everyone at the Red Bird chattering a mile a minute trying to figure out what had gone on. Said 'Good Lord, did we have to arrest half the county?'"

She laughed and crooked a leg under herself before sitting at the table. "I don't know about you but I'm still beat. Did he say if he wanted me to come in today? What day is it, anyway? I lost track."

"Saturday. He did say Brad misses us and we can have him back anytime we get through running all over the country chasing cults down. He said take the weekend off cause Monday is going to be hell. The phone hasn't stopped ringing at the office. Dailies want to know what's going on in Cedarton. He's putting them off till he can get this week's issue out, then they can have at it. Wants to wait till Monday because by then we'll know more about what the law is going to do with everyone, and the paper can go to print on schedule."

Their eyes met across the table. "Maybe I ought to call Mac." She didn't make a move to do so.

"I think that's a good idea. You can tell him all about our buddy Couch. Oh, by the way, they never ran him down. Seems he's disappeared along with Mac's old buddy Kimble."

She raised her brow. "That's interesting."

"I called Tinkerbelle and Burt. Guess it's pretty crowded down at the county jail this morning. She said they borrowed a wagon from the Fayetteville police and hauled every last one of those yahoos in. Don't know what they're gonna do with them. Some are in county over there, the rest in Harrison."

Her phone jangled. The number wasn't immediately familiar, but she picked up anyway. A woman's voice she didn't recognize asked to speak to Jessie West.

"You have her. Who is this?"

"Alicia. Alicia Woodson." She barely spoke above a whisper.

"I'm sorry, who?"

"I'm the attorney. We met. I can't find Jeff."

"Wait. What? Jeff, your husband. Yes, of course. Tell me what happened." Her mind went in circles. Why was the woman calling her?

"This morning when I got up— sometimes I fall asleep before he comes to bed and when I woke up he wasn't here. I mean not here anywhere. And I've looked all the places he sometimes retires to. And when I called nine-one-one no one answered. I didn't know who to call, except I remembered you." The distraught woman finally took a breath.

"Take it easy, Alicia. Dal's here with me. We'll be right there."

She disconnected. "Come on, get dressed. That was Alicia Woodson. Her husband's missing. He's blind and she can't find him. Thinks something happened. I think she must've tried to call nine-one-one when we were all down in the valley. Stupid Couch doesn't know anything about running the department or he quit caring. Anyway, she's terrified. We need to get up there and help her. You might be the only lawman not tied up in that cult mess."

Both in the Jeep, he cut ruts in the yard and headed toward the mountain road to the Hermitage. "Why did she call you?"

"Alicia and I got acquainted. Well you met her when you took Mac there to get her take on him being a witness for Kimble's preliminary hearing. I think she panicked. Who could blame her? He's blind. My God, how terrifying."

On the way up to the Hermitage on the mountain above Cedarton she explained to Dal about the Woodsons and how Jeff had been blinded by an IED in Afghanistan.

"Oh, yeah. I'd forgotten. Nice lady. Wonder why she thinks he's in trouble? Maybe he just went walking or something."

"I don't think he'd do that without telling her. She's scared to death, so there's probably more has gone on up there than she told me over the phone. But we do need to hurry."

A few minutes later he skidded to a stop in the circular driveway in front of the large historical home recently purchased by the attorney and her husband. The guy probably just took off for some peace and quiet. What hell it would be to be blind and not be able to just go for a walk without checking in with someone.

"A veteran? Any chance he's armed out there in the woods somewhere? It happens with these guys."

She jumped out of the Jeep and headed for the house without answering his question. God, the woman was fearless. He caught up with her, took her arm.

"Jessie, slow down. Let's take it easy. We'd better approach with a bit of caution."

Giving him one of her looks, she twisted free, ran up the steps to the verandah porch. "Alicia, it's Jessie West and I've brought help."

Without hesitating, she grabbed the doorknob in the center of a huge door and stopped cold. "It's locked." Finger on the doorbell, she held it down a long time. Still no reply.

The guy could be in there and in real trouble. Dal took out his phone. "Jessie, what's her number?"

"Number? I don't know."

"Course you do, it's in your phone. Settle down, honey. Let me see if she'll answer her phone. Give me the number, or better yet, you call her. She knows your voice."

"Dal, what's this about?"

"If he's reliving something in a flashback he could be armed and holding her, thinking she's the enemy. So we would be the enemy too. We have to be careful."

This time her look was one of embarrassment. "Sorry, I'm not even thinking straight. I keep imagining what she must be going through not knowing where he's at."

While she talked she punched redial from the earlier call, kept her eyes pointed toward Dal, and after a while shook her head. "She's not answering. Should we break in?"

"Not yet. I'm going around back and see if maybe there's a door open. You keep talking to her through the door just in case she's in there listening but afraid to open up."

"Alicia, it's me. Jessie West. You called earlier. I brought a deputy with me. Let us in and we'll see if we can help you find Jeff."

Dal moved around the corner of the large porch that circumvented three-fourths of the house. He stopped to peer in some windows, but could see no one. Where the hell had the woman gotten to? Surely she wouldn't take off on her own after calling Jess.

A gun barrel. Pressed into his back. He froze, turned his hands outward, forced himself to breathe.

"I need some identification."

Oh, shit. He had no badge, no nothing to prove who he was. Well, in truth he did. Cause all he was was a man with a driver's license standing on her porch and her thinking someone had snatched her hubby. For the first time since returning to Cedarton he experienced a nakedness. No way to prove who he was, even to himself. Hell of a note.

Jessie stepped around the corner and halted. "Alicia, that's my friend Dallas, and he's here to help you. Put down the gun, honey. We'll find Jeff." She held out a hand.

His brain screamed at her to stay put, to be careful. The woman's eyes were wild, flashing somewhere between fear and fury. A very dangerous place to be. Especially while holding a semi-automatic. Locked and loaded.

"Sweetie, we're here to help you." With that the crazy-ass woman walked right up to Alicia and laid a hand over the hammer of the weapon. Granted, she did sort of stand to one side, but Dal's heart slammed around in his chest. Afraid to move for fear the woman would react while her finger was on the trigger. She didn't. By then the gun was pointed toward the floor.

Everyone on that porch let out a breath you could've heard off down in the holler. Dal took the gun, jacked out the cartridge, and lowered the hammer. Jessie grasped Alicia's arm and together they went inside through the open double French doors.

By the time Jessie seated Alicia on a leather couch, the woman was sobbing so hard she couldn't speak. A jug of whiskey sat in a tray on a nearby table. Dal tucked the .45 in his belt and poured three healthy slugs into the glasses sitting around the jug.

He took a deep draught of the best damned bourbon he'd tasted in a while. Jessie sipped at hers and Alicia downed two fingers in one long swallow.

Dal perched on the edge of a chair near her, finished off his drink, and studied first one of the women then the other. Jess would give him a heart attack one of these days, the crazy-ass shit she pulled. He couldn't help admiring her guts. Yet she needed some training in self-preservation. Alicia stopped crying, set down her glass and leaned forward, hands clasped together, elbows on her knees.

"I apologize for that." Alicia gestured with an empty hand. "I've been half out of my mind. He knows not to go off without letting me know. It's something we've agreed on since the day he came home from the hospital." Her voice evened out a bit, but still vibrated.

"Why do you think someone took him? Is it possible he fell down somewhere nearby and you just can't find him?" Dal finished off his drink, but kept the glass in his hand, thumb rubbing around the rim of the crystal to make a singing sound.

She shook her head. "No. I've been everywhere in the house, all over the yard, and through the barn." She smiled with a tremor on her lips. "He likes the barn. Says he can shout as loud as he wants to without disturbing the neighbors like when we lived in New York."

Dal studied her for a minute. A damned strong woman, but that's what it took to live with a wounded warrior. "Do you mind if we look around again? Maybe we'll see something to show us what may have happened to him."

"Sure, I guess that would be okay."

Jessie rose and moved to sit beside Alicia. "I'll stay here with her, if that's okay."

Dal nodded. "I need to ask you one more thing and I don't want to upset you. Does he suffer from PTSD, flashbacks, that sort of thing?"

"The blindness. Sometimes if something happens quick like, he panics, doesn't know where he is. Can't get his bearings. The doctors told me that's common with all people who are blind, whether they've fought in a war or suffered some other trauma."

"I'll take a look around here in the house, then. Be back soon as I can."

It probably took him twenty minutes or more to search each of the rooms and closets, nooks and crannies in the large house. Jeff Woodson was nowhere to be found. But in what appeared to be his workshop at the back where large maple trees cooled a glass-enclosed room, he found a heavy duty flashlight under the edge of the drafting table. As if it had been accidentally dropped.

What in the world would a blind man want or need with a flashlight? Thinking it might contain a signal of some sort, perhaps something that sensed objects, he turned it on and played around with it a bit. Spotted the serial number stamped in its familiar color. An issue all too well known to him. It belonged to a county sheriff's deputy.

Goddamn. Well, he knew Couch was in the wind as well as Kimble. It could belong to either of them. But why in hell would either choose to snatch Jeff Woodson? Pocketing it, he continued a search under and behind everything in the room. Near a back door that let out onto a deck, the carpet nap was crushed as if a pair of boots had rested there a while. He stepped outside on the deck that was a few feet off the ground and surrounded with a latticed rail.

No prints on the deck, but it was dry out. He moved slowly around the edge, concentrating on the growth for several feet out. Whoever came in had to leave their mark, since the deck looked out across wildflowers and an uncut clearing into the surrounding trees. Whoever came in that door had to cross somewhere and they'd have left a trail.

Didn't take long to find it.

Trouble was, if they left the way they came there would've had to be more than one to get Jeff over the high rail. There was no sign of that. They'd taken him out a different way.

Through the house and out one of the many doors. He needed help. With Colby laid up with his "flesh wound," that help had to be Nick. With luck he'd be home by now. Butt resting on the rail, he pulled out his phone and punched in the newly added number of the climber. Told him in a few words what was going on, then clicked off and went back inside.

Jessie and Alicia sat on the couch, holding hands, one soothing the other. Both glanced up and hope changed their expressions. Damn, how he hated to have to tell them what he'd found, and what he thought. But there was nothing for it but to get it done. He dug the flashlight from his pocket. Just to be sure.

Alicia took it from his outstretched hand, looked it over. "Nope, not Jeff's. He's got one of those electronic ones that beeps when he gets too close to objects. He'd have no need for this." She looked up at him, knuckles going white around the casing. "Someone did take him, didn't they?"

He dropped on his knees next to her. "Take it easy. There's no blood, not even evidence of a struggle, so he's not hurt."

"But why?" Her eyes filled with tears. "What are they going to do with him? I don't understand."

"That's what you're going to have to tell me. My best guess? Something to do with the case against Sheriff Kimble and Arthur Couch. Or maybe you're involved in investigating something connected. Are you involved with anything at all to do with the charges being brought against either of them?"

"Yes, but— wait a minute. No one knows about any of that. It's all privileged information."

"Maybe so, but the ones being charged may know things and they may have been able to find out, well, things. Mac has hired you. Maybe they think or know he has information that could be detrimental to them. Or perhaps someone else connected to the cult? Think, ma'am."

"But how would they know that? And what good would it do them to take Jeff?" The answer must've occurred to her before she got the question out because she pinched her lips closed with the fingers of one hand and her eyes grew wide.

Dal patted her arm and rose, favoring the bad leg. Damn thing felt like a hot poker was being held under his skin. Didn't take well to all the climbing and racing around the countryside on foot. Still had some more to do, though. A car skidded to a halt out front. And here was his help.

"Dal?" Jess rose and took him over to the windows looking out across the valley. "You think Couch has Jeff, don't you?"

He nodded. "Or Kimble or both. And she probably knows why. Only she's not telling cause it's privileged."

"Is that Nick?"

"Yep. Can you stay here with Alicia? She hadn't ought to be alone. Besides, if she gets a call offering an exchange, you'll need to be here to make sure it's recorded. I know you can do that, can't you?"

She cradled his cheek in one palm. "Of course. But you need to be careful. Please."'

Turning his mouth, he kissed her hand. "You know me."

"Exactly, that's why I asked you to be careful. Don't go doing anything dangerous. Or if you do, please be very careful."

"And the same goes for you. Don't take off on your own for any reason. Stay in touch with me and if someone calls, let us know immediately. You got it?" He gazed into her eyes.

Knuckles rapped on the door and Dal signaled Alicia to remain seated. "This is Nick Snow, and he's going with me. We're going to bring Jeff back. Meanwhile, you might go through your records. You said you have an office here, so do you have everything you've put together on this case?"

"Yes, everything's here."

"And you're not working for anyone else who might have a connection to this mess? Just the one file?"

"You know I can't tell you anything except yes or no. I'm afraid it's yes. But I—"

"Okay, listen to me, both of you. No matter what, do not agree to meet with those people or make a trade. If they contact you, record the conversation. Do not argue with them. Tell them you'll make arrangements to do what they ask. Then call me or one of the deputies. Got that?" He turned to stare hard at Jessie. "Do not leave this house, no matter what they say. I'm going to send a deputy up here soon as I can find someone. He'll make sure you're safe. Promise me, Jessie."

He lifted her chin and doubled the earlier stare. "Say it."

"I promise to stay here."

Not sure if he could trust her, he limped to the doorway and went with Nick across the verandah and to the beat-up Volvo. With a grim smile he rattled the keys to her Jeep in his pocket. She wasn't going anywhere unless she knew how to hotwire the thing, but that was a distinct possibility. Time he gave up thinking he could keep her safe or control her even in a small way.

But one thing was clear. He loved her and he couldn't do a damned thing about that.

16
CHAPTER

"Where do we start?" Nick stopped out of sight of the house. "You think they've hurt the guy?"

"Haven't the slightest idea, but they took him easy without knocking him around. So, knowing his history, they had to put him out quick. Probably chloroform or something similar. I think they want him all in one piece. Alicia probably knows more than she realizes. What she does know frightens these people. But what she can prove is more dangerous."

"You have any idea where to start?"

"Let's go down to the sheriff's office. I want to go through Couch's desk. He may have left information there, since he didn't expect all this to happen so quickly. Or maybe there's a clue as to where he might be hiding out. He managed to disappear awful fast when we closed in. Him and Kimble both."

Nick drove for a while without saying anything. It wasn't until he parked in the empty lot behind the sheriff's office that he broke the silence. "Is this legal?"

"Probably not, but it's a little late to worry about that. I've been posing as an officer of the law for the past few days, so what the hell? You got time to quit." He glanced at Nick, who shook his head. "Okay. Why don't you pull around back so it's not so obvious we're here?"

Nick nodded, and once they were fairly well hidden from the main thoroughfare, Dal led him to the back door.

Locked. Not a bother, though, just one of those door knob locks. He glanced at Nick, held out his hand. "Give me your credit card."

"I don't have a credit card. I thought you knew I live off the grid."

"Well, shit. I don't have one, either. Driver's license ought to work, huh?"

"I'd think so. Just don't break it in two."

While Nick kept watch, Dal slipped the card between the jamb and the door, slid it down carefully, and disengaged the latch. "You'd think they'd keep the sheriff's office more secure. Can't believe nobody's here. If Mac was still in charge there would be."

Nick made a noise deep down in his throat. "Maybe they'll fire Couch after this."

"We can only hope."

The place was dark with no lights on, the heavy growth of trees in the square keeping out the morning sunlight. Couch's office—Mac's actually—was fairly neat, though a scattering of files lay off-center on his desk, one open like he might've been checking on a case when interrupted.

Dal picked up the phone and checked the last few calls, three from the same number. One he wasn't familiar with.

Till now. "Got your phone?"

Nick took one out of his pocket.

"Call this, see who answers." Dal held up the phone while Nick obliged.

Dal scanned a few pages in the open file. A few familiar names. A deposition signed by Alicia Woodson requesting the presence of a list of deputies who served under Mac to act as witnesses.

"What the hell is Couch doing with this? I don't think it's legal for him to have a copy of an attorney's deposition. Look who's signed it."

"That the lady whose husband has been snatched?" He held out the phone. "No answer, just a message that the mailbox is full."

Dal nodded, paged through the file some more. "He's got copies of all sorts of legal papers from her files. How the hell did he get these? And if he already had this file, how come he would need Alicia's cooperation? I don't get it."

"Must be more to it than a file, then. Anything there that might explain them grabbing a blind man? I gotta tell you, that flat pisses me off. Least they could do is pick on someone who can fight back."

"Yeah, well, bad guys seldom play fair. I'm not an attorney, so I don't know the value of all the scraps of paper here. I do know he shouldn't have these." He held up a wad of papers, tried the drawers in the desk, and found nothing of any value. The upper left hand drawer was locked. Must be a good reason for that.

It only took a few seconds and his Barlow pocketknife to break into it. "A half-empty bottle of Dewars. Nothing else. Our sheriff must like an occasional snort."

While Dal went through a small filing cabinet, Nick strolled around the room checking out the photos on the walls, along with awards from several organizations. He stopped at one. "Hey, come take a look at this."

Dal rose with a thick file in his hand and joined Nick. "That's Couch and who are the other two? That's a cabin behind them." All the men held stringers of fish, some quite large.

"There's a sign there in the background. Can you read what it says?"

Nick put his finger on the framed photo. "He needs a place to hide, it might be this isolated cabin."

"Yeah, a fishing resort." It took him a while, but Dal finally made out the letters on the sign. "Blue Springs Lake. Never heard of it."

"I know it. You think it's worth checking out? It's about twenty miles south of Hooper Valley." Nick snapped his fingers. "If the cultists kept going the way they were when we stopped them, they'd be there."

"An ideal spot to hole up. Stay and wait for buyers. A better place to hold a hostage. Call that number again. If someone answers, ask them who they are. If they won't tell you just ask for Arthur. See what happens."

On the other side of the room behind the desk was another picture. The same three men with signatures scrawled under each figure. Arthur Couch, Robert Kimble, and who was that other guy? The signature was unreadable. It was someone he'd seen recently but he couldn't place. Dal took the picture off the wall, removed it from the frame, and slipped it inside the thick folder. He'd figure out who he was. Both photos were taken at the same fishing resort.

This entire case had been masked to look like something it wasn't. Worry about the cult, get everyone so concerned that the trafficking of children wasn't noticed.

But why take Jeff? To blackmail Alicia?

Or maybe Jeff knows something. Something they want kept quiet.

That's the only answer that fits. So Kimble, Couch, and the head honcho are still free. He'd seen that face somewhere before. It'd come back to him.

"So all we have is a file stolen from Alicia Woodson, a kidnapped veteran, and nearly twenty kids we don't know where they came from or worse, where they were destined to go. Oh, and we mustn't forget, a religious cult led by at least two crooked cops and fashioned after a goddess so obscure only a few people ever heard of her."

Nick rested half his butt on the corner of Couch's desk. "But what we really need to concentrate on is where the heck did they take Jeff Woodson and why? Between the FBI, the US Marshals office, Immigration, and who the hell knows who else, we can only hope all the rest will be straightened out."

"Except for the one guy they don't know about. Don't you really want to know what's going on here?" Dal looked at Nick. "I itch to catch up with Couch and Kimble and be the one who locks handcuffs on their wrists. But, hey, I don't have any of those. I don't even have the right to arrest the SOB."

Nick eyed him with a steely glare. "No, but we can find them. Cause I think you and I both know they're the best bet for having snatched Jeff Woodson. Everyone else involved is in custody."

"Not everyone."

"Who's left?"

"I don't know who." Dal held up the file. "But this guy is a good suspect." He sat at the desk, opened the file. "I think what I'm doing is illegal. These folks are trying to turn The Rising Moon into a legal church. Good God, no pun intended. Talk about a way to launder all the money earned from trafficking. I'm taking this back to Alicia so she can clear up some stuff for me. Privileged information be damned. This is what they want before anyone like me gets his hands on it. Did you know you can plant a church? Holy shit." He found a leather binder, slipped the file inside it, and zipped it up.

"Come on, I want to find that fishing resort. Couch and Kimble aren't smart enough to have come up with this all on their own. They may be in charge of the Rising Moon folks, but they didn't organize finding buyers for the kids, then finding the kids and getting them sold and delivered and on their way out of the country. And then organizing a church to hide all the money made from such a hellish scheme. There's not even anyone looking for those poor kids. Those two don't have the brains for all that. This guy, well, he's got big plans for legalizing or covering up the whole thing under the guise of a church. No longer a cult that everyone sneers at. This is fricking unbelievable."

"Well, you said yourself the resort would be a good place to hold a hostage. They were headed in that direction, so it follows that it would also be a good place to hook up with the buyers of those kids. Oh, by the way, no one ever answered the number you gave me."

"I'll call Duggan, have him see if he can put a trace on the calls, then we're going fishing."

Jessie stood at the kitchen window, the aroma of coffee filling the room. She poked around in the unfamiliar cabinets until she found coffee mugs, then located sugar and cream. "What do you take in yours?"

Alicia didn't answer and Jessie turned to see her sitting at the table, crying.

"Oh, honey. They'll find him, I know they will." She handed the woman a napkin and she dried her face.

"I just can't help thinking about Jeff. You'd think he's gone through enough without something like this. We can't even imagine how he's feeling, trapped somewhere with someone who's going to do God only knows what to him. The worst part would be knowing he's helpless to do anything to take care of himself. He can't even see what's coming."

Jessie patted her hand. What else could she do or say? She filled the mugs, took them to the table, then fetched cream and sugar.

"You know, when he first came home I felt so bad for him. He'd always been so active, played on a local ball team, we went to movies at least once a week. He loved mysteries and could always figure them out before the end. One of his favorite evening things was to watch the sun go down. He had hundreds of photos of sunsets and sunrises. Worst thing was, he could no longer do his job. Blind people can't design buildings and so he spent a lot of time after he finished rehab practicing what he learned. He got to where he could get around our part of the city very well, even though it drove me mad to have him go walking alone."

Jessie took a sip of the coffee, watched Alicia through the steam from her mug. "You told me he's an artist. Must have been really difficult for him to take up that. I can't imagine."

Alicia's sad little smile told Jessie how much she loved Jeff. "He's amazing, simply amazing. Considering what happened to him, he's so sweet and thoughtful. But he hates like hell to ask me to help him do anything. I have to be really careful to keep from upsetting him. Oh, God, Jessie, what if they hurt him... or kill him? I can't imagine life without him, but what I really can't imagine is never forgetting what they did to him. What terror he suffered. I already have bad dreams about him being in that dreadful explosion that blinded him."

"Dal and Nick will find him. I know them. They'll never stop till they do. It's in their DNA"

Jessie's phone rang and she snatched it up. "Dal? Where are you?"

"On our way to a fishing resort. Listen, ask Alicia why or how Couch got hold of her file on Mac. What good it would do him, would you?"

"Hang on, I'll put you on speaker." She laid the phone on the table, asked Alicia the question.

Alicia stared open-mouthed at Jessie. "I haven't the slightest idea how he got it. As to why, I suppose some of it could be used to hurt Mac's case, that is if it ever goes to trial. From what I can tell, most of this is trumped up. There's no evidence anywhere that Mac took bribes from anyone."

"Well, we found copies of the file on his desk at the sheriff's station."

Dal related what they'd found and why they were on their way to the Blue Spring fishing resort. It sounded like they really expected to find Couch and Jeff there. She smiled and nodded at Alicia.

"You be careful. And please let us know as soon as you do."

"We will. Did the deputy arrive yet?"

"Haven't seen him. Want me to go look?"

"Nah, just let me know if he doesn't show up soon. And Jessie?"

"Yes?"

"You keep your promise and stay put. Please?"

"I will. Bye."

She disconnected and dialed Tink. She picked up on the second ring. "Hey friend. How are things going with the cult thing?"

"Oh, Lord, girl. What a frickin mess. Let me tell you, don't ever try to spend an hour in a room filled with a dozen agents from the FBI, ICE, DEA, and US Marshals. It would blow your mind. I saw and heard things you wouldn't believe. I think I know the size of every penis in the damned room."

Jessie chuckled. "I hear that. Has anyone heard from Couch?"

A long silence, then, "I guess I don't know. Is he missing?"

"Are none of them aware that he's a part of the cult and disappeared before they gathered them all up?"

"I just figured he was at the station holding down the fort, since all the deputies are involved in handling this mess. He's not here, though, if that's what you need to know."

"Did you not get a call from Dal to send a deputy up to the Hermitage to keep an eye on Alicia till they can find Jeff?"

"What is going on, Jessie? I have no idea what you're talking about. Why are they looking for Jeff? Just what's going on?"

"I think you need to come up here if you can, Tink. We need to talk some more. Sounds like there's a lot going on those boys down there aren't aware of. Where are the kids?"

"They sent all of them to DHS in Fayetteville first thing this morning."

"Are you sure they arrived?"

"Why wouldn't they? Jessie, you're scaring me."

"Tink, call DHS in Fayetteville, make sure those kids made it over there, and get your butt up here soon as you can. And you might bring someone with you. I think we're gonna need an extra deputy."

Jessie hung up, gazed out the window.

"What's happened?" Alicia stared at her.

"Not sure, but everything's going to be okay. Help is coming up here, then we'll figure something out. Right now, I'm starving. What's in the fridge? Don't get up, I'll fix it." She forced a smile. "Don't mean to panic you, but I can't cook, so...."

She lifted her shoulders in a shrug.

Alicia rose. "Well, never fear, I happen to be a great cook and the larder is full. What do you want?" She swung open the door of what turned out to be a freezer filled with prepared meals. "Name it, I've probably got it. Arranged in order so Jeff can— can—" She hugged herself and hunched forward, a huge sob escaping.

Jessie ran to her side, put an arm around her waist. "Come on, you need to lay down. You're exhausted. We're going to find him."

The grief Alicia had held back rolled from her like gigantic waves of pathetic sobs. Jess supported her to a couch in the front room and helped her stretch out. Her heart ached for the woman because she understood what it was like to love so completely, to care more for someone else than she did for herself. She sat on the floor and held Alicia's hand while she cried, and when she finally quieted a bit, she found the bathroom, wet a washcloth, and took it to her, folding it and placing it on her forehead.

We will find him and bring him back to her. I will personally see whoever took him punished if I have to do it myself.

Appetite gone, she went out onto the verandah to wait for Tink to arrive. She knew exactly where Blue Springs Lake was and as soon as her friend arrived, she was headed there to join Dal and Nick. This story would not end till she could write about the rescue of Jeff and capture of that prick Arthur Couch.

Nick pulled the noisy Volvo to the side of a narrow, weed-infested road and turned off the ignition. "It's about half a mile yonder. Hate to say this, but it doesn't look like a vehicle has used this road in a long while. We may be wrong about where this guy lit out to."

"If he didn't drive, then what? Is this a private lake?"

"No, it's just a well-kept secret. Mostly hikers come in from the other side on a trail that joins the Ozarks Cross-Country Hiking Trail. They camp and fish here."

"I can't imagine Couch hiking, can you?"

"Nope. There are some cabins that were once used by a lot of people. But after the dams were built along the White River those lakes became a more popular spot to fish and boat. Easier to get to. And this one sort of died out in popularity. If they're here they walked in, cause there's no other road except this one."

"Well, sooner we get in there, sooner we'll know." Dal climbed out of the car. He still wore the pistol Nick supplied when they raided the caravan. He slipped it from its holster on his thigh, checked the magazine, and nodded.

"Ready?" Nick dragged a rifle from the backseat. Glanced at him. "Might need something long-range, you never know."

"You never know." He liked this guy more and more. "Well, let's get in there and finish this. Say, Nick?"

"Yeah?"

"We gonna take him alive." It wasn't a question. They needed answers only Couch might have. "Kimble may be with him, and we can't discount that he may have some other cult members who slipped through the net."

"Could be one hell of a fight. We'll take them alive if we can."

"Kneecap em if we have to."

Nick had started to walk along the road and Dal followed, kicking up grasshoppers in the tall, dusty grass.

"Dangerous."

Dal leaned forward to make sure he'd heard. "What's dangerous?"

"Oh, not double-tapping em in the gut."

A shiver went through Dal's spine. He'd hate to have ever gone up against this guy. He was iron hard. "Bet you're a good enough shot to hit any of them just about anywhere you want with that rifle."

"Maybe." Nick didn't say anything else till they neared the blue crystal lake that shimmered in the afternoon sunlight. A row of dilapidated cabins slumped around one edge of the water, looking deserted as could be. On the far side of the water a couple of small tents were the center of movement, but that was far away. Hikers, probably.

Dal hauled up behind a large sycamore tree and Nick chose one nearby. After a pause he signaled that he was going around the back and pointed toward a beat-up boat near the shore that would make good cover. Flashed five fingers, then moved. Dal nodded, hunched down, and moved in fits and starts, using thick brush as cover till he was hidden from view. Nick had disappeared into the woods back of the cabins.

Other than the clicking and birring of insects, it was so quiet he hated to breathe for fear of being heard. Nothing stirred but a few birds. He waited the five minutes Nick had signaled, then moved slowly toward the end cabin. The two of them entered front and back in the same moment, remaining quiet. Nothing there save signs of animals.

Some twenty minutes later Dal went through the front door of the third and last cabin to meet Nick coming in the back way.

"Empty. No sign anyone's been here in a while, save old Mister and Missus Coon and maybe a rat or two." Dal holstered his gun and slid down against the wall. The damn leg hurt like hell, but he wouldn't admit it to Nick, who could run all day and not be winded.

Nick peered through the back window into the woods. "What now?"

"It was a good guess. Reckon where that peckerwood got to?"

Nick kept looking around, keeping an eye out. "Afraid he's probably long gone by now."

"That begs another question. Where is Jeff Woodson? I still think the two of them are holed up somewhere close with Woodson. They want those files. Their world has come apart and they'll try to put it back together somewhere else." Dal rubbed his face. "Someone else must have him. Couch had him, he'd be hanging around to get something in return." His phone vibrated against his leg. He pulled it out. "Jessie? You okay?"

"We just got a phone call. I think you need to come back here. Unless you found someone or something?"

"Nope, nothing. Who called?"

"Don't know, but she claims to have Jeff and she wants to deal."

"She? Who the hell she? And deal for what?"

"She won't say. She'll only talk to you."

"Me? I can't make a deal with anyone."

"Dal, I told her you had a phone with you, she should just call you, but she called Alicia's number and will only talk to you on her phone. Sounds weird, doesn't it?"

"We're coming back. She calls again, you ask for proof of life. You get her to let you talk to Jeff and you make it clear that if anything happens to him I'm coming after her and I won't stop till she's caught."

"I'll tell her that."

"Okay. And by the way, you might tell her I have what she wants and we can make a trade. See you soon. Please, Jessie, stay put."

She'd disconnected before he got the final words out. She was going to do something stupid. He just knew it. If she even got a clue who this woman was, she'd take off to find her cause that's the way she was.

He slipped the phone back into his pocket and got to his feet. Goddamn, he'd be glad to get back to the car. There were times when he yearned to lay hands on the guy who'd pulled the trigger in that back alley in Dallas and tried to cut him in half.

But then he shut his mind up till the thought was no longer there. He'd get this done and behind him, then he'd take Jessie to bed and fuck her for a week without stopping. Dear God, let that happen. Holding her always took away the darkness.

"You okay buddy?" Nick crossed the rotting floor, eyes on Dal so he must've failed to feel the wood give underfoot. His leg crashed through and he screamed with pain.

Dammit. He shouted Nick's name, and next thing he was on his knees next to him trying to get him free. Fingers prying at the broken boards. Digging out pieces.

"Stop." Nick hammered on his back. "Stop. Just wait a minute. Something's in my leg."

He couldn't see down in the hole. It was too dark. Where the hell was his damn flashlight? There. He fumbled it loose from his belt, switched it on. "Hold still, Nick. Don't move. Dammit. You've got a nail in your thigh. It's bleeding pretty bad."

Fingers worked his belt loose. Were they his own or someone else's? Didn't matter, he had it loose, fastened around Nick's leg tight till the blood stopped squirting.

Telephone in his pocket.

Punched first contact. *Emergency.*

Where the hell were they? Oh, yeah. Blue Springs Lake, fishing cabins. He shouted the message once, then again, dropped the phone on the floor, and grabbed Nick's arm.

"Steady, just hold still. They'll be here."

It took forever. Nick's head on his shoulder started trembling. Going into shock. He loosened the belt a bit but the blood spurted. He had to tighten it again. He'd lose his leg if they didn't get here, do something for him. Sirens from far away. Closer and closer slow like a snail's pace. Talking to Nick, who no longer responded.

Boots clomped across the floor. He drew in a deep breath, glanced up to see Mike Henley. Thank God. Thank Mike.

"Move back out of the way, Dal."

"He's bleeding. Tied my belt around his leg. Where is everyone?"

"Coming. I heard the call and was closest so I came in my car. Always carry some medical supplies. Figured it was best if I get here instead of going back to come with the responders."

He worked all the time he talked. Both hands were bloody when he raised up. "Okay, help me get him out of there so we can lay him down. Take his shoulders. I've got his legs."

Dal scooted around, put his hands under Nick's arms, waited till Mike said go, then lifted slowly. His flashlight lay on the floor, the beam spilling out across the bloody boards. "Is he okay?"

"He will be. We'll have to keep pressure on that and he'll need a tetanus shot and stitches and some time in the hospital, but you need to settle down yourself. You're white as a sheet."

Dal chuckled. "Some trick for an Indian, huh?" He shook so hard he leaned back against the wall of the ramshackle cabin. "Last time I saw that much blood, I was laying in it."

Why in the hell had he said that? He never talked about that, didn't figure most folks here even knew about it.

"Dal, you okay now?"

"Hell, I'm fine. It's him we got to worry about."

"Why in God's name did you come inside this rundown place?"

Why indeed? Dal didn't remember, but he thought Nick walked across the floor to him instead of going out and around. Didn't matter now, but it was a good question. Just something people do sometimes. Something stupid. Even the smartest forget.

The yellow responder truck barreled up to the cabin, parked next to Mike's vehicle, and men poured out of every opening. Lights on top flashed and whirled, lighting up the early evening shadows that appeared to walk out of the trees to embrace the rushing rescue workers.

Over an hour later, Dal left the hospital in Harrison and walked across the lot to Nick's Volvo. They were keeping him for a couple of nights so Dal was going home. He had the phone in his hand before the world came crashing down around him.

Alicia Woodson and Jessie were waiting for him to talk to the woman who said she had Jeff. Holy fuck, how could he have forgotten that? Her phone rang and rang, till finally voicemail answered.

Climbing into the Volvo, he threw the damned thing into the seat, started the beat up old vehicle, and headed north toward Cedarton, a good forty-five minutes away going flat out. And the Volvo wouldn't go flat out. But he gave it a try, hoping to God the old engine didn't throw a piston through the hood.

He must've tried Jessie's phone a dozen times during the hour it took to roll into the front yard at the Hermitage. He bounded up the steps and ran inside without knocking before he noticed he was still covered in blood.

Alicia sat on the couch, Tink next to her, and when they saw him, both of them covered their mouths to hold back a scream.

Alicia threw her arms around Tink. "It's Jeff, he's dead. What did they do to him? What happened?" She went to pieces, sobbing hysterically.

"Tink, tell her this isn't Jeff's blood or mine. Nick had an accident. I'm sorry I scared her. I couldn't get hold of Jessie and I came from the hospital fast as I could. Did you hear from the woman who called about Jeff? And where the hell is Jessie?" Even as he asked a dark dread crept over him.

Before she could reply, the answer to his question hit him like a sledgehammer. "She went after him, didn't she? Tell me she didn't. Where did they tell her they were? When did she leave? Could you please answer me?"

But she did—of *course* she did.

"I will, Dal, soon as you hush."

He stopped talking, stood in the middle of the floor, and stared at her. Alicia stopped sobbing so loud, but continued to cry. "It was you they wanted. Where were you?" The words were nearly indistinguishable.

Dal ignored her. "Tinkerbelle?"

"The woman called back, asked for you. Jessie told her you had gone and she would have to deal with her. I mean, you know Jessie. She got right down in her face, so to speak. Told her it was no use her being stubborn, that she would be the one to get her what she wanted and so she'd better talk to her."

"So, what did she want?"

"Some files from Alicia's cases. She would trade Jeff for them, so Jessie got Alicia to put together some legal files, worthless stuff from the cases she specified, then she took them where the woman told her to go."

"Where did she tell her to go?"

"She wrote it down." Tink untangled herself from Alicia's grip, fetched a piece of paper, and handed it to him. He read it. "Do you know where this is?"

Tink nodded. By now tears poured from her eyes, but she was trying to hold it together.

"How long ago was that?" He, on the other hand, was about to lose it.

"It was a little after six."

"Two and a half hours and she's not back yet? Why the hell didn't you just give her what she wanted? We could've gone after her and got everything back when we caught her. Why try to fool her?"

"That was Jessie's idea. Besides Alicia couldn't or wouldn't tell us which file it was."

Of course it was Jessie's idea. Why had he thought any different? That black dread he knew so well filled him, blotted out everything but a need to track down and kill.

He had the files the bitch wanted. Out in the Volvo, cause he'd pinched them from Couch's office. Every damned thing they wanted. They'd damned well better trade Jessie and Jeff both for them or someone would be cleaning up a blood bath.

"Dal, you have to go find them."

"That's what I'm trying to do, but I need to know where this woman is. Where she told Jessie to meet her."

He paced the floor, limping and grumbling. Where in the world could the woman be? He knew that name, could not put a finger on where he'd heard it. As if out of his control the heel of his hand hammered at his head.

Do something. Don't let this happen again.

He whirled, stomped to Alicia. "You listen to me good, woman. I don't know what you've gotten yourself mixed up in, but you'd better tell me where this woman might be or your Jeff will die."

She screamed back at him. Nothing he could understand.

"You damned well know cause I have a big fat file I took from Couch's office. Bainbridge and planting a church to cover all their foul doings. And maybe, just maybe, I can go get Jessie and your husband home safe. You understand me?"

Tink tugged at his arm. "Dallas, take it easy. Stop. Calm down. You're terrifying her."

He jerked from her grip, shoved her away. "Too damned late for calm. You get some answers out of her and get them now. I'm going to try to wash Nick's blood off me. Where the fuck is the bathroom?"

She pointed him in the right direction, and when he left she was sitting beside the hysterical woman talking to her.

In the luxurious room he stared for a long moment into the mirror. Someone glared back at him that he did not know. A man covered in blood, the blood of someone who didn't even have to be involved in this, except he chose to be. And that man lay in a hospital while that, that woman out there....

He bit off the thought.

Cursing, he filled the basin, stripped out of the bloody shirt, and scrubbed with a bath brush. Over his chest, under his arms, then up and down both till his skin burned. Bloody water swirled around and round in the sink.

"Dal."

He jumped. Eyes wide, Tinker stood in the door, a clean tee shirt in her hand. "You okay?"

He shook his head. "Hell no. What's that?"

"Alicia wanted me to give you this so you wouldn't have to wear that." She nodded toward his discarded clothing heaped in the floor, wet with bloody water.

"Get a mop or something, Clean up this mess. I've got to go after Jessie before she gets hurt. She tell you where?"

Nodding, she handed him the shirt. "Bainbridge. You and Jessie followed Couch... the missing girl? Rebecca?" She gulped and broke off.

He was already shaking his head, mute now. Too terrified, too angry to dare speak or touch this woman.

"You go on, I'll clean this up. Git, now. Take care of my friend. She thinks she's invincible."

He slipped on the shirt, tugging at the bottom which barely covered him. He cursed, then began issuing terse orders "You call one of the boys, I don't care which one, but not Colby. Tell them I need backup out at the Bainbridge place. Better alert the responders, cause some folks are gonna get hurt out there."

"Dal, you be careful."

"It ain't me you need to worry about. Gotta go. You two stay here, no matter what, you hear me?"

"I hear you."

When he left she was cleaning up the mess he'd made in the bathroom.

17
CHAPTER

Jessie cut the lights and parked Alicia's borrowed pickup half a mile up the road from the farm. A sliver of moon shimmered in the last light of the setting sun. It was still easy to see the sky but shadows crept under the trees. She left the file on the seat, shut the door silently, hunkered low, and scurried toward the house where lights glowed in the windows.

It hadn't been hard at all to recognize the voice of the woman who'd called and threatened Jeff. She'd heard it before, and at the time remarked on her unusual tonality. Too bad for the bitch.

At the edge of the porch, she took the steps carefully so as not to make a sound. Alicia's .45 Dal had left for them was in her pocket, but damn she'd hate to have to use it. What she'd told Nick was true. She had shot someone, a man she had once loved who came after her with murderous intent. She despised the idea of doing it again, but she could if threatened.

At the largest of the front windows she paused, heart slamming around in her chest.

God, they'd hear that. A deep breath, then another, and she put an ear against the wall, listened for conversation, then peeked around the frame. Inside, a man sat in a chair but no one else seemed to be in there. He appeared to be staring at the floor. She darted to the other side of the window and worked her way to the front door. If luck was with her, it wouldn't be locked. Country folks seldom locked their doors, but maybe kidnappers might and child traffickers might.

Stop, Jessie. Just do this.

She gripped the knob and turned it slowly. The latch popped and the door snicked open. Holy shit. Even country kidnappers didn't lock their door. Good to know. Inching through a skinny slit, she tiptoed into the room where the man sat. His head raised.

"What do you want now?"

Had to be Jeff. Sure wasn't the man of the house. Course, for all she knew, he could be dead and the woman now in charge. A woman she remembered well.

She crept closer to him. "Jeff? I'm here to help. Don't say anything. Just stay right where you are. Where is she?"

He opened his mouth and she touched his lips with her fingers. "My name is Jessie. Can you hear me?" Be dumb to talk above a whisper till she found out where the rest of the kidnappers were. It was said the blind developed sensitive hearing. She certainly hoped so, for she dared not speak any louder.

He nodded.

That was a relief. "Are you tied up?"

He shook his head.

"Okay. You stay right where you are for a minute. Can you do that?"

He nodded again.

"Good. I'll be back for you."

Hard to know where they were. Guess they weren't afraid to leave a blind man unguarded. Still not sure if she was dealing with more than one person, she took her time going from one room to the other. Though lights were on throughout the house every room appeared to be empty.

Finally the low hum of conversation from behind a closed door in the very back corner of the house. Had to be a bedroom unless these folks had some strange nooks and crannies, cause she'd been through just about every kind so far.

One step away from the door, the floor creaked underfoot.

She stopped short, listened.

They kept talking so they hadn't heard.

Her heart had nearly stopped.

The smartest and safest thing she could do would be go get Jeff, put him in the car, and leave. Then she could worry about what to do about these assholes. Congratulating herself on doing the smartest thing, she turned and headed back toward the main room where the man hopefully still waited for her. Headlights swept across the windows, the sound of a car. She scurried into one of the back rooms.

Waited.

Listened.

Lots of loud talking, but she couldn't make out the words or recognize the voice since it was all mixed in with the others. Sounded like two men now, angry at the funny-voiced woman.

She had to get to Jeff and quickly for it sounded like they were fixing to light out. No telling what they'd do to him or with him.

Where the heck had Dal and Nick got to?

If she dared call the Hermitage she could check on what was going on there, but they'd hear her. Might as well just go on and hope for the best. Tired of trying to move slow, she hurried into the front room. His chair was empty.

Now what?

They must have him or he got scared and hid somewhere.

Enough of this shit. She pulled out the .45, pointed it at the floor, and scooted toward where all the action was taking place. As she neared the door, it popped open, startling her till she jumped back. The man who pulled it open jumped too. She raised the gun.

"Stay put, right where you are. What'd you do with Jeff?"

He didn't stay put, but backed up and slammed the door.

Startled, she tried to open it, but couldn't. Locked or blocked. She hammered on it, yelled Jeff's name.

"You back off, or we'll kill him." The woman's weird voice.

"Wait. Did you bring the files?" One of the men.

"Oh, sure. She came here with a gun and brought the files with her." Another sharper-voiced man.

"What's the matter with you? You wanting to get this man killed?" Weird woman.

She couldn't resist a reply. "What's the matter with you? You wanting to kill a hero, a veteran? A wounded one, at that. You must be really nice folks to do something like this."

"We are nice." The sing-song voice of the first man.

Evidently they didn't understand sarcasm. "If you're so blamed nice then send him out here to me and we can argue this out when he's safe."

"You slide the files we asked for under the door and you can have him. Don't know what a woman wants with a blind man, but hell, we're easy to get along with. She can have him back, and remind her everything we discussed is privileged. She can't go blabbing it anywhere." This from one of the men.

She knew that voice. The prick Couch. That meant three men in there. The woman's husband, Couch, and someone she didn't know.

That unknown voice joined in. "Let's just shoot this son of a bitch, then her and get the hell out of here. Enough of this fucking around. We need to end this. Now."

The last few sentences faded behind Jessie cause she ran out on the front porch. The room, just opposite the front room, had a window and she eased over to it. Bent down to peer in.

"Jessie, what the hell are you doing?" If a whisper shouted that one did.

She covered her mouth to keep from hollering out loud. Arms grabbed her waist hard and dragged her around the corner of the porch.

"No time now, Jess. How many in there? Are they armed? Where's Jeff?" Dal's words sharp, his breath hot against her neck.

"Four, I think, and yes. They know I am. Jeff's in there with them."

"Good work. You got em cornered. Now, just what did you intend to do with them?"

"I almost had Jeff clear, then Couch and some other guy showed up. Where have you been?"

"We have been looking all over hell and creation for that asshole."

"Well, I've got him."

He put his arms around her, held her close again. He was trembling all over, whether from anger or fear, she wasn't sure. For a long time, he didn't speak. Finally, he took in a shaky breath. "Who else is in there, do you know?"

"Missus Bainbridge, her husband, Couch, and I'm not sure about the other man."

"You could've been killed. What were you thinking?"

"I was thinking about a blind man caught up in this mess and no one to help him out of it. I recognized her voice on the phone and I couldn't help but try to find him. I couldn't help it."

He hugged her all the harder. "I know you couldn't help it. I just wish you'd be more careful, is all."

"So, what are we going to do?"

"I've got backup coming."

"They're fixing to leave. They want the files they think I have or they'll kill Jeff and leave."

"They won't kill him long as they think you have the files. How come you don't have them?"

"I do, well, not really. We fixed up a fake file to trade. It's in Alicia's truck. Never got the chance. My plan sort of backfired."

"Uh huh, well, we've got to keep them here somehow till backup comes. I'll go get your fakes and you go to that door and start bickering with them. Stall them long as you can, then give them the fakes. We have to keep them here till the guys arrive, but they have to think you're here alone. I'll radio them and tell them to come in quiet. We have to save that young man in there. And Jessie? Don't do anything stupid."

She hurried back inside, tapped on the door. "I'm back. I had to go get you your files from the car, but they're too fat to go under the door. You'll have to open up for me."

"First you throw your gun through in here. And don't try anything. We're armed too, and I'll shoot this hero of yours. Now, I'm cracking the door open, put your gun through."

Dal returned with the files, handed them to her. "Stay back and slide that gun in on the floor."

She nodded.

"Okay, but I'm not giving you the files till you let me have Jeff. I don't trust your asses."

"Gun." The door creaked open a few inches and she pushed the barrel through. "It's stuck, open it some more."

"Christ, Taylor. Let's just kill both of em, get the files, and get out of here. I'm tired of playing games with these hillbillies."

Words gritted under her breath. "Who you think you're dealing with, you asshole?" She yanked the gun back. "You don't go calling folks names in the midst of making a deal. That isn't the way it works. You want these files, now you apologize. Don't you know anything about political correctness?"

"Geez, you just called me an asshole."

The woman intervened. "Will you two stop this bickering? Listen, I've got a gun pointed at your hero's head. I open the door, you give me the files. Is that clear?"

"Jeff? Answer me."

His voice, loud and strong. "She's not lying, but—" Scuffling, stuff hitting the floor, shouting, all followed by a gunshot.

Dal pushed her aside and hit the door with his shoulder. It wasn't latched and he stumbled into the room, Jessie at his back. Jeff stood over one of the men, a gun in his hand, and it was pointed pretty well where it needed to be. Crouch lay slumped against the wall, blood pouring from his upper arm. Another door from the room stood open and the others were gone.

"I hope that's the cavalry." Jeff's amusement carried a touch of panic.

"Yep, if you can call us that. Looks like you've got the situation pretty well in hand."

Dal knelt beside Couch. "He'll live, if I let him." He yanked the whimpering man to his feet, drilled the barrel of his gun into his belly. "For two cents you'd try to escape, you asshole. You don't know how bad I want to put a bullet through your brain."

She leaned her head against his shoulder, the muscles tense and hard. "Dal, honey." The tone of his voice since he'd arrived and the way he'd acted had put that old fear in her. The one that kicked in when he let himself go.

Jeff spoke from the center of the room. "He ought to know not to touch a blind man. Told me right where he was. But I'd appreciate it if you'd cover him, just in case. And let me know where I am."

Jessie left Dal's side and went to Jeff, took his hand, and placed it through the crook in her elbow. "I'm Jessie, and he's covered and the real cavalry is on the way."

"The woman's gone and the other men, I'm afraid. Who are these people and what did they want with me?"

"I imagine Alicia can explain it to all of us when we get back there."

"Would you mind if I sat down? It's been a nerve-wracking day."

She dragged a chair to him keeping an eye on Dal, who had calmed down considerably. "A chair. On your right."

Jeff located the chair and lowered himself into it.

Four deputies pounded through the door, weapons drawn.

"We're fine. About damn time you all got here." Jessie laid her hand on Jeff's shoulder as if they shared a joke no one else was privy to. And indeed they did.

"The hell of it is, she got away. We've got Couch, but Kimble, Taylor, and Susan Bainbridge escaped." Dal paced the floor at the Hermitage after having finished giving a blow by blow of what had gone on at the Bainbridge farm an hour or so earlier.

He was still having trouble remaining calm. Jessie's close call when he had no control over the situation fed a fear inside him that he wanted gone. Hell of it was, it wouldn't leave. So he just kept pacing and talking.

"What about Couch?" He didn't see who asked the question.

"Les and Burt accompanied him to the Federal Building in Fayetteville. The bastard needed some patching up, but thankfully we had Mike, our star EMT, with us and he did the honors. It was just a flesh wound."

A chuckle traveled around the room and Dal turned to stare out the window. Something clutched at his gut and he wished he could see the humor, but it went over his head.

Jessie finished the explanation. "Yeah, Jeff disarmed that son of a bitch Couch and the fool shot himself in the scuffle."

Alicia wrapped her arms around the man in question. "And if you ever do anything like that again, I'll... well I'm not sure what I'll do."

He leaned close and whispered something to her. She kissed him and whispered back. He laughed.

"I'm thinking we need to leave these two alone." Dal moved to Jessie's side. Slipped an arm around her waist. "And if you ever do anything like that again" —he pointed at Jeff— " whatever he said."

That got a laugh out of everyone in the room and the anger trapping him let go. He leaned his forehead against the top of her head. Wanted only to get out of here and go home. Wherever that was.

Tink sobered first. "Hey, don't you think, since that crazy woman and her small following are still running around out there, we ought to leave a deputy here till we catch them? I'd be glad to stay here if it's okay with Alicia." She gazed at the couple sitting together on the couch. "I promise to be very discreet. You won't even know I'm here."

"That's not a bad idea. We can send someone out to take over when Burt comes back from Fayetteville, since romance is definitely in the air." Dal grinned at his favorite deputy.

Tinkerbelle blushed. "You're just a mess, Dallas. But I wouldn't mind Burt coming out here to help with guard duty. Everyone else will probably be out looking for our escaped couple. Wonder where they got to, anyway?"

Dal wished he knew too. "One thing, though, Tinkerbelle, you be real careful and if she shows up you draw first, cause she's got a lot to lose, and from what I saw of her she wouldn't mind taking a shot at you. And I don't want Mac on my butt, especially since I really don't have any say so anyway. I think it's a good idea to have your husband join you till she's caught. It's called having your back as opposed to taking care of the helpless woman." He sent a long look Jessie's way. "And lock this place up tight."

Joining hands, Alicia and Jeff stood. "You're welcome to stay long as it's necessary, Tinker, but Jeff and I are going to go to bed. It's been one heck of a day. There's three bedrooms on the second floor. You and your husband just make yourselves at home."

Dal laughed. "Sounds promising all the way around. We'll go on. The staties and I reckon just about every law enforcement bunch in the state are looking for the Bainbridges and Kimble, so I think we all deserve a night off. I'm going to see Nick. I'll tell him you all are thinking of him."

Everyone said their goodbyes and he took Jessie's hand. "You're coming with me, whether you like it or not. I can't afford another scare like the one you gave me tonight."

"I'm coming with you. I'm bushed. After we see Nick, let's grab something to eat in Harrison. That place we ate the last time? I'm starved."

"Okay, as long as we can go back to your place afterward. I'd like to lay us down somewhere for a while, and do what people do in bed."

"You mean sleep?"

He swung her arm. "No, my sweet, I do not mean sleep. I may tie you up to the bed."

"Sounds interesting."

"May be." He sagged and held on to her. "Goddammit, Jess, if you do something like that again, I can't be responsible for what I do."

The damn leg was on fire, but there was nothing wrong with any of his *other* parts.

"I had to do it. There was no choice." She leaned her head against his shoulder and he put an arm around her. They walked in silence out to the Jeep.

"You look whipped. I'll drive if you like."

He was only too happy to let her. The sun set, orange streaks against purple. The hollers rested in darkness, creeks reflected the sky's brilliance in what seemed only a flash of time before stars filled the sky. The lights of Harrison brightened the horizon ahead.

He rolled his head to watch her profile against the window glass. Looking at her when she didn't know he was doing so pleased him somehow. Her innocence and studied concentration revealed secrets about her she might never show otherwise. How much she cared about the smallest things, how she could make funny faces when deep in thought. How goddamned beautiful she was in an unpretentious sort of way. And how he wanted his arms around her. And if only she'd stop running into danger full blast.

He drew in a deep breath. Was he truly falling for her in a way he'd vowed not to do? Or was he just lonesome and could get over it? Not sure if either or both were true, he laid a hand on her thigh and rubbed. She didn't turn to look at him. Never did that while driving. Odd, the things he noticed about her.

She pulled into the parking at the small hospital, getting as close as she could to the entrance. Grateful for small favors, he climbed out and limped along beside her to the door.

"What floor is he on?"

"Second."

It was the first they'd spoken since leaving the Hermitage. How easy it was to be with her without yakking all the time. He let her go through the door first and she went to the bed where Nick was propped up watching something on television. They hugged and she kept hold of him for a minute, massaging his shoulder.

"Hey, good to see you guys. How's it going?" He punched a button on the bed and the television went off.

"It's going, buddy. How's the leg? You scared hell out of me. I always thought you were invincible." He wouldn't tell Nick about what had happened. Not yet anyway. The poor guy might blame himself and there was no use in that. None at all.

Nick laughed. "You thought so too, huh? They tell me I'll survive. That may have been the dumbest thing I've ever done." He looked up at Jessie. "How's my best girl?"

"Doing good. Wish we'd a caught that witch though."

They spent half an hour or so visiting, Dal lounged in a chair, Jessie perched on the edge of the bed. She glanced at Dal, stood, and gave Nick a peck on the cheek.

"I've got to go feed this guy before he caves in. Are they letting you out tomorrow?"

"So I hear."

"We'll come pick you up, then, unless you have other arrangements." She reached for Dal's hand. "Let's go eat so I can take you home and put you to bed."

He grinned. "Sounds good to me."

They told Nick goodnight and left.

In the Jeep, she stuck the keys in the ignition, then leaned back to look at him. "Why don't we go on home and I'll run in and pick up something at the Red Bird and we can relax at home and eat."

"Oh, damn, I love you."

"Better be careful what you say, Mister, I may hold you to it."

Jessie lay in bed beside Dal, watching him sleep. Moonlight filtered in through the window reflecting on his face, accenting the high planes of his cheekbones. What would it be like to be married to him? To be *with* him, on a long-term basis. What a surprise to even think that. Neither of them had an inclination toward such a thing.

Yet since his return after being gone so long, her feelings against it had, if not changed, at least eased off. Surely it was just that old true adage absence makes the heart grow fonder that she suffered from. Once they began to see each other more often, battled about cases, disagreed about almost everything, and satisfied their mutual lust on a regular basis, she would no longer have the inclination. For sure he wouldn't. He'd always made that very clear.

Yet, this night, when she still felt so attached to him, cared so much for him, she snuggled close and shut her eyes in contentment. There were much worse things than loving this man when he didn't love her.

The phone rang. Jessie startled awake and tried to reach it, but Dal was lying with his head on her belly and both arms tight around her. Fast asleep. Even after the phone kept ringing and she continued to try to get undone from his grip he didn't budge.

If Brad weren't still with Parker he'd have Dal awake by now. They'd go pick him up in the morning before he drove her friend crazy.

Shaking Dal's shoulder didn't help much. "Dal, sweetie, either answer the phone or let me go." She couldn't help laughing. "Guess you'll have to do both in order to do one." What in the world could be going on now?

Dal groaned and stirred while she wiggled and squirmed. "Answer the damned phone." His voice muffled against her stomach must have awakened him for he rolled over. "I'll get it. I'll get it."

"Okay, you get it honey." She scooted on out from under him to sit on the edge of the bed. Even though her muscles ached and her scratched skin itched, she felt good. Until the tone of his voice jarred her back to reality.

"What? When? Good God, we'll be right there." While skinning on his jeans and a clean t-shirt to replace the one Alicia had loaned him earlier, he filled her in. "That crazy bitch broke into the Hermitage after we left, demanding all the files Alicia has on the applications for her church." He paused putting on his boots. "Don't ask me, I guess we'll find out. You ready?

Carrying her shoes, she followed him out to the Jeep. "Is anyone hurt?"

"I don't think so. That was Tinkerbelle. She was pretty excited."

He crawled in behind the wheel and they were off in a cloud of dust.

"That woman must be nuttier than a fruitcake."

"I liked shithouse rat better. Okay, I know it isn't funny. At least we got some sleep. What time is it, anyway?"

"It was three twenty-five when the phone rang."

"So maybe quarter to four? Is this mess ever going to end?"

"I'm beginning to wonder."

He steered around the circle drive and skidded to a stop. Without waiting for him she jumped out and raced toward the all-too-quiet big house. She opened the door before he made it to the steps. He needed to be taking it easy instead of back out running around.

"Wait a minute, Jess. Please. Do not go inside yet."

His tone halted her in the doorway, where she held it open till he reached her, his gait uneven. He had his gun out, so she drew the .38 as well. Whatever he expected to find in there she needed to be ready. It was eerily quiet inside, the long hallway dark without lights and no windows. He went right, she went left, and they checked out the rooms. Flipping on the lights revealed a shock. Everything in the room was broken, bits and pieces lying on the floor along with a huge scattering of empty shells. Lamps, pieces of furniture, windows, all ripped into shreds.

What had happened here? "Dal?"

"Someone has riddled the place with an automatic rifle of some kind. Nothing else would do this sort of damage."

Her throat swelled with the thrashing of her heart. Would they find everyone dead? The way things looked they might. Her knees buckled and she grabbed Dal's arm.

"Take it easy. It's over. Trust me, whoever did this is long gone or they'd still be at it."

Every step they took, glass crunched underfoot.

Inside the next door two figures lay sprawled on the floor.

For a moment she couldn't breathe or move or talk. Tink and Burt both. She finally found her voice. "Dal."

"I see."

"Are they—?"

He eased forward "My God."

On her knees she checked Tinker with trembling fingers, her insides clenched so tight she couldn't breathe or speak. She was alive. With a strong pulse. She nodded at Dal, embraced with a dizziness like she was going to pass out.

He touched Burt's neck, glanced at her. "He's alive. No sign of Jeff or Alicia, though."

She cleared her throat, found a hoarseness that passed for speaking. "Their bedroom is the wing on the right." Still holding Tink's arm, she indicated the door across the hall.

He nodded. "You stay here and see if you can bring them around. Find out what happened. I'll be right back."

Tink groaned when she rolled her knuckles into her breastbone. "Come on, girl. Sit up. Tell me what happened here."

"Jessie? What? Where?"

She shook her. "Come on, wake up."

"That crazy woman. She... she busted in here, started shooting up the place. We couldn't get near her. We were right here and we couldn't stop her. It was like she was fighting an army, shooting everywhere and demanding we get her the files she wanted. I have... I had no idea what she was talking about. Alicia and Jeff were in bed. That's all I remember."

Burt rolled over, sat up, and looked around, a confused expression on his face. "You okay, babe?" He grabbed Tink.

"I'm okay except for a lump on my noggin."

Dal burst back into the room. "Both unhurt. The room untouched. Alicia said she told the woman where the files were. Said it wasn't worth hers and Jeff's lives. Said that what was in them was only information the Bainbridges had originally left with her when they hired her to establish a legal church. She's really confused why the files were so important they had to attack to get them back. I told them to stay where they are. No sense in them getting more upset. This place looks like a tornado hit it."

Tink held her head. "That bitch was crazy. She had one of those guns, you know, the kind that just keeps shooting and that's what she did, just kept shooting the walls, the furniture. Everything. I never saw anything like it except in the movies."

"Well, evidently whatever she wanted she thinks she has it. Thank goodness she didn't kill anyone. I don't think that's on their agenda. They've had chances and haven't done it. I'm not sure I give a damn what's in those files. What could be so important about establishing a church? Let the feds sort this out. I'm done." Dal shrugged and tucked his gun away.

Burt examined Tinker's head. "That's gonna need some stitches. You hadn't fought so hard, she might've let you off easier." He smiled and kissed her cheek.

"I think we'd better call in the feds, much as I hate to. This is getting to be too much for our deputies to handle. Besides, this woman obviously is involved with the trafficking. She may be the head honcho." Dal rubbed his stomach. "I'm so hungry I could eat a horse. I'll call over to Fayetteville and get those guys out here. Maybe they can make sense out of everything. I don't want to leave the Woodsons alone till that woman is behind bars." He glanced at Jessie, who sat next to Tinker holding her hand. "What time is it, anyway?

"Well, every clock in this room was killed, so I'm not sure." She took out her phone. "Looks like it's six twenty-eight. Not too early for breakfast. Tink, if you two are okay, I'm going to raid the kitchen, see if I can round us up something to eat." Dal looked like he'd been through hell and back.

He was already on the phone trying to contact the feds, not even thinking that everyone was in bed. She gave him a quick glance before leaving the room. He'd go till he dropped and there was nothing she could do about it. But fix something to eat.

Within half an hour she had bacon sizzling, a bowl of scrambled eggs waiting to go in the skillet, and had popped open a tube of biscuits and slid them in the oven. Sometimes she amazed herself. Must be the adrenaline. She was actually cooking. Might be the luxurious kitchen, the fancy glass-topped stove, or just the need to do something. Now if she could just keep from burning anything. Stay busy and keep from thinking about all this crap crumbling down around them. And feed her man. Sounded good.

A bit later she sat at the table with Tink, Burt, and Dal, all shoveling food into their mouths as if they hadn't eaten in weeks. The kitchen smelled like bacon and coffee and biscuits, none of which were burned. She'd become a cook overnight.

"Woman, you never cease to amaze me." Dal forked up eggs, picked up a biscuit slathered with butter and strawberry jam, and stuck that in his mouth, followed it all with a big slurp of coffee.

He wiped his mouth with a napkin, looked at her, and smiled. It was like everything between them had been made okay. Or at least back to normal. That she could take.

She smiled back.

Their plates were wiped clean. Though exhausted, Dal had to hang in until the feds came. Till this was finished and his life got back to normal. He was staring out the window on his third cup of coffee when three black SUVs barrel-assed into the yard and spewed out men from all doors.

"Good Lord, we've been invaded." Tinker laughed, then cupped a hand over the knot above one ear. "I am so embarrassed I'd like to hide under the bed."

"Hey, no one walks into fire from an automatic rifle." Jessie tossed the comment over her shoulder while scraping plates and loading them into the dishwasher.

"Maybe not, but we ought to've heard them coming."

Dal looked up from his coffee. "Them? I thought it was just a woman."

"Yep, but she had a man with her."

"Now is about time you told us that. Wonder where Kimble is."

Tink shrugged. "Must've been her husband with her."

She was probably right. No one had seen or heard from Taylor Bainbridge since the day he and his wife had reported their daughter missing. Which was all a lie. And Kimble had probably took off.

Boots clomped across the porch, knuckles tried to knock the door in.

Tink held her arms over her head. "Oh, Lord, let them in before my head comes apart."

Burt, who had been too quiet all morning, hopped up and went to let the crew of lawmen in.

Dal dreaded the next few hours, but was happy to see among the assemblage the familiar but somewhat battered face of US marshal Trey Ledger. For a few minutes everyone jabbered away at once, until one older guy who looked kind of like Mark Harmon on NCIS held up a hand and bellowed for silence.

He got it. "Let's get this organized. My name's Craig Morrison. I'm not a very special agent, but I have been put in charge of getting this mess straightened out. We have laws broken all over the goddamned place and it's up to me to see the lawbreakers end up in the right brig, so to speak. If someone could tell me what happened here, it would be a start."

"Now, where are" —he took a pad from his jacket pocket and peered at it a moment— "who is Missus Alicia Woodson?"

Tink poked her hand in the air like she was back in school and everyone chuckled.

"You're Missus Woodson?" You could tell by his voice he was doubtful.

"No, but I can fetch her. She's in the other room with her husband Jeff. Do you want him too?"

The agent stared at Tink like she was an alien from outer space. "She's in the other room. What other room? There seems to be ten or twelve rooms in this place. One of them pretty much destroyed. What the hell kind of party did you folks have?" Before Tink could reply, he waved a hand toward her. "Never mind. Please, if you would, go fetch her. I do not need her husband right now."

Tink waved at him again. "If he wants to come with her, may he?"

Morrison raised his shoulders, swiped a hand over his white hair, and nodded. "By all means, if they are tied together somehow he may come with her."

"He's blind." Tink's voice came out harsh, shaming the man. "After what they've been through, I don't think it would be nice to leave him alone in there. Do you?" She stood on her tiptoes and stared into Morrison's face.

"For God's sake." Morrison gestured toward one of the younger agents, who appeared to be his partner. He wore a jacket with FBI on the back and sort of kowtowed to Morrison. "Would you go with Miss Whatever?" Again a wave of his hand. "And fetch the Woodsons?" He put an accent on fetch like it was a word foreign to him.

What a self-important prick. Dal wanted to bust the guy in the mouth. After what had happened over the past few days they didn't need to deal with this horseshit.

The FBI agent returned with Alicia and Jeff, and Tink trailing along behind. Morrison's manner changed immediately.

He introduced himself to both of them. "Sorry for all the inconvenience. Is there a room where we can talk? I just have a few questions to ask you that might be better discussed in private."

What seemed like hours later, following private discussions, the intake of several pots of coffee, some joke telling among lawmen, and a lot of impatience, Morrison seemed satisfied. As for the rest of them, they were in the dark about what was going on. Morrison received a phone call while they were all milling about. He talked for a while, put the phone away, and said something to his partner, the FBI guy, who nodded and took up residence in a vacant chair.

"Hunt will remain with these people until this gets sorted out." Morrison gestured to the remainder of men.

One by one they filed out of the house, crammed themselves back in the SUVs, and left.

Tink rubbed her palms together. "Well, I don't know about the rest of you, but I'm satisfied. Case solved and all that. Oh, by the way, you might be interested to know they picked up Missus Bainbridge with an automatic rifle in the backseat of her Mercedes. I shamelessly eavesdropped at the door when he called several of his cohorts into the private room where they could talk."

"If that don't beat all." Dal looked around the room at the Grace County deputies who had assisted in bringing in the culprits. "Congratulations everyone. I know Mac will be proud of you for solving this confusing case. So why don't you all go home and get some sleep?"

Nervous laughter went around the room. "No, really Dal, what's up?"

He gestured with open hands. "What would I know? I'm not even a deputy of this fine county. Let the FBI take care of it. Two fugitives are still at large. Maybe they'll fill Mac in soon, then we'll be able to celebrate whatever it is that we have done. Jessie and I are going home."

18
CHAPTER

She and Dal enjoyed Honey Buns and coffee that morning and lingered in the quiet for a while. She finished off her breakfast, rose, picked up the phone, and dropped on the couch to call Mac. Dal refilled his cup and stepped out on the front porch. The window framed him leaning against a post gazing out across the hills. He hadn't yet told her if he was going back to Frog Pond or staying here. Except that he had told everyone when they left the Woodsons' earlier that they were going home. It would break her heart all over again if he left but, with the troubles seemingly behind them, she had to be prepared for that.

Mac picked up and grumbled a hello.

"Hey, guess you heard we're back."

"Sure did, and I'm relieved. Tell me all about it. I can't wait till I can read that paper of yours."

It took about fifteen minutes of nonstop talking to fill him in, then answer some questions.

"Well, gal, I'm happy you all came through unscathed. What about that danged Couch and Kimble? Both of em. Nearly unbelievable that Colby was the only injury to our boys and I understand he's fine. Tough as a cob, that boy is. Sure hope we can keep him on the force. Sorry to hear about Nick. Hear he's still in the hospital. I don't know him well."

"No one knows Nick too well. He's a good guy, just likes to steer clear of folks. Dal and I are going to go over to Harrison this morning and pick him up. Depends on how he's getting along whether he goes home. He lives alone so I don't know what his plans are. Seems like everything may get back to normal soon. I guess we'll have to wait a while to see how this shakes out with the feds."

"Feds. Pfaw."

She agreed wholeheartedly, told him goodbye, and hung up, then joined Dal on the porch and sidled up against him. He curled an arm around her. Like they had always been together.

"Guess we still have the weekend off, since technically you don't have a job anyway." She tilted her head and gazed up at him. His viridian green eyes glistened down at her.

"Did you have anything in mind?"

"I'm going to call Nick at the hospital and see what time they're going to turn him loose. We need to go get him."

"Do that now, would you?"

"Sure." Curious she tilted her head, pulled out her phone, found the number, and dialed. After she found out Nick was being released shortly, she told Dal.

An hour later they had the climber and his crutches in the front seat of the Jeep next to Dal. She leaned forward on her elbows between the two men to chat with them while Dal drove back to Cedarton. The top was rolled down and the summer sun kissed her shoulders and the back of her neck, tossed her pony tail this way and that. It felt good to not have anyone chasing them or to be doing the chasing. She could almost relax.

During the drive Dal related some of their adventures with the Woodsons, catching Nick up on the Rising Moon and the capture of Susan Bainbridge.

"Taylor, the husband, got away along with Kimble. Wouldn't surprise me if the two of them don't start something up again to keep carrying on that trafficking business. Amazing how they used a cult to cover up their real business."

Nick leaned back and stared up at the blue sky. "Did you ever find out why they went to such lengths to get those files back?"

"The feds spent a lot of time with Alicia Woodson, but you know that stuff is privileged. Information shared between a lawyer and her client. I reckon they could get the Bainbridge woman to talk. If I know the feds they figured out a way."

Nick craned around to look at Jessie. "I know you're curious. I'll bet you could find out more about it if you tried."

Dal laughed. "You're right there. She's good at prying stories out of people. We need to just turn her loose on them."

They all laughed some more, then Jessie sobered and gazed out across the mountains. They were right. She'd give a lot to know what was in those files that meant so much to the Bainbridges. All she'd overheard for sure was that the two were planning on starting an honest to goodness church and had Alicia doing the legal work for it. Jessie turned her silent musing out loud.

"A church would be a heck of a good way to launder all the money trafficking brought in. Right out in the open with no taxes involved or any questions asked. You know, if the feds can get their hands on Alicia's files, the real ones, I'm thinking those guys will be busted. Course they'll have to catch them, but I think their trafficking days are over."

The two men were silent for a while, then Dal whistled. "Good God, you're right. Always knew you were smarter than you act."

"Hey." She laughed and smacked him on the shoulder. "You didn't think of it."

"No, I'll admit my mind has been on other things. But you're right on the money. Establishing a legal church would take care of that, while the cult members could continue to hide out the kids till they're sold. Once the feds get hold of the information in Alicia's files, plus pry the rest out of those cult members, that should put an end to their plans. Wonder where Kimble and Bainbridge disappeared to, leaving poor Susan to take the heat?"

"Poor? She shot up the Woodsons' house with a dangerous weapon."

"And the two men took off, cowards that they are."

At Red Rock Nick convinced them that he could handle himself very well and said he'd like to be alone. No offense intended.

Much as she liked him, she was relieved to have the rest of the day alone with Dal. He must've felt the same cause he drove right back to her cabin without asking her what she had in mind. So when they arrived, before she opened the door to get out, she asked him what he wanted to do.

"Thought we might take a long walk in the woods other side of the creek. We could take along a quilt so we can" —he gave her a lazy look— "lay in the shade and take a long nap." He tickled her nose with the tip of a finger.

"Sounds good to me. When we come back I'll fix us something to eat."

"Oh yeah, about that. You been taking secret cooking lessons or what? That breakfast was damned good."

"I think it was all the pressure, but I'm willing to try again."

"Well, I guess we'll have to see after one of us goes shopping."

She laughed. "There is that." They were dancing all around the elephant in the room, so to speak. What Dal was going to do now that Mac had his job back and things were settling down. "For right now, I'll go in and grab us that quilt. Be right back."

She found their Keds and they sat on the steps side by side and slipped into the shoes, then he gathered up the quilt and they strolled out across the yard hand in hand.

Behind them a horn beeped over and over. A dog barked. She turned in time to catch a flying fur ball. Brad hit her in the chest, wiggled and squirmed and licked her face. Parker climbed out of his Rover.

"Had to bring that animal back to you before one of us had a fit. And I think it would've been me. What y'all up to?" He eyed the quilt with a wide grin. "Looks like I might've interrupted something. Sorry about that, but Brad, there, since you dropped him off with me the other evening, he's stolen one of every pair of shoes I've got so I can't spare anymore. Heard you were back, so...." Parker stared ruefully down at his feet, encased in a brown slip-on and a white sneaker. "Where do you reckon he got to with all my shoes?"

Still holding the excited pit bull, she laughed so hard her belly ached. Dal joined her and Parker glared at them, trying to keep a straight face.

"No use in making fun of me, after what I've been through with that fella. I ought to get hazard pay." He ruffled Brad's ears and neck. "Well, you kids look like you might have plans, so I'll go on home and leave you be." The way he stood there gazing at them, she couldn't let him leave.

"Tell you what. Let's go back up to the house and visit a while. We probably can entertain you all day with stories of our adventures."

"You sure?" He looked from Dal to her and back again.

Dal turned toward the house. "Course we are, we were just going for a walk. We can do that later. I understand we have the weekend off."

Parker got between them, grabbing an arm with each of his, and led them across the yard and back into the house.

Good thing her one dalliance with him when they were both having a rough time hadn't ruined their friendship. Next to Dal she loved him the best, and then came Mac, with Nick moving right up there. Besides, maybe he'd have some insight as to what motivated the Rising Moon folks to do what they were doing.

Parker laid down his sandwich and took a sip from the beer bottle. "*Masque of the Rising Moon*? How creative. And worshiping a pregnant goddess. That beats them all. Did you check her out, this goddess, see if she really exists?"

Dal wiped his mouth with a napkin. "Yes, she does indeed. She's Sumerian. But I thought we had the weekend off." He covered Jessie's hand with his and for a moment got caught up in her expression. Staring at him like that brought on lots of memories.

Parker chuckled. "Figured you'd be curious and google her."

"That's precisely what we did. Some of the stuff we saw was so upsetting I don't even want to think about it." She took the last bite of her sandwich and grabbed her computer. "Glad I thought to plug this in this morning."

Finishing his beer, Dal rose to sit by her side on the couch. Pointed. "See, here it is. She does exist. Sumerian goddess of the rising moon. It sounded too dumb to be true till we checked it out."

Jessie read on. "And to think Couch was a state trooper for years. And Kimble a sheriff. It's plumb embarrassing, I would imagine. Probably involved with child trafficking that entire time. I hope they nail their balls to a tree."

"Whoa, hope I never cross you." Parker shook his head. "And Jessie, I think you're spot on about them creating a legal church being a good way to launder the money coming in from trafficking. Who would've ever thought of that? It'll make a heck of a story once they can prove it. It constantly amazes me the godawful things human beings will do."

"Then you see a kid like Colby, serving three years in Afghanistan, coming home a hero and continuing to fight the bad guys. And Nick." Jessie wiped a tear from her eye and closed the laptop. "Don't want to do anymore today. Just want to sit out on the porch and think about all the good people in our lives."

Dal rubbed her cheek with his thumb. "Don't cry, darlin. It's all gonna be okay."

"Those poor kids. Poor babies." She broke down and he put the computer on the coffee table and took her in his arms.

Holding her that way, catching the expression of concern and care on Parker's face, a fist squeezed his heart. People loving people. It was a strange and beautiful sight to behold.

How did anyone live without it? How had he gone off, left everyone who cared for him, denied he gave a damn about them? Why had he been so ignorant about what life is really about?

People were who they were. Somehow he'd have to learn to handle it when Jessie put herself in danger. He didn't want to lose her, but if he went back to Frog Pond, that's exactly what would happen. So somehow he had to keep her safe, have her back when she went off on one of her wild tangents.

He buried his face in her hair, breathed her scent, rubbed one hand up and down her arm, whispered her name.

"You two need to take a nap. You're plumb wore out. I'll just let myself out. Thanks for the lunch, Jessie." He leaned down and kissed the top of her head.

The door closed. Evidently he let Brad in because the little pit bull leaped up on the couch and included himself in the loving, poking his way onto Jessie's lap and licking Dal where he could find skin.

Laughing, he picked her up, Brad nestling in her curves, and carried them to the bedroom. She refused to let go when he laid her on the bed, so he crawled over top of her and they stretched out side by side.

"Looks like you've regained some of your strength. What are we gonna do?"

"About?" He twisted a lock of her hair.

"This. Us. You can't leave again. You just can't. If you do I'll—"

"I'm not going anywhere. Now stop crying. Brad is very upset." He rubbed her back for a long time. "We do still have to talk though."

"Oh, sounds serious."

He didn't answer, just kept massaging her back.

The little dog licked her face free of tears, then wiggled around till he found a hole between them where he could fit, curled up, and stared at her with soulful eyes.

He couldn't take his eyes off her till she finally relaxed and fell asleep, then he did the same.

Drawing in a breath, he came out of a nightmare, left behind dark fears, and settled into her arms. She murmured something and held on tight.

Sometime during the day Brad had gone elsewhere. The clock read 7:15. They had slept away the afternoon. Her wiggling to get fixed aroused him.

Her blue eyed gaze fixed on him and he fingered her tousled hair back out of her face. "You are so gorgeous when you first wake up."

"And how am I the rest of the time?" She reached to run her fingers through his long glossy hair. "Are you going to cut it?"

"Want me to?"

"Only because it means you're coming back to me, to Cedarton, to the sheriff's department. I think it's pretty sexy."

He laughed. "Oh, you do, do you? Well, I don't know. Maybe I ought to tell Mac he can't be the fashion police for his deputies. How would that be?

"Oh, crap. I'd like to see his reaction to that."

"You and me both."

"So?"

"What?"

"If you can handle my fits and starts, then I guess I can learn to handle yours."

"Mine? I don't have any fits and starts."

"Oh, right. Who was it who took off from the Bainbridge's and almost got herself killed? Jessie, I can't handle the thought of you getting hurt. It's like someone throws me in hell. I need to be able to protect you. I know what facing death is like and I don't want it to happen to you."

"Oh, sweetie. You can't control everyday life. Everything that happens. We never know when we'll face death. Neither you or me. Everyone feels that way to a certain extent. You just need to realize that. I've seen you come apart when something scary happens to me. I've also seen you under pressure when you do all the right things. The brave things. We can do this together or separately, long as you don't leave again." She slid closer, kissed him. "Now, let's go get us something to eat."

It was almost nine that night before they returned to the cabin. She drove the Jeep and parked near the front porch, ran around, and opened the door.

He laughed. "Never heard of the woman being gallant."

She took his hand and led him through the lit yard. Brad stood on the porch, wagging all over.

He followed her to the door and waited while she unlocked it. Inside she flipped on a light, looked up at him, eyes dark with desire. Together they walked through the house, shed clothing on the way to the bathroom, and stepped into the shower.

Tongue dry from the ride, he tilted his head and opened his mouth to the cool water. Her arms crawled around his waist from behind, hands sliding low, lower, till she gripped his growing erection.

Yep. He'd definitely thought about it and reached a decision. He would go with whatever she wanted.

He sucked in a feeling of passion and joy, propped himself against the wall of the shower with both hands, and released himself to her ministrations. As soon as she brought him to the edge where he thought he might go blind or slide to the floor, she turned loose and circled in front of him. Knelt and slithered up the entire length of his body like a snake enveloping every inch of his water-slick skin until his prick was caught pointing upward between them. At any moment it would spring forward and shove her backward.

A funny uh sound emitted from his throat. Where it came from he had no idea. One thing was for sure. If he lifted his hands from the wall he'd fall flat on his butt, or worse, smash her to the floor.

With him pinned firmly against her she moved up and down so his prick slipped from between her legs up over her belly and between her breasts, then back down again. Soapy slick. What a sensation. If a small woman could ever overpower a man his size, this was the way to do it. He could do nothing but prop himself, close his eyes, and enjoy the hell out of what she was doing. The feel of her wet flesh against the swollen tip of his penis drove him wild. Each time she skinned up, then back down all hell broke loose inside him and his poor prick beat to the rhythm of his hammering heart. Sure every time he would manage to poke inside her only to be dragged away again, he moaned with passionate despair. Felt good but felt dreadful, all at the same time. His throbbing balls begged for release.

He tried to say her name, plead for release, but only made that weird uh sound again, so gave that up as well. At last she backed into the corner, slid down to the floor. Dropping painfully to his knees he cupped her butt. She hooked her legs around his waist and he plunged inside her. Her orgasm sent shudders through them both and he came inside her. The world spun to a halt, caught fire, went off in every direction till he had no notion where he was. Just that water poured over him and she hung on while he clutched her, muscles flexing and trembling.

A long while later, or at least it seemed that way, she repeated his name weakly several times. He came back to the world he'd left and rolled off her. She let out a long sigh.

"Are you okay? I thought I was going to have to call out the first responders again."

"Jesus, woman. You trying to kill me? I think I'm going to have to sleep right here."

She smacked his bottom with the flat of her hand. "Water's getting cold and I can't turn it off from here. Can you help me up?"

"I seriously doubt it." He made an effort to roll over and get to his knees, then his feet. "I think we're in bad trouble here."

She managed to get to her knees, then chuckled. That grew to a laugh and he joined her. First thing he knew she had collapsed across him. "Teach us to make love after going without sleep for three nights and climbing bluffs and chasing around after a bunch of crazies. We're not getting any younger, you know." She shifted a little. "What is that? What the hell is that?"

"It's me— I mean him."

"Wait, you just wait a minute." She struggled to her feet, shut off the water, then joined him back on the floor of the shower. "Okay, so you'd been celibate how long before you came home?"

"Nine months, three weeks, and six days. Till the other night, that is. I'd tell you the hours, but I need you to do something for me."

She straddled his lap and eased him into her warm, moist, sweetness. "This time let's go easy and slow. Okay?"

How in the hell did he always get in this predicament with her? The thought flew away and he nibbled over to her breast. Her smell, her taste, the silk of her skin, the pearl-like nipple in his mouth, so nice. So damned nice. She made a purring sound and settled all around him.

He was home.

Velda Brotherton writes from her home perched on the side of a mountain against the Ozark National Forest. Branded as *Sexy, Dark and Gritty*, her work embraces the lives of gutsy women and heroes who are strong enough to deserve them. After a stint writing for a New York publisher, she has settled comfortably in with small publishers to produce novels in several genres. She enjoys reading mysteries, but it never occurred to her she could write them until Dal Starr and Jessie West emerged from her background in the newspaper business, and the *Twist of Poe* mysteries were born.

Facebook: Author Velda Brotherton
Twitter: @veldabrotherton
http://www.veldabrotherton.com

www.ingramcontent.com/pod-product-compliance
Lightning Source LLC
Chambersburg PA
CBHW030633020726
47493CB00006B/1694